D0966595

One Secret Summer

Also by Lesley Lokko

Sundowners
Saffron Skies
Bitter Chocolate
Rich Girl, Poor Girl

One Secret Summer

Lesley Lokko

First published in Great Britain in 2010 by Orion Books,
an imprint of The Orion Publishing Group Ltd
Orion House, 5 Upper Saint Martin's Lane
London WC2H 9EA

An Hachette UK Company

1 3 5 7 9 10 8 6 4 2

A CIP catalogue record for this book is
available from the British Library.

ISBN (Hardback) 978 1 4091 0170 3
ISBN (Trade Paperback) 978 1 4091 0171 0

Typeset at The Spartan Press Ltd,
Lymington, Hants

Printed in Great Britain by
Clays Ltd, St Ives plc

The Orion Publishing Group's policy is to use papers that are natural,
renewable and recyclable products and made from wood grown in
sustainable forests. The logging and manufacturing processes are expected
to conform to the environmental regulations of the country of origin.

www.orionbooks.co.uk

Acknowledgements

Grateful thanks are due to a number of people whom I never actually met during the writing of this novel but whose works were both inspiring and insightful. Chief among those is the award-winning journalist and reporter Rageh Omaar, for his autobiography, *Only Half of Me: British and Muslim; the Conflict Within* (Penguin: 2006); John Burnett, for his book, *Where Soldiers Fear to Tread* (Heinemann: 2005) and Scott Peterson, for his account of war in *Me Against My Brother: At War in Somalia, Sudan and Rwanda* (Routledge: 2001). For once, this novel *wasn't* written in a remote cottage in the Scottish hills but in Accra, Johannesburg and Houston during the final phase of the US presidential race, which in itself was a war of a different sort. Big thanks to Kevin and Carol McNulty for their warmth and hospitality (and far too many great dinners!). I would also like to thank Nicola Trott, Lihua Li, Tim Soutphommasane and the Praefectus of Balliol College, Professor Diego Zancani, for their immense generosity and time in showing me around Holywell Manor and Balliol College, Oxford. Thanks too to Poppy Miller and Janice Acquah for their help in understanding the torment and joy of drama. In Accra, thanks go to the GNO team – Wild Lizzie, Nana Amu, Natasha, Poem and Vera – as well as all the usual suspects, Vic, Patrick, Sean, Elkin, Joe, Delta Kilo and Irene; the glorious guys at Chain Gang, especially Raila, and Sunshine, and finally, in Biriwa, Carsten, Marcel and Rudi. In Jo'burg, Kate, Paloma and Paris have made me a very special home in all senses of the word, a huge thank you to them – and the same goes to the Jozi 'new crew' – Trev T, Veronica, Caroline, Eva, Rootie, Moky, Jutta, Chiluba, Denise and Krisen. Kay Preston (yet *again*) and Margie Wilson continue to show me the light; Kate Mills, Lisa Milton, Susan Lamb, Gaby Young and the whole Orion team are, as always, wonderful. A big thank you to my sister, Debbie (and especially to those wonderful people at Skype); to Megs, Lois, Nick, Paul and Mae-Ling, and finally to my father and stepmother, whose unequivocal love and support this year has been the most significant of my life.

In memory of Charles

PART ONE

Prologue

Mougins, France, June 1969

The dull, mechanical sound of metal hitting the earth came to the young woman as if from far, far away. She watched in silence, arms wrapped tightly around her waist, as the two men scooped out a small, shallow hole in the ground, pausing only to wipe their faces or mark out the limits of the dig. An owl whooshed past, his gentle enquiring call puncturing the balmy night air. The smell of olive and pine trees drifted up to her from the valley below; she knew already the scent would be with her for the rest of her life.

Finally it was done. One of the men called out something softly in their own language to the other. She watched as the small bundle was passed carefully to him, already wrapped in the white muslin sheet that was their custom, and placed into the ground. A tiny stifled sound escaped from her throat but was swallowed up in the soft 'thwack' of earth as they quickly began covering the hole up again. It took them almost no time at all. The ground was patted flat, the flagstones replaced, stamped over, made new. In the morning they would begin the work of resurfacing the driveway . . . in a few days, no one would ever know what lay beneath. Buried, disposed of, forgotten. She would never see the men again. That was part of the deal. Neither looked at her as they walked past; that, too, was part of the deal. She turned and watched them as they put away the shovels in the small lean-to at the top of the drive, and then they were gone. She waited for a few moments and then walked slowly back into the house and bolted the door behind her. Her teeth were chattering. She poured herself a brandy and took it into the living room. She couldn't bear to go upstairs.

She curled herself up beside the empty fireplace where she'd slept for the past six nights, clutching her drink. It took her almost the entire glass to stop shivering. She forced herself to think of what would happen next.

Alongside the new driveway, in the morning something else would be delivered. Something that would put an end to the nightmare that had begun a week ago and make everything all right. Everything. Nothing would have changed; it would never have happened. No one would ever know. She took one last swallow of brandy, willing herself desperately to believe it. No one *could* ever know. If it ever came out, she would be finished. They would all be finished. There was simply no other way, no other choice. This was how it would be. Always.

1

JOSH
Mougins, France, July 1973

The ground underfoot was hot in that delicious, beginning-of-the-summer-holidays way; air electric with the sound of insects pulsing thickly with banked-up warmth. Overhead the intense blue sky yawned endlessly towards the horizon. Josh Keeler, four years old and marching along the path with all the determination of a seasoned jungle explorer, could scarcely contain his excitement. Ahead of him, his two older brothers, Rafe and Aaron, danced their way around the reassuringly solid shape of Harvey, their father. Trailing behind, in a pretty flowery dress of the sort she only ever wore on holiday, Diana, their mother, brought up the rear, humming to herself in a way that she never did in London.

The pink oleanders that lined the path to the pool swatted his face as he hurried after them, anxious to keep up. His whole body was suffused with anticipatory joy. This year he was going to learn how to swim. His brothers were already strong swimmers; they'd had lessons at school. Josh was just about to begin. It was hard being the youngest, especially when Rafe and Aaron took no more notice of him than they did of Buster, the family dog. He longed to be like them; for them to like him. He couldn't understand why they didn't.

It was almost as warm inside the silky envelope of the pool as it was outside. He felt the gentle pressure of his father's hand cupping his chin and tried to remember what he'd been told about frogging his legs to keep his body level with the surface of the water. Rafe and Aaron were clowning around confidently at the far end of the pool, scrambling in and out of the water and diving in off the side. It would be years before he could do any of that, he thought to himself miserably as he struggled to stay afloat. A few seconds later, he heard Rafe shouting. He felt his father's attention leave; his fleshy, breathing presence momentarily disengaging itself as he turned towards Rafe. The water pushed away from him as Harvey lunged out. There was a sudden lull, as if he were falling, and then everything seemed to happen at once. Water rushed up at him, covering his mouth and nose. He panicked, swinging his arms wildly above his head as his legs dropped and the water closed over his face again. He burst through the surface, clawing at the air, but there was nothing to hold on to. He opened his eyes, caught a glimpse of Aaron staring calmly at him before he went under again. No one moved, no hands came out to hold him. It was quiet there in the swirling depths; his lungs were almost bursting with the desire to breathe. He was afraid to open his eyes. The taste of chlorinated water filled his mouth, bubbling upwards painfully through his nose. He felt the hot smarting of tears behind his eyes; shame flooded over him like a stain. It wouldn't do to cry in front of Aaron. Or Rafe, for that matter. It simply wouldn't do.

2

MADDY
New York, September 1991

The Greyhound bus slowly lurched its way into the Midtown Bus Terminal just before dawn. Amongst the thirty-odd passengers gathering their possessions and preparing to disembark was a young woman who was still fast asleep. She lay curled up in her seat, swathed in her black overcoat, only a fiery mass of red curls visible, tumbling halfway down her back. The woman who'd been sitting next to her for the past sixteen hours paused in the task of pulling her bag from the overhead locker and looked down at her. She smiled indulgently and touched her lightly on the shoulder. 'Wake up, honey,' she murmured, bending down. 'We're here.'

The girl's eyes flew open. For a brief, incomprehensible second, she struggled to remember where she was. She looked around her in bewilderment at the darkened, ghostly interior of the bus, passengers pulling their suitcases and bags from the overhead lockers, a child whimpering somewhere near the front. Where the hell was she? A sudden lurch in the pit of her stomach brought it all rushing back. New York. New York City! She'd finally arrived! She struggled upright and hurriedly pushed her hands through her hair, pulling it into a ponytail, furious with herself. She couldn't believe it! She'd been awake for almost the entire journey, taut with anticipation, every nerve in her body waiting for that moment when she'd look out of the window and see Manhattan emerging out of the early morning mist, right there in front of her – and she'd missed it. She clambered out of her seat, grabbed her coat and bag, still brushing the sleep from her eyes.

'You know where you're going?' Shirley, a plump, recently divorced woman who'd boarded the bus in Franklin, the next stop after Marshall-town, smiled down at her. Shirley was in her early fifties and on her way to stay with her eldest daughter in New Jersey. She was full of advice about New York City, most of it incomprehensible to eighteen-year-old Maddy Stiller, who'd never been further than Chicago and only once at that.

Maddy nodded, hoping she looked and sounded more certain than she felt. 'I . . . I have the address right here,' she said, patting her bag. 'My mom said to take a cab.'

'You do that, honey. Best thing to do. There'll be plenty of them across the road. Just give the driver the address and make sure he's got a NYC sticker in the window. You never know,' she added darkly. 'Well, I hope everything works out for you. I'll be looking to see your name in lights one of these days. You take care, now, Maddy. Everything'll turn out fine, you'll see.'

'Th . . . thank you,' Maddy mumbled, cheeks red with embarrass-ment. She watched Shirley pick up her suitcase and navigate her way confidently through the crowd. She felt a sudden wave of loneliness. As recent an acquaintance as Shirley was, she was the only person she'd spoken to since leaving home. Although she'd have been quite happy to ride the thousand-odd miles from Iowa to New York in silence, Shirley, it was soon clear, wasn't. Shirley was what Martha, Maddy's mother, would have called a 'talker-stalker' – the kind who wouldn't shut up until she'd wormed every last piece of information out of you. She wasn't unkind – just persistent. By the time they reached Des Moines, she'd established that Maddy Stiller had gone to Meskawi High School in Marshalltown, that she was the only daughter of Frank and Martha Stiller and that Frank had disappeared one Sunday afternoon when Maddy was fourteen. Just disappeared. He'd got up early as usual, went out to feed the cows and then came back into the kitchen and announced he was going into Des Moines. He'd driven the white pick-up truck down the road, turned left instead of right and gone all the way to Chicago. He'd left the pick-up truck in the parking lot at O'Hare International Airport with instructions on the windscreen to call Mrs Martha Stiller of Dewey Farm, Marshall County, Iowa. Martha had driven out with Ron, their neighbour from across the way, in tight-lipped silence. A few weeks later a letter arrived for Martha and a postcard for Maddy. From San Francisco. Maddy read the few lines and then burned it. Apparently there was someone else 'involved'. Maddy didn't know what that meant. Poor Martha, everyone said. No one ever said 'poor Maddy'. 'Oh, we heard *all* about it, honey. Your *poor* mother. Just goes to show, doesn't it? You can just never tell about people, can you?' Maddy looked down at her hands. When people brought up the topic of her father's disappearance, which they usually did as soon as they heard her surname, she never knew what to say. Along the long, flat tongue of Interstate 88, Shirley managed to worm out of her that she'd won a four-year scholarship to study drama and that, aside from her school trip to Chicago, it was the first time she'd ever left Iowa. 'Oh, my,' Shirley breathed, clearly impressed. 'You must be very talented.' Maddy's stomach lurched again and again. Talented? No, she wasn't talented. She just wanted to get out of Iowa, that was all. She still couldn't get over it all. Less than three months after she'd made the application to Tisch, here she was. It felt like a dream.

'These yours?' The brusque voice of the driver interrupted her thoughts. He pointed to the two rather battered suitcases left standing in the hold.

'Yes, those are mine,' Maddy nodded hurriedly.

'Here . . .' He tossed them unceremoniously towards her. 'Ain't got all day,' he said, slamming the hold doors shut. 'Let's get this show on the road!' He slapped the side of the bus and stalked off.

Maddy struggled awkwardly to get them out of the way. She stood on the edge of the sidewalk, clutching her handbag tightly to her chest, trying to ignore the burning sensation of fear in the pit of her stomach, looking around her for a sign – any sign – of where to go and what to do next. People were streaming in and out of the subway station across the street. The sound was deafening. It was nearly 7 a.m. and the entire city seemed to be on the move. People thundered in and out of the narrow hole in the ground, no one speaking, not looking at one another, no eye contact . . . nothing. Bodies rushed past one another, a tangled, indistinguishable mass of people in which unfamiliar details jumped out

8

at her – a skullcap here, a long flowing white robe there; the pitch-black face of a young boy wearing a baseball cap turned backwards, stopping to grab a paper-wrapped bagel; two women in diaphanous black tents, only the slits of their eyes showing, large woven shopping baskets visible through the sheer black material – she'd never seen anything like it. She stood there on the other side of the road, too stunned to do anything other than stare. She thought of her last glimpse of Martha, standing bravely beside the bus stop, waving at the Greyhound as it lurched around the corner, and the tug of tears crept into her throat once more. She'd turned her head to wave but the corner was already made and Martha was no longer there. Her stomach lurched again, dangerously. She had to get a cab, find the address of the Tisch halls of residence and phone her mother. And find a bathroom. Her stomach, always the most precise register of her nerves, was dangerously close to revolt.

There was a constant line of yellow cabs crawling up the street. She tried to remember what Shirley had said – was it the yellow light to the left or the white light in the centre that indicated an available ride? She couldn't remember. She shuffled along, her suitcases banging awkwardly against her legs and hips, looking for the end of the queue. Several times someone simply stuck out a hand in front of her, jumping into the cab she'd had her eye on. There didn't seem to be a queue. She tried waving a hand like everyone else, but as soon as the cab swung over, someone else simply popped out in front of her and sped off. No one paid the slightest bit of attention to a slender young redhead whose face carried the painful outward expression of her nerves. She was close to tears by the time it happened for the tenth or eleventh time. Didn't these people have any manners? A cab sped up the road towards her. She looked quickly left and right – no one else seemed to be waiting. She waved frantically at it like she'd seen everyone else do. It seemed to work – he appeared to be making straight for her. She stepped down off the sidewalk, determined not to let anyone else grab it before her, still holding on to her suitcases. She heard a sudden screeching of brakes, felt a rush of cool air sweep past her head and then the sound of someone shouting, 'Oh! Oh, my *Gawd*!'

She hit the kerb face first, catching her knee on the edge of one of her damned suitcases. She lay in stunned silence, the sounds of traffic and pedestrians rushing over to her receding slowly into the background as their voices rose. 'What the hell was she trying to do?' 'What happened? Did I do something? Did *I* hit her?' 'Jesus!'

She tried to lever herself off the ground, her face hot with embarrassment and her cheeks already sticky with tears. She'd tripped over one of the blasted suitcases. Someone bent down to her. 'You OK?' He knelt down so that his face was on a level with hers. He helped her to sit upright, squinted at the cut and pulled out a clean handkerchief, placing it firmly against her eyebrow. 'You've cut yourself – just a scratch, nothing to worry about. When you get home, splash lots of cold water on it. It'll help the cut close quicker.' He had a nice voice. Maddy closed her eyes as he applied a gentle pressure to her forehead. 'It'll stop bleeding soon, don't worry.'

'Darling, she's fine. We're going to be late.' A young woman's impatient voice broke through the babble surrounding her.

'Just a minute. She's bleeding.'

'It's nothing – it's a small scratch, that's all. Just put a plaster on it.' The young woman looked down at the dazed Maddy. 'We're going to miss the first act.' She was beginning to whine.

A middle-aged man bent down, and together they helped Maddy to her feet. 'Will somebody get this girl a cab?' he growled at the small crowd that had gathered to watch. Seconds later, a cab appeared. The driver jumped out, picked up her suitcases as if they were dust, and Maddy was helped into the back seat. Still holding the young man's handkerchief to her forehead, she leaned back against the plastic seats, handed over the scrap of paper with the address of Gramercy House, the first-year hall of residence, and tried not to cry. The cab pulled smartly away from the kerb and was soon swallowed up in the traffic. She lifted a hand and tried to brush her tears discreetly away. It wasn't quite the arrival she'd planned.

3

NIELA
Hargeisa, October 1991

Fifteen years after leaving Hargeisa, the Aden family returned. Not as the prosperous professionals they'd become, Hassan Aden complained bitterly to anyone who'd listen. No, they were returning as refugees from a war they hadn't anticipated and knew nothing about. *Refugees!* He spat the word out. Refugees with nothing but the suitcases they were able to carry and the few possessions they'd grabbed as they ran. Not even the old second- or third-hand pick-up truck in which they were driving to Hargeisa belonged to them. Back home in Mogadishu there were three cars in the driveway, including the brand-new Mercedes, which he'd been forced to sell for next to nothing. *Next to nothing!* Hassan's voice rose in pained indignation. Next to him, swathed in dusty black with only her eyes showing, his wife remained silent. On the back seat, nineteen-year-old Niela Aden and her two younger brothers sat squashed together, exhausted and irritable – and scared.

The truck groaned its way up the escarpment. As they rounded one bend after another, the first signs of the city began to appear – low whitewashed buildings, but with their walls and windows blasted open. As they drove slowly along deserted streets into the centre of town, everyone fell silent, even Hassan. The road was pitted with gaping craters that the driver kept swerving to avoid. Every single building they passed carried the scars of recent battles – even the street lamps had been blasted apart. They hung above the road dangling the remains of a bulb from a crooked, wavering arm. Niela swallowed. Although she could barely remember Hargeisa, it was obvious this wasn't the small city of citrus groves and calm, peaceful streets that her parents spoke nostalgically about. This was worse than Mogadishu. Hassan gave the driver directions in low, wary tones. They turned left and right down one pockmarked street after another until they finally pulled up in front of a yellow wall, it too marked with wounds. 'Wait here,' Hassan instructed. Niela watched him walk up to the wrought-iron gate and rap authoritatively on it. From somewhere beyond the wall a dog barked, a low, menacing burst of sound. A few moments later, a small hatch in the gate opened. '*Salaam alaikum*,' Hassan said. 'Is Mohammed Osman at home?' There was a quick muttered exchange and then the gate was hurriedly opened. Suddenly her mother, who had remained silent for almost the entire journey, began to cry.

There was a thin trickle of water coming out of the shower head but it was just enough. Niela stood, letting it dribble its way through her thick curly hair, across her shoulder blades and down the backs of her legs. She turned her face up, revelling in the simple but forgotten sensation of water running down her face. It had been three days since she'd had a shower. Unbelievable. She, who showered three or four times a day at home! As the family fled northwards, her mother had shown her how to wash herself quickly at the side of the road with nothing more than a flannel and a small bottle of drinking water. Under her arms, under her breasts, between her legs. Her mother displayed no shame, squatting by the side of the road, hitching her black burqa up around her waist. Niela didn't know where to look. She'd never seen her mother squat before. But there was no other option. She'd pulled down her jeans and joined her.

She wrung the last drops of water out of her hair and stepped out of the shower. She scraped her hair back into a ponytail, shook the dust out of her jeans and pulled on her one clean T-shirt. She wondered where everyone was. Her father and brothers had been shown a room on the other side of the courtyard. She and her mother had followed the young servant girl, who shook her head wordlessly whenever she was addressed. She opened the bedroom door cautiously. The house was arranged around a courtyard. In its centre, long since dried up, was a fountain surrounded by pretty blue and green tiles. There was a single orange tree and several large terracotta pots that had obviously once held plants. In one, a long, thin green stem protruded from amongst the brown, decaying leaves, clinging on to life. She shivered suddenly, despite the heat. Hargeisa, like Mogadishu, seemed to belong to the dead.

She turned away from the courtyard and walked along one of the outside corridors that led to the kitchen and probably where her mother was to be found. As she approached, she heard the low murmur of voices from within one of the rooms. She stopped; it was her father's voice. He was arguing with someone – Mohammed Osman, perhaps? She looked around quickly – there was no one about. She stepped a little closer.

'Get them out, Hassan,' she heard the man say. 'You have family overseas, isn't it? What about your brother in Vienna? He can take you in, surely?'

'Why should I leave? This is my country!' Her father's voice was angry.

'Not any more, Hassan. They've taken over everything, I'm telling you. At least you have a choice. D'you think I would still be here if *I* had such a choice? Don't you think I'd be gone too?'

'But where should we go?'

'Go to Vienna! Get out! Go to Europe, America . . . wherever you can! I'm telling you, Hassan. Go now, before it's too late. This place is finished.'

'Niela!' Niela jumped guiltily. Her mother was standing in the door-way of one of the rooms. She'd been so intent on the conversation she hadn't heard her approach. 'Come away from there!' her mother hissed at her, gesturing to her to move away from the window. 'Come here!' Niela moved away as quickly and quietly as she could. Her heart was thumping. Move? To where? She couldn't imagine her parents – especially not her father – leaving Somalia. Yes, they'd been abroad before – they'd visited their Uncle Raageh, her father's younger brother, in Vienna several times, and one summer Hassan had taken the family to France, where Niela practised her schoolgirl French, ate ice cream every day in place of lunch and developed a crush on the neighbour's son . . . but that was on *holiday*. At the end of their three or four weeks abroad, they'd boarded the plane and come back to Mogadishu, to the chauffeur-driven Mer-cedes and the large, comfortable house in the suburbs. She'd gone back to the International School, where her best friends were German and American and Senegalese – daughters of diplomats or successful busi-nessmen like her father. She and her friends swapped notes and pictures of the places they'd been. The thought of *not* coming back was unthink-able. But the unthinkable had suddenly come to pass. The gunmen who roamed the suburbs neither knew nor cared that Hassan Aden had worked hard his entire life to provide his children with the best education he could, or the most comfortable home within his means. They grabbed the cars and seized the house, together with the seven Aden pharmacies spread across the city that he'd spent the last decade building up. It was all gone. Everything. Not even the signs outside the pharmacies remained. Hassan came running home one afternoon with as much cash as he could lay his hands on stuffed into a small leather suitcase and ordered them to pack. They fled with whatever they could carry, and that was it.

'Didn't I tell you to stay in your room?' her mother hissed at her.

'But . . .'

'No buts! It's dangerous!'

'Uma, we're inside—'

'Come and help me prepare food. Your father and your brothers must be starving.'

I'm starving too, Niela wanted to say, but didn't dare. Instead, in silence, she followed her mother through the small gate to the kitchen. Together they set about preparing the simple meal of rice and beans. The little servant girl who'd let them in darted about, following instructions.

There was no sign of either of Mohammed Osman's wives. *Insha'allah*, her mother answered, whenever Niela asked a question. *If God wills it.* Sometimes, Niela thought to herself angrily as she rinsed the rice under the tap, she wished she had even just a fraction of her mother's faith. Ever since the bombs started falling on Mogadishu, she'd begun to have serious doubts about where His attention lay.

4

JULIA
Oxford, October 1991

'Burrows? Is that with a "w" or a "gh"?'

Julia looked blankly at the porter. She could feel her hackles beginning to rise. 'Sorry?'

'Your surname. The spelling.' His pen hovered above a list. 'As in William S.? Or as in a mole's abode?'

'B-U-R-R-O-W-S.' She spelled it out briskly. How the hell else was she supposed to spell it?

'School?' he asked, his lip curling in the faintest of sneers.

'School?' Now she really was confused. School was a good four years away. What the hell was he on about?

'What school did you go to?'

'What's that got to do with anything?'

He looked up at her. His eyes flickered over her, silently assessing her accent, her coat, her shoes and, of course, the all-important name of her school. 'Rooming lists. We put the name of your school next to your name. It's an old Oxford tradition.' *And one that wasn't about to die either*, his expression implied. Despite the sort of student they let in nowadays. Like Julia.

'Kenton.'

'And where's Kenton?'

Julia's face began to redden. Behind her, she heard someone snigger quietly. 'Newcastle,' she muttered.

'Ah.' His voice carried with it about as much snobbery and disdain as could possibly be packed into a single syllable. 'Of course. You're in

Room 11. Top of the stairs, turn right. Next, please. Ah, Mr Fothergill-Greaves. We've been expecting you . . . Eton, isn't it? Excellent, sir . . .'

Julia was summarily dismissed. She picked up her bags and turned, her cheeks flaming. Two young men who were standing in line behind her looked her up and down as she walked past. Their expressions were as clear as if one or the other had spoken. *Who the hell are they letting in these days?* Determined not to let them get the better of her, she raised her chin and marched past them, biting down fiercely on the urge to snap at them. The three years she'd spent at university in Nottingham had taught her one thing: when feeling overwhelmed, say nothing. Nothing at all. She lugged her case up the stairs, turned right as instructed and walked down the corridor to Room 11. As soon as she opened the door, however, she forgot all about the porter and the snobbish looks the two young men had given her. She stood in the doorway, half afraid to enter. Her room at Holywell Manor, Balliol's graduate residence, was everything she'd ever dared hope for. Small, cosy, charming . . . exactly as she'd pictured it. There was an apple tree outside the window, still heavy with fruit. She let her case drop to the floor and moved hesitantly into the centre of the room. She looked around her, suddenly overwhelmed with emotion. She'd done it. She was finally at Oxford. She'd beaten twelve other hopefuls to win a place on the coveted year-long Bachelor of Civil Law degree. It was the start of the Michaelmas Term. Ahead of her lay eight weeks of lectures and tutorials and then she would go back up to the small house in Elswick that had been left to her when her grandmother died, a few years earlier. She opened the window and leaned out, breathing in the scent of freshly cut grass and autumn flowers. Up and down the narrow lane in front of her cars came and went as students were dropped off and parents said their fond farewells. The lump in her throat swelled suddenly. She quickly pressed her fingers against her eyes. She'd promised herself – no tears, and certainly not on her first night. But it was hard *not* to cry. She could just picture her father's face, his ruddy cheeks reddening even further with pride. What wouldn't he have given to see her at Oxford? What wouldn't *she* have given to see her parents again? She closed the window abruptly and turned away. She looked at her watch. It was almost six thirty. There was a welcome dinner for all new postgraduate students that evening. Time to unpack her belongings, take a bath and prepare herself for the evening ahead. After her brief encounter with the snobbish porter, she had a feeling that finding a place for herself at Balliol was going to be much harder than she'd thought.

It took her less than half an hour to hang up her clothes, put her books on to the bookshelf and change the bed, replacing the university standard-issue sheets with her own eiderdown and the patchwork quilt that had been hers since her thirteenth birthday. She smoothed it down and plumped up the pillows – the room was already beginning to feel like her own. She closed the wardrobe door and turned to the last item on the bed – the photograph of her parents. She stared at it for a moment; it had been beside her bed for the past seven years, so much a part of the furniture and her surroundings that she sometimes looked at it without seeing. She ran her finger along the scrolled edge: Mike and Sheila Burrows, Mike's arm around his wife's shoulders, both looking quizzically into the camera. Her nan had taken the photograph one afternoon as they'd come back from a Sunday walk down by the river. Julia remembered it as if it were yesterday. Mike had bought the camera for Julia's fourteenth birthday. She and Annie, her best friend, had joined the after-school photography club. It was Annie's idea . . . there was some boy she had a crush on who was also in the club; Julia could no longer remember his name. She'd gone along more out of loyalty than anything else but she'd discovered she actually liked taking photographs, and Mike, always on the lookout for the little hobbies and interests that would open up the world for Julia in a way that hadn't happened for him, had bought her the camera. She looked into her father's face. Sandy brown hair, blue eyes . . . a strong, stern face. There was nothing in it, no sign of the tragedy that had followed. At the time, it was still two years off. She put the frame down with trembling hands. Now was not the time to think about it. She had to focus on getting through the evening ahead. Time to take a bath, wash her hair . . . think about something else instead. She pulled off her shirt and wriggled out of her jeans, pushing her shoes off impatiently with first one foot, then the other. She grabbed her dressing gown from where she'd hung it and opened the door. There was no one about. She walked down the corridor to the bathroom, wondering where everyone was. Holywell Manor was suddenly quiet. She looked at her watch again. It was half past seven. The dinner was at eight. She had half an hour to change into the dress she'd bought specially for the occasion, do something with her straight, dark brown hair and possibly even put on some make-up. Not that she had much –

she'd never been the sort to paint her face. A touch of mascara and a dash of lipstick – those were the limits she'd stuck to for most of her adult life. She'd never paid much attention to her looks. After what had happened to her parents, it seemed silly, trifling . . . almost blasphemous. She gave herself a little shake. Stop. Stop now, before it's too late.

Fifteen minutes later, having forced herself to calm down, she opened the wardrobe door and looked at herself in the inside mirror. She smoothed down the stiff, unforgiving fabric. It was no use. She looked like a meringue. The pale yellow dress that had seemed so right in the shop window suddenly looked overdone, too fussy and frilly by half. She pulled her lower lip into her mouth in dismay. Fuck it, she muttered to herself, pulling a brush through her hair. She had no time to change, and besides, she'd nothing to change into. It was the yellow meringue or nothing. She thrust her feet into her new white shoes and grabbed her handbag. She hurried down the stairs and pushed open the front door, wondering where everyone was. It really was rather odd. Apart from the odd Chinese student who'd looked at her blankly as she walked down the stairs in her frock and already uncomfortable shoes, she hadn't seen a single person in Holywell Manor. As she hurried down Broad Street, she noticed that all of Oxford seemed strangely quiet. There appeared to be no one around.

She stopped outside the wooden door leading to Balliol College and pushed it open. She stepped into the domed archway and caught her breath. It was her third visit to the college, but there was something about the golden stone buildings and immaculate lawns that sent a shiver of excitement down her spine. The beadle looked up from his post as she approached. 'Can I help you?' he asked briskly.

'Er, yes, I'm here for High Dinner,' Julia said, wondering why he was looking at his watch.

'High Dinner? Started half an hour ago,' the beadle said. 'You're late.'

'Half an hour ago?' Julia felt a cold ripple of embarrassment. 'I thought it was at eight? It said so on the prospectus . . .'

The beadle shook his head. 'Dinners always start at seven thirty. You can slip in the back, I suppose. There's a door over by the north side.'

Julia looked across the quadrangle, following his finger. She'd have given anything to turn around and run straight back to Holywell. But the beadle was looking at her expectantly. She couldn't chicken out. Not on her first night. There was nothing for it. She had to go in.

'Thanks,' she muttered, walking off with as much dignity as she could muster. Her shoes were killing her and her stomach was churning with nervous embarrassment. She peered through the small window in the doorway. The dinner was indeed in full swing. The hall was vast and filled to the brim with students, mostly in black evening jackets and long black dresses, stunning in their simplicity. Not a soul in yellow or a frill in sight. She suddenly longed for the cosy friendliness of Nottingham. Although she'd always been something of a loner, especially after what had happened, she missed being known, having a friendly face almost everywhere she turned. She was the only one from the small group of friends she'd made who'd gone on to do a postgraduate degree. Here she knew no one, and what was worse, no one seemed in a hurry to know her either. On the raised platform at one end of the hall were the Fellows and Masters, all dressed in long black and purple gowns. Someone was giving a speech. Her heart sank even further. She pushed down on the handle, hoping to creep in without making a sound, but the door was jammed shut. She tried it again, harder this time – perhaps it was locked? She pushed a third time, there was a loud crack and the door suddenly gave way. She stumbled into the hall, all hopes of making a quiet entrance dashed. Several hundred heads turned her way. Crimson-faced, her heart thumping so loudly she was sure everyone could hear it, she only just managed to stay upright as she hurriedly closed the door behind her and slid on to the end of the nearest bench. The speaker, who'd stopped as soon as she came crashing into the hall, resumed his speech. She looked down the table and suddenly caught the eye of someone she dimly recognised. It was the man who'd been standing behind her in the queue at Holywell earlier that afternoon. His expression then had been one of disdain. Now it was disdain mixed with amused incredulity. He turned his head and murmured something to his neighbour. They both looked at her and sniggered. She'd obviously got it all wrong. She looked back down at her plate. She'd lost her appetite, and not just for food.

An hour later the whole interminably pompous, stuffy dinner was over. She hadn't spoken to a single person other than to ask someone where the toilets were. She walked back alone down Broad Street, fighting back tears, limping slightly from the blister that had formed almost as soon as she'd put on her new shoes. She turned left on to Parks Road and was almost halfway down when she realised she'd taken the wrong turning. She stopped at the corner of Parks Road and Museum Road – which way was it? She tried to remember how she'd come. Left or right? She turned left on Museum Road and then right on Blackhall Road and then suddenly found herself at a dead end. She walked back, turned left on to Keble Road and stopped. She was well and truly lost. Her shoes were killing her. Where the hell was Holywell Manor? She turned round to face the direction from which she'd come and began limping back towards the traffic lights.

'Lost?' someone shouted out cheerfully. Julia looked up. Christ . . . it couldn't be? Him again? She put up a hand to touch her hair in exactly the sort of self-conscious, girlish gesture she despised in others.

'No, I'm . . . I'm just taking a stroll,' she said as nonchalantly as she could.

'Yeah, right. Turn right at the end of the road. There's a sign. You'll find life a lot easier if you follow them.' The two men laughed indulgently and rode off without saying another word.

Julia stared after them, fists clenched. She hobbled to the end of the road and looked at the sign he'd pointed out. *Holywell Manor.* An arrow pointing straight ahead. How the hell could she have missed it? She walked back down St Cross Road, her cheeks flaming and the horrid taste of tears already in her throat.

5

MADDY
New York City, September 1991

Her head still throbbing from the pain of the cut on her forehead and with a bruise the size of Iowa beginning to show up on her knee, Maddy got out of the cab at Gramercy Hall, the NYU residence hall for freshmen students, and looked nervously around her. Washington Square was full of cars and cabs. There seemed to be hundreds of students being dropped off and arriving, just as she was. The cab driver helped her with her cases and soon she was given a room number, a key and a swipe card, which, the Resident Adviser told her, was worth more than her life. Without it, she wouldn't be able to attend classes, borrow books, eat, sleep or study. 'Don't lose it,' he said sternly, waggling it in front of her face. 'What the hell happened to you anyway?' he asked, looking askance at her forehead.

'I . . . er, tripped,' Maddy mumbled, taking the swipe card from him. 'It's nothing . . . just a scratch.'

'If you say so. You're on the sixth floor. Lifts are over there. Next.'

Maddy beat a hasty retreat. She lugged her suitcases over to the lifts and waited alongside half a dozen other new students, all studiously avoiding each other's eyes. She got out on the sixth floor and walked down the corridor of identical-looking doors until she reached Room 617. The letter from the accommodation office had told her she'd be sharing the room with another first-year drama student, Sandra Zimmerman. She wondered what Sandra Zimmerman would be like and if she'd already be there. She took a deep breath and pushed open the door. There was a girl standing near the window. Tall, dark-haired, in a smart, super-stylish black coat with a fur collar. She turned as Maddy entered the room. Maddy's heart sank. Not only was she beautiful, she was without a doubt the most fashionable person Maddy had ever seen. In her sensible black duffel coat Maddy felt like the proverbial country hick. She swallowed nervously. 'Hi,' she said in what she hoped was a steady voice. 'I . . . I guess you're Sandra?'

'Yeah, but everyone calls me Sandy. I guess you're Madison?'

'Yeah, but everyone calls me Maddy.' They looked at one another warily, sizing each other up.

'What the hell happened to your forehead?' Sandy asked finally.

'I . . . I tripped. Over my suitcase,' Maddy stammered, her cheeks reddening.

Sandy raised one perfectly shaped brow. 'No wonder. Where did you find *them*?' she asked, looking pointedly at Maddy's two large, falling-apart suitcases.

Maddy's face turned even deeper red. 'They . . . they belonged to my mom.' She glanced across the room at the two smart black suitcases standing next to the window. She and Sandy Zimmerman were clearly worlds apart.

'Well, I'm going downstairs to get a bottle of wine,' Sandy said, moving towards the door. 'It's our first night – might as well get wasted. What d'you prefer? Red or white?'

Maddy could only stare at her. Wine? She couldn't remember the last time she'd had a glass of wine. 'Er, whatever,' she said as nonchalantly as she could possibly manage. 'Should . . . would you like me to . . . how much?'

'How much?' Sandy's brow wrinkled.

Maddy's stomach was twisting itself in knots of embarrassment. 'I just meant . . . would you like to share? The cost, I mean.' It was one of the things Martha had lectured her sternly about. *Always pay your way, Maddy. You may not have much, but it doesn't cost you anything to be generous. Remember that.*

'It's only a bottle of wine,' Sandy said, shaking her head. 'Don't worry about it. Besides, Daddy's paying.' She waved her credit card at Maddy and disappeared out of the door.

Maddy sat down on the edge of the bed as soon as she'd gone, overwhelmed and suddenly very lonely. She'd been in New York all of three or four hours, she'd fallen over, hurt herself, found her way to her new home and was now confronted with a roommate who was so far removed from anything or anyone she'd ever encountered before . . . It was all too much. She got up, wrapping her arms tightly around her, and pushed open the door to the adjoining bathroom. She stood in the doorway, slightly dazed by the white tiles and the scent of industrial disinfectant. She locked the door behind her and leaned against it for a moment, her eyes closed. She missed her mother; she missed the farm; she missed the animals and the view from her bedroom window. She missed everything. She opened her eyes and looked at the toilet bowl in the corner. Gleaming white, solid, pure. She stumbled towards it and knelt down, breathing deeply. It took her a few moments to ready herself. Then, in one smooth, much-practised gesture, she tucked her hair behind her ears, leaned forward and stuck her fingers down her throat.

Five minutes later it was all over. She straightened up, a profound sense of relief flowing over her, calming her immediately, bringing back a sense of order and control. Her eyes were streaming with tears but her head was clear and sharp. She got up and walked over to the sink. She rinsed her mouth and scooped up a little water in the palm of her hand. She passed it over her face, wincing as her fingers brushed the cut. It really was nothing – a crust of dried blood, a little bruising, nothing to worry about. Her face stared back out at her, startlingly white in the harsh bathroom light. She looked at herself, trying to imagine herself as others might see her. Lightly freckled alabaster skin; a wide, full mouth; brown eyes set fractionally too far apart. She wasn't even pretty. Certainly not beautiful.

Not like Andrea Halgren or Lindy Myerson – or Sandy Zimmerman. 'Unusual' was what people usually said. 'Striking', if they were pushed. And in a good mood. She had the sort of face that showed everything, every emotion, every thought, every nuance. The sort of face that told its own story, hid nothing, left nothing unsaid. She desperately wished it weren't so. 'You're so damned *sensitive*,' was what her father always said. Sensitive. Temperamental. Moody. Highly strung. He had a long, detailed list of negatives, which generally began with her character and ended with her looks. Fat. She was fat. That last comment had tormented her for the past few years. She could still feel the heat rise in her cheeks every time she remembered it. 'Just look at them damned thighs, Madison Stiller. You'll be bigger than the cows if you don't watch out!' She'd been helping him with the early morning milking. In summer. In shorts and a T-shirt. She'd looked down at her thighs in horror and promptly burst into tears. 'What the hell's the matter with you?' her father had shouted after her as she ran from the shed. 'It's only a joke. Where are you going? We ain't done here!' She fled upstairs to her room and peeled off her shorts, anxiously examining herself in the mirror. Fat? Was she really fat? She looked at herself in distress. She had to be. If her father said so, it must be so. She'd eaten almost nothing in the days that followed, much to Martha's distress.

'I don't know what's got into you,' she said crossly, removing yet another almost untouched meal from the table. 'It's hanging out with those two, that's what's done it. I never liked Lindy or Andrea, for that matter. Will you look at her, Frank?' She appealed to her husband. Frank looked up from the newspaper he was reading and grunted. When he looked back down again, the subject was closed. Maddy's worst fears were realised. She *was* fat. He thought so.

But she couldn't go on eating next to nothing. The following morning in her science class, she'd been called on to come up to the chalkboard. She'd got up from her seat a little too quickly. There'd been a rushing, singing sensation in her head and then the next thing she knew, she was lying on the ground. She'd fainted. She'd had almost nothing to eat in a week. Ironically, given Martha's reservations, it was Lindy who'd provided the answer. 'My sister does it,' she'd said airily. 'That's exactly what you need to do.'

'What does she do?' Maddy asked, half-fearfully.

'It's easy. You eat what you want and then you just throw up.'

'How?'

Lindy shrugged. 'You stick a finger down your throat. It's easy, I swear. My sister uses a piece of thread. Look, I'll show you.'

'Yeeugh! You're so *gross!*' Andrea squealed.

Lindy was right, though. It *was* easy. At home that night, Maddy practised for the first time. She'd eaten a little more at supper than usual, despite her feelings of revulsion. She went to bed early, pleading a headache, and then locked herself in the bathroom. It took three or four tries before she managed to make herself sick – and then it all came rushing up. One and a half sausages, two spoonfuls of mashed potatoes, carrots. She could hardly breathe with the effort of trying to make herself sick, but the feeling of calm and control that descended upon her once she had been was like nothing she'd ever experienced. From then on, it was easy. She would wait in her room until her parents had gone to bed, then she would creep downstairs, open the fridge door as quietly as she could and stuff whatever she could find into her mouth. She would stand there savouring the taste and feel of biscuits, ice cream or anything else she could lay her hands on, and then, when she couldn't possibly cram anything else into her stomach, she would creep back upstairs and into the bathroom to bring it all back up. When her father disappeared, it was the first thing that ran through her mind. It was her fault. She was fat and ugly and he'd finally decided he couldn't stand it any longer. He was so sickened by the sight of her that he'd had no option but to leave. How else could she explain it?

'You OK?' Sandy was sitting on the bed when she finally emerged from the bathroom. 'You look kinda weird. Here, have some of this.' She held out a tumbler full of dark red wine. Maddy took the glass and took a cautious sip. Her mouth tasted of antiseptic mouthwash and bile. The wine was warm and rich. 'Cheers,' Sandy said, lifting her glass. 'Welcome to New York.'

'Er, cheers,' Maddy murmured. She took another sip, trying not to stare. Sandy had tossed her coat casually to one side; she looked at it curiously. *Donna Karan. DKNY.* Maddy had never heard of Donna Karan. Or DKNY.

'So where you from anyway?' Sandy asked conversationally.

'Iowa,' Maddy mumbled, looking into her tumbler.

'*Iowa?*' Sandy's voice rose incredulously. 'Like, the Midwest?'

Maddy nodded, embarrassed. Sandy made it sound like a disease. 'Are you from New York?' she asked quickly, wanting to change the subject.

'Sure am. Upper East Side. My mom wanted me to stay home for freshman year but I was just *dying* to get away. I'm going home this weekend, though. You should come with. One of my friends is having a party Friday night. Why don't you come?'

Maddy hurriedly swallowed of the rest of her wine. Twin surges of excitement and fear rippled through her. A party. A weekend at someone's home. She felt as though she'd stepped on to the set of a film. She'd only been gone from Iowa for a day and a half and already her life felt as though it belonged to someone else.

6

NIELA
Hartishek, October 1991

It took the Adens almost a week to make it to Hartishek, the sprawling refugee camp just across the Somali–Ethiopian border. They drove into the camp before dawn. No one spoke, not even the driver, as they wound their way slowly through the maze. As the light came up, the sprawling mass of tents and shacks revealed itself to them, a vision of hell. A thin pall of smoke hung over everything – in front of the makeshift shelters women cooked on tiny stoves over coal fires. Hassan looked around him, too stunned to do anything other than stare. It was Niela who ordered the driver to stop. She wound down the window and asked a young man wandering aimlessly in front of them if he could direct them to the UNHCR HQ. He pointed out the dusty two-lane track that led to the centre of the camp. 'But don't expect them to give you anything,' were his parting words. 'They've run out of everything. Useless.' He spat the word out bitterly.

'What d'you think he means?' Niela asked her father as she wound up the window again. 'Run out? Run out of what?'

Hassan shook his head helplessly, unable to answer. Niela repeated the directions to the driver, her heart sinking. For the past three days, the whole family had focused on getting to Hartishek, somehow imagining it to be the end of their journey. Now that they'd arrived, it was clear that this was only the beginning.

A few hours later, they stumbled out of the UNHCR offices with a tent, a few blankets and a small parcel of food that was intended to last them the weekend. Hassan's shoulders were slumped. The process had defeated him. The aid workers who staffed the various agencies that had been set up in Hartishek to deal with the thickening stream of desperate refugees seemed unable to distinguish between him, a prosperous, educated, middle-class Somali with a string of degrees and a successful business, and the nomads who wandered in off the Ogaden every day with their goats. They spoke to him as if he'd never held a fork or knife in his life, except perhaps in killing. His university degrees meant nothing to them – bought, most likely, one young girl's expression implied. Again, it was Niela who stepped in to spare her father any further humiliation. She collected the blankets and food, found the way to the bare patch they'd been allocated in between what felt like a million other people and dispatched her brothers to find water. On instruction from Hassan, she paid off the driver out of the cash they'd brought with them and told him to return the truck to Mohammed Osman. She watched him drive back down the dusty road, biting down hard on the impulse to run after him and beg him to take her away – *any*where. Anywhere would be better than this.

Their new neighbours, an extended family from south of Mogadishu, immediately offered what help they could. It took them a couple of hours to erect the tent. Niela and her brothers arranged the bedding and the few personal effects they'd managed to bring with them. By midafternoon, when the sun was finally beginning to lose its ferocious heat, the Adens had a new home. A tent, but still a home. It was hot and dusty and the constant noise surrounding them was deafening at times, but it was also a comfort of sorts. Here in the camp they were literally one family amongst thousands – but there was unexpected solace in the thought that they were all experiencing the same displacement and confusion together. No one here was spared. Doctors and lawyers rubbed shoulders and shared the ablution block with watchmen and taxi drivers – here they were all equally dispossessed. And, as Niela reminded her mother, at least they were safe. There were no marauding militia, no random gunmen, no gangs. The burly UN soldiers who patrolled the borders of the camp looked as though they meant business. Raageh and Korfa discussed their guns excitedly. They were still young enough to treat their escape from Somalia as an adventure, but there was something in her mother's silence and the set of her father's mouth that worried Niela. She had never seen her father – or her mother, for that matter – in that light. Without his pharmacies and the automatic deference his successful businesses afforded him, he seemed lost. It was painful and frightening to watch. Now that they'd finally arrived in Ethiopia, his task was to get the family from Hartishek to Addis Ababa and from there to Vienna, but Niela was already wondering if he had the necessary strength to continue their fight. Her uncle, Hassan's younger brother Raageh, who lived in Vienna with his Austrian wife, was doing everything he could to secure their visas, but the bureaucratic processes by which Somalis were allowed to leave Ethiopia seemed insurmountable. It was only their first day, Niela thought, swallowing hard. Perhaps her father would recover from the shock in the next few days.

As she lay awake that first night listening to the faint sound of her father's worry beads being passed from finger to finger and the soft, shallow breaths of her mother, a feeling of terror stole over her. In the corner of the tent was a small transistor radio, a couple of cooking pots and two or three books her brothers had thought to snatch as they fled. Those objects, unwitting symbols of the life they'd left behind, were all they had to reassure themselves of where they'd come from, and, more importantly, Niela suddenly saw, what they were. Now, more than ever, they had to hold on to those things. If they didn't, they would soon be lost.

But if there was terror at where they'd found themselves, there was also something else. In the first few days after their arrival, cut off entirely from the routine of family, friends, school and work, they were free to roam around the vast, tented camp city that stretched to the horizon. Niela's mother began to insert herself into the community of veiled women who organised the food in the camp, either for their individual families, or, more often, for the small clusters of neighbouring tents that grouped themselves according to a whole set of criteria that Niela had hitherto never understood – language, class, relations, extended families, tribal ties . . . anything that would bring some sense of order or community to the place they now called home. After a week, Niela began to see that for all its ramshackle air, the camp was surprisingly well organised. Former shop-owners, teachers, mechanics, builders and doctors were all trying to make for themselves a life that bore some marginal resemblance to what they'd left behind. There were makeshift clinics and schools; barbers set up chairs under sheets of tarpaulin; enterprising tailors operated pedal-driven sewing machines and women clubbed together to cook. Anything to avoid having to wait meekly and helplessly for handouts. Some families profited – those that had been lucky or clever enough to understand that they would be leaving Somalia for years rather than months and had thought to bring with them things that would really help: jewellery and cash, which were infinitely more useful than food and clothes. Sadly Hassan had had no such foresight, but by the end of their first week, it had somehow been established that his knowledge of medicines and drugs could usefully be traded for other things – cigarettes, food and precious toiletries.

To her surprise, Niela's gift for languages and the written word was equally useful. She was able to help a few of their neighbours who could neither read nor write to compose letters to the various agencies in charge of refugees, make appeals, push for one commodity or another and generally move their precariously slow cases forward. It didn't take much, she noticed with a growing sense of awe, to swap one existence for another. In Mogadishu, where she'd lived all her life, she'd been a normal, regular high school student with relatively liberal parents and a nice comfortable home. Three meals on the table every day and clean clothes folded away neatly in the chest of drawers that stood in the corner of her bedroom. She'd had posters on her wall of pop stars and actors, and the pretty lace coverlet that was spread carefully across her bed every morning by one or other of the maids in the house had come from a shop in Paris. Twice a week there were fresh flowers on her dressing table and on Friday nights, she and her friends watched the latest videos brought over from England and America. Sometimes her mother made them popcorn. But that was then. In less than a month, the world she'd grown up in had changed. Her two best friends – Sally-Anne Parkinson and Helga Neustrop, daughters of the Australian and Danish ambassadors respectively – disappeared with their diplomat parents as soon as the fighting broke out and she hadn't heard from them since. The International School had closed its doors; the few Somali students who attended it had long since fled. There was nothing left of that life now. Nothing at all. At some point in their flight from the capital they'd stepped across an invisible line where everything they'd ever known had been traded for a tent, a few blankets and a collection of memories, which, if they were to survive, they'd do best to forget.

7

JULIA
Oxford, October 1991

It took Julia a second to work out that the hands on her alarm clock were pointing to 9, not 7. It was quarter to nine! She leapt out of bed, stubbing her toe on the edge of her desk as she fumbled for her glasses. Quarter to *nine*? She grabbed her dressing gown from the back of the door and stumbled down the corridor. Her first tutorial was at 9 a.m. She'd overslept. Oh, God.

Fifteen minutes later, her mouth still tasting of toothpaste, her hair hurriedly brushed and shoved into a ponytail and a sweater thrown over the T-shirt she'd been sleeping in, she ran out the front door, trying to remember where the Faculty of Law was and, even more importantly, how to get there. Room C/2/4. Where the hell was C/2/4? Was there a floor marked 'C'? Was it on the second or fourth floor? She ran from one floor to the other and down one corridor after another, growing increasingly desperate. It was almost quarter to ten by the time she finally located it. She stood outside the door for a few minutes, hastily trying to compose herself. She scraped back the tendrils of hair that had come loose, wishing she'd thought to look in the mirror before leaving her room . . . too late. She opened the door cautiously and entered the small seminar room. Six pairs of eyes swivelled round to meet hers. She looked at the ground and slid into the nearest seat. Her cheeks felt as though they were on fire.

'Ah, Miss Burrows, I take it?' The elderly professor sitting at the front of the class looked at her from behind his glasses. 'Seminars start at nine a.m. on the dot. Difficult, I know, but there we have it. Now, where were we . . . ?'

'I'm sorry, sir. It won't happen again. I . . . I got a little bit lost trying to find the room.'

'Lost? Again?' A low murmur, meant for her ears only, came to her from the man sitting to her left. She felt her face turn an even deeper shade of red. There was no mistaking the voice. Him. *Again?*

For the next half an hour, she concentrated fiercely on following the professor's low, soft voice, ignoring the quivering panic that kept rising in her as the morning unfolded and she realised her grasp of jurisprudence was even shakier than she'd feared. At Nottingham she'd always been amongst the top four or five students in her year; here at Oxford, she understood immediately, things would be different. Aristotle's Golden Mean; Aquinas and Hobbes; Dworkin and analytic jurisprudence . . . the phrases flew out of the professor's mouth and seemed perfectly comprehensible to everyone else in the seminar room except her. She struggled to keep up, noticing out of the corner of her eye that she was the only one writing practically everything down – everyone else sat upright and alert, nodding every now and then, jotting down a word here, a name there . . . no one seemed to be drowning in a sea of information as she was. 'In short,' Professor Munro said, getting up and lighting his pipe as a way of making his point, 'anything that concerns the way a society is organised is political.' Julia's hand stopped mid-sentence and a ripple of pain ran up and down her spine. *Anything that concerns the way a society is organised is political, Julia.* It could have been her father speaking to her. In a flash she was fourteen years old again, standing next to him in his shed at the bottom of the garden, helping him stuff envelopes for the by-election amidst the smell of ink and printer's chemicals that never quite left his hands. Mike Burrows was a printer and a trade unionist at the *Newcastle Herald*, just like his father; a stout, fiercely independent man with a strong social conscience and the intellectual fervour of the self-taught. He was fiercely ambitious – the opportunities that were open to Julia's generation hadn't been available to him, and Julia had grown up somehow knowing that there was a future 'out there' that would be different for her. But it was more than that. Mike was different from most of the men who lived in the streets around them. There was something about him that kept people at arm's length. They came him for advice or support, not for a drink or a game of cards. At least once a month there was someone whose life came spiralling out of one of the neighbouring houses and whose children ran in fear of what they'd seen. Hanging around the living room listening to their talk, rubbing a foot surreptitiously against her shin, Julia caught a glimpse of something she'd never seen in her own home – a husband who beat his wife; a man who came home drunk every night; a man who was going to lose his job. Mike was asked to 'speak' to them. One day there was a woman Julia recognised as Mrs Glenby from the other side of Elswick Road. Her daughter, Winifred, was in Julia's class. The snivelling, fear-distorted face was of the kind she'd never seen in her own home. The image burned in her mind's eye for months afterwards.

Although Sheila, Julia's mother, had never had a career of her own, she was just as ambitious for Julia. Together they went to the local library every Saturday with a list of books they'd selected that week and handed it over to the librarian. They read together in the evenings whilst the radio was on in the background – classics for Julia and a Catherine Cookson or the occasional Agatha Christie for Sheila. Mike didn't hold with watching TV every night. The soft tones of Radio 4 were the backdrop of Julia's teenage years.

And then one day everything changed. It was a Friday evening, six weeks before Julia's O level exams. Mike and Sheila were driving back from their weekly grocery shop. Witnesses said the small red van had come up Park Close at a ridiculous speed. There was a sudden, deafening screech of brakes as it rounded the bend and then the driver lost control of the vehicle. He was drunk. The van skidded across the intersection on the wrong side of the road and ploughed headlong straight into them. Mike was crushed against the steering wheel. He died almost immediately. Sheila was rushed in a shrieking ambulance to the nearest hospital but it was too late. She died an hour later. Julia was still at school when it happened. It took over an hour for the message to reach her. By the time she and her grandmother arrived at the hospital, they were both gone and Julia's entire world was turned upside down.

She struggled to breathe, sitting amongst all the intelligently nodding heads, none of whom had any idea what Professor Munro's words had brought on. The tightness in her chest made it impossible to write. She set her pen down quietly and turned her head to look out of the window. Through the thin veil of tears she could just make out the tops of the trees lining the Cherwell River and the rise of Headington Hill beyond. She sat very still for a few moments, waiting for her heartbeat to return to normal and for the world to right itself again. She could feel her neighbour's eyes on her but she simply didn't have the strength to do anything other than studiously ignore him. It was in moments like these that the weight of how differently her life had turned out to most people she knew hit her with all the force of a speeding truck. She closed her eyes briefly again at the inappropriateness of the metaphor she'd unwittingly chosen.

*

'Bad luck losing your way like that on your first day.' Someone spoke to her as they made their way out of the seminar room an hour later.

Julia turned. It was the tall, thin young man with a prominent Adam's apple whom she'd noticed sitting at the front of the class. She looked at him warily. 'Should've looked it up on the map last night,' she said tightly. 'My own bloody fault.'

'Oh, I wouldn't worry about it,' he said airily, quickly. 'Everyone misses something in the first couple of weeks. I'm Dominic, by the way.' He held out a hand. 'But do call me Dom.'

Julia hesitated. The five other students in the class had rushed ahead, chatting excitedly. They all seemed to know one another, although she couldn't understand how that was possible. They'd been at Oxford less than a weekend. No one had even bothered glancing her way, except for that awful pompous bloke she'd met the night before, and then it was only to say something sarcastic, so why did this Dominic – Dom – seem to want to have anything to do with her? But her manners got the better of her and she reluctantly held out her hand. 'I'm Julia.'

'I know. Munro called out the names this morning and you were the only one not there.'

'Oh, go on . . . rub it in, why don't you?' Julia asked sharply and then regretted it as soon as she'd spoken. She was being defensive, as usual. There was just the faintest possibility he was only trying to be kind.

Dom's eyebrows rose in mild protest. 'I wasn't. I was just intrigued as to who you might be, that's all. I know most of the others on the course. We were all undergrads together,' he said, pointing to the group of students ahead of them. 'Except Keeler, of course. He's a bit older but his younger brother was in my class at school.'

'Who's Keeler?'

'Aaron. The blonde guy. Sitting next to you. The one you kept throwing hateful glances at.'

Julia flushed crimson. 'He . . . he was rude. About me being late,' she said weakly. 'He's just so . . . so bloody arrogant.'

'Ah, yes. Well, comes with the territory. Good looks, famous mother, place at Oxford practically guaranteed . . . I'd probably be just as pompous. He takes a bit of getting used to but he's all right really, underneath it all. I blame his mother, personally.' Julia looked up at him again. There was something odd about his cheery voice. Was he envious, perhaps? She couldn't yet tell. And who was Keeler's mother?

'Who's his mother?' she asked.

'Diana Pryce. Can't you tell?'

Julia looked at him incredulously. Diana Pryce? Diana Pryce was that man's *mother*? She remembered the day she'd first seen Diana Pryce on television. She was a lawyer, a QC, if Julia's memory served her right. She'd campaigned for the release of two hunger-striking Irish political prisoners for years without a glimmer of hope, and then all of a sudden, in a flurry of publicity, their convictions had been overturned. She'd watched the proceedings every night for a week, sitting beside her father. 'Damn fine woman that,' Mike had said admiringly. 'She never gave up. That's something to be proud of, Julia. Never give up.' Julia remembered staring at the fuzzy image of an immaculately dressed woman in high heels holding tightly on to the arm of one of the prisoners, whose emaciated face bore the dazed look of someone whose life had been turned upside down. She shook her head disbelievingly. Diana Pryce was Aaron Keeler's mother? 'I'd never have guessed,' she said faintly.

'Oh, stick around Oxford for a couple of weeks and you'll hear it all the time . . . that's all anyone ever says about him,' Dom said. 'Must be a bit of burden, if you ask me. Always being compared to her. There's three of them – three brothers. They all went to Eton. Heavenly Creatures – that's what we used to call them. You know the type – good-looking, sporty, clever. The sort you love to hate.' He looked down at her. 'Anyway, sod the Keelers. We've got library induction in about an hour. Shall we go and have a coffee somewhere? Have you been to the Bodleian yet?' Julia shook her head. 'Come on, then. There's a coffee shop across the road and then we can go over together. Don't worry, there's no ulterior motive here. I'm as queer as they come.'

Julia's mouth dropped open in protest. 'It never crossed my mind.'

'Good.' He grinned at her. 'So . . . shall we?'

'All right then,' Julia said, still a trifle uneasily. Although she'd warmed to Dom in the five minutes they'd been chatting, she was still baffled as to why he'd chosen to speak to *her*. After all, no one else had. Aside from the arrogant Keeler, no one else had so much as looked her way since she'd arrived, so why had Dom? She risked a quick upward glance. There was nothing in his expression that gave her a clue. He held the door open for her, and somewhat uneasily, she led the way. They followed the noisy group ahead of them down the stairs and out of the faculty building, Julia still puzzling over the fact that Dom appeared to want to be her friend. Why? It didn't make sense. Mind you, she reminded herself quickly, not much about her new life at Oxford made sense. She'd never in her life felt quite so out of place.

Although she'd been one of the very few from her comprehensive in Newcastle to go to university in the first place, there'd been plenty of people like her at Nottingham – the first in their respective families to leave home and take up a course of study that meant they would probably never return. In her year alone there'd been three or four people whose backgrounds practically mirrored her own. Oxford was different. Whatever Dom's reasons for befriending her might be, it was impossible to believe he felt as out of place as she did. No one could possibly be more unsuitable. Everything about her screamed 'working class', 'northern', 'poor' – or worse. Amongst the leggy blondes and dark-haired, curvy beauties she'd seen around her, she was an oddity with her short, boyish haircut and standard regulation outfit of jeans and a sweater. She'd never been the type to worry about her looks – in her eyes at least, she'd never had looks to worry about, so why bother? Alison, her closest friend at Nottingham, had begged to differ, but she was an engineering student so what the heck did she know? Julia had had two boyfriends whilst at Nottingham – Mike, who was an exchange student from New Haven, Connecticut, and George, a fellow law student from Doncaster – but neither had quite set the world on fire as Alison seemed to think they ought. The truth of the matter was that she'd never found anyone whose conversations were more interesting than either the novels she read in bed at night or the textbooks she read in class, and that, give or take the odd moment of tenderness or warmth, was pretty much it. Alison thought she was hopeless. Julia thought it too. And now here she was, in possession of a first-class degree from Nottingham, at the start of a one-year Masters at Balliol, sitting in a seminar room with some of the brightest, most ambitious and easily most capable students in England . . . and none of them seemed to want to do anything other than ignore her. It was almost too painful to think about.

She turned her collar up, shoved her hands in her pockets and hurried to keep up with Dom. Although she was five foot six and had always thought of herself as tall, she was clearly no match for Dom's long legs. They turned into Turl Street, heading for the Bodleian, and, to Julia's relief, soon left the others behind.

8

Within a fortnight of Julia's arrival at Balliol, two crucial bits of information had been made clear. The first, which caused her more than a few sleepless nights, was that however hard she'd worked at Nottingham to stay at the top of her class, at Oxford it simply wasn't enough. A first from Nottingham – from *anywhere*, she hastened to correct herself – meant little. In fact, it meant almost nothing. At Oxford, amongst some of the brightest and most ambitious people she'd ever met, she struggled to keep abreast. Aside from the horrendous reading lists, there were more lectures in a week than there'd been at Nottingham in a term; the list of essays they were given was endless, the list of precedents she had to look up was bottomless . . . and to top it all off, not only was the arrogant Aaron Keeler in her jurisprudence seminar class, he was also in her legal theory and civil justice classes – small, intimate groups of six or seven students where it was impossible to hide. He seemed to delight in her obvious discomfort; she'd no idea why. When she'd been called upon for the fifth time to respond to a question she didn't even understand, let alone feel confident enough to answer, and had seen his smirking face, she decided that not only was she out of place in terms of her looks, her accent and her background; now it had been very firmly proven that she didn't belong academically either. It was a crushing blow.

The second piece of information came to her in a flash, and although it was somewhat easier to stomach, it was no less of a surprise. She was sitting next to Dom in one of their many lectures, surreptitiously looking around her, when she caught sight of the expression on his face. It was such a painfully obvious mixture of longing and discomfort that she frowned, wondering who or what he could be looking at. She followed his eyes . . . and in a second, it was clear. He was staring at the back of Aaron Keeler's head. Her jaw dropped in surprise; he turned his head in that moment and caught her looking open-mouthed at him. He started to say something, then changed his mind, averting his eyes. Julia's mouth opened and closed again . . . she said nothing, but suddenly it all made sense. No wonder Dom had picked her out – she was the only person Aaron Keeler never spoke to, aside from him . . . Was it something Aaron had known since schooldays? She'd long wondered what on earth it was that drew her and Dom together – well, now she knew. It wasn't quite what she'd expected, but she'd felt such a keen stab of sympathy looking at him that she couldn't possibly be disappointed. Dom was in love with someone who wouldn't even look his way. Julia wasn't in love – in fact, she wasn't sure she'd *ever* been in love – but she did know what it felt like to be an outsider, always looking in. So that was what had drawn him to her . . . now that she knew, she felt even more kindly disposed towards Dom. Poor him. Imagine being in love *with Aaron Keeler*. She couldn't think of anything worse.

She was trudging back from one such seminar at the end of her fifth week – three more to go, she thought to herself miserably. And then she'd go back up to Newcastle and spend Christmas either with her only remaining relatives after her grandmother's death in her first year at Nottingham – a distant cousin of her father's and his equally distant wife – or she'd ring Alison, who was now down in London struggling to find her feet in an all-male engineering firm, and spend it with her and her engineer boyfriend, an equally dismal prospect. She could always spend Christmas on her own, just as she'd done the year before – although it had been such a sad, lonely time that she'd sworn never to do it again. She was lost in thought, trying not to think about how miserable she'd been, and didn't recognise the students who'd stepped in front of her as she made her way up Broad Street, clutching her stack of books and concentrating fiercely on the pavement in front of her.

'She'll never last.' A girl's voice rang out clearly. 'Her sort never do.'

'Did you see her expression this morning? When Munro asked her about Hegel. She didn't even know who Hegel was!'

Julia stopped, brought up short by the mention of Hegel. Were they talking about *her*? She lifted her head to look at them properly. She recognised Aaron Keeler's blonde head immediately. He was bending down towards another blonde, the improbably named Araminta Hedley-Tetherington. Next to Araminta – known to everyone except Julia as 'Minty' – was Keeler's obnoxious sidekick, Peregrine.

'Well, I shouldn't imagine she'll be around for much longer,' Julia heard Peregrine say. 'Her type don't stick around. She'll fail the Christmas exams and that'll be it.'

She watched Aaron stop and light a cigarette. 'Who *cares* what happens to Julia Burrows?' he asked, his voice making it absolutely clear that he didn't. 'Why on earth are we wasting five minutes talking about her?'

'I'm just *saying*,' Peregrine began, his tone aggrieved. 'I'm just speculating that she won't make it past Christmas. She's awful.'

'She's not worth bothering about. Now, who's up for tomorrow night? There's a fancy dress party somewhere in Headington. Some girl from the Poly.'

'The Poly? God, Aaron . . . you do have the *weirdest* friends,' Minty giggled.

The ripple of loathing that ran straight up and down Julia's spine forced her to a complete stop. She stood in the middle of the pavement, her breath coming in short, angry gasps. She'd never in her life encountered such unbridled animosity – and from people she didn't even know! It was clear from their voices that they hated her . . . but *why*? What had she ever done to any of them? She put a hand up to her cheek. It was warm and wet and it wasn't the rain. She wiped her face furiously with the back of her hand, trying to ignore the hard, angry knot of hurt burning its way into her heart. No matter what she did or how hard she tried, she would never fit in. Everything about her was wrong. It didn't matter how hard she worked; they all thought of her as beneath them. She brushed the tears away angrily. Her parents hadn't prepared her for *this*. This was worse than anything she'd ever imagined. She was a second-class citizen and always would be. That was the reality of the path she'd chosen. Diana Pryce could have it all; Julia Burrows couldn't. End of story. *That* was how things worked. But they were wrong about one thing. Gone by Christmas? No fucking way. She wasn't going anywhere. It was time to make them sit up and notice her – even if it killed her, she would do it. She didn't care how long and how hard she had to study. *That* was what her father had wanted from her. To fight. And if it was a fight they wanted, well, they'd got it. She would fight them to the bitter, bloody end.

9

'Stop! Stop! *Stop!*' The instructor's voice cut straight across her mono-logue. Maddy froze mid-sentence. Nothing seemed to be going right. She looked across the room nervously, her heart sinking. Bearing down upon her with all the wrath of an angry god was Mark Ryan, voice and accent coach to the hapless first-year students. Or at least that was what he called them. 'Hapless. Completely fucking *hap*less.' He was English, although there wasn't an accent on the planet he hadn't been able to master. 'Look around you,' he'd said to them on meeting them for the first time at the beginning of the semester. 'Take a long, hard look at each other. By Christmas, the person to the right or left of you will be gone.'

Well, it was nearly Christmas and now he was glaring at *her*. Maddy's heart sank, coming to an abrupt halt in the pit of her stomach. 'Just stop! You're *massacring* the bloody language!' Her mouth remained open but to her horror, nothing came out. Not a sound. Not a single squeak. Across the room, her fellow students looked on, not all of them sympathetically.

'What the *fuck* do you think you're reading?' Ryan glared at her. 'A *memo?*'

'N-no, sir,' Maddy stammered, her face on fire. She could see Sandy wincing.

'Then why the *fuck* does it sound as if you are?'

'I . . . it doesn't, sir . . . I . . .' Maddy could scarcely get the words out. She was absolutely petrified.

'It doesn't? Oh, forgive me, I must be mistaken. *Next!*' His voice was dripping with sarcasm. Maddy looked at him uncertainly. 'Next,' he spat out, looking past her to where the others waited at the rear of the studio. He bent his head to his marking sheet. She was dismissed. Just like that. She walked unsteadily to the back of the room, tears burning behind her eyes.

'Asshole,' Sandy muttered as she took her place beside her. 'Don't let him get to you,' she whispered out of the side of her mouth.

'Ms Zimmerman?' Ryan's voice rang out. His ears were as sharp as his eyes. 'Care to show the rest of us how it's done?'

Maddy looked away as a red-faced Sandy walked nervously to the front of the class. She blinked back the tears that were threatening to spill out of her eyes. This was *torture*. How had she ever imagined this was what she wanted to do for the rest of her life?

At 5 p.m., almost three hours after it had begun, the humiliation was finally over. The students traipsed dispiritedly out of the hall and disappeared as quickly as they could. Maddy and Sandy walked along the corridor in silence, Maddy too embarrassed to speak. Suddenly she heard Ryan's voice behind her. He was talking to someone, clearly about the class he'd just taken. 'Christ, what a group. There ought to be a law against them. There's one girl in particular. The Stiller girl. What a turnip. Do they make 'em in a factory somewhere out there in the cornfields? A Midwestern actress. Can you think of anything worse?' Whoever he was talking to snorted derisively. Maddy stood rooted to the spot, not daring to turn around. A door opened and closed somewhere behind her and then suddenly there was silence. Maddy's face was on fire. She couldn't even bring herself to look at Sandy. *A turnip-headed Midwesterner*. Was that what he thought of her? Was that what they *all* thought of her?

'Come on.' Sandy squeezed her arm sympathetically. 'Let's go get a drink. Don't let him get to you, Maddy. He's just an asshole.'

Still too stunned to think, let alone speak, Maddy allowed Sandy to lead her downstairs to the bar on the ground floor. *A turnip-headed Midwesterner*. How could she *ever* have thought she could act?

'Here.' Ten minutes later, Sandy slapped down two bottles of beer on the table in front of them. 'Drink up. We've only got an hour before it's Loughlin's class. And don't waste a single moment thinking about Ryan. He's just pushing you. He wants you to quit.'

'How do you know?' Maddy asked, bewildered.

'Oh, just trust me. I know his type. Don't let him get to you. You have to learn to fight back.'

Maddy stared at Sandy enviously. She and Sandy were polar opposites – they couldn't have been more different. Sandy was wealthy, worldly, confident – everything Maddy wasn't. Maddy knew just how wealthy and worldly she was. She'd been to Sandy's home. Twice. An enormous, spacious and supremely elegant apartment overlooking Central Park. Three long-haired dogs that Maddy mistook for cats, half a dozen

38

servants, summers in Europe and winters in St Bart's, wherever that was. Sandy's mother, a rake-thin dark-haired beauty, was a psychologist; her father a lawyer. In that, too, they couldn't have been more different. 'From *Iowa*?' Sandy's mother cried out when Sandy first brought Maddy home. 'Iowa?' She made it sound like the moon. Which it might as well have been for all the relevance Maddy's own home provided when it came to the Zimmermans. She'd wandered around the apartment-with-no-end in a daze. There was more artwork in the Zimmermans' living room than she'd ever seen in one place in her entire life. 'Are these *originals*?' she'd asked in a whisper as Sandy led her through and up a flight of stairs. Maddy had never been in an apartment that had stairs.

'Of course,' Sandy replied, genuinely surprised by the question. Maddy's mouth remained shut for the rest of the afternoon.

Now she sat opposite her, nursing her bottle of beer, wondering why she'd even bothered to come to New York in the first place and why, of all the things she could have tried her hand at, she had chosen acting. It was clear she couldn't act. It was all Mrs Steenkamp's fault, she reasoned, taking another swig. She was the one who'd first put the idea into her head. It was about a month after her father had disappeared. 'Why don't you come down and try out for a part?' she'd asked Maddy, more out of sympathy than anything else. Maddy had been so sick of people constantly asking her where her father had gone, why he'd gone, who he'd gone with . . . Mrs Steenkamp's invitation to join the after-school drama club had been a welcome escape. The minute she got up on stage, however, something inside her opened up. She was no longer Maddy Stiller, the only daughter of a man who'd upped sticks one afternoon and abandoned his wife and child; she was someone else. Another character. Someone with an entirely different past and history. On stage, at least, she was free. From that moment on, acting was all she could think about. At Tisch, however, she had suddenly grasped something else. It wasn't enough to want to *be* an actor – she had to prove she was good at it too. And that she seemed unable to do. 'What's wrong with me?' she asked Sandy, more rhetorically than anything else. She knew what was wrong. It wasn't only Ryan who demanded more of her than she was able – or even prepared – to give. All her instructors said more or less the same thing. Unless she was able to let herself go – truly let herself go – she would always remain where she was. A competent performer, nothing more. She worked hard, learned her lines, rarely, if ever, forgot her words . . . but she was certainly not someone who would ever set an audience alight. She lacked what others seemed able to give – depth. Only she knew the reasons why. She couldn't.

'Come on,' Sandy said, draining the last of her beer. 'It's Loughlin next. You sure you can handle this?'

Maddy nodded, hoping she looked more confident than she felt. If she was scared of Ryan, Wally Loughlin absolutely terrified her. He was a small, intense man who'd worked with all the greats from Brando to Pacino, and his classes were a mixture of torture and stunned amazement at what he managed to get out of his students, even Maddy. She spent most of her time in classes torn between the longing to take part and the longing to just disappear. She drained her bottle and stood up. Sandy was right – she had to learn how to handle the criticisms that were levelled at them almost hourly; she had to develop a thicker, tougher skin. She had to learn how to fight back and not wind up in tears almost every afternoon just because Ryan didn't think she had it in her. How did he know? Feeling somewhat braver, she followed Sandy out of the bar and together they rode the lift to the third floor, where Loughlin's weekly improvisation studios took place.

The class was already full when they walked in. Sandy found a couple of seats towards the rear and Maddy followed her gratefully. A few minutes later, Loughlin strode in. He wasted no time in organising the class. He picked out a handful of students, tossed out a few words and gave them each five minutes to come up with a two-minute sketch of whatever it was he'd thrown their way. There was a lot of nervous giggling as the ten students struggled, each in their own way, to think of something that would not only satisfy Loughlin but hopefully impress him too. A tall order. In the semester she'd been at Tisch, Maddy had never seen Loughlin impressed by anyone, let alone her. She sat with her chin cupped in her hand, watching, entranced, as he put the students he'd selected through their paces. 'Fear!' 'Envy!' 'Desire!' Someone who'd been given 'envy' to perform was suddenly required to improvise. 'Give me hatred!' Loughlin yelled. 'Burning hatred!' Suddenly the word she'd been fearing all semester slipped out. 'Stiller!' Maddy froze. 'Get up here. You're next. Gimme grief!' He glared at her as she made her way un-steadily to the front of the class. 'You've got two minutes, Stiller. Show us how it's done.'

Maddy felt her throat go dry. As always when she was nervous, she felt her body temperature begin to drop. She shivered. She closed her eyes briefly and tried to summon up the emotion he'd asked for. She couldn't.

She needed a starting point. Loughlin coughed. She tried to focus. Grief. Sadness. Tears. She swallowed. Loughlin coughed again. The palms of her hands began to itch. Grief. *Come on, Maddy*, she willed herself. *Get a grip.* 'I . . .' She opened her mouth but could go no further.

'In your own time, Stiller,' Loughlin drawled sarcastically. 'But I'm not seeing anything that speaks of grief to me.'

Maddy willed herself to concentrate. Grief. When had she last experienced it? She stood there trying to summon it up, but nothing came. She was sweating, despite the chill that had settled over her. She thought of the farm, of her mother's face the day she boarded the bus for New York . . . surely there was something there? But there was nothing; just the usual carefully constructed wall she built around those emotions she felt she couldn't handle. She could feel herself clamming up. Her mouth suddenly flooded with water as the old, familiar feeling of panic began to settle in.

Loughlin slid off his stool and walked towards her. He was a tall, powerfully built man. He towered over her, saying nothing, but staring at her intently. For a brief, absurd second, she thought he might actually hit her. 'Stiller!' he roared. Maddy jumped. Someone in the class laughed nervously. 'Grief! Anger! Fear!' Loughlin roared, jabbing his finger at her.

'I . . . I *can't* . . .' Maddy stammered, desperately trying to control her voice.

'Can't or won't?' His blue eyes flashed contemptuously at her.

She looked up at him, failure flooding her senses. She'd seen Loughlin give other students a hard time, but this was different. She stood in front of him, trapped by her own fear – fear of him, of the class, of what he was asking her to do. She felt her stomach turn over. She'd never experienced anything like it. There was a dull, metallic taste in the back of her throat that she dimly recognised as tears. *Oh God . . . please, no. Please don't let me start crying in front of him.* 'I . . .' Again she tried to get the words out, and again her mouth and tongue failed her.

'Thought so.' Loughlin looked down at her, the contempt in his expression all too clear. 'Disappear, Stiller. You obviously haven't got what it takes. Next! Anderson. Come up here. Show the rest of us how it's done.' There was another embarrassed cough from the audience.

Maddy stood still for a second, rooted to the spot, unable to take it all in. Todd Anderson, tall, impossibly handsome and impossibly gifted, strode confidently to the centre of the stage. He ignored her as he prepared himself to take on the role she clearly couldn't. There was nothing for it but to exit the classroom as quickly as possible. She fled.

It took her less than half an hour to empty her closet of her possessions and stuff them in her suitcase. Tears were streaming down her face but she couldn't feel them. Her heart was racing. She had never, *ever* been so humiliated in her entire life. Loughlin's words sang out endlessly in her ears *Clear out, Stiller. You obviously haven't got what it takes. A turnip-headed Midwesterner.* They were absolutely right. She *didn't* have what it took. Better to get the hell out now before she was humiliated any further.

Suddenly the door burst open. Sandy stood in the doorway. Her mouth dropped open as she surveyed Maddy's suitcase. 'What're you doing? You can't be serious! You're *quitting*?'

Maddy picked up a sweater, folded it and placed it in her case. She hoped her voice was steady. 'Loughlin's right. I'm not cut out for this, Sandy. I don't know what I was thinking—'

'Maddy, I don't believe you!' Sandy was incredulous. 'You've had a couple of bad days and you're going to *quit*?'

'They're not just bad days,' Maddy said defensively. 'Loughlin's right. I . . . you've got to have talent, Sandy. It's not enough just to *want* to act. I *can't.*'

'Bull*shit*. Maddy, we've only been here a couple of months! You can't quit before the first semester's even ended! That's absurd!'

'It's not absurd!' Maddy closed the lid of her suitcase with a snap. 'I'm not like you, Sandy. I'm from a *farm* in Iowa, for God's sake. I just wish I had your confidence. You grew up here, you've been all over the world . . . you're *tough*. I'm just some country hick—'

'Will you *stop* it? Listen to you! We're *all* scared, Maddy. It's hard for everybody, not just you.'

'That's not it! Of course I know it's hard for everyone. But I'm no *good*, Sandy. I can't do this. I can't! Every time he asks me for . . . for these emotions . . . I *can't!*'

'That's because you won't *let* yourself, not because you *can't*. Don't think I don't know what's going on with you, Maddy. Don't think I don't know where you disappear to every night.'

Maddy stared at her. Embarrassment rippled up and down her spine. 'Wh . . . what're you talking about?' she whispered, her voice suddenly failing her.

'Oh, come on. It's so *obvious*. You starve yourself all day long, then you

42

go and stuff your face with all kinds of shit. You think I don't know what you're doing?'

There was a sudden silence. Maddy felt her knees give way. She sat down on the edge of her bed. Her head felt heavy and there was an unfamiliar tightness in her chest. She couldn't speak. She opened her mouth to say something, but nothing came out. Shame flooded her senses. Her dirty little secret was out. 'I . . . I'm . . .' she stammered, unable to look up.

'Look, Maddy . . . you don't have to explain. I know what's going on. My mom's a shrink, remember? You need help. Quitting's not the answer.'

Maddy's eyes flooded with tears. Help? How could anyone help her when even she didn't know what was wrong? 'I . . .' She tried to speak. 'I . . . I'm OK,' she stammered, wiping furiously at her cheeks. 'I'm fine. I . . . I'm just a bit tired, that's all. I don't know what you're talking about.'

Sandy's eyes narrowed. She looked searchingly at Maddy. Finally she lifted her shoulders, spreading her hands out before her. 'OK. Fine. Whatever.' She gave her another piercing glance and then left the room. Maddy was suddenly alone. She looked down at her hands. They were shaking. Her whole body felt as though it was on fire. She'd come dangerously close to being found out and it was all her own fault. She'd made the mistake of allowing someone to get too close to her; she'd been careless, she'd let her guard down. She had to make sure it would never happen again. As much as she liked Sandy and as grateful as she'd been to have a friend in this cold, lonely city, she simply couldn't afford to let anyone come any closer. She was on her own again, just as she'd always been. It was safer that way.

10

NIELA
Vienna, January 1992

Without a shadow of doubt, it was the waiting that was the hardest part. From the mile-long queues that formed before dawn at the store where the food packs were handed out to the interminable wait for their visas to come through, each and every day was spent in anxious anticipation. Niela could no longer remember what it was like *not* to wait. But it was astonishing how quickly they adapted – Niela herself had grown so accustomed to the routine of watching her father leave every morning and return empty-handed with no new information that it had become normal to her. It was almost as if he was going to work. He rose before sunrise, dressing himself in the dark without a sound. He stepped outside the tent to pray; then her mother got up, fumbling her way in the darkness to the box of matches that sat on top of the radio. In silence she lit the stove and prepared his breakfast in the way she'd once ordered her own servants to. She served him coffee and *njera*, the sour, flat Ethiopian bread that Niela had grown to hate. He ate quickly, pausing only to wipe his mouth and pat down his beard, and then he set off on his daily journey to the UN offices, where he waited all day for the interview or the request for information that would take his family a step further in the long, arduous process of leaving. Only he knew what pride he'd had to swallow in order to make that three-mile round trip, sitting patiently in front of college students barely older than his daughter, answering their questions and demands with the correct aura of humility and the right amount of subservience that would ensure he would get his family out, intact and alive.

One morning, about three months after their arrival, Niela was squatting uncomfortably on her haunches trying to slice onions with a not-too-sharp knife when she heard the commotion. She opened the flap of the tent and peered outside. People were running down the dusty track towards the tent. She looked up at her mother.

'Keep slicing,' her mother instructed her briskly, holding back the flap to look herself. She worried constantly about men catching a glimpse of Niela – as if anyone would look at her, Niela often thought to herself with half a smile. From the three or four showers she'd taken daily in Mogadishu and her once-weekly trip with her mother to the salon, where her hair was washed, conditioned and braided, to the twice-a-week visit to the female ablutions block, where she washed her hair with soap – no conditioning oils here – it was a miracle anyone still thought of her as female, never mind anything so ridiculous as pretty. She'd long since given up looking at her own reflection.

Through the opening she could see their neighbours running towards them. In the centre of the small crowd, clutching a sheaf of papers, was her father. She dropped her knife and jumped up, ignoring her mother's reprimand, and ran outside. Her father was running towards them, his long djellabah flying behind him, his worry beads jerking from side to side. Niela's mouth dropped open. She'd never seen her father run in her entire life. *They got the visas! They're going to Austria! They're leaving!* People were shouting and laughing excitedly. Her heart began to beat faster, and she searched her father's face as it came towards her. They'd waited so long for this very moment, she thought to herself wildly. It couldn't be true. It couldn't possibly be true.

It was. After weeks and months of pleading his case, Hassan's requests had finally found their way to the right department, the right pair of ears. No one could know the private depths of strength in a person, Niela saw that night, as her parents lay awake a few yards from her, whispering to each other. God alone knew what sort of understanding had passed between them in the last few months as they struggled to keep the family together. But they'd done it. Somehow, through the means and channels available to them, they'd managed to secure the visas they so desperately needed to get out of Africa to the safety of a new life.

It took them less than a week to pack up their few belongings, make the journey from Hartishek to Addis Ababa and from there, at long last, to Vienna. As the plane carrying the Adens and a few other families, whose shocked, dazed expressions revealed their status as refugees more clearly than any travel document possibly could, flew steadily northwards, Niela looked down on the finger of water that was the Red Sea and felt a part of her slipping away, sloughing off. For the third time in as many months a new, different side of her was struggling to emerge – now, for the first time in months, there was a sense of optimism mixed in with the pain she'd been struggling to contain.

11

Vienna. A city, a country, an entire *continent* buried under a suffocating blanket of snow. It was winter when they arrived. Days contracted to become brief intervals between the longest nights Niela had ever known.

She came out of the warm, steamy fug of Uncle Raageh's apartment each morning into a seizure of cold. His large, comfortable flat was on the first floor of an old building on Wallnerstrasse, close to the Volksgarten and the Rathauspark, both jewel-encrusted landscapes under layers and layers of glittering ice. Every morning on their way to German language classes that Niela and her brothers were required by law to attend, they walked down by the River Donau, muffled in clothing borrowed from neighbours and friends to protect them from the cold.

'Ich fahre. Du fährhst. Er fährt.' The teacher paused in her declensions to look expectantly at the class of foreigners sitting patiently in front of her. *'Jetzt bitte wiederholen Sie . . .'*

Niela joined in the chorus. After three months, she was finally beginning to get her tongue around the difficult language. She no longer stood in silent embarrassment at the supermarket, pointing dumbly to things she couldn't name. She no longer had to shake her head in frustration when someone spoke to her. Like a complex piece of music, the individual notes had slowly begun to fall into place. It helped that Ayanna, her cousin and so far, at least, her only friend, only spoke German and a little English. Niela dimly remembered the fuss that had been made when her Uncle Raageh had declined to marry the young Somali girl who'd been chosen for him and had married an Austrian girlfriend instead. She couldn't understand how anyone could possibly have objected – his marriage to Ulli had produced Ayanna, not only the most beautiful young woman Niela had ever set eyes on, but also one of the nicest. Ayanna was twenty, only a couple of years older than Niela, but she might as well have come from another planet. She was in her second year of a psychology degree at university. She still lived with her parents – hers was the large, almost empty room at the end of the corridor that had been given over to the Adens' suitcases – but she spent most of her time at her boyfriend's flat on the other side of the city. Niela regarded her comings and goings with amazement. Ayanna wasn't married and yet *she slept at her boyfriend's home?* And he wasn't Somali either! He was Turkish. Uncle Raageh seemed unperturbed. She overhead her father asking him one day how on earth he could let it happen. 'Oh, they all do it, Hassan,' Raageh said, laughing. 'What'm I to do? I can't stop her. Better we know where she is.' Niela didn't hear her father's reply. She wasn't sure she wanted to.

*

By the time spring was over and the city emerged from under its blanket of snow, the Adens, each in their own way, had begun to settle in. Hassan found work, although it was nothing even remotely like that which he'd been qualified to do. He no longer had a profession. His profession had become the task of putting food on the table for his family. He left every morning to work in the Turkish wholesaler's, where he managed to find a bookkeeping position, and returned every evening. His work had no place in their lives. He did not speak of it, and neither did they. The refugee housing authorities had found them a small flat in Simmering, to the south of the city. Niela's mother spent her days cooking and cleaning, much as she'd done in Mogadishu, though without the help of half a dozen servants or the support of her close-knit community of friends.

In June, after almost four months of the government-mandated language courses, Korfa and Raageh were deemed fluent enough to begin school. Niela's position was more precarious. She was too old for high school, but her German wasn't yet good enough to sit the entrance exam for university, even if they'd have been able to afford it. It was a strange hiatus. The past was no longer available, but the future was too uncertain to believe in. Suspended between two worlds – one to which she no longer belonged and another to which she couldn't – she waited. As her German improved and the boys were swallowed up by school, it fell naturally to her to become the family's eyes and ears, to interpret the what was happening around them and to do whatever she could to make sense of their new lives. She struggled against it at first. With her father and brothers gone from morning to evening, she couldn't bear the routine of helping her mother prepare the flat every day for their return, cooking, cleaning, fussing around the men when they came home at the end of the day. She began to look around for something else to do.

The relationship between her uncle and her cousin fascinated her. Her Uncle Raageh was a lawyer. After a particularly hard day in court, he would come home, loosen his tie and, if Ayanna and Niela happened to be around, beckon them into his book-lined study. 'Come. Set up the board. I've had a hellish day. Let's play.' The three of them would play chess, Niela and Ayanna on one side, Uncle Raageh on the other, until Tante Ulli came in with wine and cheese and the game was abandoned in favour of talk. Niela, who had always considered herself close to both her parents, was astonished to find a different sort of closeness here. With Uncle Raageh and Tante Ulli she talked about other things. Life. Politics. Sometimes even boyfriends. She could feel her cheeks turning hot with embarrassment as Ayanna and her mother discussed things that Niela couldn't even imagine *thinking* about, much less talking to Saira about. Although she loved her parents dearly, it came to her slowly, listening to her aunt and uncle and cousin, that the aloof inflexibility her father displayed back in Somalia, so useful back at home, would be of no advantage to him whatsoever in Europe. Here it was all about change and adaptation. How to move *with* the times, not fight against them. As she sat between her parents one night and at the dining room table with Ayanna and her uncle and aunt the next, she had the strong, uncomfortable sensation of her two lives coming together, not in harmony, but in collision. Something would have to give. And soon.

12

'Can you type?' The middle-aged woman sitting opposite Niela looked at her suspiciously.

Niela nodded vigorously. 'Yes. Quite well,' she added with a confidence she certainly didn't have.

'And file?'

Niela nodded again. The woman looked her up and down, pursed her lips and made a sudden decision. 'OK. I'll take you on for a month and then we see how it goes. *Gut?*'

Niela felt a quick surge of relief. 'Oh, *thank* you, Frau Henschler. Thank you.'

'*Nichts zu danken*. Let's see how you get on. You can start on Monday morning. Nine a.m. Please be on time.'

'I will, yes, of course. Th . . . thank you again,' she stammered, getting up as the older woman rose to her feet.

She left the small office, resisting the temptation to punch her fist in the air. She'd found a job! After five months of getting her head and tongue around the language, she'd found a *job*! She couldn't believe it. She'd been walking down Simmeringhauptstrasse as she did every morning to pick up groceries for her mother when she'd decided on the spur of the moment to take a short cut through the cemetery on the other side of the road. It was strangely peaceful inside the cemetery; more like a park than a place to bury the dead. She strolled amongst the beautifully tended graves and flower beds, pausing every now and then to read the inscriptions and wonder about the lives behind the headstones. She'd emerged on to the main street on the other side, an area she'd hardly ever been through. There the buildings were mostly industrial, small-scale family-run businesses – the odd factory or two. She was walking past one such building when she noticed a sign in the window. *Help Sought. Clerical Position. Must be able to type and speak English fluently.* She'd walked straight in almost without thinking. Half an hour later, she had the job.

'A job?' her mother said, pausing in her task of peeling onions to look suspiciously at her. 'What do you mean? What sort of job? What'll your father say?'

'What d'you mean? What does he have to do with it?' Niela was genuinely surprised.

'You should have asked him first.'

Niela stared at her mother incredulously. 'Uma, we need the money. Besides, I can't sit at home all day long.'

'It's your father's job to provide money, Niela, not yours. And you're not sitting at home all day long. There's housework to be done. Meals to put on the table. You're supposed to be helping me in the kitchen, not going out to work!'

'Uma, I was meant to go to *university*,' Niela protested, still incredulous. 'I don't want to spend my days cleaning and cooking.'

'Things are different now, Niela.'

'But I can't sit around waiting for ever. It's been almost a year since I had anything proper to do—'

'You don't call this proper?' Her mother pointed with her knife at the dish she was preparing. 'What *do* you call it then?'

Niela's mouth opened, and then she shut it again. It was no use arguing with her mother. Since they'd arrived in Austria, she'd been aware of a growing distance between them; something to do with the way Niela had had to take over certain tasks – shopping, running small errands, dealing with the bureaucracy of their housing, dealing with the authorities. It wasn't exactly as if her mother resented it, but something had changed in the balance of power between them. Nothing seemed to anger her mother more than the suspicion of patronage. Niela had no idea how to explain to her that just because *she* spoke German and her mother didn't, and because *she* seemed more able to negotiate their new existence, it didn't mean that Saira had lost any of her authority. On the contrary. She looked at her mother and sighed. 'I don't want to argue, Uma,' she began, hoping her voice sounded more conciliatory than she felt.

'Argue? Since when do you argue with *me*?' Her mother was beginning to climb slowly and mightily into her anger.

Niela sighed again. Whatever she said these days seemed to strike the wrong note. She forced an apologetic smile to her face. 'I'm sorry, Uma. I . . . I'm just tired, that's all.'

'*Tired?* Try cooking and cleaning all day and then come and tell me you're tired. I don't know what on earth you get up to, gallivanting around the city all day. You and that cousin of yours. I don't know what's got into you, I really don't. And I don't like it, Niela, not one little bit.' The resentment seemed to push up against her throat. 'I don't know what your father will say about this.'

It was on the tip of Niela's tongue to say he probably wouldn't notice, or care, but now was not the time for confrontation. She listened with half an ear for a further five minutes and then, as soon as she could, she mumbled an excuse and left the kitchen. She walked down the corridor to the tiny box room that was hers and closed the door. She lay down on the bed, fully clothed, listening to the faint sounds of the city outside the window. A bus chortled past; there was the distant drill of road works; a child cried out. After the steady thump of mortar and gunfire that had been the backdrop of their life in Somalia, the sounds outside their Viennese flat were soothing, even peaceful. A sign of normality in a world that had temporarily gone mad. The argument – if it could be called such – with her mother lingered in her mouth and mind; a faintly unpleasant, unsettling taste. She wished she could shake herself of the feeling that worse was about to come.

On Monday morning at 9 a.m. on the dot, just as instructed, she was waiting outside Bünchl u. Sohne, hopping nervously from one foot to the other. Frau Henschler unlocked the door and nodded at her approvingly. Herr Bünchl was already in his office, she said, walking briskly down the corridor to the office where Niela was to work. The smell of slightly burned coffee wafted through the air. 'You can hang your coat up here,' Frau Henschler said, pointing to a small cupboard. 'Tea room is in there. We have a break at eleven each morning. Coffee and biscuits are provided.' She opened the door to a small office. Two women looked up as Niela came through the doorway. 'Lisel and Margarethe. This is Niela, the new girl. She's starting today.' Frau Henschler made the introductions. Lisel was in her early thirties, a cheerful peroxide blonde with a piece of gum wedged permanently between her lips. She waved cheerfully at Niela as she took her seat opposite. Margarethe was older, and more reserved. She greeted Niela pleasantly enough but it was clear that there would be no easy hand of friendship outstretched towards her. She had been working at Bünchl u. Sohne for almost twenty years and she ruled the roost. Niela didn't mind. Her aunt Rawia, her mother's oldest sister, was remarkably similar. Most of her life had been spent pandering to her aunt's idiosyncratic behaviour; Margarethe would be no different.

Despite her mother's objections, Niela's job brought about a new kind of peace in the house. Saira no longer pursed her lips in silent disapproval when she walked through the door each day and Raageh and Korfa took it in turns to see who could hug her first. She'd taken a step away from the family; they both regarded her with something approaching awe. There was a tacit agreement between her and Saira that her father wouldn't see the money this new venture brought in. Every week she handed her mother an envelope, which supplemented Hassan's meagre salary and the amount given to the family by the government in a way that was unacknowledged yet welcome. It was indeed the Somali way of doing things – quietly, without confrontation, and most importantly, without loss of face. She was beginning to see how important it was, not just for her, but more significantly, for the family.

She'd been at Bünchl u. Sohne almost three months when, one rainy Thursday afternoon, Lisel stopped by her desk and asked her if she was coming with them to the annual company Oktoberfest party in Mistelbach. Niela looked up at her in alarm. 'What's Oktoberfest?' she asked.

'It's the beer festival. It's great fun. Herr Bünchl organises a bus for us . . . it's a laugh. Come on, join us!'

Niela shook her head. 'It's very kind of you, but . . . I . . . don't think so. I don't think my father would agree to it.'

'Why ever not? What's wrong with Oktoberfest?' Lisel asked, genuinely puzzled. 'I mean, *everyone* goes. It's a national holiday!'

'Well, I'll . . . I'll ask, but I really don't think he'll allow it.'

'Go on, ask him. We'll make a day of it. You *never* come out with us!'

'So you don't think I should even *ask* them?' Niela regarded her cousin doubtfully. Ayanna was applying silver eyeshadow to her eyelids. She stepped back and looked at the effect in the mirror. She shook her head firmly.

'Absolutely not. Just say you're staying here.'

'But what if they call and want to speak to me? What if my dad speaks to your dad and—'

'Niela, will you stop worrying! Have a good time for once in your life! Just call me when you get back to Vienna and I'll come and meet you at the tram stop. No one will even notice you're gone!'

'Well, if you're sure,' Niela said reluctantly. Even as she spoke, however, a small thrill of excitement was running through her. 'But what'll I wear? I've never been to a party here before.'

'It's Oktoberfest. Wear what you want. How about this?' Ayanna pulled out a black V-neck sweater with the word 'Fame' splashed across the front in sequins.

Niela looked at it dubiously. 'Isn't it a bit . . . well, low?' she asked anxiously.

'Low? It's a *sweater*!' Ayanna laughed at her. 'Look!' She held it up against her. 'There's nothing low about it. Wear it with a pair of jeans. It's fine. Nice and simple. It's Oktoberfest, not the opera. Here, try it on.'

Niela slipped her shirt over her head, pulled on the sweater and turned to face herself in the mirror. She looked like any of the young girls she saw every morning on their way to and from school, jobs, university. Except for her skin colour, she thought, she looked pretty much like everyone else.

'You've got such a lovely figure,' Ayanna said admiringly. 'I don't know why you cover it up all the time.'

Niela's face grew hot with embarrassment. She quickly pulled off the sweater and put her shirt back on. She picked up her bag. She was about to tell a lie to her parents and the thought filled her with dread. 'I'll . . . I'll call you later,' she said, making a beeline for the door before Ayanna could question her further. 'And don't say anything to anyone . . . please. I'm still not sure I'll go.'

''Course you'll go. I'm going to a party at Pratern. If you get back in time, why don't you come and join us?'

Niela didn't reply. The thought of lying to her parents, going to Mistelbach *and* then possibly joining Ayanna at a party in Pratern was enough to make her feel ill. 'See you,' she mumbled and opened the door. She ran down the corridor. Her aunt was in the kitchen but she didn't stop to say goodbye. She wanted to get back to the familiar atmosphere of the flat in Simmering, close the door of her bedroom behind her and bury her head in her pillow. Something was about to happen. She could feel it. Deceiving her parents was only part of it.

'Here. Try it. It won't bite, you know,' Lisel giggled, handing her a tumbler of beer. 'Or turn you into an alcoholic or whatever else it is you guys are afraid of.'

Niela took it cautiously. 'We're not all like that,' she said mildly. 'Some of us drink. My dad does. Occasionally.'

'Just not you.'

'Oh, I've had wine before. And champagne once.'

'*Ach*, I'm only teasing,' Lisel laughed delightedly. 'You're right. Alcohol's bad for you.' She lifted her glass and drained her beer in almost a single gulp. 'Another one?'

Niela had to laugh. She shook her head. Whilst it was true that she'd tried wine before, she'd never even tasted beer – and she wasn't sure she would ever again. It was definitely an acquired taste. Cold and sour. She looked on in astonishment as Lisel poured herself a fourth glass. She was still nursing the same tumbler one of the factory workers had handed her when they arrived. She looked around the enormous tent. It was hard to see why everyone was so excited about Oktoberfest. They'd spent the better part of the morning on a coach, Niela trying hard to suppress the knot of panic in her stomach at the thought of what would happen if she were found out.

13

The party went on for hours. It was almost eleven by the time the coach finally pulled into the square in front of Stefansdom in the centre of town. Niela was almost asleep, her head lolling uncomfortably against the windowpane. Her tongue felt as though it was stuck to the roof of her mouth. She glanced nervously at her watch. Fortunately it was only a short walk from Stefansdom to Uncle Raageh's. She followed the others off the bus and made her way quickly across the park.

Ayanna's bedroom light was on. She'd either arrived back from her party or was on her way out. Niela breathed a sigh of relief as she opened the front door. It took her a second or two to work out who was standing in the hallway, waiting for her as she came through the vestibule. Her legs suddenly turned to jelly. It was her father. They stared at one another for a moment. Behind him, Niela could just make out her mother's silhouette. She opened her mouth to speak, but nothing came out.

'Come here.' Her father spat the words out.

'Hassan,' her mother began, lifting a handkerchief to her eyes. 'Hassan, I beg you—'

For a split second, Niela thought he would hit her there and then. Her aunt appeared behind him, looking in bewilderment from one to the other.

'Whose bright idea was this?' she asked Niela in German. 'Ayanna's?'

Niela shook her head, terrified. 'No, it was mine. I—'

'Shut your mouth!' her father roared at her suddenly. 'And don't you *dare* speak that language in front of me!'

'Hassan, please.' It was her uncle this time, pushing his way past his wife. He laid a placatory hand on his brother's arm. 'This isn't the time or the place. It's nearly midnight. Come. Come inside. Let the girl explain herself. She's—'

'Whore.' Her father shook his head in disgusted disbelief at her. '*Whore!*'

'Hassan!' Her mother cried. 'Stop it, I beg you!'

'Please! Come inside. Please!' Uncle Raageh was just as distressed. 'Let's talk about it inside.'

'Is this how we brought you up? To sneak around like a common streetwalker? No sense of decency? Of shame?' Her father was climbing into his anger. Niela knew his rages. There would be no turning back, no going inside to discuss things calmly. She began to tremble. *I've done nothing wrong.* She spoke the words to herself alone. *I've done nothing wrong.* She hung her head and stood in silence, listening to her father's wrath and threats. She was to come home immediately. She would be put under lock and key. She was no longer allowed to leave the house. *That job of hers – he'd known it from the very start. Trouble. He could sense it. Walking out of the house one morning without so much as a word to anyone.* He raged on and on. Somehow, from some depth of understanding she didn't even know she possessed, Niela saw that his rage was not directed at her alone. She avoided her mother's eyes and concentrated instead on the floor, waiting for the flood waters to recede.

Uncle Raageh took them home. It was almost one in the morning by the time they pulled up outside the flat in Simmering. From the way her mother hustled her out of the car and up the steps, leaving the two men to talk alone, she knew she was in for a lecture from her as well. She followed her into the sitting room, unsure as to how much more she could bear. But her mother surprised her. 'Niela,' she said, turning to her, gesturing to her to sit down. Her voice was soft. 'This is not the way to go about it.'

'Go about what?' Niela was confused.

Her mother slowly unwrapped her veil as she sat down. She patted the space next to her. 'I know this is hard for you. It's hard for all of us. Especially your father. It's not easy, you know . . . a man in his position. You've shamed him, and in front of his brother, too.'

'But I haven't done anything!' Niela cried, tears of frustration springing to her eyes. 'All I did was—'

'Lie. You lied to us, Niela. Is that not enough?'

'But only because you won't let me *do* anything. I'm not allowed out of the house! I can't make friends. I can't go anywhere, meet new people, get on with my life—'

'Niela, Niela. In time. *Y'ani* . . . you want everything *now*. It won't work that way. Not with your father. I should know. I've been married to him for twenty-five years. There are other ways to get what you want. It doesn't always have to be a confrontation.'

'What d'you mean?'

Her mother regarded her thoughtfully. 'Niela, you're nearly twenty years old. I know things haven't worked out the way you wanted – the way we wanted. But that's life. We have to make another life now. *You* have to make another life.'

'How? How can I when I'm shut up in here all the time?'

There was silence for a moment. Then her mother turned to her, taking her hands in hers. 'Niela. There's been an approach . . .'

Niela stared at her, her heart tightening. 'What d'you mean, "an approach"?' she asked fearfully, disengaging her hands.

'It's a distant relative. On your father's side. He's—'

55

Niela jumped up from the couch. 'No! *No!*' Panic rose in her throat. She couldn't believe her ears.

'Niela—'

'No!' She backed away from her mother, almost knocking over the small side table that stood between her and the door to the corridor. 'I won't do it! I won't!'

'It's only an approach, Niela. He's a very respectable man. He lives in Germany and—'

'You can't make me!' Niela almost screamed the words. The door to her brothers' bedroom opened. Korfa and Raageh's heads appeared. She swept past them, tears blinding her, and pushed open the door to her own room. She flung herself down on the bed, past caring what her father or anyone else thought. She couldn't believe it was happening to her. They were arranging to marry her off! *She* – of all people! She who'd had dreams of going to university, taking up a profession, choosing her own husband if and when the time came. Now they were preparing to hand her over to a complete stranger – never mind the fact that he was a distant relative! What had it all been for? The exhortations to do well in school, to study hard, the trips to Europe and the future that she'd grown up thinking was hers? They'd never stopped her from doing *anything* back home – so why now? The questions went round and round in her head until she thought it would explode. She heard her parents arguing in the sitting room; heard the opening and closing of doors, the sound of her mother's voice, pleading with her father. She heard her mother's words, 'there's been an approach', swelling and receding in her mind the way conscious thought expands and contracts in the last few moments before sleep – and then she slept, too exhausted to think or dream.

PART TWO

14

NIELA
Vienna, October 1992

If she'd thought, even for a split second, that she could talk her way out of trouble, Niela was sadly mistaken. Overnight, she'd become a prisoner in her own home. She was forbidden to leave the house without someone accompanying her. With Korfa and Raageh at school and her mother in the kitchen, there was no possibility of escape. She lay in bed all day, too stunned to think.

One morning, about a week after she'd been caught, Saira came into the room. She pulled back the curtains briskly and turned to Niela. 'It's time to get up,' she said, lifting the counterpane from the bed. 'We have some news for you. Hamid will be here on Saturday. It's time to prepare yourself.'

Niela stared at her. Her mouth had run dry. 'P . . . prepare myself? Uma . . . I can't do this. I *can't*. Don't make me, please. I beg you.'

'Niela, stop being so dramatic.' Saira regarded her calmly. 'And stop thinking only of yourself.'

'Why are you doing this to me?' Niela began to cry.

Saira clicked her tongue against the roof of her mouth as she always did when irritated. 'What are you talking about? You have done this to yourself. No one is doing anything to you. It's for the best, Niela. Everything will turn out for the best.'

'No . . . it won't. I don't want to be married, Uma. Why is Abba doing this to me? Why do you let him?' she sobbed.

Saira regarded Niela for a moment or two, then sighed. She sat down heavily on the edge of Niela's bed. She reached across and patted Niela's hand awkwardly. 'He's afraid.'

'Afraid? Afraid of what?'

'Of the future. Of what's going to happen to you. To us.'

'Uma . . . this isn't going to be for ever.' Niela lifted her tear-stained cheek to look around the room. 'We won't always be here.'

'Oh, Niela. You're so young. You're naïve. What's going to change? We're exiles now. We can't go back. This is it.'

Niela stared at her. 'No. No, it's not,' she said stubbornly. 'Things will change.'

'Your father is nearly sixty, Niela. *He* cannot change. He cannot adapt, not like you children. His life is over. Yours is just beginning.' Her mother looked at her almost fondly. 'Do you really think your father would marry you off to someone unsuitable? Someone who wouldn't care for you? He will make the right choice for you. For us. Trust us. Everything will turn out just fine. You'll see.' Saira got up slowly. 'Now, dry your eyes and wash your face. I want you to get up. Your future husband is coming this weekend. There are things you need to do. Get dressed. We're going into town.'

There were things about her mother that still had the power to shock Niela into silence. She followed Saira in mute astonishment as she led her through the maze of trams and buses that took them to Meidling, a district of Vienna that Niela had never seen or heard of – until now. How had Saira found it? This was a different city to the one she'd comé to know. Here there were no coffee shops or smart, expensive boutiques. The buildings had none of the opulent glamour of the 1st Bezirk where Ayanna lived, or even the modern apartment blocks of Simmering. Here the buildings were run-down and industrial-looking, the streets were narrow and crowded, made even more so by the makeshift kiosks and market stalls that lined the roads. Nigerians, Ghanaians, Turks, North Africans . . . and Somalis, too. Her mother moved from one shop to another with ease, stopping to chat with someone at this stall, tasting fruit at that one, exchanging a bit of gossip with a woman in a headscarf who smiled fondly at Niela. 'Don't you recognise her?' Saira asked, prodding Niela in the ribs. 'From home. Mrs Qureisha. No, you don't remember her?' Niela shook her head, bewildered. How had her mother found out about Meidling, and why hadn't she said? Saira chatted excitedly to the women who owned a fabric shop halfway down the street. Yes, she was about to be married, Saira said, looking proudly at her only daughter. The women smiled at her, equally proud. 'He lives in Munich,' Saira said, pronouncing the word with some difficulty. 'A good man. A relative on my husband's side.' They nodded knowingly. *Yes, a good match. So difficult these days. The young girls . . . their heads get filled . . .* They looked from one to the other. *What can we do? So far from home. You can't control what they get up to.* Saira's grip on Niela's arm confirmed that her own daughter would do no such thing. Niela listened to them, her head swimming with fear.

The flat was cleaned, swept, polished and cleaned again. For two days, Niela and Saira did nothing but dust and wipe, making sure that every surface was spotless, every square inch gleaming. Niela threw herself into the task as a way of distracting herself from what was about to come. She watched herself going through the motions of getting up, getting dressed, getting on with the day as if she were watching someone else. Saira's food preparations began – sacks of rice appeared in the kitchen, along with bags of onions and cartons of chopped tomatoes. Hassan came home on the Thursday before Hamid's arrival with bloodstained packets of meat that he'd crossed town to the best halal butcher to get. Korfa was recruited to help him cut it up; Niela walked past, a lump the size of an orange in her throat, making it impossible to speak. One of Saira's friends from Meidling arrived on the Friday . . . from the tiny kitchen came the smells and sounds of home. Uncle Raageh appeared that night for supper. He was unable to look Niela in the eye. Hamid would be staying with him, as was the custom. Niela ate supper that night alone with Saira and Mrs Qureisha, listening to the sound of the whisky bottle being opened and closed as Hassan and Raageh celebrated the upcoming match. She went to bed with tears in her throat. Saira's awkward attempts to placate her had failed. She lay in bed that night, unable to sleep or think of anything other than the fact that her life, as she knew it, was over.

15

Hamid Osman and his sister Fathia were ushered deferentially into the living room. Niela was seated alone in the dining room, separated from her parents and the two visitors by the bookcase that divided the small room. She caught the briefest glimpse of a short, rotund figure dressed in white as they passed. Korfa and Raageh were in their room – after the introductions had been made and the business of marriage had been concluded, they would be called to come forward and eat. She could hear the sister's high, nasal voice. Her heart sank. She'd overhead her mother telling Mrs Qureisha that at least Niela wouldn't be alone for the first few years of her marriage. Fathia Osman had recently joined her brother in Munich, *al-Hamdulillah*, thanks be to God. Much better for Niela to have company, someone to talk to. After all, Hamid was a busy man, *al-Hamdulillah*. Well off. His own businesses. Niela would lack for nothing. She'd listened to the two of them in the same state of stunned silence. *Munich. Germany. A husband. A sister-in-law.* The facts paraded themselves one after the other.

She looked down at the material of her dress. It was black with gold embroidery. Saira and Mrs Qureisha had chosen the fabric. Niela hated it. She sat with her hands folded in her lap, her heart beating wildly in her chest, wishing she were anywhere but in the dining room of the small flat in Simmering, waiting to meet a man she'd never set eyes on who would take her somewhere to begin another life. She felt the nausea of fear in her stomach every time she thought about what it would actually *mean*. A husband. A wedding night. Her stomach twisted itself into knots. Her mother had made light of her objections. *What's to fear? He's a good man, Niela. He will look after you. We know the family. It's all for the best.* What hope did she have of persuading them otherwise? What objections could she possibly make?

'Niela?' Her father's voice penetrated the veil of fear. She looked up. He was standing in the opening beside the bookcase. 'Come. Hamid is ready to receive you.'

She stood up. There was a faint ringing in her ears as she followed her father through to the living room. She saw Fathia first. A round face, head covered with a lacy white scarf; small, dark eyes that darted from right to left as she scrutinised Niela up and down; small mouth, pursed lips indicating pinched displeasure – Niela took in the details automatically. She let her gaze slide off the woman and brought it to rest on Hamid. He was short – shorter than Niela. And fat. His skin was dark and gleaming, bursting with good health. A beard. Flecks of grey amongst the tight black curls. Niela's whole body shrank from him. He was smiling at her and nodding his head. She dropped her eyes and looked at the ground. Her father was speaking; there was a corresponding laugh from someone. Saira murmured something to Fathia – yes, all was as it should be. Their daughter was pleasing to him. Negotiations had been successful; Hamid had delivered his side of the bargain. They began to discuss the wedding. All was well. No one asked Niela anything. She stared at the ground. Her eyes were smarting but she stubbornly refused to lift them. She couldn't bear the thought of anyone seeing her tears.

The *aroos* – the wedding – was planned for the following week. There was no time to waste. Hamid had a string of important business meetings to attend; better to get everything over and done with as quickly as possible. Niela would return to Munich with them as soon as the two-day celebrations were over. Hassan brought out a bottle of whisky and carefully poured himself, Raageh and Hamid a glass, as was the custom for men. Saira and Fathia sipped at the sickly sweet lemonade Saira had prepared that afternoon. Niela remained silent throughout, willing the whole thing to be over, longing to escape to her room.

Finally, just when she thought she couldn't stand it a second longer, Hamid stood up. He was tired; it had been a long day. He thanked Hassan and Saira for their daughter's hand and their hospitality. The speech had the formal, rather stilted qualities of a successful business transaction. After it was over, Hamid and Fathia left with Uncle Raageh, and Niela and Saira were left alone. 'Come,' Saira said to her when the menfolk had disappeared downstairs. 'I want to show you something.' Niela followed her mother into her bedroom. There was a suitcase on the bed. Saira opened it, revealing yards and yards of the sheerest, finest silk in a dazzling array of colours and patterns. Niela remained mute. 'It's for you,' Saira said, holding up a piece of pale lilac silk. 'For your *guntiino*. It's the custom, you know. Three changes of outfit. Mrs Qureisha will sew them for you. Niela, will you stop looking so glum,' she admonished sharply. 'This has cost Hamid a fortune, you know. Try to show a little gratitude.'

'Did I ask for anything?' Niela muttered stubbornly.

'That's not the point. You're engaged now. Stop acting like a spoilt child. You're behaving like your cousin.'

'Why don't you marry *her* off to that fat old man?' Niela asked bitterly. 'If you're so keen to have a wedding.'

'Niela!' Saira's exasperation boiled over. She snatched back the silk, stuffed it in the suitcase and snapped it shut. 'I've just about had enough. Go to your room.'

Niela turned without a word and left the room. She ignored Korfa and Raageh's worried glances and walked straight down the corridor to her room. She shut the door firmly behind her and leaned against it, breathing heavily. In a week's time, her life would be over. The wedding was scheduled to begin on Friday afternoon. Hassan had organised the rental of a community hall in Meidling where the *nikkah* would be performed in front of practically the whole Viennese Somali community. A day and a night of feasting and celebration, followed by an elaborate luncheon the next day for family and close friends. Hamid had reserved a hotel room for the wedding night, and early on Sunday morning, after saying goodbye to her family, she would set off for Munich and her new life as his wife. She pulled the coverlet up over her face to try and blot out her thoughts.

16

The day of her wedding dawned early. Niela woke with the first shaft of light. She'd forgotten to draw the curtains the night before, and every now and then, a ray of sunlight emerged from behind the low grey clouds and came to rest on the carpet. There was a small, escaped feather lying on the bedspread. It stirred and flattened gently as her breath rose and fell. She lay still, trying not to think about what would happen next. She could hear the sound of her mother moving about in the kitchen, pots being clattered around, the fridge door opening and closing. In an hour or so, Saira's friends would start arriving, Uncle Raageh would bring his car round to the front and the business of loading it up with food and drink would begin. The day she'd been dreading all week was finally here.

There wouldn't be much she would remember. She didn't know when she'd first stumbled upon the trick of seeing herself from a distance, watching herself go through the motions of some fearful activity or another. Perhaps it had started with the war. She could clearly recall walking down the road to the house one day and hearing the by now familiar 'crack' of a rocket exploding somewhere close by, followed by the high-pitched whine of an engine and people's screams. She'd stopped, the hair at the back of her neck rising in awareness of the potential danger she was in. It took only a few seconds – suddenly she was no longer there, in her own body, sweat seeping from her pores. She was somewhere else, watching herself in a long, slow series of moving images,

64

walking calmly to the side of the road. She hid behind a row of black plastic dustbins and waited for the engine sound to draw near. Gunshots rang out; there were more screams. Niela crouched behind the dustbins but *she wasn't really there*. She could hear the jeep approaching – people shouting, crying, begging. It passed right in front of her, men with guns swinging wildly from its sides, shouting, gesticulating and firing into the air. She'd waited there for almost an hour, her legs aching with cramp, until she slowly came back down to earth. The film stopped; she returned to herself. She walked on. At home, Saira was hysterical with fear. She was not to go out alone again. Ever.

As she allowed the women to dress her in the pale lilac *dirac* that Saira had shown her, the same sensation of leaving her own body returned to her. She watched the proceedings almost dreamily, her mind anywhere but there. She saw faces turned towards her in delight, heard the ululating cries of the women and the hearty, suggestive laughter of the men. Hamid gave a speech; the imam recited verses from the Quran. There were tears from some of the women, but not from her. She repeated her vows in a flat, obedient voice, devoid of emotion. She wasn't really there. Hamid's grip on her arm was proprietorial. She stared at the thick fingers with their smattering of hair and his pink, buffed and polished fingernails. Sweetmeats and the soft, floury delicacies that her mother and Mrs Qureisha had been preparing all week were pushed into her mouth. She sat in the high-backed chair with the lacy veil covering her face as cameras went off, one after the other. *A good match. Yes, a very good match. Pity about the bride, though. Why doesn't she smile more? Silly girl, anyone'd think she was going to a funeral.* She heard the muttered comments as if they were directed at someone else. She was not the one being addressed.

Her parents were amongst the last to leave. The wedding party broke up in fits and starts; people left, were called back to have one last drink, one last chat. They came and went and came back again. Niela's gaze drifted every now and then to the large clock at one end of the hall: 9.56; 10.07; 11.13. It was past midnight when the swing doors finally banged shut and she was alone with Hamid. His car was waiting outside, he told her, helping himself to the last of the whisky bottles that remained. The women had cleared the tables and the younger men had stacked away the chairs. There was almost nothing left of the party that had taken up the better part of the day – brightly coloured streamers, a collapsed balloon, an empty Coke bottle or two. She got up stiffly and picked up the bag containing her overnight things. The folds of her long ivory *dirac* swirled about her legs as she made her way across the empty hall to the exit. It was her third change of clothing that day but she couldn't even recall the colour of the previous two.

It was chilly outside. She waited by the front steps of the building as Hamid brought the car to the entrance. Aside from their vows, they'd barely spoken to one another all evening. He leaned across and opened the door for her from the inside. There was a moment's awkwardness as she fumbled with the handle and then she slid inside the car, placed her bag at her feet and was enveloped in the darkness that smelled of cigar smoke and the pungent aftershave she'd come to associate with him. 'Fasten your seat belt,' he said to her as he pulled away from the kerb. She did as she was told in silence. He didn't speak again until they drove up in front of the hotel.

She didn't even have the luxury of fear. He was shorter than she but twice as strong. She was barely inside the small hotel room when his hand was on her waist, pushing the thin fabric of her dress up her body to lay claim to her skin. She tried not to panic, remembering what her mother had told her. *Submit and it will get easier, insha'allah.* He fumbled inexpertly with her clothing, tugging impatiently at the offending *dirac* and then at her bra underneath. She had no recollection of how they moved from standing in front of the bed to lying on top of it, but when she had gathered her wits sufficiently to understand what was happening to her, it was too late. He was heavy. He pinned her arms to her sides, his mouth leaving a wet, sticky trail across her skin. Was he kissing her? She had no idea. She twisted her head to one side, looking away from him. He didn't appear to notice. Her legs were shoved quickly apart; she felt the weight of his belly against hers and then the thing she'd feared most – his hands on her, parting the way. She lay very still, her heart beating almost inside her mouth, waiting, waiting. When he finally thrust and pushed his way inside her, the scream seemed to have come from someone else, somewhere else. He clamped a hand over her mouth; her ears were filled with the sound of his grunting and panting so that her own answering screams were drowned. There was a wrenching upheaval inside her as her entire body convulsed and turned. She tried to bring her knees up to her chest to push him away, but his large, heavy body was in the way. He must have sensed her resistance; his hands gripped her arms, those buffed and polished fingernails digging painfully into her skin. She twisted her head to the left and to the right, bruising her lips against his beard, trying desperately to avoid his mouth. He rammed himself into her over and over again, saying things . . . calling her names . . . his voice a roar in her ears. An extraordinary tension seemed to come over him; he stiffened, gasping for breath, and then suddenly, almost as quickly as it had started, it was over. He convulsed like an animal in pain and then slid from her, rolling over on to his back, gulping in air like a man about to drown. After the noise that had surrounded her for the entire duration of his assault, the silence was shocking. She rolled away from him, curling herself up into the tightest, smallest ball, and stuffed her fist in her mouth. Pain spread from the centre, between her legs, through her limbs, up across her stomach and breasts, all the way to her mouth. She could feel the mattress shuddering slightly as he fought to bring his breathing back under control.

'Go and take a shower.' The command came from him in the manner of someone speaking to a servant.

Niela rose and stumbled towards the bathroom. She was too stunned to think. There was blood on her thighs as well as a trail of rapidly drying wetness that had come from him. She turned on the tap and stepped inside. After a few minutes she realised that the salty taste of the water was the brine of her own tears.

They drove away from Vienna early in the morning. Niela did not look backwards, not once. It was Hamid who lifted a hand to her parents in farewell, not she. She sat beside him, her profile turned away, chin set against the anger that was building dangerously inside her. Fathia sat in the back, alternately munching on the sweets Saira had packed for the long journey, or chattering away to her brother. Neither said much to Niela, which suited her just fine. The radio was tuned to a Somali news programme; she listened with half an ear, and tried not to think about what lay ahead, or what had happened the night before. Hamid drove impatiently, keen to return to his business interests in Munich, or so she gathered from his comments to Fathia. Niela had only the vaguest idea of what it was he did; he was a businessman, not a professional like her father or Uncle Raageh. The dialect he and his sister spoke was harsher than the language spoken in her home – another sign of the times. Back home such a union would have been unthinkable. Here, in exile, the impossible had come to pass.

Austria came and went in long, empty expanses of fields, rivers and hills, occasionally punctuated by towns and villages, sometimes a city or two. Graz. Innsbruck. Klagenfurt. All passed before her eyes in silence. They drove through Switzerland in a few hours, stopping at the border with Germany for the night. This time, to her immense relief, he made no move towards her. He slept on his back, snoring loudly. She lay awake for hours, unable to sleep, watching the pattern made against the flimsy curtains by car headlights as they swept past.

In the morning she was awake long before him. She got out of bed without making a sound and collected her things. She crept down the corridor to the bathroom and took a shower. She dressed quickly and slipped back into the room to stow away her bag. She was almost out the door when his voice stopped her.

'No trousers.' He said it in German. She turned in surprise. He was still lying in bed. His white singlet had risen up over his belly; the mound of it was very dark against the white sheets. 'No trousers,' he repeated, yawning as he spoke. 'You must not wear trousers. Go and change.' Niela opened her mouth to protest, but before she could utter a single word, he flung back the covers and got out of bed. 'No trousers!' he half shouted at her. 'Skirts.' He picked up his suit from the back of the chair and began to dress. The conversation was over. Niela silently pulled out a skirt from her suitcase and opened the door. He didn't even look at her. She walked down the corridor, her heart thumping against her ribcage. She hadn't even thought of it – would he demand that she veil herself as well? She pulled off the offending jeans with trembling fingers and put on a skirt. When she walked into the dining room to join him and Fathia, neither of them said a word. She picked at a piece of toast in silence, fighting back the urge to scream.

It was nearly dusk by the time they finally drew up outside a small suburban house somewhere on the outskirts of the city. Niela had finally fallen asleep, lulled by the hum of the heater and the steady drumbeat of rain against the windows. She woke with a start; Hamid had switched off the engine and was busy taking their suitcases out of the boot. She opened the door cautiously. A small garden with a wire fence separated the house from the neighbour. A short flight of steps to the front door – a brick house, flat-roofed, two storeys. She quickly took in the details. Up and down the street the houses were identical. Even the front doors were painted a uniform shade of dark grey. Hamid and Fathia led the way; Niela followed behind them, carrying her overnight bag. The house was warm at least, she noticed, as soon as they stepped inside. It was crowded in the way of most Somali homes – too many couches and chairs, too many small side tables, shelves crowded with pictures, almost every square inch of wall space taken up with framed photographs of relatives and landscapes of home. She looked around her and swallowed nervously. Home. This was home.

Fathia showed her through to the bedrooms. 'I sleep in here,' she said, pointing to the second door down the corridor. 'When we clean tomorrow, I will show you where everything is. You and Hamid will sleep in here.' She opened the door to a medium-sized bedroom dominated almost entirely by the double bed. Hamid brought Niela's suitcase into the room. 'Tomorrow,' Fathia said. 'We can arrange things tomorrow.' She and Hamid left the room, arguing mildly over whose turn it was to place the weekly call to their parents in Mogadishu and Niela was left alone. She sat down on the edge of the bed with her hands in her lap. She was too exhausted from the long car journey and from the effort of trying not to think to do anything other than sit. She was still sitting there an hour later when Hamid came through. 'It's time to eat,' he said briskly, walking over to the wardrobe and pulling out a pair of worn slippers. 'Tomorrow you will cook.' She got up wordlessly and followed him through to the dining room. She'd hardly eaten anything all day. The simple meal of rice and chicken stew that Fathia had prepared was a welcome distraction. She accepted the plate from her sister-in-law and was just about to raise her fork to her mouth when she noticed Fathia's frown. She glanced at Hamid. He hadn't yet raised his own. Fathia sat opposite him, waiting patiently until her brother had taken his first bite. Then she nodded at Niela. *Yes, you may begin.* Niela felt her whole body tense with rebellion, but again she said nothing. She swallowed her pride, along with a mouthful of rice, and concentrated on her food.

She submitted to Hamid that evening just as she'd done on her wedding night, waiting only for it to be over. Fortunately for her, he was tired from the long drive . . . the whole thing was finished in a matter of minutes. He rolled away from her with a satisfied sigh and fell asleep almost immediately. Niela lay in the dark, listening to the sound of his snores, trying to summon up memories of happier times. If she didn't, she seemed to understand instinctively, she would succumb to the silent lethargy that had gripped her ever since her parents had announced what they intended to do. Somewhere in the back of her mind was the image of an aunt, one of her father's younger half-sisters, back in Mogadishu, who'd almost died of despair when her husband took a second wife. She no longer remembered the details . . . she'd been too young to properly understand what had happened or the significance of her sorrow, but there was something about the still, despairing sadness that had over-taken the normally vivacious girl that brought her own circumstances to mind. Her aunt had once been a lively, pretty young woman with a temper and a strong, confident laugh. She'd seen her in the living room one day, sitting in silence, her face turned away from the others, drawn against some private grief that only she could see. 'What's the matter with Aunt Soraya?' Niela had asked her mother. 'Why is she crying?'

'Shhh! Don't disturb your aunt, poor thing. See what happens when you love someone too much?'

It was too much for a twelve-year-old to understand. But now, lying next to the stranger who'd overnight become her husband, Niela couldn't shake the image of the young woman sitting for hours alone in the living room or out on the veranda, her lips moving to a sentence only she could hear. If she wasn't careful, she too would wind up like that – though not for the same reasons. If her aunt's misfortune had been to love someone too much, Niela's was the opposite. She barely knew Hamid but she hated him already.

In the morning when she woke, Hamid was gone. She got out of bed and ran to the bathroom. She stood under the shower for a long time, washing away every last trace of sweat and semen from her body, trying to rid herself of his touch. She shuddered as she dried herself on the towel she'd brought from home. She wanted nothing of his to touch her. Absolutely nothing.

She finished dressing and opened the bedroom door. From the kitchen came the sound of pots being cleaned. Clearly, Fathia was already up. Niela walked down the corridor to the kitchen. From Fathia's disap-proving expression as she entered, it seemed as though she'd been up for hours. There was a place laid for her at the dining room table. 'Have your breakfast,' Fathia said grudgingly. 'But hurry up. There's a lot of cleaning to be done.'

She wasn't joking. As soon as Niela had finished her coffee and washed her plate, Fathia appeared in the doorway with a broom. For the rest of the morning, Niela swept every inch of the house. It was as though the two of them had been saving up the dust. She swept the rugs, mopped

70

the tiles, moved furniture, polished the endless tables, wiped the chairs and picture frames, rubbed the brassware until it shone like a mirror . . . and still Fathia's demands kept coming. *The bathrooms need cleaning. The wardrobes need airing. The sheets need washing. Have you forgotten the ironing?* By lunchtime, Niela's arms were aching. Back in Mogadishu she'd barely lifted a plate. In Vienna, under her mother's watchful eye, she'd quickly learned how to clean a small flat, but Fathia's demands were of an entirely different order. They ate lunch together in the kitchen at a small table, neither speaking much. Niela answered her questions about whether or not the bathroom mirrors had been wiped or whether she'd remembered to starch Hamid's shirts with a curt 'yes' or 'no'. She refused to rise to Fathia's bait. What did she think? That Niela had never swept a floor in her life? She felt a small thrill of satisfaction when, after the day was finally over, Fathia was unable to think of a single thing further for her to do. Niela had done everything she'd asked, and more. There wasn't a speck of dust to be had, anywhere. Niela folded away her apron and stowed the cleaning supplies underneath the sink with a faint smile of bitter satisfaction lurking around the corners of her mouth. She walked back down the corridor, conscious of Fathia's eyes on her back. She held it very straight until she'd closed the door. Then she leaned against it and finally gave vent to the tears that had been building inside her for what seemed like a year.

Slowly, against her will, a kind of order began to impose itself on her life. She missed Korfa and Raageh more than she could put into words, but aside from the short, stilted telephone call that took place twice a week when she answered her mother's endless questions with a brusque 'fine', Vienna began to recede from her memory. She could no longer recall the exact layout of the flat – did the bookcase separating the dining room from the living room face inwards or out? What colour were the kitchen tiles? Mogadishu was still as clear in her mind's eye as if it had been days since they left rather than years, but Vienna was fading fast . . . as if she'd never really been there or intended to stay. Hamid worked long hours. During the week he was up long before her. He prayed in his study at the end of the corridor. Saira's relief at hearing there was a sister in Munich to keep her daughter company was misplaced. Fathia required a servant, little else. Certainly not a friend. She was in her late forties, unmarried, with no prospects of ever being so . . . the private disappointments that surely must have been hers had long since hardened into the pursed lips and tightened expression that greeted Niela every morning across the kitchen table.

Hamid wasn't unkind. In his own distant, unfathomable manner, he behaved in the only way he knew how. He went to work, he prayed, he was a stalwart member of the small Munich Somali community . . . he provided food and shelter for his young bride as he should . . . what more could the girl want? He performed his side of the bargain – now so should she. Niela sometimes heard him arguing with Fathia. *Why does she go about with such a long face? Can't she produce a smile every once in a while? What have we done to her?* Fathia's answers were always the same. *It's the way they are, these young girls nowadays. Spoilt, every one of them. Don't worry, she'll learn.* Niela turned away, her heart sinking. How anyone could think she was spoilt was beyond her.

Twice a week she and Fathia went by bus to the supermarket. Niela looked out of the window at the suburbs sliding past. Once or twice she caught a glimpse of her own face – a tightly held mask of contained emotions. Seeing her face as a stranger might, it surprised her. She'd never given much thought to her own appearance. She supposed, in a kind of distant, disinterested way, that she was pretty enough. In high school she'd been as much sought after as her two best friends, Sally-Anne and Helga. The three of them had made a striking trio – blonde, blue-eyed Helga; Sally-Anne with her green eyes and curly auburn hair; and Niela, dark-haired, dark-eyed, dark-skinned. Charlie's Angels, some of the other kids called them. For a brief summer, Niela had yearned for long shiny blonde hair like Helga's, but that was more out of curiosity than anything else. Her own hair had to be washed, conditioned and braided once a week by a hairdresser; Helga and Sally-Anne simply stood under the shower and ran a brush through theirs. She'd heard her mother's friends exclaiming over her – *look how pretty she is, Saira. Lucky you. You'll have no trouble finding a husband for her, none at all.* She'd listened to the comments with a smile on her face. Her mother's friends were wrong. There would be no traditional arranged marriage for her. She was going to university when she finished high school. *She* would have a career and be independent in the way Saira had never been. *That* was her future. Not the one her mother's friends dreamed up.

So much for those dreams now, Niela thought to herself miserably as she followed Fathia around the supermarket, pushing the trolley. What sort of a career was *this*?

17

One morning about a month after her arrival in Munich, she walked into the kitchen to find it strangely silent. She looked around her. Fathia wasn't yet up. She set the breakfast table, wondering what was wrong. Her sister-in-law was always in the kitchen before anyone else. She made the tea, wondering if she ought to go on and prepare breakfast itself. She stood there uncertainly for a second. Perhaps Fathia had overslept? She made a cup of tea and walked down the corridor. She hesitated for a moment, then rapped on the door to Fathia's room.

'Come.' She heard Fathia's voice. She opened the door and stepped inside. She'd only ever been into her room to clean it. Now, with the curtains drawn and the faint, sour smell of sweat in the air, she resisted the temptation to turn away.

'Are you all right?' she asked, setting the cup of tea down on the dressing table.

'Sick. I'm sick. My throat.' Fathia's voice was a painful croak. 'You'll have to go to the pharmacy for me. I need medicine.'

Niela's heart jumped. Alone? She would finally be able to leave the house on her own? 'Of course,' she said in what she hoped was a solicitous tone. Her heart began to beat faster.

'Bring me paper.' Fathia pointed to a notepad on the desk by the window. Not even a 'please', Niela thought crossly as she handed it over. Not a single 'thank you, Niela, for bringing me tea'. Or '*please* go to the pharmacy for me'. No, with Fathia everything was a command. *Bring me this. Bring me that. Fetch this, fetch that.* But the thought of going outside the house on her own for the first time in four long, miserable weeks was enough to push the irritation out of her mind and she left the room excitedly. 'Don't delay,' Fathia croaked out as she shut the door. Niela didn't bother to reply.

Muffled in clothing that added another dimension to her body, she ignored the frost on the ground and almost ran all the way down the street. It was only early December but the trees were already stripped bare. She kicked her boots in the sludgy pile of frozen leaves that had settled between the edge of the pavement and the road, breathing in the icy air, tasting the scent of the first moment of freedom at the back of her throat. The bus trundled into view; she boarded it and smiled widely at the driver. He smiled back, momentarily confused. Her face felt strange – it had been weeks since she'd had a smile on her face.

She stopped at the bakery at the entrance to the small shopping centre and bought herself a cream bun. She bit into its soft creamy centre hungrily . . . Fathia favoured the sticky, sickly-sweet baklava and dates that she bought in industrial quantities and which Niela hated. She stood in the cold until she'd finished it, licking the last dollops of cream off her fingers in pleasure.

'You look as though you enjoyed that.' Someone spoke to her. Niela jumped. She hadn't even noticed the young man standing behind her in the line. She swallowed the last bite and quickly wiped her mouth. 'Sorry, I didn't mean to startle you.' He smiled down at her. His face was partially hidden by his woollen hat and the scarf tucked up around his chin. His eyes were blue, she noticed. He looked kind.

'I . . . no, I was just . . .' she stammered, not knowing quite what to say.

'You've got a bit of cream . . . here . . .' He pointed to the tip of his own nose.

Niela immediately put up a hand to her face. 'Here?'

'No, just there . . . yes, that's it.'

'Er, thanks.'

'Not at all.'

They stood for a moment in slightly embarrassed silence. 'Cold, isn't it?' he said finally.

Niela nodded. 'Yes, yes it is.'

He looked down at her and smiled. 'I don't suppose you're from round here, are you? Originally, I mean.'

Niela hesitated. He was the first person she'd spoken to in Munich other than shopkeepers and checkout girls. She was starving for conversation with someone – *any*one – but she was both shy and afraid. She looked around her quickly, as if half-expecting Fathia to appear suddenly from behind one of the shop façades. 'No,' she said. 'Not from here.'

'So where are you from?'

'From Somalia.'

'Have you been here long? You speak such good German. My name's Christian, by the way.' He held out a hand.

Niela hesitated again. Why was he so interested in where she was from

74

or how well she spoke German? She risked a quick upwards glance. He was tall, with dark brown hair, and blue eyes that crinkled at the corners and the shadow of a beard that showed up beneath his skin. He looked to be a little older than she was . . . late twenties, perhaps even thirty. She looked back down at her feet. Why had he suddenly decided to talk to her? 'I was in Vienna before I came here,' she said finally.

'Ah, Vienna. That's the accent I hear. Nice city,' he said conversationally. 'What's your name?'

'Niela.'

'Nice to meet you, Niela. Do you work around here?'

Niela shook her head. 'Look, I . . . I'd better go. I have to buy some things,' she said quickly, casting a quick, furtive glance around her again. 'I . . . goodbye,' she said abruptly, not knowing how else to end the conversation.

He lifted a brow. 'Oh, sure . . . well, goodbye. Nice to meet you, Niela. I work in the bank on the corner.' He lifted a hand and pointed it out. 'Maybe see you around one of these days?'

Niela nodded, anxious to get away. She raised a hand awkwardly in farewell and, without waiting for anything else, almost ran across the square to the supermarket. Her face felt flushed – how long had it been since she'd seen or talked to anyone other than Hamid and his dreadful sister?

'What took you so long?' Fathia demanded as soon as she walked in the door. 'I've been waiting for *hours*. What were you doing?'

'Nothing,' Niela said shortly. She unpacked the few groceries she'd bought – a bunch of bananas, some oranges and a string bag of sweet tangerines – and the medicine Fathia had asked for. She took it without a word and disappeared into her room. Just as there'd been no 'please', there would certainly be no 'thank you'. Niela stowed away the fruit and picked up the broom. The floor needed sweeping and she wasn't about to wait for a command.

The memory of the brief conversation stayed with her all day, a small ray of pleasure, despite her awkwardness and the momentary panic his attention had induced. Christian. She tried to picture his face, muffled as it had been by his thick woollen scarf and the hat he wore pulled down low over his forehead. Blue eyes, she remembered. Deep blue with a smattering of something else . . . green? Brown? She couldn't quite remember. Thick, dark brows, a long, straight nose and a mouth that opened to reveal a line of teeth marred slightly by one that overlapped the other. She felt a sudden, unexpected rush of tenderness. Korfa too had had such a tooth that defied all attempts by the orthodontist to correct it. Like Niela, who'd suffered the indignity of braces for two long, uncomfortable years, he'd hated the dentist. Thinking about Korfa produced a painful ache that was now in some unidentifiable way bound up with her five-minute encounter with a young German bank clerk called Christian. A small sound of irritation escaped her lips. The realisation that she was still capable of feeling something other than mute resignation was an unwelcome surprise. She didn't want to think, to feel, to miss *anything* about the person she'd once been. She didn't want to think about Korfa or the reasons why a total stranger would express an interest in where she was from or who she might be.

18

Was it him? Niela averted her eyes, casting them downwards as the young man behind the counter looked up. No, it wasn't. Yes, it was. Recognition dawned on his face as she inched forward in the line.

'Hello.' He smiled at her as she approached. 'It's Niela, isn't it?'

She nodded, almost too afraid to speak. 'I . . . I've come to see about opening an account,' she said, hoping her voice was steady. 'A savings account.'

He nodded, still grinning at her. 'You'll have to see that lady in the corner over there . . . she'll set it up. But then you can come back here, to me . . . I'll take the deposit from you and get you started.'

'Th . . . thank you.' Niela turned away. There was a lump in her throat. It had taken her almost a fortnight to summon up the courage to slip away from the house. She'd waited until Fathia was in the shower, then she'd scribbled a hasty note – *Forgot something at the supermarket. Back in half an hour.* She'd put it on the dining table, grabbed her coat and the keys that were lying on the console in the hallway and slipped out, her heart beating wildly inside her chest. She ran all the way down Lindenallee. She was in luck; a few seconds later, the bus swung into view. Within ten minutes they were pulling up outside the shops. There it was. On the corner. Sparkasse. The bank. She put her hand in her pocket and fingered the notes nervously. Four hundred Deutschmarks – a last-minute gift from her mother. She glanced at her watch. She'd been gone for fifteen minutes. Fathia would have come out of the shower by now and would probably have seen her note. She had reason to be nervous. Of the two of them, Fathia was by far the greater threat. There was something about Niela that set Fathia's teeth on edge – was it Niela's faint, barely there insolence when addressed? Or her ability to withdraw into herself so that Fathia's rants slipped off her like rainfall? Or the fact that Niela was married to her brother . . . not that you'd call it a marriage, Niela thought to herself bitterly. There was nothing marriage-like about their situation. Hamid spent more time with his sister than he did with his bride – which suited her perfectly. The only time she was forced to be with him was in bed, and fortunately that happened seldom and was over almost as soon as it started. One unforeseen advantage of marrying someone so much older. The *only* advantage. Hamid was nowhere near old enough to drop dead any time soon, more was the pity.

The lady Christian had pointed out looked up as she approached. Niela cleared her throat and explained what she'd come for. At most, she had another thirty minutes to accomplish her task. But what *was* her task? What had she really come for? The money could just as easily sit in the bottom drawer of the wardrobe, as it had done for the past month. She had to be honest with herself. She'd come because she was lonely. Achingly lonely. So lonely that at times she talked to herself just for the pleasure of hearing another voice that wasn't Fathia's shrill, nasal squeak or Hamid's low, irritated bass. Christian was the first and only person to have spoken to her in six weeks, and that was the reason she was here. Not the four hundred Deutschmarks. Or a savings account. She took the papers the woman had given her, quickly filled them out and then walked back to Christian's counter and handed them over. She waited patiently as he typed in her details, looking up at her every few seconds with a smile.

'There you go . . . that's it. Here's your savings book. You bring it every time you want to make a deposit or a withdrawal, along with your ID card.' Christian pushed a little booklet back across the counter. 'All done.'

'Thank you.' Niela picked it up and slid it into her bag. There was a moment's pause. 'Well, goodbye, then.'

'Can you hang on for a few minutes?' he asked suddenly, lowering his voice. 'I'm finished here in about ten minutes. We could have a coffee . . . if you're not too busy, of course?' His eyes were smiling.

Niela hesitated. She shook her head. 'I . . . I'm expected back at . . . at work,' she lied quickly. 'I'm sorry. I . . .'

'Well, how about tomorrow?'

She shook her head again. The chances of getting away two days in a row were slim. Already she was dreading having to face Fathia when she got home. 'I'm sorry,' she repeated miserably. She shouldn't have come. There was no way to explain to him why she couldn't go for a coffee. 'But . . . maybe but I could meet you on Friday?' she said, brightening suddenly. On Friday both Fathia and Hamid went to mosque. 'If you like,' she added quickly.

He pulled a quick face. 'That's almost a week away! No, it's fine. I finish early on Fridays . . . would two o'clock suit you?'

Niela nodded. She clutched her bag tightly. It was nearly three o'clock. She'd been gone almost an hour. 'I'd better go,' she said nervously. 'I . . . I'm late.'

'See you Friday.' There was a smile on Christian's face that almost made her cry. She couldn't remember the last time anyone had smiled at her. Half blinded with tears, she hurried to the door.

She was right. There *was* hell to pay. Fathia's shrill, angry voice followed her all the way down the corridor and into her room. Where had she been? How *dare* she go out on her own without telling anyone. Didn't she understand Hamid's instructions? She wasn't to go *anywhere* on her own. Munich was a dangerous city . . . It went on and on. Niela remained absolutely mute. Saying anything would only prolong the outrage. Eventually, just as she'd predicted, Fathia ran out of steam. She couldn't prove anything – Niela had gone to the shops. Luckily she'd had the foresight to actually buy something . . . two pints of milk. They'd run out the night before. She threw Niela one last filthy look before slamming the bedroom door and flouncing off down the corridor.

The room was quiet after she'd gone. Niela lay down on the bed, savouring the sudden silence. There was a warmth in the pit of her stomach that Fathia's voice had failed to extinguish. She'd spoken to him for all of fifteen minutes but she now had a friend. She felt as though she'd known him all her life . . . which, considering this new life was all she had, wasn't quite as crazy as it sounded. Friday. It was Monday. Four more days. For the first time since arriving in Munich, she had something to look forward to.

She met him at two o'clock, exactly as planned. It was easy. Fathia left for the mosque around one thirty; with any luck, she and Hamid wouldn't be back until well after six. It struck Niela, as she walked down Lindenallee bundled up against the cold and the light dusting of snow that had begun falling that morning, that the weekly visit to the mosque and the Somali community centre next door was Fathia's only outing, other than going to the shops or the post office. She couldn't remember how long her mother had said Hamid and his sister had lived in Munich . . . two years? Three? She'd heard Fathia's stilted German . . . it couldn't be more than that, surely? After all that time, she'd made almost no friends, had no job, nowhere to go . . . no wonder she'd wound up such an embittered, lonely old prune. But she didn't feel sorry for her. Not in the slightest. Fathia got what she deserved. If she'd tried being just a little bit kinder to those around her, some of it might have rubbed off. Maybe. On second thoughts, probably not. Niela actually smiled to herself as the bus pulled up next to the bank. She was still smiling when she walked into the coffee shop and saw Christian sitting there, two large cream dough- nuts arranged on a plate in front of him. He looked up as she approached and grinned. 'I took the liberty,' he said, pointing to the doughnuts. 'Cream, with jam.'

Everything after that was easy. She ate her cream doughnut and half of his; drank two cups of coffee and chatted away as if the whole afternoon were perfectly normal. As if she were just meeting a friend. As if she hadn't had to wait until her husband and her sister-in-law had gone to the mosque. As if she hadn't sat in the bus on the way over, her stomach heaving with fear, and above all, as if she were free to meet Christian again. 'Where d'you work?' he'd asked her.

The lie slipped out easily enough. 'I'm a translator at the Somali community centre,' she said. 'In Sendling.' It was the only place she knew in Munich other than the house and the shopping centre where they sat.

'That's miles away. D'you take the bus?'

'No, my hu . . . a friend picks me up every morning,' she stammered. 'How long have you worked in the bank?' She quickly changed the subject.

'Too long. I'm saving up. I want to go travelling. Africa. Asia. The Far East. I want to see the world, don't you?'

It was on the tip of Niela's tongue to say that she too wanted to see the world. She too wanted to go travelling. For Niela and her friends back in Mogadishu, the routes were different. People here wanted to go to places like Africa and South America, the further off the beaten track the better. Niela longed to visit New York. London. Paris. Berlin. Well, here she was. In Munich. But she wasn't here as a tourist, taking in the sights. She was married, a prisoner in her husband's house. And what was worse, one Friday afternoon whilst her husband had left the house to pray, she'd slipped out and come to a small bakery to meet a man she barely knew. It didn't sound good, even to her own ears. She prayed he would never find out.

19

The first slap caught her off guard. She staggered backwards, stunned by the force with which he'd hit her. The second sent her tumbling to the ground. She caught her shoulder against the chest of drawers as she fell; the pain shot through her, cutting off her speech. 'Whore!' For the second time that year, the word reverberated around the room. He bent down, panting, and grabbed her by the hair. A third slap, and a fourth. She tried to push him away but it only seemed to enrage him further. 'Is this what I brought you here to do?' he screamed, yanking her head backwards so hard she was afraid her neck would snap. 'Sneaking around like some common whore! We should have known it! I knew there was something wrong with you!'

'I . . .' Niela opened her mouth to protest, but the slap he administered split open her lip. She could feel the blood on her tongue. He'd lifted his hand to deliver yet another blow to the side of her head when the door opened.

'Hamid . . . that's enough.' Fathia stood in the doorway. 'Stop it. She's bleeding.'

'Do you think I care?' Hamid's fury was nowhere near spent. '*Whore!*' He whacked Niela across the face once more, his own features contorted with ugly rage. Niela felt her whole body go slack. There was a faint singing in her ears . . . she'd almost passed out, she realised, as she tried to get up from the carpet.

'Hamid . . . stop.' Fathia was not about to be put off. She stepped in between the prostrate, bleeding Niela and her brother, who was incandescent with rage. 'Enough. I'll deal with this.'

Hamid stood above her, still panting, his chest rising and falling, spittle showing at the side of his mouth. Niela kept her eyes firmly on the carpet. She didn't dare lift them. There was a bubbling sensation in her stomach, as though she were about to vomit. She heard Fathia usher her brother out of the room, heard his angry tirade as she led him down the corridor and into the living room. The drinks cabinet opened; she could hear its telltale squeak. The pounding in her head was almost as unbearable as the pain shooting up and down her arms, her face, her shoulder . . . everywhere. She brought a hand up to her lip. It was sticky to the touch. The scent and taste of blood was still in her mouth. She swallowed painfully. What the hell had happened? She'd come back from her weekly trip to the café – the house was empty, as usual. She'd eaten alone in the kitchen, turned on the television and watched the news and then gone to bed around 9 p.m. It wasn't unusual for Hamid and Fathia to return from the mosque at that time, sometimes even later. She'd been standing by the chest of drawers, folding away the day's laundry, when she heard his car pull up. Instead of going to the kitchen as he usually did, she'd heard him walk down the corridor to the bedroom. It hadn't occurred to her until the door flew open that there might be anything wrong. She'd turned, seen him in the doorway, his entire body quivering with anger . . . and she knew. She'd been caught. She tried to turn away but he'd blocked her path. He raised his hand and dealt her the first stinging blow.

The door opened again. Niela looked up in alarm. It wasn't Hamid. It was Fathia. She held a glass of a pale golden liquid in one hand and a pad of cotton wool in the other. 'Come.' She beckoned to Niela. There was no expression on Fathia's face as she dipped the cotton wool in the whisky and brought the sodden pad to Niela's face. The sharp sting caused the tears to jump straight out of her eyes. Fathia was surprisingly gentle. She worked in silence. She cleaned Niela's mouth and eyes and dressed the cut on her shoulder. When she was done, she put away the empty glass and threw away the soiled cotton pad and turned to her. 'Go to sleep. In the morning everything will be all right.' She closed the door behind her. Niela sat on the edge of the bed, her legs still shaking. Her mouth was swollen and bruised and already the vision in her left eye was beginning to blur. She touched the lid cautiously. It was almost closed. The large gold signet ring that Hamid wore must have caught her just above the eyelid. It was painful to touch. She sat there for what seemed like hours, too afraid to lie down, too afraid to sleep. She had no idea what would happen next. She heard Fathia's voice again. *In the morning everything will be all right.* How? She'd never been hit in her entire life. She couldn't imagine her father lifting a hand to her mother, or anyone else for that matter. What on earth was she supposed to do now? Wait until the next beating? She tried to stop the tears falling – the salt stung like hell – but she couldn't. She could feel them sliding, soft, salty and silky, down her cheeks, underneath her chin, soaking into the fabric of her nightdress. She had to do *some*thing. But what?

'Niela?' The look of alarm on Christian's face was genuine. 'Niela! What the hell happened to you? Are you all right?' He ignored the frown his manager gave him and put up a hand to touch the glass screen separating them.

Niela's heart was racing so fast it hurt. 'Christian . . . I need to withdraw my savings,' she stammered, past caring what the others in the line behind her thought. 'Right now. Everything. I need to close the account.'

'What's wrong?' Christian turned to the teller next to him. 'Cover for me for a second, will you?' He started to get up but Niela stopped him.

'No . . . don't. Please. Just give me whatever's in my account. I don't have very much time.'

'But where are you going? What's happening, Niela?'

'I'll . . . I'll explain later. Just give me everything I have. Hurry, please.'

Christian's eyes searched hers; there must have been something in her expression that convinced him she was both serious and desperate. He counted out a bundle of notes, put them in an envelope and slid it into the tray. She signed the slip and stuffed the envelope in her handbag. 'Can you meet me outside at lunchtime?' he asked her, his eyes still searching her face.

Niela looked up at the clock behind him. She'd been gone for thirty minutes. Any second now, Fathia or Hamid would come looking for her. 'I . . . I can't,' she stammered, her face flooding with heat. 'M . . . maybe later?' She turned away before he could say another word or see the tears that were building up rapidly behind her eyes. She had to get out of the bank as quickly as she could. She couldn't believe she'd managed to escape. She'd been kept under lock and key for two days, ever since the beating. She'd lain in bed all day, her thoughts drifting dangerously low. That morning, she'd heard the front door bell and Fathia's answering grunt. It was the man who'd come to check the gas meters. He'd asked Fathia to accompany him to do the reading. Niela knew the meters were kept in the basement. As soon as the door closed behind them, she jumped up. She hadn't consciously formed a plan. All she knew was that she had to get away from there as fast as she possibly could. She turned on the shower in the bedroom – that would buy her an extra fifteen minutes or so – and hastily got dressed. She grabbed a small bag, shoved a sweater and some underwear in it and the photograph of her parents and brothers that stood on the dresser and was out of the front door in seconds. She'd run all the way down the road, praying the bus would come along soon. It did . . . before she knew it, she was running up the road towards the bank.

Now she hurried out of the bank and crossed the road without looking left or right. Any second now she would feel a hand on her shoulder or hear Fathia's voice. There was a bus waiting at the stop on the other side of the street. Marienplatz. She had a vague recollection that that was in the centre of the city. She ran across the road and boarded it. She had no idea where she was going or what she ought to do . . . head for the central train station? If she did make it there, where would she go? A few seconds later, the driver started the engine. Niela gripped the handle of her bag tightly. From here there'd be no going back. If Hamid or Fathia ever caught her, she was finished. *This is it*, she thought to herself wildly, as the bus pulled out into the traffic. *This is it.* But what was it? Where would she go?

She stood looking up at the destinations clicking their way up the departures board. *Click. Whirr.* Stuttgart. Berlin. Hanover. Bonn. Another set of clicks and whirrs as trains began to pull out of the station. She bit her lip. Stuttgart? She didn't even know where it was. To the left of the board were the international departures. London. Amsterdam. Barcelona. Madrid. She looked around her. It was the week before Christmas. There were holidaymakers and tourists everywhere. Young couples, grandparents, families . . . everyone on the move, going to or coming from home for the holidays. She felt the tug of tears in her throat and the by now familiar churning of panic. She had neither family nor friends and nowhere to go. She looked at her watch. It was nearly eleven o'clock in the morning. Fathia would have noticed her absence by now and called Hamid. But they would never find her. Neither of them would work out that she'd taken a bus into the centre of Munich and from there another bus to the train station . . . no, they would never find her. She was free. Unless she made the decision to return, no one would ever hear from her again. She looked back up at the board. London. There was a train leaving for London in less than an hour. Via Paris. She swallowed. She knew no one in London. For that reason alone, it seemed a good place to start.

20

JULIA
Oxford, January 1992

It was dark by the time the train finally pulled into the station. Snow was falling lightly on the tracks, like icing sugar. Julia hauled down her case and moved into the corridor. She shoved down the window and opened the carriage door, shivering in the cold. There were only a handful of people on the platform; it was the second day of the new year and term wasn't due to begin for another ten days or so. There wasn't even a ticket collector at the barrier – he, like almost everyone else she knew, had better things to do in the days following New Year's Eve. She didn't. She'd gone back to Elswick for Christmas and had spent it in miserable silence with her aunt and uncle, begging a headache and leaving early the day after Boxing Day. She hated Christmas – a season whose sole purpose seemed to be to remind her just what it was she'd lost – her parents, her grandmother, her roots. She couldn't wait for it to be over. She'd gone to a friend's house in Elswick for a New Year's Eve party – one of the few friends she still had – but there too she'd felt out of place and out of sorts. There were only two other girls in her class who'd gone on to university; neither had returned to Elswick since they'd all left school. Rebecca, in whose house the party was being held, worked in a travel agent's. Aside from the usual cheery 'how're you?', there didn't seem to be much to talk about. Julia stood to one side, nursing a beer for most of the evening, and left shortly after midnight. After a day spent on her own in what had been her grandmother's house, she packed her small suitcase, unable to stand the silence and the memories any longer. Now, arriving at an almost deserted Holywell Manor, she almost wished she'd taken Dominic up on his offer and gone to stay with him instead. She had only the vaguest idea of where Dom lived – he kept referring to it as a 'bloodthirsty leech of a country pile' – but she'd overheard someone saying once that his father was an earl. Not that she had any clearer an idea of what exactly an earl was. And, being Julia and her father's daughter, she'd been too embarrassed to ask. Well, whatever it was and whoever *his* father was, it was clear Dom was posh. A Christmas spent in the country with posh parents? She wasn't sure she'd have coped. Not that she'd coped much better on her own, she reminded herself briskly as she got off the bus on the high street and walked down Longwall towards Holywell in the deepening snow. She skidded once or twice as she rolled her suitcase behind her. *That* would be the icing on the cake, she thought to herself bitterly, pushing open the wooden gate to the Manor. A broken leg.

She made her way up the stairs, relieved to see there was no one about. She wasn't sure she could have faced anyone – not even the three scrupulously quiet, scrupulously polite Chinese graduate students who, as far as she could work out, were the only other students at Balliol who seemed as out of their depth as she did. And at least they had each other. She often came across them in the kitchen, chattering animatedly amongst themselves in Cantonese or Mandarin, Julia couldn't tell which, of course. As soon as she entered, they stopped, guiltily, as if they'd been doing something wrong. No matter how often Julia smiled at them, or how many times she said 'hello!' as brightly as she could, she'd never managed to get more than a timid smile in return and soon she gave up altogether. Now not even they were around. The Manor was deathly quiet.

She opened the door to her room. It was exactly as she'd left it. She felt a sudden, unexpected surge of warmth at the sight of her patchwork quilt and the collection of pens she always kept on her desk. Her single room, small as it was, was more of a home to her than anywhere had been in the past few years and she was glad of it. She dragged her case to the centre of the room, eased off her boots and padded across the floor. She pushed open the window a crack and perched herself on the ledge.

A few inches from her face, snowflakes fell in steady floating swirls. The grounds to the right of Holywell were already blanketed in white. All was quiet, still, serene. She breathed in the cold winter air, taking it down into her lungs, forcing out the sadness that lay at the bottom. She was back; she had a few days of comforting solitude before the Lent Term commenced. Best to take full advantage, she thought to herself. She had a lot of reading to do, and although she'd got through the Michaelmas Term without actually failing anything, there was still a long way to go to the top. At the moment, two people on the course held that spot. Douglas Parks and Jonathan Roddington-Palmer. Before the end of the year, she'd sworn to herself grimly, there'd be another name added to the list. Hers. It wasn't enough just to be at Oxford – she wanted to be up there, counted amongst the best. She knew she was easily as good as them . . . it was just that they were so damned confident. When she was called on to present an argument or defend a point of view, Julia's hands would go clammy; she could see them wincing at her accent and the way she kept tucking her hair behind her ears. She had none of the smooth, easy sophistication of the rest of them, and of the four women on the course, she was the only one who was neither blonde, flirtatious nor charming. In fact, she'd overheard one of their tutors saying that she was 'entirely devoid of feminine charm' – she hadn't known whether to be pleased by the comment or dismayed.

She closed the window with a snap and turned round. It was almost six o'clock. Aside from a rather soggy cheese and tomato sandwich on the train she'd had nothing to eat all day. Her stomach was rumbling. She'd left some dried pasta in the kitchen downstairs and possibly a jar of pesto in the fridge . . . she'd only been gone a couple of weeks . . . surely it would keep that long? She threw her suitcase a glance; she'd unpack when she'd eaten and then she'd get down to work.

There was someone in the kitchen; light was spilling out from underneath the door and she could hear the banging of pots and pans, the slam of a cupboard door and then the fridge being closed. Whoever it was, they were making one hell of a racket. It didn't sound like one of the Chinese students. She opened the door cautiously, wondering who else could have come back to Oxford the day after New Year . . . and why. She put a hand to her mouth as soon as she saw who it was. Aaron Keeler. He had his back to her, but there was no mistaking the tousled thatch of blond hair or the broad sweep of his shoulders. He turned as she walked in, and his look of surprise matched hers.

86

'Oh. It's you.' He immediately turned back to filling his pot.

'Yeah, and Merry Christmas to you too,' she snapped, unable to help herself. She too turned away before he could answer and opened the cupboard where she kept her small stash of groceries. She blinked. Her bag of dried fusilli was gone. Aaron Keeler was holding it above his pan of boiling water. Her pan, as a matter of fact. Come to think of it, she'd never ever seen him in the kitchen. 'Excuse me,' she said icily. 'I think that's *my* pasta.'

He looked down at the contents of the packet he'd just emptied, which were now swirling around merrily in the pan of boiling water. He shrugged. 'Sorry. Didn't have your name on it.'

'You can't just come in here and . . .' Julia began hotly, aware that her indignation had both raised her voice a notch *and* deepened her accent. *Ye can't joost cooome in 'ere.* She winced. 'What I mean is—'

'I know what you meant. Fine. *You* have the bloody pasta then.' He shrugged off her complaint. 'I'll just nick someone else's.' He crossed the kitchen and opened another cupboard. 'Ah. M and S. Much better.' He held a packet aloft. 'Happy?'

'Look, I didn't mean it like that . . . there's more than enough for both of us,' Julia said, her cheeks reddening. Christ, he was arrogant!

'Don't worry, wouldn't *dream* of robbing you.' He busied himself with finding another pot. Julia was left standing in the middle of the kitchen, wishing she'd shut her mouth. It there was one thing she couldn't bear being accused of, it was being mean. Stingy. Ungenerous. She'd never been stingy in her entire life! And his faint but unmissable emphasis on 'you' spoke volumes. He'd rather rob someone else – someone who could afford it. She felt her temper begin to rise.

'Look,' she said hotly. 'All I meant was it would've been polite of you to *ask*, that's all. I don't care about the bloody pasta. You can eat the whole packet for all I care! And in fact, whilst you're at it – here, you can have the rest of my pesto too.' She yanked open the fridge door. Her jar of pesto was gone. She whirled round. It was standing next to the cooker, a teaspoon already stuck inside it. She glared at it, then at him, and then, without trusting herself to utter a single further word, she stalked out of the kitchen and made her way back towards her room, her hunger momentarily forgotten. She'd sooner starve than argue with Aaron Keeler over food! She pushed open the door to her room, slammed it loudly behind her and threw herself on the bed. Her heart was beating fast. She couldn't help it – there was just something about the way he was that set her teeth on edge. Everything about him – from his assured good looks to the sneer that hovered permanently on his lips. *Don't worry, wouldn't dream of robbing you.* Ugh! She glanced down at her hands; they were clenched tightly shut. She let out a small sigh of exasperation. Not only was she angry, she was hungry too. And unless she waited another hour to make sure Keeler was out of the way, it looked as though she'd stay that way all night. It was too bloody much! What the hell was he doing back here anyway? A quick image of him floated up in front of her eyes. He was tanned. She'd been too angry to take it in at the time but he had the telltale T of slightly reddened skin across his forehead and nose . . . He'd either been on a beach or on the ski slopes somewhere. Whichever, he looked alarmingly healthy and . . . she stumbled across the thought . . . alarmingly attractive. Urgh! She rolled over and buried her head in her pillow.

It took a few minutes for the realisation that there'd been a knock at the door to penetrate her consciousness. She raised her head, wondering if she'd misheard. There was nothing. She got up, still clutching her pillow as if to ward off whomever might be standing there, and cautiously opened the door. There was no one. The corridor was empty save for the unmistakable scent of warm pasta and pesto. She stood uncertainly in the doorway for a few minutes – should she go back to the kitchen? He'd obviously come down the corridor to her room . . . what was she supposed to do now? Go back after him? She stood there for a few minutes, catching her lower lip in her teeth, then she turned and walked slowly back into her room. Damn him, she thought to herself for the umpteenth time. He'd wrong-footed her, and there was nothing she hated more than not knowing how to behave. Had he come to apologise and offer her a plate of food? Or had he come to gloat? Knowing Keeler, probably the latter. But that was the problem – she didn't know him at all. Not really. Not in the way that would answer the question. She opened her suitcase and rummaged through it until she found her nightdress. She was too tired, too hungry and too upset to think about it any further. She opened the door again, looked quickly up and down the corridor to make absolutely certain he wasn't around and marched to the bathroom to brush her teeth. Enough. She'd had enough. And the second term hadn't even yet begun.

What had started out as a silent animosity born largely out of mutual disdain between Julia Burrows and Aaron Keeler had, by the time Lent

Term ended, escalated into an almost full-scale, no-holds-barred war. In the week following the pasta 'n' pesto incident, as Dom liked to refer to it, Julia had been surprised to see Aaron coming to and from the Balliol law library with almost as many books as she. Now he was rarely seen in the MCR without his nose buried in a book. Julia was puzzled. His first term had been spent largely in the bar. 'Well, that's because you've got his goat,' Dom told her smugly when she mentioned it as off-handedly as she could. 'Look, he's spent his life coasting on his mother's tails. Now it's down to him. And with your marks shooting spectacularly upwards, my dear . . . well, it's no wonder. If there's one thing those damn Keeler boys can't stand, it's being beaten. Doesn't matter what it is. Rowing, rugby, reading . . . it's all the same to them. I think you're putting him under pressure. He looked as though he'd bust a gut when you won that argument in class yesterday.'

'Me?' Julia said, hoping the right note of self-deprecation had entered her voice. Although she'd sooner have died than admit it, the thought of finally giving Keeler a run for his money was immensely gratifying. Immensely.

'Yes, you. And don't look so surprised. Even Munro's had to reassess his opinion of you. You were in quite splendid form this morning. And don't pretend you don't know what I'm talking about, either.'

Julia had the grace to blush. 'Pure luck,' she said, as airily as she could.

'Bollocks. I've hardly seen you all term. You're always in the bloody library. With Keeler, I might add.'

Julia's blush deepened. 'That's not true,' she muttered.

'If you say so. Anyway, that's not why I'm here. It's my birthday next week. Yes, yes . . . I'll be twenty-three, can you believe it?' He looked down at her. Julia resisted the temptation to laugh. Dom still looked eighteen. 'Anyhow,' he continued, frowning, as though he'd read her mind, 'I'm having a dinner party. No, not here . . .' He waved a dismissive hand around the MCR. 'At home.'

'At home? What . . . in Norfolk?'

He nodded, a trifle sheepishly. 'Mother insists. She's fed up hearing all about the people on my course. She wants to meet you all too. She knows a few people already, of course. From Eton. But she's ever so keen to meet you.'

'Me?' Julia echoed faintly for the second time.

'Mmmm. I rather think,' Dom lowered his voice apologetically, 'that she has hopes. High hopes.'

Julia looked up at him uncertainly. 'Of what? Oh, oh . . . I see. Um, well . . .'

'Oh, do say you'll come. It'll be fun, I promise. We'll go down on the train on Friday morning and come back on Sunday.'

'Er, who else is coming?' Julia asked.

'Um, well . . . I did invite Keeler,' Dom had the grace to admit sheepishly. 'I *had* to. I know he wasn't in my year but he's an old Etonian. Mother would've killed me if I hadn't.'

Julia was silent. A weekend in the countryside with Aaron Keeler? She wasn't sure she could stomach it. The thought of it was already making her feel ill. But it was Dom's birthday and she knew how much he'd like to have them both there . . . if for entirely different reasons. She was curious, too, about Dom's home. He said very little about it, or his parents, whom he referred to affectionately as 'Mother' and 'Sir'. Hayden Hall, the Barrington-Brownes' ancestral home, lay close to the sea in Norfolk. 'It's massive,' he'd said to her gloomily once. 'And there's no escape. I'll inherit the whole bloody lot when Sir goes. They're just indulging me at the moment, I'm afraid.' He'd stared into his half-empty glass of beer with such intensity that Julia was moved.

'Indulging you? What d'you mean?'

'Law. Doing the postgrad year. This is just a pastime, really. When they go, I'll have to take over the bloody estate. I spend the rest of my life worrying about how to keep it up. You've no idea what it takes to run one of these country piles.'

'No, I don't suppose I would.' Julia smiled gently.

'I don't mean it like that. It's just . . . well, I don't seem to want *any* of the things they want for me.'

'Wife, children, a country pile, stuff like that?'

He nodded glumly. 'In a nutshell, yes.' Julia hadn't known what to say. She looked up at him now. 'Of course I'll come,' she said simply. 'Wouldn't miss it for anything.'

'Thanks, Burrows,' Dom said with feeling. 'It'll be a bit . . . well, you know what I mean.'

Julia nodded slowly. She'd never experienced it herself, but unrequited love had to be one of the very worst things to suffer. Particularly as in Dom's case there was absolutely no hope of his feelings ever being returned. Judging from the way women threw themselves at Aaron Keeler's feet and the way he reciprocated, he probably hadn't even *noticed* Dom. Or his suffering. She hesitated for a second – she wasn't the type to go around hugging other people, even if they were friends – and then tucked a hand in his arm. 'You'll have to help me find something to wear, though,' she said, allowing herself a smile. 'I've only got one evening dress. It's yellow. It's awful.'

'Ah, yes . . . the Yellow Meringue, as I believe you called it. Yes, well . . . I'll do my best. Black, I think. Mother says, you can't go wrong with it.'

'Help me spend some of my grant money this afternoon, then. I haven't bought new clothes in ages.'

'It shows.' Dom only just avoided her gentle shove. 'Thanks, Burrows,' he said again as they headed out of the MCR. 'Really. And don't worry about Mother. Deep down, you know, I think she . . . er, *knows*.'

'Mothers usually do,' Julia said softly. It took her a few seconds to swallow the sudden lump in her throat.

21

Dom insisted on paying for first-class tickets for himself and Julia the following Friday. Aaron, Peregrine and David – the three old Etonians at Balliol who'd been invited at Lady Barrington-Browne's express request – were going down the following morning by car. Despite her reservations about spending a weekend with Aaron Keeler and her nerves about spending a weekend on a country estate – what should she wear at dinner on the Friday night? How should Lady Barrington-Browne be addressed? Which fork did she use for fruit and did she have to drink tea with her little finger sticking out? Dom answered her questions patiently. 'Just be yourself. Mother will love you, I promise' – Julia was excited. For the first time since she'd arrived at Balliol, she felt as though she'd carved herself a niche. A little on the small side, to be honest – the 'niche' consisted of herself and Dom – but still, it was lovely to have something to look forward to at the weekend other than the law library. She'd thoroughly enjoyed the afternoon spent looking for a dress, too. In the end, Dom's 'infinitely superior taste' (his words) won out. She emerged from Selfridges with a simple black dress and a pair of 'killer heels' (also his words).

They took the train to Paddington and then a black cab across the city to Liverpool Street, where they boarded a second train to Norfolk. A driver would be waiting for them in Swaffham, Dom told her. From there it was a half-hour drive to Hayden. As the train pulled out of Liverpool Street and began to gather speed, Julia's excitement grew. How long had it been since she'd had fun . . . real, *proper* fun? She couldn't remember, which in itself was a sign of sorts. The countryside around Cambridge rose up around them in swathes of light and iridescent green; the banks of gorse showing the first yellowish haze of flowers. The wide, open Norfolk skies were blue and clear; after the gloom of Oxford Julia suddenly felt more alive than she'd done in months. She sat in the plushly comfortable seat, her nose pressed against the window, not wanting to miss a single detail.

At Swaffham, a uniformed driver met them off the train. With her mouth hanging open, she followed him and Dom out of the small station and into a splendidly shiny black car whose cavernous interior reminded her of the train. 'Is this yours?' she mouthed at Dom, unwilling to let the chauffeur see just how impressed she was.

'Well, it belongs to the family,' Dom said, looking slightly discomfited. 'I hardly ever use it myself.'

Julia turned to look out of the window. She'd had no idea Dom came from quite such wealth. They were almost halfway to Hayden when she noticed the low wall running along one side of the country lane. 'Don't tell me that's your boundary wall,' she said, half joking.

Dom looked even more discomfited. 'Um, yes. I told you . . . it's a leech of an estate. You've no idea how much it costs to run.'

'No, but I'm beginning to,' Julia said primly. She turned her head once more. They'd been driving for about fifteen minutes at roughly forty miles an hour. She made the swift calculation. At least ten miles, with another twenty-odd to go . . . She swallowed. Hayden Hall was bigger than all of Elswick. As they finally entered the gates and she saw the majestic line of oaks standing like furry light green sentinels along the sweep of the driveway, she was rendered speechless. There was a blinding flash of sunlight reflecting off the car's bonnet as they turned into the enormous circle and pulled up in front of the pale gold façade of the Great Hall.

'Here we are,' Dom cried, opening the door. The chauffeur came round to Julia's side and opened hers, helping her awkwardly on to the ground. 'At last!'

'I'll bring the bags up, sir,' the chauffeur murmured as he closed the door behind Julia.

'Thanks, Neil. Come on, Mother's waiting. She'll have been waiting all afternoon, I promise you.' Dom held out an arm. With her mouth still open, Julia took it and together they climbed the many stairs.

'Dominic!' A woman's voice rang out as they walked down what seemed to Julia to be an endless corridor filled with paintings, furniture, doorways and yet more paintings and sculpture until they finally turned into a private sitting room at the end. Lady Barrington-Browne rose as they entered. She was tall and exquisitely slender, dressed in a quilted skirt and jacket that Julia dimly recognised as Chanel – though quite how she recognised that was beyond her. She kissed her son carefully on both cheeks and then turned to Julia. 'And you must be Julia. How lovely of you to come.' She held out a hand. Julia didn't know whether to shake it or to curtsy . . . Lady Barrington-Browne solved the matter by clasping her hand warmly. Her blue eyes regarded Julia with evident sympathy. 'Dominic tells me you're an orphan. How dreadful. Dominic is *so* very fond of you and I must say, I can see why. Welcome to Hayden Hall, my dear. You must make yourself at home. Immediately. Come.' She led the way to three of the plushest, most comfortably upholstered sofas Julia had ever seen. 'Will you have some tea, my dear?' Without waiting for an answer, she rang a small silver bell and seconds later, as if by magic, a maid appeared with an equally silver tray. Julia took her cup with hands that shook only a little. Despite the enormous gulf in class between them, there was a warmth in Dom's mother that she felt herself responding to. When, half an hour later, Dom's father appeared in the doorway and greeted them both in a distant, formal way, it was clear which one of his parents had had the greater influence. There was a gentleness in Dom that was entirely his mother's; his father barked out a couple of routine questions – all going well up there, I take it? When are you back for good? – and, having gulped down his tea, rose and announced he was off to his study. 'Do come down for dinner, won't you?' Lady Barrington-Browne said to his rapidly departing back. There was a grunt of a reply and then he disappeared. She turned to both Julia and Dom and beamed. 'I think that was a no. Well, I'll just have to have you both to myself. How *lovely*.'

*

Over dinner, served by two uniformed servants in a beautifully appointed dining room overlooking the vast lawn and a lake to the south of the house, Lady Barrington-Browne managed to draw out details of Julia's childhood that she herself had forgotten. Was it the wine, perhaps? No sooner had she taken a couple of sips of the most delicious red wine she'd ever had than someone appeared with a crystal decanter and replenished her glass. There was poached salmon and tiny just-in-season potatoes with a sprinkling of dill. 'Everything we eat comes from the farm,' Lady Barrington-Browne said proudly. She looked at her son. 'It's quite an enterprise, darling. You'll have to go through it all with Father before you go back. You'd be amazed at how well it's doing.'

Dom grunted, much like his father. Julia hid her smile. She looked past Lady Barrington-Browne to the trees framed in the window behind her. She felt the presence of the house and the weight of its history like someone standing at her shoulder. It was strangely comforting. 'It's lovely here,' she said suddenly, without meaning to.

'Isn't it?' Lady Barrington-Browne followed her eyes. 'I still remember the day my husband brought me here for the first time. It was hard to say whom I loved more.'

'Mother!' Dom looked up from his plate. 'That's a terrible thing to say.'

'Perhaps,' Lady Barrington-Browne demurred. 'But quite true. One day this will all be yours,' she said, smiling at him. 'And your children's.'

'Mother.' There was a faint warning in Dom's voice.

'All right, all right.' She lifted her wine glass almost defiantly. 'I just want you to be happy, darling.'

'I *am* happy, Mother.'

'I know you are. And you've brought Julia to visit. I'm *so* pleased.'

'Mother.' This time the warning was clear.

To cover her confusion and embarrassment, Julia suddenly found herself recounting a trip to a stately home that her parents had taken her on when she was six. All she could remember about the outing was needing the bathroom, she laughed. She had no recollection whatsoever about the house. Dom looked at her gratefully; his mother reached across the table and gripped Julia's forearm. 'You poor, poor girl. Losing them both like that. What a terrible shock it must have been. You must look upon us as family, dear Julia.'

'Oh, I . . . I didn't mean it like that,' Julia stammered in embarrassment. 'I . . . I wasn't . . .'

'Of course not. But I must say, you're by far the most interesting person Dom's brought home in a very long time. It's usually the Etonians . . . the ones who're coming down tomorrow. What are their names again? Ah, yes . . . Aaron and Peregrine. Quite dull, I find.'

'Mother, that's enough. Right. I'm going to show Julia the chapel and then we're off to bed. It's been a long day.'

'Of course, darling. It's a lovely chapel, Julia. Quite soothing. You must light a candle. Sleep well, won't you? I'm going riding tomorrow morning but I'll see you at lunch. Mrs McCallum's organised the menu for tomorrow night; it's all perfectly under control.'

'As always. Night, Mother.' Dom bent and gave his mother a kiss. 'Come on.' He turned to Julia. 'She's right. The chapel's wonderful. Puts you in a wonderfully serene state of mind.'

It *was* wonderful. Small, but exquisitely formed. The air was thick and sweet with the scent of lilies; as they pushed open the heavy oak door, Julia again felt the comforting weight of centuries of wealth and tradition. She followed Dom down the nave until they reached the altar. Rows of tea lights stood on either side of them. She followed his lead and lit one, placing it carefully in the holder on the top row. The thin, flickering light grew steadily stronger, sending shadows dancing across the stone floor and walls. She'd never been particularly religious – both her parents were lapsed Catholics – but there was something beautiful and moving about being in the presence of God, which was the only way she knew to describe it. Her lips moved in a silent prayer, but for once, there was little pain or sorrow attached. The family chapel was peaceful; when she got up a few minutes later, the world suddenly seemed lighter, clearer. She followed Dom out into the cold night air, her hands stuffed in the pockets of her coat. She slipped one into his arm and together they crossed the courtyard in companionable silence. She was glad she'd come; it had been a long time since she'd been enveloped in the warmth of a real home, as vast as this one was. It was a warmth that stayed with her all night.

22

The following afternoon, she and Dom were in the drawing room playing Scrabble when a maid entered to say the first guests had arrived. All morning she'd heard the sounds of preparation coming from the vast kitchen below the entrance hall – the clang of pots and pans, muted shouts, bottles being brought up from the cellar. She'd seen two uniformed maids trotting back and forth between the kitchen and the formal dining room on the first floor with plates, cutlery, armfuls of fresh flowers and bottles of wine. 'How many people are coming?' she'd asked in amazement.

'Oh, a dozen or so. There's the Balliol lot and a couple of other old Etonians. You'll really like Simon – he's been crewing round the world for the past couple of years. Then there's my cousin and two friends of hers. Keeler rang this morning and asked if Minty could come—'

'*Minty?*' Julia's face fell. 'God, anyone but her. She's awful.' The memory of walking behind Minty and Aaron and listening to them discussing her still rankled.

'What could I say? I know she's a royal pain in the arse, but she and Keeler are practically joined at the hip these days.'

And now here she was. Julia could hear her voice before she actually appeared. 'Ooh, isn't this just *divine?*'

She winced, getting up from her position on the floor. 'Well, just make sure I go easy on the champagne tonight,' she said darkly to Dom. 'Otherwise I might give in to temptation and slap her one.'

Dom grinned. 'In that case, Burrows, I'll be plying you all night. You slapping Araminta Hedley-Tetherington? Now that I *have* to see.'

'Dom . . .'

'All right, all right. Keep your hair on. I'm only teasing.'

'Christ, how the other half live.' Aaron Keeler suddenly appeared in the doorway. Julia looked up. His eyes narrowed as he caught sight of her. She ignored him as best she could. Behind him, peering eagerly around the room, was Minty, followed by Peregrine and David, the impossibly foppish fourth member of their little set. Julia's heart sank. She'd so thoroughly enjoyed herself in the past twenty-four hours that the dinner party was a rude reminder of how difficult the rest of her stay would be. She felt Minty's eyes range over her jeans and sweater, coming to rest on her socks. In her neat little twinset with the requisite pearls strung around her slender neck, Minty looked as though she'd stepped off another planet. Planet Wealth. *Oh, stop it,* Julia muttered to herself, clearing away the remains of their Scrabble game. She couldn't afford to let Minty ruin what had so far been the most enjoyable weekend she'd had in years. She followed the newly arrived guests out of the drawing room and escaped to her room as quickly as her footsteps would carry her. It was nearly four. A few more hours until dinner. She'd spend most of them reading, she thought to herself, and then she'd take a nice long bath and get ready. She almost laughed out loud. Get ready? She'd never spent more than ten minutes getting ready for anything. Tonight might be different. For the first time in ages, she felt a sudden impatience with the jeans and sweaters that were her staple wardrobe. She looked at herself in the mirror on the wall next to her bed. She really ought to do something with her hair. Shoulder-length, perfectly clean, perfectly manageable. She'd had the same cut for almost ten years. Not that you could really call it a cut . . . it fell away from her face in a straight line to her shoulders. Nothing to it. Tonight, however . . . she took a handful of it and piled it on top of her head. She turned her profile this way and that. Her ears suddenly looked very bare. Earrings? She didn't possess any. She let her hair drop again. She was being silly. Who cared what she looked like? There was no one present whom she wanted to impress.

At quarter to eight on the dot, she opened her bedroom door and peered out. There was no one about. Dom had phoned up to instruct everyone to be in the drawing room for drinks fifteen minutes before dinner. She walked a little unsteadily down the corridor in her new high heels, trying not to think about her shoes, her dress, her hair and – most difficult of all – her make-up. She'd experimented with a little mascara and eyeliner, not sure whether she liked the effect or not. It wasn't as if she'd never worn make-up before . . . more that she just wasn't used to it. She put a hand up to her lips . . . yes, she'd remembered to put on lipstick too. She crossed the Great Hall, her heels making a loud clacking sound on the marble floor, and walked down the long corridor towards the sound of voices and music.

'Ah, Julia . . . there you are.' Lady Barrington-Browne, the picture of slender elegance in a dark blue silk dress, patted the seat beside her. 'You look lovely, my dear. Come and sit next to me.' Julia avoided Minty's jealous glare and crossed the room, uncomfortably conscious of her every step. She perched on the edge of the sofa and gratefully accepted a glass of wine. She took a larger sip than was perhaps necessary and looked around the room. Aside from the four people she knew, there were six or seven others, all in evening dresses or black dinner jackets, dotted around the room. They all knew each other, of course . . . they'd either been to the same nursery schools, boarding schools or university halls. The well-trodden path, as Dom often put it. In one corner, standing by the window with a drink in hand, was Aaron. He was alone; Minty had been waylaid by a girl in a long emerald-green dress who'd been at boarding school with her, or so the conversation went. Quite why Minty's voice carried so much further than anyone else's was a mystery to Julia. She seemed to think it necessary to speak several decibels louder than everyone around her. 'Ooh, did she really? Oh, how *ghastly*! No! I can't *imagine* her . . .' And so on. Julia took a further sip of wine, enjoying the warmth it spread through her, bolstering her rather shaky confidence just that little bit more. The clock struck 8 p.m. Lady Barrington-Browne clapped her hands. A maid appeared, followed by another. The guests turned and began to make their way towards the dining room. Dinner was about to start.

'A *printer*?' Minty's voice carried all the way down the long, elegantly dressed table. 'What's a printer?'

Julia was on her third – or possibly fourth or even fifth – glass of excellent red wine and the question neither surprised nor irritated her. She could feel Dom's eyes on her as she lowered her glass. 'A printing press. Newspapers. He worked for the *Newcastle Herald*.'

'Oh.' Minty seemed stumped by the answer.

'He was in the union.' Julia had no idea why she threw that little detail in as well.

'A unionist?' Peregrine couldn't help himself. He was staring at Julia as though she'd just mentioned that her father had been in jail. For murder.

'Mmm. All his life.' For once, Julia was enjoying herself. She couldn't have said why, but the uneasy looks the others were giving each other around the table amused her. Christ, they'd led such sheltered lives. 'Bit of a firebrand, actually.'

'I'll say.' Aaron's muttered remark reached her ears alone. She turned her head slowly to look at him.

'Something wrong?'

He frowned, as though not quite sure how to respond. Dom, fearing that a situation was about to develop that might even end in the promised slap, suddenly launched into a diversionary anecdote about something that had clearly happened a decade earlier at school. Julia's attention drifted. She took another sip. She'd ceased to care what they thought about her. In for a penny, in for a pound, as her father would have said. She smiled to herself. She'd never thought the day would come when she'd be able to think about him, or her mother, for that matter, with a smile on her face. It had been nearly ten years since they'd gone, and although time had certainly dulled the sharpness of the pain, it hadn't gone away. Now, all of a sudden and when she'd least expected it, a smile had crept in. The day she'd been waiting for had suddenly arrived. 'Excuse me,' she said quickly, putting down her glass and standing up.

Dom looked up at her, frowning. 'You all right?' he asked, concern tingeing his voice.

'Yes, I'm fine. Just need a bit of fresh air, that's all. No, don't get up. I'll just step outside for a minute.' She pushed back her chair and walked quickly to the end of the room. The French doors led out on to a long, wide balcony. She pushed them open and stepped into the inky darkness. She wrapped her arms around herself and took a deep breath. The weekend had turned out to be far less of an ordeal than she'd feared. She'd experienced something else alongside the good food and wine and the wonderfully comfortable bed. She struggled to put it into words – graciousness? The gulf that separated her from Dom and his background was neither as wide nor as intractable as she'd thought. There was a grace in the way they handled and displayed their wealth that had disarmed her. Perhaps – she hesitated as the thought came to her – perhaps the constant out-of-placeness that characterised her every waking moment at Balliol was her problem, not theirs? Perhaps she wasn't quite as out of her depth as she feared? Dom had teased her often enough about it – *you don't carry a chip on your shoulder, Burrows, it's a bloody great boulder. You ought to try putting it down every once in a while. You'll wind up with a slipped disc.* She couldn't help herself; she giggled out loud.

'What's so funny?' A voice suddenly materialised out of the darkness behind her.

She whirled round. It was Aaron Keeler. She felt the weight of the boulder reassert itself. 'Nothing,' she said tightly. What the hell was he doing there? She heard the worrying into flame of a match; he'd come outside for a cigarette.

'Smoke?' He held out the packet.

Julia hesitated. She wasn't much of a smoker – the odd one or two at a party, nothing more. But she didn't know what to do with her hands, and Aaron's proximity was unnerving. She could smell his aftershave – a subtle, tangy scent that brought her father to mind. 'Thanks,' she muttered, taking one. He bent down to give her a light; for the briefest moment as their hands touched, there was a spark that ran straight through Julia, leaving her slightly dizzy and drawing on her cigarette as if it might save her, keep her upright. She was furious with herself. It was the wine. Or the fresh air. Or both.

'So . . . a printer and a trade unionist. What does he do now? Retired, I suppose?'

'He's dead. They're both dead. Killed in a traffic accident when I was fifteen.' It came out more abruptly than she'd intended. She looked away, flicking the ash from her cigarette over the balustrade.

'Oh. Shit. I'm sorry. I . . . I didn't know.' Aaron's voice was suddenly gentle.

'Why would you?'

'No, really. I'm sorry. It . . . it sort of explains things, though.'

'What?' She turned back and eyed him suspiciously. He was looking down at her with the strangest expression on his face. She was aware of a sudden increase in her heart rate.

He gave a small shrug. She looked up at him. They stared at each other for a second, then his hand came out, catching her off balance. He touched her arm, producing a second wave of tiny electric shocks running up and down its length. 'I don't know . . . You're . . . you're so . . .'

But whatever it was he was going on to say about her, he was suddenly cut short. 'Aaron?' It was Minty. Her voice was plaintive. 'What're you *doing* out there?' There was the sound of the door being opened and Minty stepped out. Aaron drew back from Julia and the shocking, unexpected moment of intimacy was lost. He turned around; in a flash, Minty's hand was on his arm, pulling him away. Julia felt as though she'd been slapped. Her face was hot and her hands were clammy. She didn't wait for another second. She tossed her cigarette over the edge and quickly walked back into the dining room. She slid back into her place beside Dom, her heart racing.

'Have you been smoking?' Dom asked, his eyebrows going up in surprise.

'Just the one,' Julia said tightly. She reached for her wine glass. Her hands were still shaking. What the hell had happened to her out there? She *hated* Keeler. But the surge of emotion he'd drawn out of her so easily and quickly had nothing to do with hate . . . the opposite. For a brief, mad second when his hand came down on her arm, all she could think about was being pulled close. From the far end of the room she could hear Aaron and Minty coming back in. Minty was laughing at something he'd said, and as they returned to the table and took their places again, Julia glanced up briefly, caught his eye and was forced to look away. She'd never given much thought to it – who *cared* if they were a couple or not – but she was horrified to find herself gripped by a feeling that was suspiciously close to jealousy. She couldn't help herself; she stole another quick glance down the table. Aaron's hand was resting casually on Minty's in almost the same place he'd touched her: on the forearm, his fingers moving lightly across Minty's pale skin. His own arm was tanned and strong. He looked down the table at Julia, and again their eyes caught and held. She watched as he lifted his arm from Minty's and draped it slowly across her back, pulling her to him. He turned his head and whispered something in her ear. Minty smiled, one of those awful smiles of smug, self-satisfied possession, and she too turned to look at Julia. They were probably laughing at her, Julia thought to herself miserably, and felt the awful burn of tears behind her eyes. She got up again, ignoring Dom's puzzled frown, and practically ran from the room. The dinner party was nowhere near ending but she'd had enough. The question, the piercing look he'd given her and the briefest of touches had triggered a host of unfamiliar feelings inside her, and she wasn't sure she knew how to cope.

She walked quickly down the corridor to her room and shut the door firmly behind her, leaning against it with all her weight, as if that might lock out what it was in Aaron Keeler that she feared. As she angrily scrubbed off the mascara and lipstick she'd put on for the evening and brushed her teeth, it came to her in a flash that it wasn't just Aaron Keeler she was afraid of – it was herself. He'd exposed a moment of weakness in her and she'd been unable to stop herself from revealing it to him. She lifted her head and looked at herself in the mirror. Her eyes were reddened with tears. There was a hollowed-out trembling in the pit of her stomach and the taste of sorrow was back in her mouth. She'd been a fool – she *was* a fool. It was March – another four months to go. She would avoid him at all costs; it was the only way.

23

MADDY
New York, February 1992

Maddy pulled back the curtain for the tenth time and stared out anxiously across the sea of faces. The auditorium was packed full; there were people standing in the back row. It was the final show of the second semester, a new play by Joel Silver, and she'd somehow won the leading role. Her stomach gave a lurch. She let the curtain drop, ran her hands down the fabric of her hot-pink pantsuit and tried to remember everything she'd been taught about controlling her nerves and her breathing. It was the first time since she'd been at Tisch that she'd landed a leading role, and to say she felt sick was the understatement of the century. It was a good role – a juicy, well-crafted, complex role – all she had to do was deliver the performance she'd been working on for nearly a month to the exclusion of almost everything else. She breathed in and out slowly, holding a hand over her diaphragm, forcing herself to calm down.

The music suddenly swelled, the lights dimmed and all of a sudden, It Was Showtime. 'Break a leg,' someone whispered as the opening score faded away and the curtains peeled back. Maddy drew a deep breath, steadied herself and then walked on to the stage. All concentration in her was channelled into the single point of her performance. Sydney, her hyper-thin, hyper-rich and hyper-selfish character, took over; Maddy Stiller ceased to exist. For the next ninety minutes, she was truly someone else. And then suddenly, it was over. She delivered her last lines, there was a moment's pause and then the audience erupted in applause. Dazed and unable to see more than a few feet beyond the edge of the stage, Maddy took her place alongside the other cast members, bowed deeply and was called back twice more. She'd done well; she could *feel* it. She stumbled off the stage with everyone else, too drained of emotion to think.

Backstage, her fellow students were full of praise. Sandy hugged her as soon as she came through the wings. 'You were just *awesome*!' she cried, squeezing the breath out of her. 'And you'll *never* guess who was in the audience?'

'Who?' Maddy asked, still too dazed to speak properly.

'Althea Katzmann.' Sandy delivered the news with the air of someone giving away state secrets. 'Althea Katzmann!'

Maddy's mouth suddenly went dry. Althea Katzmann was one of New York's top casting agents. 'Are you serious?'

'Yep. She was sitting one row behind Loughlin. Oh shit, here he comes! Call me later, OK? We're all going to Jimmy's on Canal.' She rushed off, winding her scarf around her neck, and blew her a kiss from the stage entrance door.

'Maddy.' Loughlin was suddenly upon her. He stopped and for a brief, giddy second, Maddy thought he too might actually hug her. 'Good performance,' he said, smiling broadly. 'You did well.' It was probably the first and only time she'd ever seen him smile. It was such a far cry from the man who'd snarled contemptuously at her a few months earlier that it was all Maddy could do not to burst into tears.

'Th . . . thank you,' she croaked out, her eyes smarting.

'Well done. Some pretty important people out there saw it too. Keep at it, Stiller. You've got talent.' And then just as suddenly as he'd appeared, he was gone. Maddy remained where she was, wondering if the whole thing hadn't been a dream. There was a part of her that almost didn't want to believe it could happen. She held on tightly to the childish superstition that if she said something – *any*thing – she'd jinx it, or worse. She watched everyone around her scurrying about, putting things away, shutting the theatre down, high-fiving one another and tossing out congratulations over their shoulders. The evening had gone well; she knew from the horror stories that circulated around the drama department of evenings where things *hadn't* gone well. Freshmen students who'd fluffed their lines, delivered wooden or flat performances or just simply had a bad day had had their careers wiped out before they'd even started. Alongside the humiliation and the pain of their weekly classes, there was the stress of the final semester performance thrown in, weeding them out even further. Well, she'd been in New York City all of six months; she hadn't given up; she hadn't fluffed her lines or delivered a weak performance. Somehow she managed to muddle her way through, and in those moments when she felt she couldn't give anything more, Sandy had stepped in. To Maddy's immense surprise, she'd resisted Maddy's attempts to draw away. The more Maddy retreated into herself, the closer Sandy came. Perhaps it really was as she said. Her mother was a shrink; somehow she'd picked up more than her fair share of empathy. She'd said no more about the thing Maddy feared the most – that she'd guessed her little secret – and to Maddy's great surprise, the better she got at acting, the less she felt the need. By the time spring rolled around and she'd won the part of Sydney, it had been weeks since she'd crept away to the bathroom after supper or lunch. She didn't dare believe it, but . . . perhaps she really was on the way to curing herself. It didn't seem possible, and yet . . . She picked up her clothes from her locker and quickly made her way to the showers. Time to scrub off the theatrical paint, put on her own clothes and see if some of Sydney's confidence had rubbed off on her . . . hopefully for good.

24

NIELA
London, December 1992

The continent came and went in long, unbroken expanses of fields, mountains, rivers, occasionally punctured by towns and cities. Graz. Innsbruck. Basel-Mulhouse. Niela sat stiffly upright in her seat, unable to close her eyes. She stared blankly out of the window but did not see the tide of green or the snow-capped peaks as the train shot out of one tunnel after another, crossing the Alps. In her handbag was the envelope containing just under five hundred Deutschmarks. She'd opened it expecting to see four hundred, and found an extra hundred instead. Christian must have slipped it in. She'd almost wept. No tears, she'd told herself fiercely, choking back a sob. No tears. Not now, not *ever*. She stuffed the envelope into the inside pocket of her handbag and tried desperately to think of something else. London. She was on her way to London. She'd been once before, when she was twelve. She remembered very little – rain, tasteless food and, one day, a very long queue to see a building full of wax models. They'd stood patiently outside for hours and then when they finally got in and Korfa realised the scale of the deception, he'd been inconsolable. He didn't understand the concept – when Niela told him he was going to see Michael Jackson, he'd believed her. What was this lifeless waxy figure in front of him? They'd had to take him out, still crying. She smiled a little at the memory. It was enough to prompt an answering smile from the older woman sitting opposite her.

Niela turned her face away. She couldn't bear another act of kindness, not now, no matter how small.

Occasionally she got up and walked along the corridor to stretch her legs. Switzerland was the kaleidoscope of images seen on chocolate boxes, one Alpine village after another, church steeples, wooden barns and fat glossy cows grazing on fields of dazzling green. At the border with France, the train slowed to a halt. In the silence that followed the screaming and shunting of brakes, she awoke with a start. The unfamiliar half-light of the train's interior revealed a dozen or more people moving towards waking in the same stunned manner. Across from her a man dozed fitfully, his chin sliding further and further down into his chest.

They pulled into Paris just before dawn. The deserted station glowed under eerie fluorescent lights. She hoisted her bag on to her back and made her way towards the Métro. She bought a baguette and a coffee and bit into the soft, floury inside hungrily. The train to London was leaving from the Gare du Nord in just under an hour. The warm air of the Métro rushed at her as she descended into its depths; from somewhere deep inside came the thin wail of a solitary busker. She bought a ticket and joined the growing swell of commuters as they began their day. She was too tired to think about anything other than making sure she got to the station on time. Beyond that the future was an empty, dark hole. She had barely enough money to last her a week, but she couldn't allow it to frighten her. She'd found a job before; she could do it again. She shoved and pushed her way out of the Métro at the Gare du Nord alongside everyone else and found the London train. She climbed aboard, stowed her small bag carefully in the luggage rack and found herself a seat next to the window. The carriage began to fill up with people: students, back-packers, a mother with a young child. As she watched them take their seats and arrange their possessions around them, laughing and chatting excitedly to those they knew, smiling at those they didn't, she suddenly felt terribly alone. No one else could be doing what she had done – no one else was on the run. She looked out of the window. Through the thin veil of tears she saw Christian's face again. *Niela, what's wrong?* She'd been unable to speak, just as she couldn't speak now. She waited, her breath coming in short, foggy gasps against the cold windowpane, willing the train to start.

Victoria station at four o'clock in the afternoon was a terrifying cac-ophony of bustle and noise. Niela was discharged, along with hundreds of others, on to the platform at the end of an enormous domed arch with train doors slamming all around them and the deafening sound of hundreds of pairs of feet hitting the ground running. She clutched her bag to her chest and made her way towards the station exit. She picked up a map from a Tourist Information booth; the bored-looking woman inside must have taken pity on her. She looked Niela over once, twice. 'Watch out for men offering accommodation. Try the hotels on Warwick Way. About a ten-minute walk.' Niela thanked her and hurried away. She crossed the road in front of the station and walked down Vauxhall Bridge Road towards the river, stopping every few minutes to consult the map. The hotels that lined Vauxhall Bridge Road looked forbidding; tall and dilapidated, they displayed neon signs for 'Swedish Massage' and 'Hourly Rates' – she held on to her bag even more tightly and quickened her pace. She turned into Warwick Way and looked nervously around her. A cluster of expensive-looking hotels – the Windermere Guest House, the Enrico Hotel, Astor Palace, Lime Tree Hotel. She stopped in front of one, a pretty little cottage-style place with a blue sign outside and four shining gold stars. She swallowed nervously and walked up the steps.

Fifty-five pounds without breakfast. Niela gaped at her. The woman behind the reception counter looked her up and down. 'Try nearer the station,' she said coolly. 'Might be more within your price range.'

'Th . . . thank you,' Niela stammered and quickly turned away. She caught a glimpse of a chambermaid pushing a trolley of freshly laundered sheets and towels. She swallowed. It had been three days since she'd had anything close to a shower – her skin felt grimy and sweaty, despite the chill in the air. The girl disappeared down a corridor. Niela pushed open the door again and walked out. She made her way back towards the station, avoiding the puddles. It had begun to rain – a fine, misty drizzle that lowered the sky and made everything around seem even more dark and grey. It was hard to concentrate for the fear bubbling nervously inside her. What had she done? She was utterly alone in an utterly unknown city. She had just under two hundred pounds to her name . . . with nowhere to sleep, nowhere to go and no one to ask for help. She looked at her watch. It was just after 10 a.m. She thought of her parents back home in the flat. Her mother would be cutting up vegetables and checking the pots on the stove. Her father would be at work. The boys would be at school. An image of Korfa bent over his German homework, tongue sticking out in concentration, flashed before her eyes. She stopped. The stab of homesickness that rippled through her made it impossible to move. Nothing for it but to stand still and let it burn itself out.

The Comfort B&B on Vauxhall Bridge Road was twenty-five pounds a night. Niela handed over the money for four nights. That was all she could afford. She was left with four twenty-pound notes and three or four pounds in change. The receptionist, a large peroxide blonde whose jaws moved mechanically up and down on a bright pink wad of chewing gum, was brisk. 'Breakfast's in the basement. Two pound fifty flat rate. Starts at seven. I'd get there early if I were you.' She showed Niela to her room, pointed out the toilets at the end of the corridor and then disappeared into the lift. Niela was alone. She sat down gingerly on the edge of the bed. The room was tiny; just enough space for a single bed and a wooden built-in wardrobe without a handle. The window looked out directly on to the extension of the building next door. There was a tiny patch of sky in the upper left-hand corner – nothing else. A pair of drab, faded floral curtains hung droopily towards the ground. The bathroom was halfway down the hall. The enormity of what she'd done was beginning to sink in. She stared at the counterpane on the lumpy bed until the flowers began to run and the colours bled under the deluge of tears.

Breakfast the following morning was boiled eggs and cold toast with tea and jam. Under the receptionist's watchful eye, Niela took four slices. In spite of the sense of panic that permeated her every waking moment, she'd slept well. She knew from experience that the thing to do in the situation she found herself in was not to give in and do nothing – but rather the opposite. To do everything possible – and as quickly as possible. The weeks and months of waiting for their visas to come through in the camp back in Ethiopia had taught her what she recognised as one of life's great lessons. Keep active. Stay busy. Look for ways out. She drained her cup of tea and stood up. Her task for the day was clear – find a job. *Any* job. It didn't matter what. So long as it paid her enough to live on, the rest would come later.

She tried everything. Every restaurant, every hotel, every office . . . she even applied at the London Underground station in Victoria for a job as a cleaner. *Anything*. It was pointless. After taking her name, she was asked for references and her address, neither of which she had. She walked up and down the streets of Victoria and Pimlico, scanning the signs in newsagents' windows, employment agencies . . . she walked into hotel lobbies, two dental practices and the off-licence on the corner. To no avail. If there was work to be had, she wasn't in line.

On her fourth and last day at the Comfort B&B, she counted out what was left of her money – £2.54. She slipped the change in her pocket and walked downstairs.

'A job?' The receptionist looked her up and down suspiciously. 'What sort of a job?'

'Anything,' Niela replied honestly. 'Anything at all.'

There was a moment's pause. She seemed to be considering something. 'All right,' she said finally. She pulled a pad towards her and took out a pen from behind her ear. 'Give this number a ring. Ask for Marty. Tell him I sent you. My name's Irene.' She tore off the leaf of paper and handed it to Niela. 'You only paid for four nights. We're not a charity case, you know. You either pay for another night, or you check out before noon. You don't have any luggage, do you?'

Niela shook her head, too embarrassed to speak.

Irene narrowed her eyes. 'All right. Speak to Marty and come back and see me this afternoon. Marty'll find something for you. You're pretty enough.'

Niela swallowed. She wasn't sure what her looks had to do with anything, but she was desperate. After two days, she realised London was nowhere near as cheap as Vienna or Munich, or anywhere else for that matter. At the rate she was going, she had barely enough funds to last her until Friday . . . and then what? There was absolutely nowhere to go. She fingered the piece of paper as she walked down the corridor towards the payphone. There was a cold, sinking feeling in the pit of her stomach that she dared not name. She looked at the number, drew a deep breath and dialled.

Marty sounded friendly enough. 'Oh, Irene sent you, did she? Right, well, why don't you pop in and see me this afternoon?' he said. 'We're only just up the road. Number 84. You can't miss it. It's the one with the red door.'

Niela thanked him and hung up. Perhaps she'd misunderstood Irene's glance. He sounded decent enough . . . perhaps he was some sort of agency? Cleaners, au pairs, house help . . . that sort of thing. She could do that. She squared her shoulders. She hadn't been joking when she told Irene she could do anything. She *would* do anything. She had to.

That afternoon, at two o'clock on the dot, she walked up the steps of a rather run-down building on Vauxhall Bridge Road, about a five-minute walk from the hotel. Yes, it was the one with the red door, she confirmed, looking up and down the street. The only one. There had obviously been a brass number; a ghostly '84' remained where the paint had faded. The door was locked. There was a small buzzer to her left. She pressed it and waited.

'Who is it?'

'Um, my name is Niela . . . I spoke to Marty this morning . . . ?' She spoke hesitantly into the microphone.

There was a second's pause. 'Who sent you?'

'Irene. From the Comfort B and B. She gave me Marty's number.'

There was another second's pause. Then the door clicked open. Niela stepped inside.

The hallway was dark and damp-smelling. There was an old chair in one corner, a hatstand and a freshly laundered pile of sheets, still in their plastic wrapping. She eyed the sheets nervously. What were they doing there? Suddenly, she heard a noise from the floor above. A man's head appeared over the balustrade. 'Up here,' he said, peering down at her. 'First floor.'

Niela hurried up the stairs. There was a narrow corridor at the top and, at the end, an open door. The man who'd spoken to her was waiting in the doorway. He watched her as she approached. 'Niela, right?' he asked as she drew level. She nodded. There was something wolfish and rather predatory about his smile. She could feel her skin begin to contract in fear. 'Go on in,' he said, leering down at her. 'Marty'll be with you in a second.' His arm was lifted above his head, holding open the door. He made no move to stand back as she passed under it. The smell of sweat and tobacco emanating from him was overpowering. She slipped inside the room – it was hard to call it an office, despite the presence of a desk – as quickly as she could. Her own underarms were beginning to prickle with sweat. 'Take a seat.' The invitation came out like a command. She sat down quickly, her knees pressed hard together. Something was wrong. She wondered how she was going to leave.

'Niela?' Someone came in through the doorway. She looked up. A short, fat man with a moustache advanced into the room. 'You're the one who rang this morning?' He rubbed his hands. 'Very nice, you are. *Very* nice. Only just arrived in London, have you?'

Niela nodded, her heart sinking fast. 'A few days ago,' she said, hoping her voice wouldn't betray her fears.

He raised a thick, hairy eyebrow. 'Run away from home, have you, love?' he asked, a false note of concern in his voice.

Niela swallowed. She shook her head. 'No, nothing like that. I'm . . . I'm just looking for work. Irene didn't really say what sort of work you had . . . what can I do?'

He walked around the desk and sat down, pushing the chair closer and putting his hands in a V in front of him before answering. 'That depends on you, love.'

'Wh . . . what do you mean?' Niela asked. Sweat was beginning to trickle down her back.

'Well, we cater for all tastes here. Oral, anal, straight, threesomes . . . whatever the client wants. We charge extra for doing it without condoms, of course, but that's up to the individual girls. We cater to all tastes. Black, Asian, white . . . whatever. We're a one-stop shop, aren't we, Pete?'

The man who'd been standing in the doorway grinned. Niela felt the cold hand of fear and the hot flush of shame take simultaneous hold of her entire body. She got to her feet. 'I'm . . . I'm sorry,' she stammered. 'I . . . I misunderstood. I thought . . . I was looking for something else . . . a cleaning job or something like that. I didn't understand, I'm sorry.'

'Shame,' Marty drawled, his eyes narrowing. 'You'd be a right little earner. You sure?'

Niela clutched her bag as if it were a weapon. Sweat was pouring down her back. She nodded. 'I . . . I'm sure. I'm sorry to waste your time . . .' She moved towards the door. The man called Pete remained where he was. His hand was blocking the doorway. 'C-could I just . . .' Niela indicated his arm. 'C-could I just get past . . . ?'

He stood his ground, not moving. Niela felt her stomach turn over. There was a movement behind her as Marty got to his feet. She heard his footsteps and then, without even thinking about the consequences, she lunged at the doorway, catching Pete off guard. He put out a hand to balance himself, momentarily releasing his hold on the door jamb. In a flash, she was through. She fled along the corridor and down the stairs, tears of shame and embarrassment coursing down her cheeks. The front door was closed. Her heart missed a beat. She looked around wildly. There was a small button underneath the lock – she pushed it hard and the door buzzed open. She tumbled out into the street, ran down the steps and didn't stop running until she'd reached the end of the road. She couldn't go back to the Comfort B&B. She couldn't face seeing Irene. How could it have happened? Marty's voice reverberated inside her head. *Black, Asian, white . . . oral, anal . . .* She put her hands up to her ears. How could Irene have sent her there? Suddenly she caught sight of her reflection in a shop window. Her hair had partially come out of its ponytail and was damp and frizzy in the light rain. Her skin was dull and grey, not brown . . . and her eyes . . . ? She stopped. She'd never seen her own face so haunted and desperate-looking. She looked half mad with worry. No wonder Irene had misunderstood. She swallowed painfully. What was happening to her?

She was suddenly overcome with a longing to feel her mother's arms around her, no matter how long it had been since she'd received a hug; to hear Raageh's high-pitched giggle or Korfa's deeper, throatier laugh . . . Even the thought of her father's voice produced a terrible ache in her side that made her place her hand over it. The memories that she'd kept at bay for the past few months came flooding back. The smell of her mother's hair after she'd washed it – she would often call Niela into her room to comb and braid it. Back in Mogadishu, someone came twice a week to the house to wash and set Saira's hair, to thread her eyebrows and wax her arms and legs. When Niela was old enough, the same woman had attended to her too. But in Vienna there'd been no money for such luxuries – it was Niela who'd stepped into the role. At the time she'd regarded it as just another one of her too many chores. Now, standing at the side of the road on a wet winter's day in London, without a place to sleep or the unimaginable luxury of a hot meal, it came to her just how much she missed it all – how much she missed *them.* She fingered the change in her pocket – what wouldn't she give to hear her mother's voice again? Should she . . . ? *Could* she . . . ? Just one phone call. She wouldn't have to say where she was calling from . . . a quick call, just enough for her to know that she wasn't alone in the world, that somewhere, no matter how far away, she had a family, parents who cared about her, brothers who loved her.

There was a row of red telephone boxes just outside the station. She moved slowly towards them, as if in a trance. The one farthest away from her was empty. She pulled open the heavy door and stepped inside. The booth smelled of urine – a sour, unpleasant scent that made her want to gag. She picked up the receiver and listened to the unfamiliar tone. She pulled the change out of her pocket. After the packet of crisps she'd bought that afternoon for lunch, she had £2.12. Could she afford a pound for a phone call? She stood looking at the paltry collection of coins in her hand. No. She had no idea where her next meal was coming from. She couldn't spend a pound just to hear her mother's voice. She pushed open the door and stepped out. She took a deep breath of the fresh air and put a hand up to her wet cheek. It was 3 p.m. and the light was already beginning to fade. She had nowhere to sleep that night. Her fingers were numb with cold – in her haste to escape from Hamid and Fathia, she'd forgotten to take her gloves. She blew on her hands to try and keep them warm. She felt dizzy with hunger. Aside from her usual egg and four slices of toast, she'd had nothing to eat all day save for the packet of crisps. Her mind was racing, desperately seeking an answer. What was she going to do?

She walked slowly back to the station. She saw the sign for the toilets; she made her way through the crowd and walked downstairs. She was in luck; there was no attendant. She pushed open the door to the farthest cubicle and locked it behind her. Fortunately, the toilets were of the old-fashioned kind – the doors went all the way to the ground. With any luck, no one would disturb her. She propped her bag against the wall, undid her shoes and tucked her feet under her. Within minutes, despite the comings and goings around her, she was fast asleep.

She woke before dawn. Her neck was stiff and her back was aching but she'd more or less slept through the night. She got to her feet and unlocked the door. There was no one about. The toilets were bathed in a greenish neon light; it felt like a deserted hospital ward. She walked over to the sinks and turned on the tap. Lukewarm water spilled over her hands. She washed herself quickly and brushed her teeth. She'd survived a week-long car journey through the Ogaden Plains – she could survive this. She wet her hair and used her hands to scrape it back into a bun. She thought longingly of the money she'd spent on accommodation when she'd first arrived . . . she ought to have done exactly what she was doing now. That way she'd have been able to feed herself for almost a month. She looked at herself in the mirror and was surprised by what she saw. She'd no idea how or why, but she'd lost the hunted, desperate look of the previous day. Her face was clearer somehow. There was a determination in it that reminded her of the old Niela Aden, the person she'd been when the family fled, not the person she'd since become. She washed and rinsed out her underwear, rolling it into a damp ball and tucking it into her bag. She would find a dry patch of grass somewhere later on in the day. She took one last look at the public toilets that had been her home for the night and quickly walked upstairs. The station was beginning to stir; it was just after 5.30 a.m. on a cold winter's morning, she had nowhere to live and no money, but she was no longer afraid. She would find a job that day if it killed her.

'Address?' The girl behind the desk barely looked up.

'Eighty-four Vauxhall Bridge Road.' Niela's voice was steady.

'And you've worked in an office before, right?'

'Yes.'

'OK. I've got something for you on Gillingham Street. Sarafin's. They're a contracting firm. They're looking for general office help. Photocopying, filing, the odd bit of typing, sorting out the post. When can you start? Now? They're desperate.'

'Yes . . . yes, of course.' Niela struggled to keep her voice level.

'Great. Ask for Anna. She's Mr Delaney's secretary. She'll show you what to do.'

'Th . . . thank you.'

'Any problems, give me a ring. Who's next?'

And that was it. Niela got to her feet, still slightly dazed, and walked out of the office. She looked up at the sign again. Key Employment Agency. She would remember it for the rest of her life.

'Hi, I'm Niela. From the agency . . . I'm looking for Anna.' Niela stood in front of the receptionist, clutching the piece of paper she'd been given, still unable to believe her luck. Two hours after walking out of the station, she had a job.

'Over there by the window. Girl with the glasses.'

'Thanks.' She walked over to where the girl had indicated. 'Are you Anna?' she asked.

'Yes, that's me. You're from the agency?' Anna looked up.

Niela nodded. 'I'm Niela.'

'Great. Our last temp walked out yesterday. Follow me.' Anna stood up. She led Niela down a corridor to a tiny room with a photocopy and fax machine. There was an enormous stack of documents balanced precariously on a chair. 'Sorry about the room. We'll be moving the machines into the main office in a couple of weeks' time, but in the meantime, I've got to put you in here. It's a bit gloomy but at least you can work in peace. No one ever comes in here, not even the security guards. The assignment's only for a couple of weeks. I'm sure you'll manage. Right.' She pointed to the large stack of documents on the desk. 'We've got to get these out by this afternoon. About three hundred letters in total. You need to make two copies of each, put one in an envelope – there's the list of names – and then take them to the post office before five p.m. and put the copy on my desk. D'you think you can manage that?'

Manage? Niela stared at her. She'd have done twice that if that was what it took. 'Of course. No problem at all.'

'Fantastic. OK. I'll see you later. Any questions, just ask. Lunch is at one. I'll show you where the canteen is. There's a coffee machine at the far end of the office . . . just help yourself to whatever you want. Oh, and there's a bathroom just here.' She pointed to the door at the far corner of the room.

Niela nodded but didn't trust herself to speak. She'd had nothing to eat since lunchtime the previous day and her stomach was growling with need. The door closed behind Anna and she was alone.

At four thirty that afternoon, she lugged two large sacks of letters to the post office. There was a long queue, and by the time she got back to the office, it was almost deserted. Anna had gone home; there was a note propped up on her desk addressed to Niela. She opened it. It was a list of things to be done the following morning. She slipped the note into her pocket and walked down the corridor to the photocopy room. She pushed open the door. There was no one about. She looked around the small room quickly, an idea beginning to dawn. It was warmer than the toilets at Victoria. No one would come in, Anna had said, not even the security guards. There was a toilet with a small sink; a cushion on one of the chairs that she could use as a pillow of sorts. She could wash her underwear and her shirt in the sink and leave them to dry . . . it was far from perfect, but in the circumstances, it would do.

She opened the door cautiously and walked down the corridor towards the main office. There were biscuits in the tin under the sink and as much tea and coffee as she wanted. She carried her cup of milky sweet tea back to her cubbyhole. There were a few people still left in the office, working late. No one looked up as she passed. She closed the door behind her, dragged a chair over to it and wedged it under the handle, just in case.

She drank her tea and ate the entire packet of chocolate biscuits. She sat on the floor, her arms locked around her knees, waiting for the office to close down, when she could lay herself down and go to sleep.

25

'Don't you want to get some lunch?' Anna stuck her head round the door. 'It's half past one and you haven't had a break.'

Niela felt the heat rise in her cheeks. She shook her head. It was Thursday. She'd been at Sarafin's for a week; payday was the following day. 'No, I'm fine,' she said quickly. 'I had a big breakfast.'

Anna looked at her for a second longer than was necessary. 'Are you all right?' she asked suddenly.

Niela felt her knees give way. It was the kindness that did it. She could take just about anything, but not kindness. It floored her. 'I . . . I . . .' To her horror, she felt her eyes welling with tears. She looked away. 'I'm fine,' she said in a low voice. 'Sorry.'

Anna hesitated, then came into the room, shutting the door carefully behind her. 'Look, Niela . . . this is probably none of my business, but I have to ask. Do you have somewhere to stay? To sleep, I mean?'

Niela kept her head averted. To her horror and embarrassment, she felt the tears begin to slide down her cheeks. She opened her mouth to say something – anything – but the words refused to come.

Anna was silent for a few moments. 'One of the security guards told me,' she said finally, her voice soft. 'He saw you coming out of here very early yesterday morning.'

'It's only until tomorrow,' Niela said, her heart racing with fear. She would be sacked on the spot. 'I just . . . I ran out of money and I . . .'

'Why on earth didn't you say something?' Anna asked. She put a hand on Niela's arm. 'Look, there's nothing to be ashamed of. I've been in worse situations before, trust me.'

'You?' Niela couldn't help herself. Anna was the epitome of everything Niela wasn't – smart, well dressed, well fed . . . she looked *comfortable*, in all senses of the word. A nice, comfortably off English girl. The sort of girl Niela had been once and would have given her right arm to be again.

Anna looked at her for a moment and hesitated. 'Look, Niela . . . I'm not what you probably think. I'm from Bosnia, actually. My real name isn't even Anna. It's Amra. I came here six years ago as a refugee, with nothing. Absolutely nothing. So I *do* know what it's like. You get paid by the agency tomorrow, right?' Niela nodded, not trusting herself to speak. 'OK. Look, come down to the canteen with me. I'll buy you lunch. Don't worry, you can pay me back some other time. And I've got an idea . . . meet me out the back at five tonight. I think we can sort something out.' She paused. 'Don't worry. This is just temporary, Niela. You're a really good worker, everyone says so. It's nice having you around. Come on, dry your eyes and wash your face. I bet you haven't eaten properly in days. I remember what that was like.' Niela could only stare at her. 'Come on, then. Let's go.' Anna turned and smiled at her.

It was hard not to wolf down the baked potato with tuna fish and sweetcorn. After ten days of living on nothing but sweet tea, biscuits and stale white bread, even the smell of food made Niela nauseous. She finished the potato in minutes. Anna had the good grace not to com-ment, but simply got up, went to the counter and brought over another one. 'Not the most nutritious of meals,' she said wryly, putting the plate down in front of Niela. 'But it probably beats whatever you've been living on.'

'Th . . . thank you,' Niela stammered, her mouth flooding with saliva at the sight of her plate. 'I don't know what to say.'

'You don't have to say anything. Look, I'd better get going. I've got tons of stuff to do for Delaney before he gets back this afternoon. Here's a fiver. You can pay me back later. Get yourself an orange juice and something sweet . . . you need some energy. I've got an idea about where you can stay. Let's go together after work.'

Niela watched Anna thread her way through the tables. She looked down at the five-pound note Anna had just given her and suddenly made a vow. She would never spend it. She would keep that five-pound note for the rest of her life. She didn't need anything sweet to restore her energy. Anna's kindness had done that all on its own. She tucked the note into the back pocket of her trousers and then quickly went about the business of polishing off what remained on her plate.

Niela looked around her in bewilderment. The flat was small and com-pletely empty but it was brand new. Anna strode ahead of her, turning on the lights and taps. 'Everything works,' she said, coming back into the main room. 'No furniture, but we can find you a mattress. I'll ask the foreman to bring one up from the stores.'

'Wh . . . whose place is this?' Niela asked, almost afraid to look around.

'No one's. At least, not yet. It's part of the Horseferry Road development – the big one that we've been working on for about a year. The last phase of flats won't be ready until the summer, so that gives you about five months or so. Don't worry, it's fine. No one will ever figure it out.'

'Anna . . . how . . . how can I ever repay you?' Niela asked, afraid she might burst into tears again. 'You've been so kind . . . I don't know why.'

Anna shook her head. 'Lots of people helped *me* out when I came over. Lots of people ripped me off, too,' she added with a smile. 'But I try not to remember those bits. Anyhow, I'd better run. I'll speak to the foreman on the way out and get him to bring up a mattress. Here's the keys. That one's for the front door and this one's the side gate. Use that one all the time. The project managers don't even know there's an entrance there.'

'Th-thank you,' Niela stammered, taking the bunch from her. 'Thank you so much.'

'I'll bring you a clean shirt and a skirt tomorrow to the office. You can't wear the same clothes every single day. Oh, and you'll need a sheet and a towel. I'll bring those too. There's a launderette on the corner and a grocery store just down the road.' She paused. 'You'll be fine, Niela. Don't worry. Things will work out. You'll see.' She gave her a quick smile and opened the door. 'See you tomorrow,' she said, and then she was gone.

Niela looked about her slowly. It was a one-bedroom flat on the first floor, overlooking a central courtyard. Everything was brand new – carpets, paint, blinds, everything. There was the overpowering smell of fresh paint everywhere. She opened the door to the bedroom. The walls were a creamy yellow; the carpet was dark grey. It was absolutely spotless. She walked into the en suite bathroom, blinded by the brand-new whiteness. She turned on one of the taps – a lovely, heavy chrome affair with a long, elegant spout. Within seconds, steam began to rise. She turned it off, her excitement mounting. She hadn't had a proper wash in almost a fortnight. As soon as she got paid, she promised herself, she would cross the road to the bank, cash her cheque and then buy a bottle of shampoo. Her hair hadn't been washed in weeks. Suddenly, she heard a noise on the other side of the front door. She froze. Something was being dragged along the ground. It stopped outside the door. She heard a man cough and then the sound of his footsteps dying away. She waited for a few minutes and then cautiously opened the door. Standing propped against the wall was a mattress. She felt weak with relief. She pulled it in, shut the door behind her and dragged it into the bedroom. She quickly stripped off her clothes, turned on the taps in the shower and stood under the powerful hot stream of water for almost twenty minutes. She'd brought along a bar of soap from the office and she soaped herself over and over again until the bar was little more than a sliver. She stepped out, pools of water forming immediately around her feet, and used her shirt in place of a towel. She washed her underwear and the shirt and hung them on the towel rack, which was warm to the touch. She looked at her reflection in the mirror as if to check that it was really true, that she was really there, in a brand-new flat somewhere in London, less than a fortnight after her arrival. Best of all, she'd be there for a while. She lay down on the mattress, burrowing her head into its soft, doughy warmth. How could she ever repay Anna for her kindness? What had she done to deserve it? She lay in the dark, her mind turning over with questions. Christian too – he had helped her when she least expected it. She would return the hundred Deutschmarks just as soon as she could. It was a temporary loan – just enough for her to get back on her feet. She thought of his face, the way his eyes folded at the corners when he smiled, and of the soft brown hair on his forearms. She closed her eyes. Perhaps the world wasn't quite as bad a place as it sometimes seemed. She slept.

26

At 1 p.m. the following day, she hurried out of the office and almost ran all the way to the employment agency. There was a cheque waiting for her. She took it from the receptionist with shaking hands. As soon as she was outside, she ripped it open: £157.46. There were a number of deductions, including something called an Emergency Tax – she couldn't have cared less. She'd applied for a National Insurance number, but until it arrived, the government would take more than they needed and she would have to claim it back later. She'd listened to the receptionist with half an ear. She looked at the cheque again: £157.46 for a week's work. It seemed like a small fortune. She took it straight to the bank as she'd been told and cashed it in, revelling in the small bundle of notes and the plastic sachet of coins. She stopped at the flower seller just in front of the station and bought a small bunch of yellow tulips. Those were for Anna. She rushed back to Sarafin's. Anna looked up in surprise as she walked in.

'I just wanted to give you these,' Niela said, uncomfortably aware of the lump that had suddenly formed in her throat. 'Just to say thank you.'

Anna blushed. 'You shouldn't have,' she said, taking the bunch from her. 'Really. It's not necessary.'

Niela held her eyes very wide. She shrugged. 'It's nothing. If I could do more . . .'

'Don't be silly. You've been a real help this past week.' Anna hesitated for a second. 'Look, if you're not doing anything this evening . . . would you like to come round to mine? I've got a three-year-old son . . . it's just the two of us. Nothing fancy, maybe some spaghetti . . . but only if you're free, of course.'

Niela felt her face crease into a smile. There was a graceful generosity about Anna that touched her deeply. *Only if you're free, of course* – what else would she be? 'If you're sure . . . ?' she said, hoping she didn't sound too enthusiastic.

Anna nodded firmly. 'I'm sure. Boris and I don't often have company. He loves it. We're not far from here . . . it's the big housing estate next to Pimlico tube station. I'll give you the address. How about seven? Boris goes to bed at seven thirty, so we could have a glass of wine together, if you like.'

'Seven's great,' Niela said, feeling ridiculously happy. 'Thanks. Shall I bring anything?'

Anna shook her head. 'Nothing. Absolutely nothing. See you later.'

Niela glanced down at her new jeans: £4.99 from a shop in the station arcade. She'd found a sweater for a fiver, two pairs of socks, three pairs of panties and a new bra for a tenner . . . some shampoo, deodorant, a couple of grips for her hair . . . she felt like a new person. She *was* a new person. A week ago she'd slept on the floor of a public toilet and bathed in the sink. Today, she'd earned her first week's wages and, thanks to the kindness of a complete stranger, she had a roof over her head. Even better, that same complete stranger was now on her way to becoming a friend. She scanned the front doors: 16, 17, 18 . . . there it was – 19, Formosa Court. She lifted her hand and pressed the bell.

'Hi.' Anna opened the door almost immediately. A chubby little boy clung shyly to her legs, peering out at her. 'You found it.'

'It was easy. Just as you said.' Niela bent down so that her face was on a level with the boy's. 'And you must be Boris, right?' He nodded, still too shy to speak. He was round-faced, with bright red cheeks and dark, almond-shaped eyes. Niela drew out the orange she'd been carrying and presented it solemnly to him. He looked up at his mother as if in confirmation. She smiled and nodded.

'Better than sweets,' she said approvingly. 'Go on, take it. Say thank you, Boris.'

He held the orange between his pudgy hands as though it might bite. 'Fank you,' he said softly. He was still shy.

'Come,' Anna said, turning to go into the house. 'Come inside. It's warmer in here.' She led the way into the small living room.

Niela followed her in. She looked around in pleasure. It had been so long since she'd been inside a home – a proper home, with pictures on the walls and children's toys lying around, splayed-open magazines and a half-drunk mug of tea – she'd forgotten how much she missed it. Anna's home was small but cosy. The dining room, little more than an alcove really, led directly into the kitchen. The room was filled with the scent of onions and basil. Niela's stomach rumbled. She couldn't remember when she'd had her last home-cooked meal.

They ate quickly, all attention focused on Boris, who'd soon out-grown his shyness. He chattered away happily in his special mixture of Serbo-Croat and English, oblivious to the fact that Niela might not understand. At 7.30 on the dot, Anna picked him up and announced it was bedtime. Niela smiled to herself; she remembered the struggles the maids had had with Raageh when it was time to go to sleep. Boris had no such difficulty. He clambered on to Niela's lap and gave her a wet, sloppy kiss of such genuine affection that Niela's eyes misted over almost immediately. She felt his arms go around her neck; he touched the soft, curly mass of her ponytail in wonderment. Anna laughed and swept him off Niela's lap. 'He'll be wanting you to read him a story in a minute,' she said, tweaking his nose. 'Come on, little man. Bedtime. You can play with Niela's hair next time. He's such a little flirt. I'll be back in ten minutes or so. Just make yourself at home.' She disappeared down the short corridor with Boris in her arms.

Niela picked up her glass and wandered over to the bookcase at the other end of the living room. She looked through the titles with interest. There were a few she'd read – some texts she remembered from school: Shakespeare, Thomas Hardy, Wharton. But there were others – books in Russian, heavy-looking titles on economics and trade, a few girlish novels . . . she tugged a couple out, impressed. Anna was clearly a keen reader. As she, Niela, had once been. She thought for a second of the shelves in her own room in Mogadishu. What had happened to all the books?

'Do you like reading?' Anna had come back into the dining room.

Niela turned around. She gave an apologetic shrug. 'I used to . . . back at home.'

'Where did you say you were from again? Somalia?'

Niela nodded. 'We left when the war broke out.'

'Like me.' Anna gave a small, tight smile. She picked up her glass from the table and came over. She sat down on the couch and let out a deep sigh. 'I'm lucky,' she said, taking a sip of her wine. 'He goes to sleep easily.'

'Who looks after him in the daytime?' Niela asked.

'My neighbour. She's also from Bosnia. Without her, I don't know what I'd do.'

'What about Boris's father?' Niela asked the question delicately.

'What about him?' Anna gave a wry smile. 'He took off the minute I told him I was pregnant.'

Niela didn't know what to say. 'That must have been hard,' she said finally.

Anna shrugged. 'I'm better off without him,' she said simply. 'What about you? D'you have a boyfriend back home?' Niela's face burned. She took a gulp of wine to cover her confusion. She shook her head, unable to say anything. 'Pretty girl like you?' Anna teased. 'I'm surprised.'

'Wh . . . what about the rest of your family?' Niela asked quickly, desperate to change the subject.

'They're still in Mostar. My brother . . .' Anna's voice faltered for a second. 'My brother was shot. In the war. My parents won't leave.'

Again Niela didn't know what to say. She looked across the table at Anna. Her face was closed off; there was a tightness around the mouth that she hadn't noticed before. She wasn't the only one to have suffered through hard times, Niela thought to herself suddenly. It happened to others too. To people you wouldn't expect. She thought back to her first day at Sarafin's. She would never have guessed that the efficient-looking secretary sitting behind her desk with a formidable array of pens and pencils and a large computer screen in front of her was a refugee, just like herself. That she had a three-year-old son whose father had disappeared or a brother who'd been shot. It just went to show . . . you couldn't tell anything about anyone any more. Anna had no idea what had happened to Niela. A shudder went through her suddenly. Hamid on their wedding night. She pressed her legs together as if trying to physically block the memory.

'Are you all right?' Anna's voice came to her, sounding concerned.

Niela forced herself to relax. It was all in the past now. There was nothing Hamid or Fathia or her family could do to her now. It was behind her. 'Sorry, I was just thinking . . . I have two brothers. I . . . I miss them.'

Anna nodded. 'It's hard,' she said after a moment. 'I mean, English people are very nice, don't get me wrong. I came here with nothing and they gave me everything. Papers, a place to stay, language classes . . . they were unbelievably kind. People talk about being a refugee now, but those were the hardest years of my life. And most people I meet,' she waved a hand in the air, 'they can't relate to that, you know what I mean? My father was an accountant . . . I'm not someone who grew up in a refugee camp. But it doesn't mean anything to them. They hear the word "Bosnia" and they think I'm some Eastern European mail-order bride.'

Niela gave a small half-smile. 'I would never have guessed, you know. You sound so English.'

Anna smiled. 'When I got here, I changed everything. My name, my accent, my past . . . everything. It's the only way you'll make it, I promise you. I don't know what your war was like, but ours was terrible. I've seen things I shouldn't have seen, I know about things that I shouldn't have to know about, ever.' She stopped suddenly. 'Oh, why are we sitting here talking about it . . . listen to us! We say we want to forget everything and then all we do is constantly bring it up.' She shook her head. 'Silly, really.'

Niela was silent. She couldn't articulate it the way she would have liked, but Anna was wrong. It wasn't silly. It was necessary. In ways she was only beginning to grasp, the disintegration of who she was – Niela Aden, seventeen-year-old schoolgirl – which had started the moment they fled Mogadishu, might now be halted. She'd lived with it for so long . . . all those months of not knowing whether they were coming or going, where they would go, how they would get there, who they would be . . . it had become normal to her, just as the waiting had been normal, or the sense of impending doom. And that was the dangerous part. For the first time ever, on the strength of a few minutes of conversation with someone who'd been through it too, she grasped intuitively that there was hope. If Amra could reinvent herself so completely and succeed, so could she. It wasn't a matter of luck or circumstance. It was a matter of will. What was it her mother always used to say? Good things come to those who wait. Her mother was wrong. Good things come to those who grab them.

PART THREE

27

JULIA
London, September 1996

Julia made her way carefully down the path towards Gray's Inn, conscious of her heels sticking awkwardly in between the stones. The line of clipped trees bordering the path fell away from her; in the distance, beyond the brick wall that separated Gray's Inn from the main road, she could see the top decks of a long line of red buses, crawling along. A tiny shiver of excitement ran through her. She pressed the buzzer on the front door and stood back, waiting for the door to open. The discreet brass plaque gave little away. *Bernard, Bennison & Partners. Barristers.* The words sent a small thrill running through her. She was about to start her year-long pupillage with one of the most prestigious law firms in the country. The door opened; she walked in. 'Can I help you?' the receptionist asked pleasantly.

'Er, yes. I'm Julia Burrows. I'm starting my first six today.'

'Oh.' The girl looked momentarily confused. 'Yes, yes, of course. Burrows. We've got a name badge for you. If you don't mind signing right here . . . ?' She slid a piece of paper across the counter. Julia signed her name and tried not to think about the girl's telltale slip. It was always the same, though not at the Oxford Pro Bono Publico where she'd worked for the past four years. In the shabby offices just off Turl Street there'd been lawyers like herself – working class, fiercely dedicated, a hundred per cent committed to what they did. But although she'd thoroughly enjoyed her time there, her heart was set on becoming a barrister. For that she needed a London-based pupillage, and after three interviews and a month of waiting, her dream had finally come true. She'd sold the small house in Elswick that her grandmother had left her and whilst it wasn't exactly worth a fortune, it was the only way she could afford to continue her training. During the year-long pupillage, she'd be paid an absolute pittance – another one of the reasons why working-class girls like her rarely became barristers . . . they simply couldn't afford to live and work in London on what was effectively a student stipend. It was harder than she thought to sever her ties with Elswick. The day the house was finally sold, she walked up and down the streets where she'd spent her childhood, looking at the rows of almost identical houses whose occupants she no longer knew, wondering if she would ever come back again. The cemetery where her parents and her grandmother were buried was on the other side of the Tyne. She tenderly placed the three bunches of flowers she'd brought with her on their graves and stood up, wiping away her tears. In all likelihood, she knew, she would never return. The following morning she caught the train back to Oxford, packed her bags and said goodbye to the three people with whom she'd shared a house in Headington for the past four years. Dom, ever loyal, drove her down to London. She stayed at the Barrington-Brownes' Chelsea townhouse for a fortnight whilst she looked for a place to live. The flat she found in an ex-council block just off the Euston Road couldn't have been more different from the Barrington-Brownes' four-storey house on Cadogan Square, but she didn't mind. Chelsea made her nervous, she told Dom when they went together to look at it. Claire and Alison, the girls with whom she would be sharing, seemed nice enough. Claire was a nurse at UCH, just up the road, and Alison was a postgraduate student in fine art. Dom wrinkled his nose at the tiny room and the state of the garden, of course, but Julia couldn't have cared less. A new chapter in her life was about to start and she couldn't wait.

'If you'll just come this way . . .' The receptionist came around the desk. She looked Julia up and down quickly, sizing her up. Briefcase – too shiny; shoes – too new; suit – decent but hardly designer. In her own navy blue skirt and pink shirt opened at the neck to reveal an impressive string of pearls, *she* looked as though she was the trainee barrister, not Julia. She followed the bobbing blonde ponytail down one wood-panelled corridor after another. Men and women in suits floated in and out as they climbed the stairs to the office where Julia would be working. 'Good morning,' the receptionist murmured quietly to each one, for which she received a quick, pained smile. It was so different from the relaxed atmosphere at the OPBP; would she *ever* fit in? Julia wondered to herself, then quickly tried to suppress the thought. She was shown into a large office and given a desk by the window. There were two other trainee barristers in the room. She shook hands with each: Daniel, a tall, imposing man from Nigeria, and Christopher, a short, rather earnest-looking young man who seemed surprised to see a woman. She quickly stowed her things away and was led back down the corridor. 'You'll be working with Harriet Peters,' the receptionist told her. 'Third door on the left, just down the hall. She's expecting you. Good luck,' she said pleasantly and disappeared. Julia nervously smoothed down her skirt and tapped on the door.

'Come in.' She pushed open the door tentatively. Seated behind an impressively polished desk was a formidably stern-looking woman. She took off her spectacles and peered at Julia. 'Harriet Peters. I'm the senior counsel in charge of the family unit. Gerald and I thought it would be a good place for you to start. We're a new section in the firm. There are some who think family law is a complete waste of time – doesn't bring in the sort of cash or cachet that corporate law does. I, of course, think otherwise. I've no interest in your own feelings on the matter except to say that whilst you work for me, I expect a hundred and ten per cent loyalty to the cause and nothing short of devotion. When you do your second six, assuming you get that far, of course, you can take your skills into whatever area of the law you choose. Now, I see from your CV that you spent a considerable amount of time at the OPBP. You'll be familiar, therefore, with the sorts of issues we tackle. The case I'd like you to clerk on . . .' Julia listened as Harriet outlined in exacting detail what it was she'd be doing for the rest of the week. After she'd finished, she handed over a stack of files. 'Library's on the fourth floor,' she said briskly. 'Report back to me after lunch.' And that was it. Julia hastily got to her feet, aware that her heart was racing with a mixture of extreme excitement and extreme trepidation. One thing was abundantly clear: Harriet Peters wasn't about to give anyone – least of all another woman – a break. A first from Oxford meant nothing, or so her expression implied. Julia Burrows was there to *work*.

For the rest of the week, Julia did nothing but run from her office to the law courts, her arms piled high with Harriet's legal briefs and notes. When she was asked to do something other than fetch and carry, she spent hours in the library on the fourth floor. The view over Fleet Street was the only respite from dusty tomes and leatherbound books that had been so well thumbed the gold lettering was gone from their spines. Harriet wasn't joking. By the end of her first month, Julia was so tired she could barely stand. She'd never done as much reading in her life. Aside from doing the background legal research for Harriet's briefs, she drafted skeleton arguments that Harriet invariably tore up anyway, checked facts and precedents, looked up rulings, edited and typed up case notes and did whatever else Harriet saw fit to throw at her during the day. In her second week she found herself struggling up Fleet Street with a mountain of Harriet's dry-cleaning in her arms. Patsy, Harriet's PA, smirked at her as she came in through the door. It was clear that picking up the dry-cleaning was one task she was only too happy to pass along.

But it wasn't all work. On Friday evenings, the pupils and other junior barristers met at the Cittie of Yorke pub just up the Gray's Inn Road. Harriet was never to be found at any of the social events, not even the High Dinners. No one seemed to expect her either. From the little she was able to glean from others, Julia learned that Harriet was single, in her late forties, lived in a frightfully smart part of Chelsea and drove a frightfully smart car. Once a month she went to Ireland to a luxury spa buried deep in the countryside. Aside from a passion for horses – she owned two thoroughbreds – there was nothing else to know about Harriet Peters other than the fact that she was brilliant and one of the hardest taskmasters in the firm. Like almost everyone else, she'd been at Cambridge, done her sixes at one of the city firms and been at B&B ever since. She was practically part of the furniture. She was the only female senior partner although no one could ever accuse her of pandering to the fact. She had a trim, neat figure; wore her hair short and expertly cut. She applied the occasional dash of lipstick and, once, just the faintest trace of perfume as she walked by . . . There was certainly nothing overtly feminine about Harriet Peters. No one could ever have accused her of charm.

One Friday evening after a particularly long day in court, Julia was crossing the quadrangle of the High Court, half-buried under the weight of documents, when Harriet, who was walking several paces in front of her, deep in conversation with someone else, turned.

'Drink?' she asked, causing Julia to nearly drop her case.

'Drink?' Julia repeated, frowning. She wasn't sure what Harriet meant.

'Yes, a drink. Would you care for a drink?' The person Harriet had been speaking to quickly excused himself and the two women were left in the middle of the courtyard, Julia staring at Harriet as if she couldn't believe her ears.

'Um, yeah . . . smashin',' she said, wincing. Even to her own ears, the Geordie phrase sounded out of place. 'That'd be nice.' Was it her imagination or was there the faintest of smiles playing around Harriet's lips? Julia couldn't be sure. She staggered into the private bar in the basement of the High Court, too astounded to take in her surroundings.

'Coat, madam?' A flunky suddenly appeared. 'And your documents?'

Julia handed everything over gratefully and followed Harriet to one of the upholstered booths. She'd heard about the bar – open only to senior members of the Law Society, which included every judge, peer and law lord . . . and certainly *not* eager pupils a fifth of the way through the first six. She looked about her cautiously. She recognised half a dozen faces – over there in the corner by the stained-glass window was Lord Musgrove, the firebrand Labour peer . . . and there, standing by the bar with a large whisky in hand, was Anthony Chessington, the head of Libertas. And wasn't that Grant Foster, the famous divorce lawyer? The sound of wine being splashed into a glass brought her abruptly back to her senses.

'Cheers,' Harriet said when the waiter had obsequiously removed himself. She took a long, measured sip.

Julia quickly did the same. 'Cheers,' she said, swallowing more than she intended in order to hide her confusion. She was sitting with Harriet Peters in a booth in the private bar underneath the High Court . . . drinking wine. Had the world suddenly turned itself upside down?

'What a day.' Harriet rummaged around in her expensive-looking handbag and pulled out a packet of cigarettes. 'Want one?'

Julia shook her head. She was almost too astonished to speak. Harriet Peters *smoked*? 'No, I . . . I don't smoke,' she stammered.

'Good thing too. Don't start. Silly habit.'

'My dad smoked,' Julia offered suddenly, she'd no idea why.

'Mine too. Bloody miner. Died of lung cancer, the silly bugger.'

Julia stared at her. A miner? Harriet Peters's father was a *miner*? No, she'd misunderstood. 'Did you say he was a miner?' she asked faintly, just to be sure.

Harriet nodded. 'Mmm. We're from Snaresborough. Mining town. All miners up there.'

Julia was too astonished to speak. All of a sudden, the north was back in Harriet's voice. 'I . . . I'd never have guessed,' she said finally, practically draining her wine in a single gulp.

Harriet smiled, blowing a cloud of smoke away from her face. 'No, I don't suppose you would. Oh, we're not so different, you and I. We're more alike than you think.'

'You don't sound as though you're from Snaresborough,' she said finally, unable to think of anything else to say.

Harriet signalled to the bartender for another round. 'Years of practice, my dear.' She gave a wry smile. 'It was different in my day. When I did my pupillage, there were sixteen of us and I was the only woman and the only one from a working-class background. Things have changed a bit since then . . . perhaps not as much as we like to think, but that's another story. I've been doing it so long I've forgotten what I used to be like. I don't know you very well, Julia, but you don't seem to have changed a thing about you. It's an admirable quality. Let people take you as they find you. I didn't have the confidence for that twenty years ago, but you have. Don't lose it.'

All of a sudden, Julia found herself close to tears. It was the hardest thing about losing both her parents – there was no one to talk to, not the way she and Harriet were talking now. Her father had always been full of stories and anecdotes, small snippets of information, homilies that at a deeper level were really instructions to his only child. He was the one who'd always told her to be proud of her roots, proud of who she was. How many times in the past few years had the longing to talk to him overwhelmed her? It was the cruellest twist of fate that just when she needed him the most, he was no longer there. She muttered something incoherent to Harriet and ran into the toilets. She had the strong intuition that unexpected confidences aside, tears would not be welcome in front of Harriet. She was right. When she emerged five minutes later with reddened eyes and nose, Harriet was gone.

'She left this for you,' the bartender said, handing over a scrap of paper. *Trial application for Hardy vs Matthieson at 9 a.m. tomorrow. Hand in at High Court.* Julia gave a rueful smile. There was a reason why Harriet Peters had the reputation she had. She had a feeling it would be a very long time before she caught a further glimpse of the woman behind the façade. A miner's daughter from Snaresborough? She shook her head in disbelief as she collected her coat. She would never have guessed. *You don't seem to have changed a thing about you, Julia. Don't lose it.* Harriet's words rang loudly in her ears. It was the closest anyone had come in the past few years to understanding just how hard it was to feel perpetually out of place. Harriet, of all people. Clever, smart, über-professional Harriet. Julia felt suddenly buoyed by the unexpected confession. If Harriet could do it . . . well, why couldn't she?

28

MADDY
New York, November 1996

'Maddy? Cover for me, will you, honey. Table 12. I gotta go take a pee!'

'No, no . . . Carla, don't. I've got my hands full . . . I can't—!' Too late. Maddy looked on despairingly as Carla whacked down a plate on to the counter and disappeared down the hallway. Carla was three months pregnant; you couldn't argue with that. Maddy sighed and picked up the order. Her own table had been waiting for fifteen minutes – a lifetime in the service lexicon of most New Yorkers. Not only would she *not* get a tip, she'd be lucky if the boss didn't deduct the cost of their much-delayed breakfast from her salary. She held the plate above her head and pushed her way through the crowded bar area towards Table 12, where a man was sitting, his face hidden by a large salmon-pink newspaper. 'Good *morning*,' she sang cheerfully, setting the plate down carefully. 'Sorry about the wait. I've taken over from your waitress for a minute. I've got eggs-over-easy, bacon on the side, grilled tomatoes and hash browns.'

'Thanks. Um . . . could I possibly trouble you for some ketchup?' The man lowered the paper. He was English.

'Absolutely. Back in a second.' She turned and hurried back to the bar. 'There we go. Anything else I can get you, sir?' She blushed even as the words came out. She'd slipped into character without even thinking – an *English* character to boot!

'You're English?'

Maddy shook her head, aware that the colour was still up in her cheeks. 'Sorry, no. I was just showing off.'

He looked puzzled. 'Showing off?'

He was really rather good-looking, Maddy thought to herself, trying not to stare. Blond, blue-eyed; a square, determined chin, broad shoulders, finely tapered fingers . . . There was something oddly familiar about him, but she couldn't place him. She dragged her eyes away from his face. 'I'm an actress. Well, sort of. I played an English girl once, at drama school . . .'

'Well, you sounded pretty convincing to me. You must be quite an actress.'

133

Maddy had to smile. 'Oh, absolutely. So much so, in fact, that I'm a waitress. I'm just waiting for my agent to call.' She was a little taken aback by her own lightness. There was something easy about him, she thought to herself. His face was full of boyish charm. She was quite used to customers flirting with her – it seemed part and parcel of the job. She'd studied the part of a waitress diligently – the gum-chewing, wisecracking sassy redhead with a sharp retort and a sexy, swinging walk. After nearly three years, she had the repertoire down pat.

'Well, I hope he does.'

'She. Thanks.' She gave him a quick, jaunty wink and made her way back to the counter. Her own customers were waiting and Carla, likely as not, would scoop up the tip. You couldn't argue with a pregnant woman, Maddy reminded herself.

'Here.' To her surprise, half an hour later Carla stuck a ten-dollar bill into Maddy's apron pocket. 'From Table 12,' she called out over her shoulder as she rushed back to the kitchen. 'The English guy.' Maddy looked at it, rather bemused. It was an exceedingly large tip. Especially since his breakfast had hardly come to much more. She looked over the heads of customers clustered around the bar, but he was no longer there. She shrugged. Shame. She'd have liked to have thanked him. Oh well. She picked up her coffee jug and wound her way across the floor. She hadn't exactly lied to him; she *was* waiting for her agent to call. Virginia was just about the only person left on the planet who thought that Maddy might one day find fame and fortune as an actress, not a waitress. It had been nearly two long, tough years since her final-year performance at Tisch. Her mother had come to New York and sat in the audience, entranced as her only daughter transported her and a couple of hundred other people somewhere else entirely. The hardest thing of all, Maddy often thought to herself, was that she'd actually been *good*. She'd lost count of the number of auditions she'd gone to, the number of casting calls, the promises to call her back, the days and evenings sitting waiting by the phone . . . In two years she'd had one commercial and a pilot for a sitcom that had eventually been cancelled. She'd done the community and neighbourhood theatre workshops, she'd put her picture on every board that she thought might help . . . nothing. Nothing ever came of anything. Virginia, touchingly, refused to give up, but there were days when even she tapped her pen against her teeth and proclaimed it a mystery. It was partly the fiery red hair, she mused, and what she called

Maddy's 'unique' looks . . . quite what she meant by that was anyone's guess, least of all Maddy's, but the bottom line was that the work simply wasn't there for a redhead with the kind of porcelain skin and hazel-green eyes – set fractionally too far apart – that looked a little strange with dyed brown hair. She just wasn't 'marketable' enough. End of story. Except it wasn't, of course. Like Virginia, although for different reasons, perhaps, Maddy stubbornly refused to give up. She couldn't. New York was her life now. She'd found herself a tiny studio apartment on the wrong side of Fort Green in Brooklyn; there was barely enough room for a sofa-bed and a desk, but it was hers. After a year of living in crowded apartments with half a dozen other aspiring actors, actresses and models of every description, she'd finally managed to save enough to plonk down three months' advance rent. Sandy, who was the only person she'd kept in touch with since graduating from Tisch, had fared no better. Too Jewish-looking; too 'ethnic', which pretty much meant the same thing, Sandy said bitterly; 'a touch too much character in your face, honey' was how casting agents usually put it. Only unlike Maddy, Sandy wasn't poor, and she lived in a large apartment in the East Village that her father had bought for her whilst he waited for her to come to her senses and get married.

'Fat chance,' Sandy scoffed over a bottle of wine. 'And certainly not to any of those nice Jewish boys my mother keeps inviting over.' Maddy and Sandy still met every other week, usually at Sandy's apartment, where they both drank far too much and wound up in tears, over the dismal state of either their love lives, or their careers, or both. This hiatus was interrupted every once in a while by an overexcited phone call from Virginia. There'd be a flurry of readings and preparation, followed by a period of fasting and then bingeing and making herself sick . . . and then Maddy would go off for the audition and sit by the phone until the rejections finally arrived and then the whole cycle would repeat itself. If it hadn't been for the atmosphere at the restaurant, Sunshine's, which she genuinely enjoyed, and the thrill of living in New York, Maddy wasn't quite sure what she would have done. Going back to Iowa was out of the question. But there was still a chance, she reminded herself firmly. She'd been to two auditions for the same role only the week before. The girl they'd originally picked had had to cancel. It was all a bit last minute, but 'if everything goes well, honey,' Virginia growled down the phone, 'you could be onstage on Saturday night. You'll be playing opposite Bette

Midler.' Maddy had had to sit down to stop herself from falling over. *Bette Midler?*

She refilled coffee mugs that afternoon with an automatic, vacant smile, her mind and stomach churning over together in unison. *God, let me get this part*, she whispered to herself as she pulled her pad from her apron and a pencil from behind her ear and prepared to take yet another order. *Let me get the part. Please God, please, please, please.* Despite her resolve, she was beginning to wonder if she'd ever do more than write out a meal order and balance a tray on her head. *This* was what she'd slogged her guts out for four long years for?

29

The Englishman was there the following morning when Maddy began her shift. This time he was seated at the bar. A dark blue suit and a shirt unbuttoned at the collar; well-polished shoes and a newspaper. He lowered the paper as she passed and their eyes met. They smiled tentatively at one another. He looked slightly the worse for wear. There was a faint shadow of a beard beneath his skin and his eyes were heavy with sleep.

'Heavy night, huh?' she asked as she poured him a cup of coffee and flipped open her order pad.

He looked at her and grinned sheepishly. She caught her breath and had to look away. ''Fraid so,' he said, in a voice still tinged with sleep.

'I . . . I guess it'll just be coffee, then?' she stammered. His charm was unsettling; she wasn't used to it. New Yorkers were many things, but usually not charming.

He studied the menu, then shook his head. 'Veisalgia,' he said firmly. 'Remedied by foods rich in cysteine.' He smiled at her.

Maddy stared at him. 'Sorry?'

'Veisalgia. It's the medical term for a hangover. Cysteine is what the liver uses to break down alcohol, and eggs are rich in it. That's why you often crave an omelette after a heavy night.' He laughed suddenly, showing a row of perfect white teeth. 'Now I'm showing off.'

'You're a doctor?' she asked, smiling.

'Guilty as charged. I'm here for a conference, actually. Hence the long night. My paper's not until this afternoon, so I nipped out to get breakfast.' He looked at her. His eyes were the colour of cornflowers or the sky on a warm summer's day. 'Did she ring, by the way?'

'Who?' Maddy was confused.

'Your agent.'

'Oh, she'll ring me soon, I guess,' Maddy shrugged, trying not to sound despondent.

'Well, I'll cross my fingers for you. What's your name? Just so I can say I knew you back when.'

'Maddy. Maddy Stiller.'

'Nice to meet you, Maddy Stiller,' he said, gravely formal. He held out a hand. 'I'm Rafe. Rafe Keeler.'

'Nice to meet you, Dr Keeler.' His hand was warm and firm. From the corner of her eye she could see Carla frowning at her. 'Well, I'll . . . I'll just get your eggs, then,' she said hurriedly. 'How d'you like them?'

His eyes came to rest on her own. There was a moment of frank appreciation so swift she thought she'd imagined it. 'Whatever you suggest.'

She could feel her cheeks tingling. 'I . . . I'll be right back,' she stammered and fled. His charm unnerved her. She rushed into the comparative safety of the kitchen.

'He's cute,' Carla stated baldly, coming in behind her.

'Who?' Maddy kept her voice as neutral as possible.

'Oh, *chica*. Don't gimme that. You know who.'

'You think so?' Maddy kept her voice as neutral as possible.

'Doesn't matter what I think, honey, *you* think so. *Hey!*' she yelled suddenly, pointing to the plate the short-order cook had left on the counter. 'Didn't you hear me say "scrambled?" Do these look *scrambled* to you?'

Maddy grinned. Carla's reputation in the kitchen was fierce. Deservedly so. She slid her own ticket quietly under the flap and hurried out. Being on the sharp end of Carla's tongue or under the microscopic gaze of her brown eyes weren't places she particularly wanted to be, certainly not today. For reasons she couldn't quite fathom, Rafe Keeler had unnerved her. She grabbed her own order of scrambled eggs and walked quickly back to his table.

He glanced up at her from his newspaper as she placed it carefully in front of him. 'Thanks. This should do the trick.'

'Let me know if you need anything else.'

'I will.' He folded away his newspaper and began to eat.

Twenty minutes later he signalled for the bill. She hurried over, slid the tab across the bar and was just about to turn away when he spoke. 'Um, look . . . I know this might seem rather sudden, but I was just wondering . . . I'm here in New York for a couple of days and I don't really know anyone other than my colleagues and I'm sort of fed up hanging out with them. The conference is over this afternoon . . . would you like to have a drink with me afterwards? Tonight?'

'A drink?' Maddy was so surprised she nearly dropped her tray. 'With you?'

'Er, not quite the reaction I was looking for,' he deadpanned, lifting his eyebrows. 'Is it too awful a suggestion to contemplate?'

'No, I didn't mean it like that . . . I just . . . you took me by surprise, that's all.'

'Well?'

'Sure . . . er, why not?' The words were out before she could stop them.

'You will?' Now it was his turn to sound surprised.

There was something warm and open about him. It wasn't the sort of thing she normally did. Four years in New York was a long time and she'd kissed more than her fair share of frogs. Sometimes more than kissed, she thought to herself with a sudden pang. But he seemed different. And it wasn't just his accent. 'Why not?' she said again, trying to sound more offhand than she felt. 'There's a little bar just around the corner on Canal Street. Joey's. You can't miss it. About halfway down the street.'

'Great. What time d'you finish?'

'Around seven.'

'Seven thirty, then? Unless you need to go home first . . . ?'

'No . . . seven thirty's fine. I . . . I'll see you then.' She flashed him a quick smile and hurried back to the kitchen. Her mind was already racing ahead. She had a grey flannel sweatshirt in her bag and a pair of jeans – hardly appropriate attire for a date. A *date*! How long had it been since she'd been on a date? She didn't want to think.

By 7.25 p.m. she was ready. She checked her reflection in the tiny washroom mirror one last time. She brushed her hair and carefully applied a dab of lip gloss. She'd borrowed a white shirt from Carla that was several sizes too large but it looked marginally more date-like than a faded college sweatshirt. She fluffed her hair out, blotted her lips and picked up her bag. It was cold outside, but the bar was only a couple of steps away. She checked her watch – 7.29. A few minutes late. A girl's *always* gotta be a few minutes late. Another unfathomable New York rule. The blue neon sign gazed steadily at her from above the entrance. She hurried up the steps, and pushed open the door into a blaze of music and voices. He was already sitting by the bar, his body half-turned towards the door. She made her way towards him, conscious of his eyes on her as she approached. His smile was one of cautious relief.

'Hi,' he said, sliding off the stool as she came up to him. 'I wasn't sure you'd actually show up.' He pulled out the bar stool next to him. 'What can I get you?'

'I'll have a whisky,' Maddy said, hopping on to the stool as elegantly as she could.

'Ah, a whisky drinker. Single malt, without ice. Am I right? You look like you know a lot about whisky.'

He wasn't. Maddy knew less about whisky than she did about wine, and she knew nothing about wine – but he wasn't to know that. She cast about quickly inside her head for a character on whom she could base herself for the duration of the date . . . someone fun and feisty, someone who would know about whisky and wine and all of that sophisticated stuff. Ah . . . she had it! Nora in *The Thin Man*. Within seconds, she knew exactly what to do, right down to her hands. She aimed just the right teasing note of banter at him and watched as he responded. It was an old trick of hers – and it worked. Every single time.

'Cheers,' he said as the bartender slid two glasses across the counter top. 'I'm deeply grateful. You've saved me from another interminably dull evening with my colleagues. And from sitting alone in my hotel room, watching CNN.'

'How did it go?' Maddy asked, taking a sip of her whisky. It was warm and smooth. Note to self: single malts. She hurriedly swallowed her smile.

'The conference? Oh, fine. Managed to get my words out in the right order and answer a couple of questions. No one pays much attention really.'

'What was it about?'

He looked at her. 'You don't really want to know, do you?'

'I do,' Maddy protested with a smile.

'New surgical advances in the removal of pilocytic astrocytomas.'

'Oh.'

'Told you so.' He was smiling back at her. 'But enough about me. Did you get the part?'

Maddy shook her head ruefully. 'My agent hasn't called. I guess that means no.'

'That must be hard. Constantly auditioning, I mean.'

'No harder than removing poly-whatever-you-call-thems. So, you're a surgeon?'

He nodded. 'Neurosurgeon. The brain,' he added helpfully.

'I know what neurosurgery means,' Maddy said tartly.

'Sorry. Habit.'

They smiled at each other. Somehow a kind of ease had been established between them. His humour was light and teasing and he offered her the facts of his life easily, generously. Within half an hour, she'd found out that his father was a brain surgeon, like him, and his mother a well-known lawyer. He had a younger brother, Aaron, who was a lawyer, like his mother. The following March he was about to spend three months in Switzerland under the guidance of one of the most famous neurosurgeons in the world. He'd wanted to be a brain surgeon as long as he could remember. 'My mother took us to see Dad operate when I was about thirteen,' he said. 'Aaron fainted as soon as he made the first incision.'

'I hate blood.' Two whiskies had Maddy bold.

'It's funny. It's not about blood. At least, I don't remember seeing any blood. I just remember seeing Dad in his robes and his mask. He looked like a god to me.'

'Is that why you chose it?' Maddy asked, a teasing note in her voice. 'All-powerful?'

He had the grace to laugh. 'Dunno. Maybe. I just thought it would be more interesting than being a GP or a gynaecologist or whatever. The brain's an amazing organ . . . you can't imagine.' He stopped and gave a self-conscious laugh. 'There I go again. Patronising you.'

'You're not,' Maddy protested. 'It's interesting. I've never met a neurosurgeon before.'

'And I've never met an actress. Enough about me. Tell me about you.'

Maddy shrugged. 'Not much to tell,' she said, trying to match the lightness of his tone. 'I'm from Iowa. I grew up on a farm. I came to New York five years ago to study drama at Tisch. I started working at Sunshine's when I was a sophomore and I sometimes think I'll be there for ever,' she said, smiling a little to take the sting out of the words.

'No you won't.'

'How do you know?' Maddy asked. There was something wonderfully invigorating about his deep, confident English baritone. He sounded so much more . . . she searched for the right word . . . *sincere*. Yes, that was it. His confidence was sincere. He was talking about her immediate future but he seemed to be giving another, deeper kind of reassurance.

'It's written all over your face,' he said matter-of-factly, and there was no trace of flattery in his voice. 'You'll make it. You just have to have more faith in yourself.'

Maddy flinched, as though he'd touched her. He could not have known it – how could he? Those were the very words her father had said to her before he disappeared. *Have more faith in yourself, Maddy.* She no longer remembered the exact conversation – was it before or after dinner the night before? Or was it at breakfast the day he left? – but she remembered the words as if he'd spoken them yesterday. And now here was someone else come to voice the same opinion. *Have more faith in yourself.* She looked at him out of the depths of childhood, her own private darkness. It was all there. The flattened landscape around the farm where she and her father walked in spring and fall, marking out the boundaries of their land; the clump of trees at the edge where he taught her which mushrooms to pick and which to avoid; the soft, rubbery feel of a cow's teat in her palm for the first time as he showed her how to milk. The sensations, memories came flooding at her as she looked across the polished surface of the table at Rafe, watching the expression on his face change as it mirrored her own. They were smiling at each other. He laughed suddenly, rubbing his palm against the taut contour of his thigh. She reached out and touched his arm. She felt the thrilling tension that had taken hold of her since that morning suddenly begin to burn its way up her body. He must have felt it too. He grasped her hand, covering it entirely with his broad, capable fingers. He turned her hand over in his. His touch was light but firm; Maddy felt as though her whole body was on fire. 'Come on,' he said, his voice very close to her ear. 'Let's get out of here.'

*

He touched her hesitantly at first, as if seeking permission. He pulled the white shirt over her head, burying his hands in the fiery cloud of her hair. Out of the corner of her eye and the tiny portion of her brain that wasn't totally consumed with desire, she noticed that the door to his hotel room wasn't even properly closed. He followed her gaze and in a single, fluid gesture that barely disrupted his exploration of her body, he kicked it violently shut. Maddy giggled. His fingers traced a light, teasing pattern across her skin, pausing here and there, his touch generating responses she'd forgotten she was capable of, skin hardening and contracting. He entered her slowly, at last, making both of them gasp. It really was so out of character, she thought to herself wildly in the last moments before a final, sharp surge of pleasure rose, engulfing her completely. But she was glad she'd agreed to meet him for a drink, however surprised she'd been by her own response. She wouldn't have missed this for the world.

30

NIELA
London, November 1996

The Tube rumbled its way across town, each bend accompanied by a deafening roar of scraping metal and brakes. Niela held on to the strap above her head with one hand, fighting to keep hold of her newspaper in the other and read it at the same time. At Liverpool Street the doors opened and she fought her way out with everyone else. There weren't many things she disliked about her job, but not being on time was certainly one of them. She walked up the escalators and emerged at the top with a sigh of relief. It was November, but whilst the weather above ground was damp and cold, the Underground was a hot, humid place that smelled principally of sweat. She'd been in London nearly five years, and although there were days when it felt as though she'd only just arrived, there were also days – like today – when she caught sight of herself in some shop window or on the side of a passing bus and had to stop for a moment to take it all in. So much had changed – *she* had changed. Beyond recognition. No longer the desperate, naïve refugee who'd arrived with nothing more than the clothes on her back. With Anna's help, she'd found herself a permanent job, a place to live, somewhere to call her own. It had taken a while, but slowly, month by month, she'd begun to create a world that was entirely of her own making, no one else's. Whilst she still missed her family with an ache that was often unbearable, she followed Anna's lead and buried that part of her so deeply that it was almost as if that Niela no longer existed. Somehow she knew that those things had happened – she'd been married off by her parents; she'd gone to Munich with a man she barely knew and whom she hated; she'd run away from him and from everything familiar – but at another, deeper level, the life she'd fashioned for herself since her arrival in London was *hers* in a way that her previous, other life could never have been, and it comforted her in ways she could never have imagined. Six months after she'd found a permanent job as the PA to the financial director of one of Sarafin's rival companies, she'd followed Anna's suggestion and enrolled in night classes in French and Arabic. Six months later, she'd signed up to do a part-time degree at Birkbeck College. She was astounded at the levels of support that existed for people like her. Not only were there government grants that she could apply for, the college itself had literally hundreds of small-scale schemes that made it possible for someone in her position to get ahead. Anna was a fount of information – this one would help pay her fees; that one would take care of part of her rent. This bursary could be used for books; that one for travel expenses. The studies that the war in Somalia had so cruelly cut short were begun again. It had taken her almost four years, but she'd done it. Slowly, sometimes painfully, but the important thing was she'd managed to secure herself a future. Three months after graduating, she'd had another lucky break. One of her tutors at Birkbeck had told her of a position going at the International Council for Refugees. They were looking for an Arabic/ French translator . . . would Niela perhaps think of applying? She did *and* she got the job. Now the two halves of her life were beginning to merge.

She stopped at the coffee kiosk outside the station and bought herself a cappuccino. She hurried down Bishopsgate, crossed over at Commercial Road and then walked up Shoreditch High Street until she hit Rivington Road. The Council, as it was affectionately known to those who worked there, was housed at number 4. She'd been there almost nine months, and it was safe to say she loved every minute of her job. Although it was largely deskbound and the bulk of her time was spent translating government documents into French and Arabic and, on the odd occasion, into

Somali, she liked the atmosphere, and the large, open-plan offices on the fourth floor gave her a view directly on to the gleaming buildings of the City. Her colleagues, too, were pleasant, easy-going people – Duncan, a tall, sandy-haired Scot who, somewhat improbably, spoke English, Spanish and Swahili on account of his diplomatic parents; Shaheeda, a delicate-faced Indian girl from Durban who took care of Hindi and Bengali; Azmi, from Turkey, and Ludmilla, half-Russian, half-Polish, who seemed to cover every language east of the Danube. For almost the entire time Niela had been at the Council, Duncan had been trying, unsuccessfully, to take her out . . . it had now become something of a joke between the five of them. It wasn't that she didn't like him – on the contrary, she enjoyed his dry sense of humour and his considerable intelligence – but the truth was, she couldn't even *think* about taking that kind of step towards intimacy with anyone, least of all someone she worked with. Her feelings towards men were a mass of contradictions – there was the terror and revulsion she felt at the thought of Hamid, and the guilt and regret she felt whenever she thought of Christian . . . just the memory of opening that envelope to find the extra notes was enough to bring tears to her eyes. She'd returned the money to him, just as she'd promised herself she would, but she hadn't included a contact address. Like everything else from that part of her life, she had to leave him behind.

'Oh, hi, Niela.' Jenny, the receptionist, looked up as she walked in. 'I've been trying to get you. Richard Francis came looking for you. He asked if you'd pop your head round his door as soon as you get in. Said it was urgent.'

Niela nodded, wondering why on earth Richard Francis would need to see her urgently. He was one of the Council's founders. 'I'll just put my stuff away,' she said, pushing the lift button. 'Did he say what it was about?'

Jenny shrugged. 'No idea. He's been down twice. See you later. Oh, it's Caroline's leaving drinks on Friday, don't forget.'

'I won't.' The lift arrived and she disappeared inside. She got out on the fourth floor, tossed her empty coffee cup in the bin and headed for her desk. Duncan looked up from his computer screen as she passed. 'Nice jacket you have on, Niela.' He winked at her. Not for the first time, Niela was grateful that a blush wouldn't show up on her dark skin. She smiled her thanks and quickly hid behind her own computer screen. She stowed her bag under her chair, fished a notebook and pen from her drawer and beat a hasty retreat back to the lift. Richard Francis's office was a floor or two above them, with an even better view.

Fifteen minutes later, it was hard to concentrate on the view. She sat opposite Richard, almost too surprised to speak. 'I know you're trained as a translator, not an interpreter,' he said, putting up his hands as if to ward off her protests. 'But we don't have anyone who speaks Arabic, French *and* Somali. I initially said no, but someone mentioned you. You'd be based in Djibouti, although the camp is just outside the city, half an hour's drive or so up in the hills. It's very beautiful, or so I'm told. I've got to get back to them this afternoon – they're under pressure to get things moving. We've got a hundred or so refugees arriving each day, about half of them from Somalia – you'd be perfect for the job.'

Niela stared at him. Djibouti? Her heart was racing. It was almost six years since the Adens had fled Somalia and she hadn't been back to Africa since. 'When would I leave?' she asked simply, and her question was an answer in itself.

'Good girl.' Richard's eyebrows shot up appreciatively. 'In about a fortnight, assuming we can get the paperwork sorted out in time. You'll be working for someone called Josh Keeler. He's the Red Cross architect in charge of the camp. You might need to brush up a bit on building terms, nothing too technical though, don't worry. They're turning the old Foreign Legion camp into long-term shelter.'

'And how long would I be there?' Niela asked, her excitement mounting fast.

'About a month. Maybe five weeks. Depends on how fast construction goes. You'll be there over Christmas, that's the only drawback. Sue Partridge told me you're doing a part-time degree at Birkbeck . . . that might work out quite well with the holidays and whatnot. Keeler's been there for a month already, but his Arabic's pretty rudimentary and the local workers don't understand much English.' Richard let out a deep sigh of relief. 'Good on you, Niela. I like someone who appreciates a challenge. I'll get Sophie to send you down the paperwork this afternoon. I'm sure you'll enjoy the experience . . . who knows, you might find you prefer working with people rather than paper. I'm always looking for good interpreters.' His expression seemed to imply he'd found one.

Niela thanked him and backed out of the room. She walked down the corridor to the lift, her mind racing ahead. Djibouti! A month in Djibouti! What would Anna say?

She soon found out. 'Djibouti? Where the hell's Djibouti?'

'Africa. Look . . . I'll show you.' Niela got up from the table and tugged out the atlas that sat on the second shelf of Anna's bookcase. She opened it up to the section on Africa.

'Where's Djibouti, Auntie Niela?' Boris, as ever, was quick to pick up on everything that passed between his mother and his favourite aunt.

'Here . . . d'you see?' Niela held the atlas on her knees so he could look. She traced over the page with her fingertip. 'That's Mogadishu. That's where I grew up. And see that town there? That's Dire Dawa. And that's Hargeisa. That's where we went when the war started. Look, that's Addis Ababa. That's the capital of Ethiopia. See?'

'The names are so pretty,' Anna said, coming over to take a look. 'Dire Dawa. Addis Ababa. It sounds like a fairy tale.'

Niela gave a snort. 'It was anything but, believe me. Look, there's Djibouti . . . see, Boris?'

'Is it far away? Is it further than Margate?'

Both Anna and Niela laughed. They'd been on holiday to Margate at Easter and it was the furthest away from home Boris had ever been. 'Much further,' Niela confirmed.

'Will you come back?' Boris asked, sounding momentarily anxious.

'Of course I'll come back. It's only for a month.'

'You'd better,' Anna said grimly. 'Don't go and fall in love with some goat-herder and trade yourself in for a couple of camels.'

Niela had to laugh. 'There aren't any camels in Djibouti,' she said. 'And I can't imagine there'll be any goatherds in a Foreign Legion camp, either.'

'Well, I'm just saying. You'd better come back. Or we'll come out there and get you. Won't we, Boris?'

Boris nodded solemnly and placed a possessive hand on Niela's arm. 'Me and Batman,' he said firmly. 'We're gonna come and get you.'

Niela looked at him but couldn't speak. There were times when she was reminded that although she'd lost almost everything when she'd made the decision to flee, in the two years that she'd been in London, she'd found more than she'd ever dared hope.

PART FOUR

31

JOSH
Djibouti, November 1996

Josh Keeler gave the plank of wood one last thwack with the hammer and jumped down from the scaffolding with ease. He squinted up at his handiwork. It wasn't perfect, but it would do. 'Yeah, it'll hold,' he said to the two young men who were standing beside him, waiting for instructions. 'For now, at least. Finish up that line, will you? We'll get on to the roof later.' They nodded and crouched down, lining up the planks.

He slid the hammer back into his tool belt and crossed the yard, rubbing the sweat and grime from his face. It was five o'clock and the shadows were already lengthening their way out of shape. In another hour, the sky would throw up a spectacular display of colour and hue and darkness would quickly descend. He looked back across the line of temporary shelters they'd been constructing for the past month. With any luck, they'd be finished by the end of the week. Another thirty homes; another couple of hundred desperate people in temporary shelter. He shook his head in angry disbelief, fishing in his pocket for a cigarette. He cupped his hand around it and lit up, drawing the smoke down deep into his lungs. A couple of hundred people? Who were they kidding? If the war didn't ease up soon, they'd soon be taking in a thousand a day. He'd seen it all before. The trickle that turned into a flood. They would pack ten, fifteen, twenty people into one of those houses – sod the recommendations from HQ. It was always the same. Some junior intern in an office in New York typed up official-looking 'recommendations and guidelines' and sent them off from his computer to base stations around the world. Neat, three- or four-page documents with a variety of headings in a variety of fonts, which found their way to the camps and clearings where he and his men worked. Words like 'maximum occupancy' and 'minimum living standards' would jump out at him from the noticeboards. *Refugees should . . . [wherever possible] . . . be decently housed.* The people Josh worked with had walked six hundred kilometres to reach a camp with the tattered remains of their families and their possessions stuffed in plastic bags. What on earth could the words 'maximum occupancy' or 'decently housed' mean to them? He was well aware that his disdain for the commands sent down to them from head office was dangerous. He'd wound up in one fight too many in most of the places where he'd worked. Yemen, Congo, Cote d'Ivoire, the Balkans and now Djibouti. It always started the same way. A visit from top brass to the delegation. A tour of the camp. A comment, a gesture, a rebuke. The argument would begin, voices would be raised, things got out of hand . . . and then the aftermath. It was invariably a matter of perspective as to whether he'd walked or been fired. He snorted. Even the word 'delegation' made it sound far less brutal, less confrontational. The truth of the matter was that they worked in conditions that few people could tolerate. Forget the heat, the dust, the snakes, the insects, the diseases . . . all of the stuff that HQ routinely described as 'challenging'. That wasn't the challenge. Josh worked with people who had, in their own words, gone to hell and back. People who'd lost everything – homes, loved ones, land, possessions . . . and then the other stuff, harder to bear. Dignity and hope. How did you work with them? *That* was the real challenge, not the heat. The people they were sent out to help were not the passive, helplessly grateful refugees of the TV and newspaper ads. More often than not they were aggressive, erratic, irrational – anything but passive and most of the time not even remotely grateful. The bureaucrats in Geneva talked of alleviating their pain and sorrow. Josh wondered if they'd lost their minds. How did you alleviate the pain of someone who'd watched his child die in front of him? By erecting a tent? And telling him to limit the number of people who slept in it?

'Josh!' Someone called out to him. He turned. It was Bo Johanssen. His boss. He stopped and waited as Bo walked up to him as quickly as the heat would allow. 'Hey, how's it going, man?' Bo had an easy, affable air about him that hid a ferocious temper and an almost messianic devotion to the task at hand.

Josh shrugged. 'OK. We'll have the second row finished by the end of the week.'

'Good, good,' Bo said hurriedly with the distracted air of someone who had something else to say. He hesitated. 'Look, Josh . . . I'm not going to beat around the bush. Meissler's just rung from Geneva. They . . . well, let's just say they didn't appreciate what went down last week. The guy filed an official complaint. I know, I know . . . you were provoked.' He raised his hands in admission. 'But Jesus, Josh . . . he was the head of the fucking delegation! The order's come through. You're to take a fortnight's leave. Go home. Go to London. Chill out for a couple of weeks and then come back. Oh, by the way, the ICR's found an interpreter for you . . . a Somali woman. She's very good, apparently. She'll be here a couple of days after you get back.'

Josh made a small, dismissive movement with his hand and tossed his cigarette to the ground. 'No way. No fucking way. I'm not going anywhere. There's work to be done here.'

'Josh . . . be reasonable. You punched the guy in the face – what did you expect? I'm not asking you to go and sit at home for six months. Hell, I don't care where you go. But you've got to get out of here. You need a break.'

'I don't *want* a break. I'm fine. I'll go when we finish the first phase.'

'I'm not *asking* you, Josh. This isn't a request.'

32

DIANA
London, November 1996

Diana Pryce pulled smartly into the driveway and brought her little sports car to a halt. She glanced at the clock on the dashboard – it was just after five. Her perfectly shaped eyebrows lifted in mild surprise. She couldn't remember the last time she'd been home before six. She picked up the grocery bag from the passenger seat, locked the car and pushed open the garden gate. Harvey, her husband, wasn't yet home. Some complication in his last case of the day – his secretary had rung just before she left the office to tell her he'd be late. She opened the front door, slung her briefcase and jacket on the table in the hallway and plucked out the letter that was sticking out of her handbag. She walked downstairs to the kitchen. The housekeeper had gone home already, but a beautifully rich, fragrant fish stew was simmering in the oven and the table had already been set. Rafe was coming for dinner. There was something he wanted to tell her, he'd said when he phoned her in chambers. He'd just come back from New York. From the excitement in his voice, Diana guessed there was more to share than his holiday snaps. A strange tremor ran through her as she put the letter she'd been carrying around all day on the table and walked across the kitchen to the sink. She filled the kettle, looking out through the enormous sliding doors to the garden beyond. The lawn, a brilliant green sweep of carefully cut grass, fell away down to the oak trees at the bottom of the garden, now turning pale gold and red in preparation for winter. She loved the garden. It amused Harvey greatly – she who couldn't tell one end of a bulb from the other! Where had it come from, this sudden love of plants?

The cold water suddenly spilled over her hand, bringing her back to her task. She turned off the tap and plugged the kettle in. Her movements were slow and thoughtful, though her state of mind was anything but. She eyed the letter on the table as she waited for the kettle to boil. Five minutes later, she sat down at the table, a cup of tea at her side, and picked it up. She slid a finger underneath the sealed flap and pulled the wafer-thin pages out. Josh's handwriting leapt at her. *Sometimes at night you can hear the shells landing across the mountains, so close you think they're landing here, in the camp. In the morning, the refugees walk across the desert, some of them carrying their dead. The stench is unbelievable. London seems very far away.* She put the letter down again and looked out across the garden. Josh was in Djibouti, somewhere close to the Horn of Africa. She'd had to look it up when he told her where he was going. She'd long since lost track of the places he'd been. Gaza. Goma. Srebrenica. Sarajevo – a list of the world's most troubled spots. Wars, famines, conflicts, camps . . . wherever there was trouble. Neither she nor Harvey understood it. Josh was a brilliant architect; everyone said so. His tutors, fellow students, strangers . . . everyone. He could have worked anywhere, done anything. After graduation he'd turned down every single one of the jobs he'd been offered at some of London's top firms and had gone to work for the Red Cross instead. Diana was baffled. After five years' worth of training he'd gone off to be little more than a volunteer? He didn't need a degree in architecture for *that*. It wasn't so much that she thought the work he did was valueless; on the contrary, when he'd signed up to work in Bosnia that first summer, she'd been proud of him. It was something to drop into a dinner party conversation – yes, their youngest had gone out to Bosnia for the summer. Quite courageous of him, really. *Of course, he's always had a social conscience, even as a little boy. Always sticking up for the underdog.* But after Bosnia he didn't come back. After Bosnia he went to Myanmar, and to some godforsaken camp on the edge of nowhere. He sent pictures of fluttering sheets of plastic, tin roofs held down by stones and old car tyres. *This* was where he lived? In bed at night she passed the pictures silently to Harvey. He put them down without comment. She put a hand over her mouth to stop herself from crying out loud. *This* was what they'd brought him up to do? She had never understood what propelled her youngest child – and, though she would never dare say it out loud, her brightest – to leave the comforts they'd provided (the beautiful home, the private schools, the hobbies, sports, holidays at the farmhouse in Mougins and elsewhere, the promise of a glittering career that both hers and Harvey's contacts would surely have secured even if his talents alone couldn't) and head out to places that weren't to be found on any map save those that chronicled tragedy. 'You're an architect, not a fucking saint!' she'd hurled at him in the middle of an argument on one of the rare occasions he'd come home. Harvey had stepped in that time and pulled her away.

'You're his mother,' he told her, gripping her upper arm. 'You can't allow yourself to talk to him like that.' He was right. She let him lead her away, in tears. Josh frightened her, that was the truth. There was something in him that she feared, because she feared it also in herself.

The front door slammed shut suddenly, bringing her back to the present. Harvey was home. She folded the letter quickly and stowed it away in her bag. She would show it to him later. For now, Rafe was coming over and it wouldn't do to spoil Harvey's pleasure in that. He was immensely proud of Rafe, as was she . . . but there were times when she wondered about the eldest two. Rafe, desperate to prove himself every bit as brilliant a surgeon as his father, and Aaron, the solicitor-turning-barrister, struggling to fill her shoes. Only last week she'd had to put in a call to Gerald Starkey, one of the senior partners at Bernard, Bennison & Partners and an old university friend of hers . . . Aaron wanted to do his second six with them . . . wasn't there something Gerald could do? Of course there was. 'Leave it to me, Diana. Only too happy to help.' Easy as that. Aaron would start with them after Christmas. She'd never had to so much as lift a finger for Josh, ever. As much as she worried about the choices he'd made, there was respect for them too. Josh would never have accepted help – from her, from Harvey, from anyone. His fierce determination to do things *his* way and no one else's caused them pain . . . but there was no denying, it also made her proud.

'Darling . . . you're home already?' Harvey appeared in the doorway. She looked up, a smile on her face.

'I know . . . couldn't believe it myself.' She got up and walked towards him, turning her face up towards him to be kissed. She leaned into his reassuringly solid frame, allowing herself the momentary pleasure of being held. His arms went around her; the faint chemical smell of the operating theatre still clung to his clothes, a scent that was at once foreign and yet familiar to her.

'When's Rafe coming?' he asked against her hair.

'At eight. Everything's ready.'

'Any idea what he wants to talk to us about?'

Diana sighed. 'No, he didn't say. But I think I can guess.'

Harvey gave a chuckle. She felt the vibrations deep in his chest. 'Ah. A woman. Someone he's met recently.'

'Mmm. In New York, I think.'

'Well . . . at least he tells us, I suppose. We always know what's going on with those two.'

Diana nodded. It was true. Rafe and Aaron were both open books. It was Josh who was closed, and secret. She knew nothing about his relationships, nothing at all. It was Aaron who'd told her that Josh had been living with someone in Amman. A Jordanian girl – Randa, Rania . . . something along those lines. She wasn't even sure how Aaron had found out. Whatever the source, she'd asked Josh about it once and had had her head bitten off as a result. She'd never dared ask again. 'I just hope it's not another Cecily,' she murmured. Rafe fell easily; he was the sort to whom trust came naturally. He didn't suspect deviousness in others because he was incapable of it himself. She'd lost count of the number of times she'd picked him up, dusted him down, consoled him and sent him on his way . . . only to see the whole thing repeat itself again and again. It didn't help that her sons were beautiful. Rafe and Aaron were carbon copies of Harvey – tall, blond, athletic . . . strong, splendidly healthy-looking young men who would age well, just as Harvey had. Josh was different, of course, dark-haired, olive-skinned, more like herself, but no less striking. Girls and women of all ages practically threw themselves at her sons; Christ, she could remember a time or two when her own friends had started behaving like teenagers in their presence! She pulled away from Harvey gently. 'I'd better go upstairs and take a bath,' she said, straightening the lapel of his jacket. 'Will you bring me up a glass of wine?'

'Good idea,' Harvey said. 'Go ahead and run your bath. I'll be up in a minute.'

Diana picked up her handbag. 'Oh, I almost forgot to tell you. I got a letter from Josh. He's coming home too.'

'Josh? Josh is coming home?'

She watched his face light up and a sharp stab of pain went through her. 'Mmm,' she murmured, turning away. 'Said something about a fortnight's leave. He should be here next week. Friday or so.'

'That's wonderful.' The pleasure in Harvey's voice was genuine. Diana couldn't bring herself to turn back round again. She made a small, incoherent sound and walked quickly out of the room.

33

JOSH
London, December 1996

Heathrow was crowded, even at dawn. He pushed his way past the crowds standing indecisively in front of screens and signs and made his way towards Immigration. He slid his passport across the desk, ignoring the officer's quick questioning glance – stamps of entrance and exit from Bogotá to Baghdad – and returned it to the back pocket of his jeans. He carried no luggage other than a battered dark green backpack that had clearly seen better days. He bought a ticket and boarded the train, tossing his backpack on to the seat opposite him. He was tired. He hadn't slept properly in a couple of days. He ran a hand over his stubble and smiled faintly. Diana would be horrified. Hopefully there would be no one at home; he needed a few hours to readjust. Coming back to England was never easy. The train shot out of the tunnel and into daylight. As they sped past the industrial sheds and yards, their corrugated steel sides dissolving in the weak early morning winter light, his feeling of dislocation intensified. By the time they pulled into Paddington, a curious sensation of distress was prickling over his skin. He was coming home. And yet he was not.

The house was empty. He slid his key into the lock and pushed open the front door. He stood in the hallway, breathing deeply. The smell of childhood washed over him, the very particular combination of furniture polish and cigar smoke from the thin cigarillos Harvey liked to smoke after dinner. There were fresh flowers on the antique side table in the hall. A rich, densely patterned Persian rug drew his eye lengthways down the corridor to the partially open door of Diana's study, which overlooked the garden. The rug was new. He didn't remember it from his last visit. They'd changed a few things, he noticed. The walls of Diana's study were now a rich buttery yellow instead of white; her desk, which sat directly in front of the window, was the same, but the high-backed leather chair he remembered had been replaced by a modern-looking one of leather and chrome. He set his backpack down on one of the hallway chairs and walked into the living room. Light flooded in from both sides. After months spent living and working in the most crudely put-together shelters imaginable, there was something disconcerting about the comfort in front of his eyes. The sofa – an enormous burnished leather chesterfield that sat five people – cost more than the row of ten prefabricated huts he'd just finished constructing. He shook his head. It was always the same. The luxury, even modestly displayed, was faintly obscene. He closed the door behind him and walked upstairs.

His old room was exactly as he'd left it. The few boxes of possessions that he'd cleared out of the flat on Marchmont Street were stacked up in the corner – mostly books and records. Nothing much else. The girl he'd been living with at the time had taken the rest. He tossed his jacket on to the bed and sat down to unlace his boots. The reddish dust of the camp still clung to the soles. He needed a hot shower, a coffee and a cigarette, in that order. He peeled off the rest of his clothing and walked naked into the bathroom. There were fresh towels on the radiator, soap, shaving foam and shampoo on the shelf beside the sink. He opened the shower door, turned on the taps and stepped in. The scalding water ran down his hair and plastered it flat against his head. He let the full stream of it run down his belly as he turned his face up towards it, giving himself over finally to the comfort of his family's home. He stepped out of the hot, steamy fug of the bathroom into the cooler air of his bedroom. He pulled on a pair of torn jeans and rummaged around in the chest of drawers until he found an old woollen jumper. He towelled his hair dry, pulled on a pair of socks and padded his way downstairs, tiredness already beginning to sweep over him in waves.

The kitchen was spotless, the only sound the faint hum of the giant stainless-steel American-style fridge. He pulled open the door and stood in bemused silence for a minute or two, surveying the contents. After the past few months of eating nothing but canned food and camel meat, the sheer magnitude of everything that was available was overwhelming. Yoghurts, fruit, fresh vegetables, wine, cheese, chocolate . . . he grabbed a pint of milk and shut the door, slightly nauseated by the surfeit of choice. He found a packet of cornflakes in the pantry and carried it to the table. He finished off two bowls, made himself a cup of coffee and lit a cigarette. He opened one of the sliding doors to let the air in and shivered in the unaccustomed cold. For almost a year he'd felt nothing but heat. He finished his cigarette and shut the door. It was time for a nap.

34

MADDY
New York, December 1996

He won't call. Of course he won't call. Why would he? Why should he? It was a one-night stand, nothing more. I know he said he would call . . . but he won't. The disjointed sentences floated around and around in her head until she thought she would explode. After Rafe left, she ate an entire tub of Ben & Jerry's ice cream, two packets of salsa-flavoured potato chips, a piece of leftover chicken Kiev that she'd brought home from Sunshine's a couple of days earlier and – for no other reason than it was there in the fridge – a bowl of cold creamed spinach. When she brought everything up a few hours later, she couldn't bring herself to look at what she'd deposited in the toilet bowl. It would have genuinely made her feel sick. She rinsed her mouth, twisted her curls into a ponytail and resumed the crazy monologue in her head. When she couldn't stand it any longer, she picked up the phone and rang Sandy.

'You did *what*?' Sandy's voice was predictably astonished.

'I know, I know. But he's really nice . . . I mean, *really* nice. He's a doctor.'

'Meaning what? That you'll hear from him again? Maddy . . . are you *nuts*? What do you know about this guy? Nothing. For all you know, he's probably married. In fact, he is married . . . of course he is. In New York for a weekend, meets some waitress in a bar—'

'No, it wasn't like that. OK, it *was* . . . but it was different.'

'Like how?'

'Like . . . like . . . I don't know. He's English. They're not like that.'

'Oh, Maddy.'

Maddy chewed the inside of her lip nervously. She'd phoned Sandy to make her feel better, not worse. 'Anyway, it's only been two days. Maybe he'll call tomorrow . . .'

'Yeah, and maybe his wife will.'

She put down the phone a few minutes later feeling even worse. Sandy was right. She was mad. Not because she'd slept with him – this was New York, after all, and Maddy was no innocent fool. It wasn't as if she'd never had a boyfriend, or a one-night stand, for that matter, although the decision about those two encounters turning out to be one-night stands hadn't been hers. She'd never had a boyfriend or slept with someone without thinking – or hoping – it would lead to something else, something more. *If that's what you want*, Sandy told her crossly, *then don't sleep with them.* She didn't know how to explain to Sandy that she simply didn't have the courage to say no. If a man she liked singled her out, she was generally so astonished that it didn't occur to her to say 'hold on' or 'wait until I've got to know you better'. Deep down she was both hopelessly romantic and romantically hopeless. She'd read enough self-help psychology books to know that the issue was somehow tied to her father's abrupt disappearance and the fear it had produced in her that everyone else would do the same – but she'd have no sooner understood what to do about it than she could bring him back. So she muddled along, oscillating wildly between elation and despair, punctuated by late-night trips to the refrigerator and the toilet and the gnawing sense that something wasn't right . . . and then she'd met Dr Rafe Keeler. Whom she knew was different, only she didn't know how. Or how to explain it to Sandy.

The phone rang suddenly, causing her to jump. She picked it up. It would be Sandy, of course, feeling remorseful. 'Besides,' she said quickly before Sandy could get a word in, 'I really don't care if it *was* just a one-night stand. It was great . . . best sex I've ever had.'

There was silence on the other end. And then a faint cough. A *male* cough. The static of an international line crackled momentarily.

'Sandy?' Maddy croaked, feeling faint.

'Um, no . . . it's not Sandy. It's Rafe.'

'Rafe.' She closed her eyes.

'Maddy.'

'I nearly fell over,' Maddy told Sandy a few hours later. 'I mean . . . I was so sure it was you.'

'So tell me this again . . . he's invited you to *London*? For *Christmas*? And he's *paying*?'

Maddy nodded. She lifted the bottle of beer to her lips, enjoying the look of stunned disbelief on Sandy's face. She felt the slow burn of excitement in the pit of her stomach. She was going to London! At first she thought she hadn't heard him properly. 'London? London, *England*?'

'Um, not sure which other London there is,' he'd said, his deep baritone voice coming down the line towards her.

'Me?'

'Well, who else? I don't know anyone else called Maddy. Do you?'

She'd blushed violently. 'But I . . . I don't even have a passport. I've never been anywhere before. I've never even been in an aeroplane.'

'Oh. Well, the plane bit's not difficult. I send you a ticket, you go to the airport and pick it up and then you get inside this big metal bird and it hurtles down the runway, gathering speed until it takes off. I can explain the principles of flight if you like . . . insofar as I can remember them, of course, but—'

'Rafe,' she protested weakly, laughing. 'I know what a plane is . . . I've just never flown anywhere before. But . . . what if I can't get a passport in time?'

'You're not a felon, are you? Haven't killed anyone lately, or been to jail?'

'No,' she said, shaking her head as if she could see him and laughing. God, she really, really liked him.

'Then it shouldn't be a problem. Can you find out and let me know?'

'Yes,' she whispered, her voice suddenly disappearing on her. They'd chatted for a few more minutes . . . and that was that. The following morning she rang the passport helpline. For $165 she could get one in forty-eight hours. She gathered together all the documentation and practically ran to the nearest passport agency offices. She waited behind the bulletproof glass window as the clerk checked her application, too nervous to even speak. Finally, the woman looked up.

'OK, Ms Stiller. Everything's here. If you'll come back on Wednesday morning, we'll have your passport ready for you.'

She left the building in a daze and walked all the way uptown to

Sandy's. It was barely lunchtime but she had to have a beer. Sandy, predictably, demanded to hear all the details – from the minute Maddy first set eyes on him until she put the phone down after he'd called a few days later. She couldn't believe it either. A good-looking, English neurosurgeon. Did such a thing exist? Clearly. Maddy happily answered all her questions. A week in London over Christmas. Even her mother was excited. 'Of course you should go,' she said emphatically. 'I'll be fine. I'm going over to the Steenkamps'. I won't hear another word.' Maddy put down the phone, her stomach trembling with nerves. Sometimes, it seemed, fairy tales *did* happen. Even to her.

35

DIANA
London, December 1996

Diana checked her reflection in the gilt-framed mirror in the hallway. She'd never quite trusted the soft, weak light that came in through the small window above the front door. She suspected it of being too flattering. She swung her head slowly from side to side, checking her new cut. Claire, her hairdresser, had persuaded her to add a few warmer, lighter highlights to her hair. She'd worn the same expertly cut bob that framed her face for the past twenty years. She brushed away a stray strand, turned up the collar of her crisp white Armani shirt and made sure the heavy silver and pearl necklace Harvey had given her for her fiftieth birthday was properly balanced around her slender neck. She turned sideways . . . the shirt was tucked into dark blue wool palazzo pants with a lovely thick hem. Patent black stiletto boots completed the outfit. Ferragamo, of course. She'd seen them in the window at Selfridges and walked straight in. Not cheap, naturally, but she'd wear them for the rest of her life. She pulled a face. She hated such phrases, especially now. At fifty-four, it sounded as though the rest of her life might arrive sooner than she thought. It was the ridiculous sort of phrase her mother had always used. She turned away from the mirror, irritated with herself. Why on earth did she have to think about her mother now? She looked at her watch. In a few minutes Rafe would be here. With this woman he'd met in New York. Once. At a bar. She'd listened to him the night he came round for dinner in pained silence. Now he was bringing her to their house. Well, at least they'd get a chance to meet her *before* Christmas lunch, she'd told Harvey that morning. She was staying for a fortnight.

'It'll be fine,' Harvey said in his typical, reassuring way. 'I know you've had your misgivings before, but she does sound rather nice.'

'An *actress*?' Diana couldn't help herself.

'Classically trained, I think. There's a difference, my love.'

'I hope so,' she answered darkly.

Well, in a few minutes she'd be here. Josh was upstairs; she hoped he would make an exception and come down. Aside from the one evening when Rafe and Aaron both came over for dinner just after his arrival, the three of them hadn't spoken. She sighed. They'd never got on, not even as children. It wasn't a question she could trust herself to answer, but it pained her nonetheless. Almost thirty years of murderous animosity between them; there would be no cure, no change. All she hoped for these days was a semblance of civility on the odd occasion they were all together – like tonight. Could Josh be counted upon to be polite? She hoped so. For everyone's sake.

She took a quick look in the living room – everything was exactly as it should be. The cushions were plumped, pictures straightened, every surface polished. The hand-knotted *gebbeh* rug with its bold geometric patterns and rich colours brought a luxurious warmth to the room. There was a chilled bottle of champagne in the silver bucket beside the chesterfield and a tray of soft, pungent cheeses that they'd brought back from Mougins. Any second now Harvey would come down the stairs, put something soothing and classical on the stereo and open a bottle of red wine to breathe. She let her forefinger rest for a second on the gleaming surface of the antique console that stood beside the door. One of the few things she'd taken from her parents' house when her father finally died. A beautiful piece; soothing just to look at. She heard a car pull up outside. She straightened one of the silver picture frames, brushed away a piece of lint from her trousers and walked to the front door, a smile of welcome fixed squarely on her face.

36

MADDY
London, December 1996

To say that Maddy felt sick was the understatement of the century. It was only her third night in London – fourth if one counted the plane journey over, which she didn't. The first two nights had appeared to her as if in a dream, out of someone else's life. She'd been too excited on the plane to even contemplate sleep. She'd sat stiffly upright in her seat, counting the hours until they landed. Rafe was at Heathrow, waiting anxiously for her to appear. She'd gone through Immigration, collected her bags and then had to rush down the corridor to the nearest toilet to be sick. She'd looked at her reflection in the neon glow of the airport toilet and nearly thrown up again. She was pale and wan and there were dark circles of exhaustion under her eyes. She'd barely slept in the previous week. She couldn't quite remember what he looked like; what if he saw her and was disappointed? What if she wasn't the way he remembered? What if . . . ? She'd walked out into the glare of chauffeurs and relatives and seen him immediately, standing at the back with the biggest bunch of flowers she'd ever seen and the widest smile across his impossibly handsome face. She almost fainted with relief. They'd gone back to his flat somewhere in the centre of town and stayed in bed for almost the entire day. They went out that evening to a nearby restaurant and he told her he was taking her to meet his parents. His *parents*? She'd met him just once . . . was he *insane*? But the circumstances were unusual; it was Christmas in a week's time and there was no question she wouldn't be spending it with them . . . it was only polite to introduce her first. Yes, he knew it was a little sudden and he certainly didn't want to frighten her off, but what else could he do? In three months' time he'd be in Basle, doing his long-awaited residency, and it would be difficult for them to meet. 'Besides, they're really easy-going. They'll love you, I promise. It'll be nice.' She'd listened to him with a mixture of fascination and horror. Did she even have anything suitable to wear?

Now, sitting next to him, her stomach churning, she watched the elegant London houses sweep past in a blur. They turned left and right down one crescent after another, Maddy losing all sense of direction and time, until Rafe finally pulled up and switched off the engine. 'We're here,' he said, turning to smile at her. 'This is it.'

Maddy looked at the house and gulped. Tall, immaculate and elegant, it was a creamy white colour with a glossy black front door. A small garden in front, a short pebbled walkway leading to the front steps and two giant planters filled with some exotic blood-red flowers on either side of the door. The garden disappeared down one side of the house. It was about as far away from the farmhouse in Iowa as it was possible to be. She looked down at her plain grey woollen skirt and tights and her heart sank. 'Rafe,' she said, her mouth suddenly gone dry. 'Wh . . . what if they don't like me?'

'Don't be daft.' He got out of the car and came round to her side. He gripped her hand tightly as they walked up the front steps together. 'How could anyone *not* like you? Hmm?' Maddy was too nervous to reply. She racked her brain for a character – *any* character – anything to help her get through the next few hours, but nothing came to mind.

The front door opened as soon as they reached it. Standing in the doorway was a petite, dark-haired woman, her arms outstretched in welcome. She lifted her face to be kissed by her son. Maddy bit down fiercely on the impulse to hide behind him. They followed her into the hallway. 'Mother.' Rafe turned to draw Maddy in. 'Mother, this is Maddy.'

His mother held out a hand. Maddy shook it. Her touch was so brief, Maddy wondered if she'd imagined it. 'Hi, it's so nice to meet you, Mrs Keeler,' she said enthusiastically, injecting as much warmth and friendliness into her voice as she could. She could practically feel the woman wince. Oh dear . . . too friendly? Too American?

'Gosh, it's been years since anyone called me that! Everyone calls me Diana. Even my sons.'

'I . . . oh, yes, of course . . .' Maddy managed to squeak.

'Where's Dad?' Rafe asked, touching the small of Maddy's back reassuringly.

'He'll be up in a minute . . . he's just checking on dinner. I thought we might as well eat downstairs, but we'll have drinks in here first. The kitchen's a bit informal for champagne, don't you think?' She smiled at Maddy.

Maddy couldn't think of anything to say in reply. She followed Rafe and his mother into the living room. It was quite simply the loveliest room she'd ever seen. Grey-blue walls; polished wooden floorboards covered in a collection of beautifully simple Persian rugs; an old leather chesterfield in one corner big enough to seat five; gleaming antique furniture scattered around, and at the enormous bay window, a pair of crushed silk curtains in a dusty rose colour. A glass bowl of giant white lilies stood on the centre table, releasing their pungent fragrance into the air. Leading off the sitting room was a dining room dominated by a long table and eight, perhaps ten chairs clustered around. An impressive mixture of paintings and photographs hung on the walls. There was a giant gilt-edged mirror above the mantelpiece. Maddy caught a glimpse of herself as she walked past – wide-eyed, obviously nervous and out of her depth. She *had* to think of something, a character, and quickly, too. It came to her in a flash. Audrey Hepburn. Gamine, wide-eyed, but charming, not gobsmacked and certainly not eaten up with nerves. Elegant, considered, feminine. She began to project herself into the role.

Suddenly a very tall, handsome silver-haired man entered the room holding a bottle of wine by the neck. He hugged his son affectionately and then turned to her. 'And you must be Maddy. Is it short for something? Madeleine, perhaps?' She shook her head, smiling in what she hoped was a charming, demure manner and was about to say, 'Madison', but he bent towards her and kissed her on both cheeks instead. 'I hear it's your first visit to London,' he said, standing back and beaming down at her.

'Er, yes, sir, it is,' she said eagerly.

'Oh, call me Harvey, please. I never bother with the "sir". Ask my wife.'

Maddy looked hesitantly at Rafe, but before she could say anything, another figure appeared in the doorway. She looked up at him. He was dark-haired and dark-eyed, as tall as Rafe but leaner, somehow harder. The sun had ripened his skin, like fruit. A beautiful rosy darkness rippled up his neck, spreading across his face. Beside her, she could feel Rafe stiffen. It was as if the temperature in the room had dropped a notch. Maddy looked from the newcomer to Rafe and back again, confused. Who was he?

'Josh, darling, don't just stand there. Do come in.' Diana went towards him, laying a hand possessively on his arm.

'Rafe.' His eyes flickered slowly over Rafe but there was nothing in his expression that even hinted at a smile or a welcome.

'Josh.' Rafe's response was equally hostile.

'And this is Maddy, Rafe's, er, friend. She's visiting London,' Harvey said quickly, making sure she wasn't left out. The man looked briefly at her, murmured some sort of standard greeting and then turned and disappeared.

'Who was that?' Maddy whispered as Diana hurried after him.

'My brother,' Rafe said shortly, picking up the champagne and expertly easing off the cork. 'Not the lawyer. The other one. Now, what'll you have? Champagne?'

'Jolly good idea,' Harvey said, carrying over glasses. He waited until Rafe had poured the champagne and lifted his glass to hers. 'Welcome to London, my dear. I hope you enjoy your visit and that you'll be back.'

'Cheers.' Rafe lifted his glass and Maddy quickly did the same. His *other* brother? Why hadn't he mentioned there were three of them? There was clearly no love lost between them; she'd rarely seen such unbridled animosity, despite the fact that he'd only been in the room for a few minutes. She was an only child; she had no experience of sibling rivalry. She looked at Rafe uncertainly. His face had relaxed back into its habitual gentle expression. Had she imagined the hardness that came into his eyes when his brother entered the room?

Harvey led the way down to the kitchen. Diana was already at the counter, bringing bowls of deliciously fragrant food to the long, beautifully dressed table. Of the younger brother there was no sign. He did not appear again.

37

JOSH
London/Djibouti, December 1996

Josh climbed the stairs to his room, two at a time. He had no desire to join them. He'd forgotten Rafe was coming to dinner. With some girl he'd picked up in New York the previous week or month, he couldn't remember what Diana had said. He'd been reading in his room at the top of the house when they arrived. He must have fallen asleep; the book lay discarded amongst the covers. Their voices in the hallway had woken him up. In the first few seconds of conscious thought he'd struggled to work out where he was. London. At home in his parents' house. He'd pushed aside the duvet impatiently and looked at his wristwatch in disbelief. It was nearly seven thirty. He'd slept for more than six hours straight. He swung his legs out of bed and stood up, narrowly missing the light that swung above his bed. He opened the door and walked downstairs. There were voices coming from below. He walked into the living room. Diana was standing next to someone. A woman. Flame-haired. Pale porcelain skin and hazel-green eyes. A light dusting of freckles across the bridge of the nose. Dark lipstick on a wide, full mouth. His mind took in the details automatically. Not beautiful, exactly, but striking. She'd looked up at him as he came down the last few steps. Her face was confused and open at the same time, her thoughts already breaking up as he looked at her, like a sky of merging and melting clouds.

The enforced break went by quicker than he'd expected. Exactly two weeks after he'd arrived, he left London the way he'd come, quietly and alone. He lay in bed for a few minutes on the morning of his departure, listening to the sound of the birds in the garden below – birds whose names he'd forgotten but whose excited twitter was still familiar. He had an early flight to Frankfurt, a three-hour delay and then a midday flight to Addis, where a driver would be on hand to meet him. It would take them almost the whole day to drive from Addis to Djibouti, but Bo wasn't putting on a plane especially for him and there were no charter flights available. He'd had his fill of London – he'd met up with the few friends he kept in touch with; seen all the films and shows he'd missed and eaten his fill of restaurant food. He longed now for the solitude of the desert and the satisfaction of getting the job done.

Harvey was in the kitchen when he descended. He looked up as Josh came through the doorway. 'You're up early,' he remarked, looking at his watch.

'Flight's at eight thirty. I'll head out in about twenty minutes,' Josh said, reaching for the coffee pot.

'I'll give you a lift to the station.' There was a second's delicate pause. 'Are you happy out there, son?'

Behind the question, Josh felt the weight of an unknown answer. As always, they seemed to be seeking something from him that he wasn't sure he knew how to give. He shrugged. 'It's fine. *I'm* fine. You can tell her that.'

'I'm not asking on her behalf,' Harvey said mildly.

'I'm fine, Dad.'

'If you say so, son.' Harvey got up from the table. 'Ten minutes? I've got an early start today – young girl with a cranial fracture. I'm looking forward to it. You're all packed?'

'Yeah. Just the one bag.' He smiled to himself. It was a typical Harvey comment. He'd never known anyone with such an obvious love of the work that was his job and yet also his life. Could he say the same about himself? Perhaps . . . but for different reasons. He looked out across the stone floor to the garden beyond the sliding doors. It was alive with damp, mossy winter growth. Everything was green. In a few days' time there would be none. Just the sandy, neutral tones of the desert and the silence that was louder than sound.

A couple of hours later, he was finally on his way. As the plane lifted gracefully into the sky, he felt the unspoken tension in him lift from within. The pilot banked to the left – below him, spread out like a giant neat patchwork quilt, the countryside to the south of the airport unfolded, mile upon mile of regularly shaped green squares, fertile and organised. It would be the last he would see of such landscapes for a while. At Frankfurt, a woman and her child boarded and sat in the seat next to his. He dozed fitfully as they crossed the length of Germany, then Italy, his sleep interrupted every few minutes by the crying of the child and the mother's low placatory murmur. The Mediterranean was spread out below them like a flat deep blue blanket, stretched tight from shore to sandy blonde shore. They crossed into Africa and the green began to give way. Now the landscape below them was lunar, a thousand shades of ochre, orange, red. There was turbulence; the great heat of the Sahara flinging up currents of air that buffeted the plane this way and that. The desert was a sea of undulating crescents of sand, great reclining figures sloping into the haze. At dusk they touched down in Addis, when the sun had fallen from its pinprick dazzle to a soft glow before sinking out of view.

He was back. The heat was a gag placed against his mouth and nose. The driver was waiting for him. A night in one of those standard international hotels that skirt every airport, even in Africa. *Salaam alaikum.* They pushed their way through the crowds of arriving and departing people, the black-veiled women and the men in long djellabahs and scarves, worry beads dangling from their hands. Yes, he was back. The driver dropped him off at the Intercontinental. It would be his last taste of luxury for a while.

167

At six the following morning, they were ready to go. He swung his bag on to the back seat and climbed in. He was impatient to get out of the city, away from civilisation. The low, mud-walled villages, pierced every now and then by the index finger of a minaret or a cluster of trees, the flashy tourist signs – *Coca-Cola, Daz, Sentou* – all swam before his eyes as they sped east towards the suburbs and the slow outline of the mountains beyond. They began the slow descent into the desert, the rocky landscape finally taking charge. Debre Zayit, Awash, Melka Werer . . . They turned and headed north, away from the Somali border and into the Yangudi Rassa National Park. The landscape changed; it became greener, hillier . . . He followed it all, eyes hidden behind shades without which he might have been blinded. The light here was fierce and alive, nothing like the watery, delicate light of Europe. They crossed the park and again it changed. Now the immense barrenness had put a stop to everything – houses, roads, shops, billboards . . . all lost, swallowed up in the expanse of bottomless eternity that lay between them and the refugee camp he called home.

38

JULIA
London, December 1996

Julia sat with her knees pressed tightly together, waiting for the door at the far end of the room to open and for Gerald Starkey to walk through it with either a smile or a frown on his face. She'd was almost at the end of her first six – would she be offered a place to continue? She could feel her heart thumping steadily in her chest. She'd done all that was expected of her; that much she already knew. Harriet would have told her otherwise. But doing what was expected wasn't the goal – at Bernard, Bennison & Partners, one had to do more. Had she done it?

The door opened suddenly. She looked up. There was a moment's awful wait and then Gerald's face broke into a smile. The relief was so great, Julia thought she might actually weep. 'Well done, Julia,' he said, walking towards her. 'Pleased to say the decision's unanimous. Harriet'll keep you on in the family unit until the end of your next six.' Outside the door, Daniel and Christopher were also waiting to see if they'd been offered full tenure.

'Th . . . thank you,' Julia stammered, not sure whether she should stick out a hand or not. She'd only ever met Gerald Starkey in passing.

'Not at all. You've earned it.' Starkey solved the problem by holding out his own. 'Oh, by the way . . . we're taking on someone next month whom I believe you already know . . . Aaron Keeler. You two were postgrads at Balliol together, or so I'm told. He's a solicitor but he's making the jump across. His mother's an old, dear friend of mine. Look out for him, won't you? Show him the ropes. I expect we'll stick him on the corporate side of things, but it'll be good for him to see a familiar face. Right, I think that's everything. Send Daniel in, will you?'

Julia's mouth fell open. She blinked, aware that a hot flush was slowly spreading its way across her face. 'Y . . . yes, sir . . .' she croaked finally. She turned quickly and walked to the door. Aaron Keeler. Oh, Christ. She walked back down the corridor to her office, distress prickling all over her skin like a rash. After the incident on the balcony the night of Dom's dinner party, she'd done her best to avoid him. She would sooner have died than admit it, but her feelings towards him had changed that night. It was as though a light had suddenly been switched on – he was no longer just the most arrogant, self-centred and pompous prick she'd ever met; he'd become someone else. Someone she wanted to talk to, be close to . . . be held by. His words had produced a longing in her to hear what he thought of her. When they'd been interrupted and Minty had come out to stake her claim, the disappointment that swept through her had rendered her speechless. She'd gone inside, her hands shaking and her head a mass of jumbled, confused contradictions . . . and then he and Minty had laughed at her, together. In collusion. The blow of disappointment was swift and complete. She'd ignored him completely for the rest of the year, hurt beyond comprehension, especially to herself. She'd only spoken to him once after that, the night their final exam results came through and she'd thrown a glass of champagne in his face.

Thinking about it even now made her heart start to race. She'd woken up early, like everyone else. She and Dom had had a coffee together in the kitchen at Holywell, not speaking much. The results would be posted on the noticeboard at the Examinations Hall on Broad Street at 11 a.m. on the dot, not a minute before. At ten minutes to, they were all gathered outside, nervously avoiding each other's eyes. Keeler was nowhere to be seen. Bang on time, the great wooden door was opened by the beadle. He glared at the twenty-odd students gathered anxiously in front of it. Seen it all a hundred times, his expression implied. Julia hung back as Dom surged forwards with everyone else. Her heart was beating fast. There were whoops of joy and muttered groans as the list was scanned. Dom was at the front. He turned his head to her, pointing excitedly at the board. 'Julia! You came first!' She felt her face flush scarlet as several other heads turned. 'Burrows came first!' Dom shouted again.

'Well done,' a girl said as she pushed her way to the front. 'You deserve it.' Julia stared after her. It was Minty. Julia's mouth dropped open. She was still staring at Minty's back when Dom came up to her and threw an arm round her shoulders.

'What did I tell you?' he crowed, looking down at her and beaming with pride. '*Knew* you'd do it!'

'Shh!' Julia wriggled uncomfortably under his grasp. 'Don't make such a fuss!'

'Why ever not? You came first, you silly cow! Of course you ought to make a fuss! Where're we going to celebrate? I *passed* . . . I can't believe it! I passed!'

Half an hour later, with a glass of beer in one hand and a glass of champagne that Dom had thrust upon her in the other, the results were finally beginning to sink in. Julia looked around the crowded pub of relieved, smiling faces and felt a sudden rush of warmth. It was just as her father had said it would be. 'Hard work, Jules. That's what it comes down to. Graft. That's what makes the difference, not what you were born with.' She felt a soft, sneaky tug of pride. That was another thing he'd warned her against. Pride. 'Doesn't ever do to be too proud, Julia. Pride comes before a fall, you mark my words.' He was right, of course.

Suddenly the door opened. She looked across the floor and saw Aaron Keeler, head and shoulders above everyone else, framed in the doorway. As always, he caught her eye. But this time, his expression wasn't as arrogant as it usually was. He nodded at her, catching her off guard. She felt a sudden rush of embarrassment. He'd come close to the bottom. He'd passed, but only just. Her father's voice came to her again. 'Generosity, Jules. Be generous to others, especially in defeat. People never remember what you do or say but they do remember how you make them feel.' She looked at the glass of champagne in her hand. She'd done it; she'd proved them all wrong. Perhaps it was time to be generous? Before she knew it, she was making her way across the room. 'Hi,' she said, stopping beside him. 'Thought you might like a glass. Congratulations.'

He looked down at her, unable to hide his surprise. Peregrine stared at her as if she'd lost her marbles. Aaron studied her, as if trying to work something out. Finally he said, 'Is this a joke?'

Julia looked up at him. 'A joke?' she repeated, puzzled.

'Yeah. Your idea of a joke.'

'Of course it isn't. I just thought . . . I just wanted to say . . .' She stopped herself short. 'Look, I just thought it would be a nice gesture, that's all. I just wanted to say well done.'

'Well *done*? For coming *seventeenth*?' There was real bitterness in his voice. Julia felt her own temper suddenly flare up. He'd passed, hadn't he? What was he so bitter about?

'There's nothing wrong—'

'Oh, *please*,' Aaron said, holding up a hand dismissively. 'Don't bother. You've had your five minutes of glory; now just piss off and leave me alone.'

She glared up at him, all friendliness gone. 'Glory? Christ, you're even worse than I imagined. I just thought—' She stopped herself, almost too angry to speak.

'What? What *did* you think?'

'Nothing,' she said tightly. 'Just forget it.'

'No, go on, Burrows. What's this all about? Did you come over to gloat? What d'you want? A pat on the back? A thumbs-up? A . . . *what the fuck!*' His shocked gasp cut through the air. Even as Julia stared at Aaron Keeler's dripping face, she wasn't fully aware of what she'd done. She looked at him, then down at her hand. The champagne glass was empty. She'd chucked it straight at him. She stared at it for a second, then, cheeks flaming and heart racing, she turned round, thrust the empty glass into Dom's hand and marched out of the pub.

That was four years ago, and she hadn't seen or heard of him since. Though it wouldn't quite be accurate to say she'd *forgotten* him, she certainly no longer thought about him every day . . . until now. Now he was coming *here*? *His mother's an old, dear friend of mine.* That was how it worked, of course. *She'd* slogged her guts out to get to Bernard, Bennison & Partners. *He'd* asked his mother to make a call. Of course. And now she'd been instructed to make *him* feel welcome? It was enough to make her weep.

39

JOSH
Djibouti, December 1996

The small plane tilted in the direction of the mountains, leaving a spittle
of white smoke trailing in its wake. It dipped suddenly, then righted itself
slowly before coming in to land. Josh stood at the open-air bar, a steaming
cup of espresso in one hand and an unlit cigarette in the other, watching it
taxi down the short length of the runway and shudder to a halt. He lifted a
hand to his eyes, shielding them from the light, and squinted at the
passengers now making their way unsteadily across the tarmac towards
him. There were seven of them, a couple of the men dressed incongru-
ously in suits. A large-bosomed blonde had taken the lead. He tipped into
his mouth the last drop of melted sugar that had settled at the bottom of
the cup, tucked the cigarette behind his ear and walked out to meet them.

The blonde had seen him, singled him out. She gathered the rest of the
brood and bore down on him purposefully. The men in suits were met by
an American army official, who immediately whisked them away. There
were four of them left. Two men, two women. From the memos that had
been flying around over the past few days, he knew that the group would
be staying for at least a month. His eyes flickered over them in turn,
coming slowly to rest on the startling figure of a young, very pretty girl in
a white tank top and a pair of turned-up jeans. She was dark-skinned,
with thick curly black hair pulled into a knot on the top of her head, jet-
black eyes under smooth, perfectly arched brows. There was something
incongruous about her in this setting. She looked like a tourist, dressed
for the sun.

'Josh? Josh Keeler? Oh, thank God!' cried the blonde as they reached
him. 'We were so worried there wouldn't be anyone to meet us!' Her
voice was a shrill nasal squeak.

He winced. 'Yes, I'm Josh.'

She was clearly the group leader. 'Nancy Shore. Cultural Adviser.
USAID.' She barked out her credentials like gunfire.

He shook each of their hands in turn. The two young Frenchmen were
sanitation engineers. He came finally to the tourist. 'Niela Aden,' she said
in a brisk, businesslike voice. 'I'm the interpreter.'

He stared at her. So she was the Somali interpreter he'd been sent. She ought to know better. 'You might want to cover your heads,' he said coolly, throwing the two women a pointed look. 'It's a Muslim country, in case you weren't aware.'

'This is Djibouti, not Saudi Arabia,' Niela Aden said tartly. 'And in case *you* hadn't noticed, this is a US army base. I don't see too many locals walking about. I've got a *dirac* with me but I'm not covering my head.'

Her sharp retort took him by surprise. He was about to say something when she suddenly walked off in the direction of the toilets. 'Hey!' he called after her. The rest of the group stood by uncertainly. '*Hey!*' She ignored him. He turned back to the other three, who were regarding him silently, their faces sallow with fatigue.

'Should we . . . should I follow her?' Nancy Shore asked nervously.

'No. Just put *your* headscarf on.' He strode off after Miss Niela Aden, his early morning calm rapidly disappearing.

Inside the building, his eyes dimmed, adjusting to the light. The lounge – if it could be called such – was full of soldiers and construction workers. He looked towards the toilets, momentarily nonplussed. He wasn't used to being ignored. Where the hell had she gone? Suddenly a female figure emerged from a doorway to his left. He blinked in surprise. Gone were the jeans and thin tank top that made her look as though she were off to Ibiza for the weekend. Instead she was dressed in a full-length pale blue *dirac*, the loose, diaphanous garment that unmarried women in Djibouti usually wore. She looked indistinguishable from any one of the hundreds of women he'd passed every day – if you didn't look too closely, that was. Even in her *dirac*, her delicate beauty was hard to hide. He wasn't the only one to have noticed either. A group of French soldiers were staring open-mouthed at her. He suppressed a small gesture of annoyance. A beautiful young woman at Camp Lemonier was the *last* thing he needed. He turned on his heel and walked back out into the sunlight. The others were still waiting uncertainly for him.

'Right. Let's get a move on. It's about a half-hour drive to the base. The car's over there. You'd better sit in front,' he said to Nancy as they picked up their bags. She was twice the size of anyone else. Within five minutes of driving off, however, he wished he'd stuffed her into the boot instead. She settled herself into the seat like an old hen, clucking in consternation at every goat, shepherd or nomad they passed in a cloud of dust. He was peripherally aware of Niela Aden, who sat directly behind him. She kept her face turned to the landscape but every now and then their eyes met in the rear-view mirror. Hers were black and inscrutable. The rocky desert slid past on either side in uninterrupted swathes of earth and dust. In front of him, the line of mountains dissolved slowly into the sky. Behind and to the right, stretching away towards the horizon, was the sea. Humps of bare-backed brown islands broke through the surface, a sandy blonde fringe here and there . . . and then everything faded into the hazy silence.

40

NIELA
Djibouti, December 1996

Through the swollen convex dome of the window, the silky blue fabric of the sea tilted gently from side to side as the little plane touched down. Niela's face was pressed flat against the glass. She was back in Africa, back home. The dusty brown mountains scored a jagged line across the horizon before disappearing into the haze. There was a brief announcement in Arabic, French and English and then the plane juddered to a halt. The doors were flung open on to an afternoon already filled with heat. Niela unfastened her seat belt and stood up. There were six other people on the flight from Addis – three of them were co-workers, sent from different offices and departments in various capacities to assist on the same project. The others were official-looking men in suits. What, she wondered to herself as she hauled down her backpack, could bring a man in a suit to this part of the world?

She followed the others off the plane, holding on to the already hot metal handrail for support. It had been a long journey – two and a half hours from London to Rome; a six-hour wait at Fiumicino followed by an eight-hour flight to Addis Ababa and then a changeover into a small plane for the final leg of the journey to Djibouti. Her legs felt wobbly as she stepped once more on to solid ground. They walked across the blistering tarmac towards the collection of small buildings that was the airport, most of them gasping in the heat. 'Oh, my,' drawled the tall, overweight blonde who'd introduced herself as Nancy as they drew level with the man who'd clearly been sent to meet them. 'It's the Marlboro Man.'

Niela followed her gaze. Standing in the shadow cast by the remains of a fluttering sunshade was a tall, lean man, dressed in jeans and a faded T-shirt. He was holding a small cup of espresso in one hand and an unlit cigarette in the other. As they drew near and Nancy pushed her way forwards, he tucked the cigarette carefully behind his ear in a gesture that brought the men at home sharply to mind. In that part of her brain that still noticed such things, she slowly took stock of a dark, wild beauty. He was olive-skinned, with intense eyes that flickered over them all in turn, coming to rest on her with a momentary flicker of impatience. She looked up into his face; in the bright glare of daylight, she noticed that his eyes held hair-thin splinters of hazel sunburst in the iris, like lights left burning in a room. He was full of light; it emanated from beneath the surface of his skin, spilling out of his pores. She looked away, moment-arily taken aback. She'd never seen anyone like him. When he spoke, his words were clipped and terse. The impatience she'd read in his face was there in his voice. 'It's a Muslim country,' he said sharply, once the introductions had been made. 'In case you hadn't noticed.' She felt her hackles rise immediately. Did he think her stupid? She turned away from him and marched off, not wanting to cause a scene. When she came back, dressed in her *dirac*, she saw she'd angered him further. She felt a sneaky pinprick of triumph. It surprised her. She'd barely spoken three words to the man and already there was an undercurrent of animosity between them that she'd never experienced before, with anyone. She climbed into the back of the vehicle, leaving Nancy Shore to sit next to him. She kept her face averted, studying the landscape – every now and then, however, their eyes bumped and met, sending a spark of an unknown, electric emotion flowing through her. By the time they drew up outside the camp, she was thoroughly and completely unsettled.

The camp itself was sparse – a few whitewashed bungalows over-looking the sea, a slightly larger one-storey building that was the office and a collection of what must once have been servants' quarters at the back. There was a yard with a drying line strung between two poles and an outside sink. Josh led them to one of the bungalows. 'You'll all be in here,' he said, pushing open the door. A narrow corridor with rooms leading off to one side and a mosquito net door that banged to and fro with the wind. 'I'll get that fixed,' he said, looking up at the hinges. 'They're all the same. Pretty much standard camp fare, I'm afraid. Toilets and showers in here.' He pushed open a door to show them. 'There's a small kitchen at the end of the corridor, but most of the cooking's done in the main building. You'll find a fridge and maybe a kettle, but not much else. Let me know if there's anything you desperately need.'

Niela looked around the room he'd shown her. It was small, with a single bed and a mosquito net tucked up around its frame. There was a rickety desk in one corner with an old chair whose stuffing had spilled out of its seat. She put her rucksack down on the ground and walked over to the window. She could hear Nancy's complaints through the half-open door. *There's no bedside light? Where can I get a pair of heavier curtains? We have to share the bathroom? No way!* She listened for Josh Keeler's response – there was none. It didn't surprise her.

At dinner that evening, Josh was nowhere to be seen. Niela sat with the others, listening with half an ear to their rambling mixture of complaints and anecdotes, and surrendered herself to the sounds of the night. The cicadas were a soft, slow murmur; the occasional high-pitched squeak of a cricket or an owl pierced the blackness; once or twice the harsh, staccato bark of a dog. The night sky was a thick lid, so close to the ground it enveloped them. She pushed up the sleeves of the *dirac*, enjoying the sensation of heat on bare arms that was particular to tropical Africa, the seamless merging of the body in space that occurs when internal and external temperatures match; no awareness of the world as separate from her skin. The woman who cooked for them was an Afar, one of the nomads of the region. If she was surprised to see a dark-skinned, Somali-speaking face amongst the foreigners, she didn't show it. As soon as she was able, Niela excused herself from the group and walked back along the corridor in the semi-darkness. She stripped off her clothes, switched off the light and lay down on the bed. The fan circled lazily above her head, sending an occasional waft of marginally cooler air across her body. Within minutes, despite the unsettled nature of their arrival, she was fast asleep.

In the morning, a piercing bar of sunlight came to rest across her eyelids, forcing her awake. It was hot in the small room; she was uncomfortably aware of the sheet sticking to her body. She picked up her watch – it was just after 6.30 a.m. She pushed the sheet aside impatiently and got out of bed. She wrapped her *kikoi* around her, grabbed her washbag and opened the door. The corridor was silent and empty. She padded barefoot along to the bathroom. She showered quickly, dressed and headed back down the corridor towards the dining room.

Josh Keeler was sitting at one of the tables on the terrace, reading a newspaper, when she walked in. There was no one else about. He looked up briefly as she entered, nodded curtly but said nothing. She poured herself a cup of coffee and slid into a seat at one of the other tables. She looked out across the flat, empty plains towards the sea. From their position halfway up the mountain, everything was laid before them. Presently, one by one, her colleagues began to emerge from their rooms, looking, if anything, worse than they had the night before. 'The heat,' Nancy muttered weakly as she collapsed into a chair, mopping ineffectually at her brow. 'I just didn't think it would be so damned *hot.*' Niela caught Josh's incredulous expression and quickly glanced away. She didn't want another reminder of the electricity that flowed over her every time she looked into his face. She made a quick mental note to steer clear of him, at all costs. There was an impatient, flammable anger welling under his skin, like oil beneath the surface of the earth. She sensed it and feared it simultaneously. She wanted nothing to do with it. She would do whatever was necessary to get the job done, nothing more.

Although she'd irritated him when they first met, by the end of their first couple of days working together, Josh was forced to admit there was more to Niela Aden than met the eye. She was good at her job, for one thing. She had a calm stillness about her that defused tension even before it arose. By the time they'd wound up negotiations for the supply of masons and carpenters for the first phase of the job, she'd won everyone over, even the grumpy tribal elders who'd viewed her with outright suspicion as soon as she approached. A woman? And a young, beautiful one at that? But she knew exactly how to handle them, a curiously deft mixture of deference and – dare he say it? – flirtation. She teased them a little, flattered them when necessary and put her foot down when she felt she had to. He watched her, slightly unnerved. It certainly wasn't his way – he was used to giving out commands and orders and was baffled by the stubborn resistance he'd encountered amongst these men. They were different. They listened to him with polite disinterest, their eyes anywhere but on him, and as soon as he was out of sight went back to doing things their way, not his. He'd been in Djibouti almost two months and to his immense frustration had achieved little. He couldn't understand it. He hadn't even been able to organise the men into work teams. There seemed to be no end to the number of people he had to consult before anything could happen. This one's uncle, that one's father-in-law, this one's cousin . . . the village chief, the headman, the elders, the clan. Christ, he'd worked in Bosnia with Mafioso of every description – Chechen, Bosnian, Russian, Moldavian . . . and somehow managed. But here in Djibouti, he was baffled. He was unable to solve even the simplest problems because he just couldn't anticipate them. Niela Aden's arrival changed all that. She moved amongst them with ease, as if she'd been there all her life. In a way, she had. As he watched her work, it struck him again and again how arbitrary most of the borders in this part of the world were. French Somaliland had turned into the French Territory of the Afars and the Issas, which in turn had become the Republic of Djibouti. They were the same people, give or take a line in the sand or two. No wonder she looked as though she was at home. She was.

On the Friday at the end of their first week, just as he was walking back to his room, he came upon her sitting on the low wall of the abandoned bungalow overlooking the sea, where he'd noticed she sometimes went at the end of the day. Without intending to, he found himself walking up to her. The sky was losing its searing whiteness and the rocky desert in front of them was beginning to turn blush-pink. Out in the Gulf of Tadjoura, the waters had stilled. The sea was stretched taut, pegged here and there to the islands. A group of labourers they'd just been working with suddenly unrolled prayer mats and bowed their heads towards Mecca. He stopped for a moment to watch them rising and sinking, the soles of their feet a dusty yellow as their prayers rose up around him, a collective groan of supplication and release, their words carried away on the wind. He moved on, towards her. She turned as he approached, but said nothing. He caught it again – that curious mixture of calm and energy that emanated from her whenever he was near.

'How long have you been doing this job?' he asked suddenly. He noticed she waited until the men had finished praying before replying.

'Not very long,' she said with a faint smile. 'It's actually my first assignment.'

'You're very good at it.' The words were out before he could even think about them. She said nothing, but looked up at him, a quizzical expression in her eyes, as if she didn't quite believe him. 'No, really. I mean it.

You know how to work with these people. Not many of the interpreters I've come across can do that.'

She shrugged. 'They're my people,' she said simply. 'We understand each other.'

'Do you still have family down here?'

'No.' She didn't elaborate. She turned the length of her profile away from him, looking out to sea. He was aware that there was more to the statement than she was prepared to give away, at least for now, and it came as something of a surprise to him that he was prepared to wait. He said goodbye and walked slowly back to his quarters, his brows knitted together in a frown of concentration. He would have to be careful with her, he realised, although strangely, he wasn't altogether displeased by the revelation. She touched him but he had no idea why.

Niela watched Josh walk away and disappear into the building where his room lay. He walked with a slow, graceful swagger, his tall, lean body completely at ease with everything around him, including himself. She was intrigued by him. After a week of working alongside him, she began to sense something else beneath the surface of his impatience. There was an intuitive compassion in him that seemed to be at odds with his brusque nature. It was clear he was good at his job. The men who worked under him respected him; she could see it in the way they looked at him or listened to him. Within a day or two, she saw that he would have eventually managed on his own, even without language . . . he was acutely aware of the subtle imbalance in power between them and he tried, wherever he could, to redress it. He had a way of asking a question that was really a provocation, which delighted them, especially the older men. After decades of being shouted at or worse, they seemed to appreciate the respect he accorded them and they returned it tenfold. And although she'd yet to see it directed at her, there was an extraordinary charm at work beneath the tight-lipped exterior and the barely controlled rage. She listened to him joke once or twice with someone whose grasp of English or French was sufficient for them to properly communicate – he had a dry, quick sense of humour and when he smiled, his whole face lit up, utterly transformed. A deep coppery glow travelled up from underneath the V of the T-shirts he wore every day, lighting his neck and face. There was a line of paler skin at his biceps where the sun hadn't reached, and every now and then she caught a glimpse of his torso as he stretched for something or jumped up on to the scaffolding, the wind tugging at his T-shirt. The almost feminine whiteness of his skin there startled her.

Now, after the brief exchange, which couldn't have lasted more than a minute or so, she sensed a shift in him towards her that she couldn't quite put her finger on. She had the sense that getting any closer to Josh Keeler would be like coming close to a flame. There was a warmth in him that she'd only just begun to see, but it was the sort of warmth that would, given the slightest chance, burn. Yes, better to keep a distance. Safer that way.

41

She was eating lunch alone the following day on the terrace overlooking the bay. The sun was blinding. The only point of colour in the bleached, arid landscape was the sea. She had just poured herself a second cup of coffee when she saw Josh walk out of his building and make his way across the yard towards her.

'I'm going into town for supplies,' he announced without preamble. 'Want to come?' She looked up at him, hurriedly swallowed a mouthful of coffee, and nodded wordlessly. 'I'll leave in about five minutes. Can you be ready?'

She nodded again. 'Sure. I'll just get my bag,' she said, getting up from her seat. He nodded without saying anything and turned on his heel.

He hardly talked as he drove away from the camp, but it didn't bother her. She turned her head to look out of the window. It was the first time she'd left the camp's confines since she'd arrived. The horizon was still and empty; it was scored across the dashboard like a slash. The hills were dotted with hard-edged boulders, glinting white in the sunlight. They changed slowly in form and aspect as the car advanced, then left them behind. There wasn't a single car travelling in the opposite direction. Aside from the odd goat-herder who looked up curiously as the car sped past, there was no one else on the road. Niela glanced at Josh's hands on the wheel. Strong, capable hands, she noticed. She let her eyes wander up the length of his forearm. It was covered in fine, silky brown hair. The sun had ripened his skin like fruit; there was an olive graininess to him that seemed very un-English to her. He wore a ragged woven bracelet on one wrist of the kind that she'd worn for a couple of months as a teenager. The kind you gave to your best friend in high school. The colours were faded. She found herself wondering briefly who'd given it to him. The vehicle gave a sudden soft shudder as they skirted over a pile of loose rocks, reminding them of the inhospitable terrain outside. 'There's water on the back seat.' Josh spoke suddenly. 'If you're thirsty.'

'Thanks.' She turned her head to look out of the window again. The landscape was almost lunar. Nothing around them but blackened volcanic rock, bleak sweeps of mountainsides, not a single tree. Far below in the bay, the choppy blue sea was puckered with rippling white waves, visible even at that distance. Cocooned in the air-conditioned interior, it was hard to fathom the heat outside. 'What d'you need to buy?' she asked after a while.

'Building supplies. Some nails and screws, a bit of rope. We're almost finished with the septic tanks but I want to put in an extra water tank before we start on the huts.'

'How long is it all going to take? The whole camp?'

'Depends. If I get the labour I need, another couple of months. There's Ramadan next week, though, and that always slows things down. I'll be glad when it's over. Fasting in this heat is hard.'

'You fast?' she asked, surprised.

'Of course.'

'I haven't fasted for years,' she said after a moment. 'I don't know why. I . . . I forget, I guess.'

'Easier to forget about Ramadan in London. Can't do that here.'

'You were in Morocco before this, right? You have the accent. I can hear it when you speak Arabic.'

He turned his head to look at her briefly. 'That's the longest sentence I've heard you say,' he said, smiling faintly.

'Well, you hardly talk much either,' she said mildly. 'Whereabouts in Morocco were you?'

'Smara. Close to the border with Western Sahara.'

'And before that?'

'Bosnia.'

'Why?' She drew her legs up under her.

'Why what?'

'Why those places? You're an architect, aren't you? Why go there?'

He gave a short laugh. 'Architects aren't supposed to work in places like that?'

'Well, I haven't met any architects who do.'

'More's the pity,' he said drily. 'Camps are human settlements. That's what we're trained to provide. You can't leave it to bureaucrats. Like our friend Nancy, for example.'

She nodded slowly. 'You're right, I suppose. We're so used to thinking about camps as temporary measures, you forget that some of them have been around longer than many towns.'

She felt his gaze shift towards her. 'Exactly. Where's home for you?'

'London. I've been there four years now.'

'And your family? I asked you before but you didn't really answer.'

She was quiet for a moment. 'They live in Vienna. I had an uncle living there. We went when the war broke out.'

'Why did you go to London?'

She didn't answer but turned her head towards the window again. The figure of a woman appeared slowly in the distance, distinguishable by her brightly coloured garb, but Niela's measure of distance was warped and they came upon her too suddenly. She herded a small flock of goats and raised her stick as they passed, in greeting or protest, Niela couldn't tell. She turned back to Josh. He didn't press her at all. She liked that about him. She took a deep breath. There was only one person she'd ever spoken to about Hamid, and that was Anna. She had no idea why she felt she could tell this man, a complete stranger and someone whom she would never see again once her job here was ended. But she could. At least part of it. 'A marriage,' she said finally. 'An arranged marriage.'

'Ah. You escaped it?'

She nodded slowly. 'The usual story. You know how it goes.'

'No, I don't. What happened?' he asked, and his voice was gentle.

To her horror, she found her eyes flooded with tears. She struggled to contain the wave of sadness that surged inside her. Just as before, he was patient, giving her the time and space to respond – or not, if she chose. She took another deep breath, hoping her voice was steady. 'I wasn't prepared for it. It wasn't the way I'd been brought up. My father is . . .' she stumbled over the words, '*was* modern. We . . . I went to an international school, I was going to go to university, normal stuff. But the war changed everything. We left with nothing.' She paused for a second, remembering her mother's words. She didn't know why, but she didn't want Josh to think badly of them. 'I think they thought it was the best they could do for me.'

'But presumably *you* didn't think so?'

She shook her head. 'No. He . . . he was much older than me. A distant relative.'

'So you ran away instead?'

'Yes. To London.'

'That takes some nerve. And now here you are, rolling around Djibouti in a Land Cruiser with a complete stranger.'

'You're not a stranger. A bit distant, perhaps.' The words slipped out without her thinking. She was surprised. She was responding to something in his tone that she couldn't place; the tenor of their conversation kept shifting. Flirtation? He hardly seemed the type. No, it wasn't flirtation. It was stronger than that, yet less. She was suddenly unsure of herself.

He laughed. 'Distant. Well, you're not the first to accuse me of it, you know.'

'It's not an accusation,' she said sharply, partly to cover her confusion. 'It doesn't bother me. I don't care how . . . no, not that, I just meant . . .'

'I know what you meant,' he said quietly.

Niela looked at him uncertainly. She was moved by his quiet assertion, but before she could say anything further, the vehicle began to slow down. They were approaching a roadblock, the first of several before the city began. '*Salaam alaikum.*' Josh kept a hand on the gear stick as he passed their documentation through the window to the bored-looking soldier. The officer peered at them curiously through the window.

'Your wife?' he asked.

'*Aiwa.*' Yes. It was simpler that way.

'OK.' He handed back their passports and slapped the roof of the car. They drove on in cautious silence.

The town was busy. It was the last Saturday before Ramadan and the shops were full of people. Josh wound his way through the narrow, pot-holed streets and finally pulled up in front of a long row of arcades, outside a shop with a bright green banner. *Ali Hassan & Sons, Purveyors of Building Supplies.* He glanced at Niela. She was sitting upright, looking around her with interest. She was wearing a light pink *dirac* that was tucked up around her knees. Her feet were still up on the dashboard; dark red toenails, he noticed. Sexy. Her bare leg was smooth and dark without a single blemish. He stopped himself quickly. 'Coming?' he asked. She nodded and opened the door.

'*Ahlan*,' he called out as he walked through the arcade and stepped through the doorway of Ali's shop.

'Joshua! *Al-Hamdulillah*!' Ali came through from the back of the shop, wiping his hands. They exchanged the traditional greeting and sat down. Josh saw from Niela's expression that she noticed and approved of the way he put his left hand on his lower right arm when they shook hands and the way he adopted the correct position on the floor. He couldn't have said why it pleased him. What did he care? In a fortnight she'd be gone.

Ali's wife interrupted them, bringing tea. She served Josh first as was their custom – he was the male guest in their home. He avoided looking at her – she was another man's wife, after all – and drained the glass in two gulps so that she could rinse it and serve the others. He liked the rituals of the culture here; slower-paced, more gracious than the back-slapping intimacy of Westerners that usually petered into nothingness. Niela chatted to Ali's wife in their language in a low tone, her face partially turned from his. He saw from Ali's expression that he was confused by her presence. But there was no time to dwell on it or explain. He had supplies to collect and he wanted to get back to the base well before nightfall.

It took them almost an hour to find what he needed and load the vehicle. There was one last handshake, a flurry of goodbyes and *salaams*, and then they were finally off. There were a few American soldiers in town, he noticed, conspicuous in their bulky camouflage uniforms and mirrored Ray-Bans. There were others, too, in khaki shorts and starched shirts.

'Who're they?' Niela asked him, pointing to a group standing by the side of the road.

'*Légion Étrangère*. The French Foreign Legion. They've been here since the sixties.'

'You seem to know a lot about Djibouti.'

'Might as well know what you're getting into.' He swung out into the flow of cars. It was almost 4 p.m. and the traffic was already starting to thicken. 'I just need to stop by one more place,' he said, turning the vehicle down one of the side roads. 'Ali didn't have any steel wire. I won't be a minute.'

The road was narrow and even more potholed than the one they'd just left. The vehicle swayed alarmingly from side to side; Niela was thrown against him as he swerved to avoid plunging into a man-sized crater. There was a tiny frisson of electricity as their bodies touched; she jerked backwards as though she'd been hit. 'Sorry, shit road,' he murmured. She said nothing but he noticed that her fingers went to the spot on her arm where they'd touched, almost as if she'd been hurt. Up ahead of them the traffic had come to a halt. He slowed the vehicle and rolled the window down, sticking his head and shoulders out to get a better look. A low, rumbling sound could be heard behind them, growing louder by the second.

'What's going on?'

He pulled himself back into the car. 'Can't really tell. There's some sort of roadblock up ahead.' A solid wall of cars had piled up quickly behind them. 'It should pass soon enough. If I don't get the wire today I'll—' His voice was cut off abruptly by an earth-shattering boom that ricocheted off the walls around them. They looked at each other warily. There was a deafening silence, then a sudden change in the fabric of sound, a distant shuddering, the sound of air being sucked up and thrown out in waves. They stared at each other, too surprised to speak. Ahead of them, all the way down the slight incline, people were beginning to get out of their cars. Some were pointing to the sky. A thick plume of black smoke drifted slowly upwards; the source was some distance away. 'What the . . . ?' Josh muttered, killing the engine and opening the door. A second, equally ear-splitting 'whumpf' hit the air. People started to run back up the street, streaming towards them. The shuddering noise grew closer, up in the sky. A high-pitched, deafening, thudding vibration in their ears. It roared overhead. 'It's a helicopter,' he shouted above the noise, pointing towards the sky. 'I think there's been some sort of attack.' Another boom split the air, followed immediately by another. People were screaming now, shoving and jostling one another, streaming past in all directions. Josh didn't hesitate. He yanked open the passenger door and grabbed Niela by the arm. The scudding, whirling noise was almost directly above them. Within seconds, the street had turned to bedlam.

She felt herself being pushed this way and that, her body shoved up against the tide of people trying to run from whatever it was that lay ahead. They were buffeted on all sides; Josh ran counter to the crowd, forcing his way through shoulders, arms, backsides, pushing against the great wave of fear streaming towards them. His grip was unwavering. A racket of blows shook the sky; screams of terror rose into the air. Niela's heart was pumping furiously, all sensation in her body concentrated on the spot where Josh's fingers gripped her arm. She followed him blindly. Somewhere in the distance she could hear the unmistakable rat-tat-tat of machine-gun fire, a sound she remembered well. A woman rushed past, shrieking, a child pressed to her breast, disappearing into the folds of her *dirac*. They came to a crossroads. There was a narrow alleyway between the shops. 'Follow me,' Josh barked. She plunged after him. He ducked; she followed. He turned once, twice. He seemed to know where he was going. Down, down a flight of stairs, running, her lungs almost exploding. His grip held her fast, almost pulling her arm out of its socket. They jumped across a ditch – there was the tangy, acrid smell of urine and spilled beer – and then he turned down yet another alleyway. He stopped for a second, looked left and right again, his hand still on her arm; she could feel his heartbeat thudding in his palm.

Suddenly the rising shriek of a police car sounded behind them, left or right, impossible to tell. With a single, wordless impulse they both scrambled up over the nearest wall and dropped down into a yard where a thin brown dog tethered to a post snarled hysterically at them. Niela only just managed to suppress a muffled shriek before Josh kicked open the nearest door and dragged her inside. He slammed it shut behind them and they collapsed against it, panting, too exhausted to speak. It was dark inside; a fanlight high above their heads let in a shaft of light that came to rest on a mound of sacks. Rice, she noted dully against the rapid-fire beat of her heart. They were in some sort of storeroom. Her arm was squeezed bloodless where Josh had held it. He released her; her fingers went automatically to the place where his had been. There was no sound in the small room other than their own jagged, raspy breath. Even the whirring helicopters had fallen silent. They stood there amongst the rice sacks and crates of bottled drinks, panting, too out of breath to speak.

'What d'you think happened?' Her whisper was unnaturally loud in the gloom. He looked at her, then at his watch. It was almost five. They'd been hiding for thirty minutes. It was hot and airless and he longed for a cigarette. Outside the door, the dog barked intermittently.

'I don't know. A demonstration of some sort that went wrong. Those were US helicopters.'

'Firing into the crowd?' Her voice was disbelieving.

'It won't be the first time it's happened,' he said humourlessly. 'Or the last.'

She sat down heavily on one of the sacks and hugged her knees to her chest. 'Yes, it happened in Mogadishu too. But the demonstrators brought the helicopters down. They shot—' She stopped, unwilling or unable to go on. There was fear in her voice now.

He looked down at her. She held her eyes wide open, as if she were afraid to cry. He felt something inside him give way suddenly, a quick surge of emotion he couldn't contain. He knelt down and put a hand out, touching her arm where he'd grabbed her earlier. 'I'm sorry,' he said hoarsely. 'Did I hurt you?' She shook her head but her fingers closed over his. He moved closer, bringing his face level with hers. His hand went up around her head, bringing it down into the space between his chin and his shoulder. He could feel the surrender in her body as she sank against him. He made some perfunctory sound of comfort, of the kind he'd used countless times before, though never in circumstances like these. She was shaking. Her teeth were chattering, despite the heat. He pressed his lips against her hair. 'Hey,' he murmured. 'It's OK. We're safe here.' She nodded but said nothing, pressing her face further into his shoulder. He breathed in the smell of her hair – its cloudy perfumed mass filled his nostrils – and his fingers sank into it of their own accord. In disbelief at himself he felt the stirrings of desire in him. His hand slid from her hair, coming to rest on the side of her neck. He put a hand under her chin and turned her face towards him. She made no protest at all. Astonished at his own boldness and the absurdity of their situation, he drew her towards him and kissed her. Her mouth was warm and sweet, tasting faintly of the tea they'd drunk at Ali's. He broke the kiss to look at her; her face was a concentration of eyes and teeth in the last remnants of light, and he was suddenly overtaken by the sort of desire he hadn't felt in years. In his mind's eye he saw again the smooth, chocolate-coloured skin of her legs, the painted toenails, the tiny hollow at the base of her neck and the faint beads of sweat on her upper lip that must taste salty on the tongue – countless details he'd taken in without even noticing in the fortnight she'd been around. She'd been on his mind, he realised, ever since she'd stepped away from him and walked into the airport building that first day, the day of their arrival.

His hand slid down her arm and stopped at the hem of the pink *dirac*. He touched it – a question? She nodded, and he placed his hand on her knee, sliding round to feel the soft, warm skin underneath. He shifted his weight so that they faced each other. He pushed the *dirac* up around her thighs – another question? She answered by allowing him to pull it away from her and slip it over her head. It was too dark inside the storeroom to see her, but his hands told him all he needed to know. She was all smooth, damp skin, firm to the touch. Her breasts were soft and full; touching them brought a sharp gasp of pleasure from her that ran through him like fire. He was gentle with her, sensing a shyness that had as much to do with her as it did with the culture from which she came. The same quiet stillness that he'd come to depend on as she worked beside him turned him on more powerfully than anything he'd ever encountered. He felt his way slowly into her body, remembering to ask her if it was all right – stupid question! She didn't answer but he felt her whole body arch, taut as a bow, just before he was properly inside her. He gave a muffled groan, sinking deeper into her, burying his face in her hair as his body began to race away from him. He brought a small cry of pleasure from her, again and again. Nothing he had ever heard had been sweeter, or so it seemed.

She heard the soft strike of a match as he leaned away from her and lit a cigarette. The tip glowed red in the darkness. The silence around them was a thick, dark blanket. He stood up suddenly and produced a small torch from somewhere. He flashed the beam around the storeroom, seeking something. He was naked; she averted her eyes. She needn't have bothered. Without a trace of self-consciousness he walked towards the door, dragging several large rice sacks behind him. 'Thought I saw these,' he said, shoving them against the door, one next to the other. 'Good. No one'll get in.' He walked back towards her and finished his cigarette before squatting down beside her. 'We'll stay until daybreak. I'll go out and see if I can find the car as soon as it's light.' He ran a finger lightly down her stomach. 'Think you can manage to sleep?' She nodded, too embarrassed to speak. She tried to cover herself with her *dirac*, but it was too hot. She was unsure of herself – should she move away from him, turn to one side? He seemed to have no such doubts. His hand lay where he'd left it on her lower abdomen, loosely connected to her body. Through her lashes she caught glimpses of him – the strong, swollen curve of biceps, the sheen of tanned skin across his shoulders, even the dark tufts of hair under his arms. Her body ached; a deep ache that brought a hot, sweet rush of tears to her eyes whenever she thought about what they had just done.

188

The first call to prayer woke them both just before dawn. Josh stirred, mumbled something into her hair, then sat up. In the growing light, Niela watched him put away his strong, lovely body; it disappeared in front of her into his jeans and crumpled T-shirt. She picked up her own underwear, fastened her bra with her back turned to him and slipped her *dirac* over her head. Dressed, she turned back to him. He looked at her and laid the back of his hand across her cheek, letting his fingers trail across her mouth, parting her lips. She was frozen with a mixture of desire and embarrassment – after all, it was the taste of her own body that was still on his hands. She sat very still, her whole body attuned to his touch. He stood up suddenly and walked to the door. He pulled the rice sacks away from it and opened it cautiously. There was a welcome rush of air. He beckoned to her and she stood up. They hadn't said a word to each other, but the sense of his withdrawal was strong. Something else had been buttoned up alongside his clothes. She stood waiting in the doorway, her own confusion mirrored in the confusion of his face.

42

Someone had procured a carton of tangerines, a rare luxury. 'Satsumas,' Nancy corrected smugly. She held out a couple to Niela. 'Go on, have some. When was the last time we had fruit that didn't come in a tin? Here, why'nt you take him a few?' She jerked her head in Josh's direction. It was no secret that Josh had little time or patience for the three other members of the team. 'Go on. You're the only one he talks to, anyhow.' She looked meaningfully at Niela. Niela could feel the heat spreading across her face.

'Thanks,' she said, balancing half a dozen satsumas in the scoop of her T-shirt. She walked over to where Josh was squatting on the ground, arguing mildly with one of the masons as he pointed out mistakes in the low wall. He broke off as she approached, squinting up at her. 'Here,' she said, holding out a couple. 'The others thought you might like some.' She offered one to the wizened old mason, who wrinkled his brow up at her, then took the fruit, holding it delicately between earth-coarsened hands. '*Shukran,*' he said, slipping it into the folds of his robe.

'*Shukran,*' Josh repeated with a quick grin. His face lit up. She held her breath. He stood up and tore off the rind with his teeth, releasing the pungent acidity into the air. She caught it on the back of her throat and to avoid her confusion, picked one up and bit into it herself. The old mason stood up and wandered off, sensing there was a break to be had. Niela sat down on the wall, facing Josh, suddenly conscious of the curve of her legs in her jeans.

'Thanks for yesterday,' Josh said after a moment. He'd asked for her help in making the electricians rip out one of the circuits they'd installed. He wanted them to redo it until he was satisfied. He was forever getting people to do things a second or third time, the head electrician had grumbled, though not without humour.

She smiled. 'I'm sure I got some of the terms wrong. They're probably installing beakers, not breakers.'

'I doubt it. Hamzeh knows exactly what he's doing. He's just trying to make a little on the side, that's all. Christ, *I* would.'

'Would you really?' she asked curiously.

'Of course. D'you know how many dependants he has?'

She shook her head. 'A couple of wives?' She hazarded a guess.

'Thirteen. His wives, their relatives, distant family.' It was his turn to shake his head. He looked out across the rocky landscape to the north. 'He had nine children. Imagine. In a place like this. How the hell d'you get enough from the earth to feed nine children?'

'It's not about numbers, it's about insurance,' Niela said simply. 'One of those nine will look after him and his wives in their old age. At *least* one.'

'But they don't, that's the problem. They all leave. He doesn't have a single child left here, did you know that? They're all gone. To the city, abroad, God knows where.'

Niela looked at him uncertainly. 'But that's how it's always been,' she said. 'You can't expect them to change things overnight.'

'No, not overnight. But if they don't, what's the alternative? Hamzeh's one of the lucky ones. He's found work. How many of the others who live around here can say the same? *That's* the tragedy of these wars, Niela. Not the camps or the loss of life or the pointless work we do.'

She gave a start at the sound of her name. 'So why do it if it's so pointless?' she asked, sensing there was something else he wanted to say but wouldn't.

'Why not? Someone's got to.'

'Doesn't have to be you.'

'Then who?' He looked at her squarely. To her surprise, she felt her temper begin to rise.

'We're quite capable of looking after ourselves,' she said tartly. 'We've been doing it for a while.'

'Oh, come off it. You lot? You know as well as I do . . . hey, where are you going? *Hey!*'

Without even thinking, she'd got to her feet. A sudden rage had blown up inside her, bewildering in its intensity. Exactly as it had been the first day she met him, he'd annoyed her so much that she couldn't think straight. She walked off.

But this time, he followed her. 'Niela! Come on, I didn't mean it like that . . .'

'Leave me alone,' she muttered, too angry to speak.

'No.' He caught up with her and grabbed hold of her hand. Out of the corner of her eye she was aware of her colleagues watching them, avidly speculating, no doubt. He forced her to a halt, turning her round to face him. 'I'm sorry. It came out the wrong way.'

'How else was it supposed to come out? Pityingly? Is that any better?'

'I just meant . . .'

'I know exactly what you meant. D'you think me stupid as well?'

'No, of course I don't. That's not what I'm saying . . .'

'Then what *are* you saying?' There was an angry silence as they glared at each other. His face was dark with some emotion she couldn't follow – not anger, though there was that too. Something else . . . Her eyes widened. His hand was still holding her forearm. He released it suddenly, but before she could do or say anything further, he pulled her to him and kissed her, hard. She tried to wrench herself free but he held her fast. The smell of him flooded her senses – it was the soap-and-aftershave scent she remembered from her father as he came to the breakfast table. Her face was pressed against his chest; the hand holding her arm slowly released its grip. She felt his other hand push its way through her hair until it touched the nape of her neck. All resistance in her faded; there was only the urgency of needing him left.

'Come,' he said against her ear. They began to walk, his hand still buried under the thick tangle of her hair. Behind them, the excited chatter of her colleagues began.

It was cool and dark in his room; the shutters were drawn protectively against the sun. He kicked the door shut with the back of his heel and led her to the edge of his bed. He sat down, pulling her towards him, but she continued to stand, her whole being poised and trembling before his touch. He lifted the T-shirt and pushed his face into the hollow of her stomach. He kissed the small, hard protrusion of her navel, his tongue sliding skilfully into the crevice. He looked up at her. She understood the gesture as he intended it and felt her knees buckle underneath her. She wanted to speak but couldn't. The wetness of tears that swelled underneath her lashes was the same wetness building up inside her, down there where his fingers touched and caressed her. There was the same wild surge of pleasure as his hand reached underneath the thin cotton of her T-shirt, barely grazing the tips of her breasts, one after the other. He entered her slowly, his eyes never leaving her face. She lost herself completely, falling, falling . . . a sensation like drowning, like suffocating, but in pleasure, not pain.

He smoked after lovemaking, drawing it deep down into his lungs and expelling it slowly, watching her through half-closed eyes, his hand lying on her stomach, stroking the spot where his tongue had trailed every now and then. She lay still, all feeling concentrated in the lower half of her abdomen, the tautly held muscles still shuddering lightly under his touch. Finally, he stubbed out the cigarette. He propped himself up on one elbow to look at her, his body hidden in the bed sheet. She felt the gentle pressure of his arms around her waist. He held her like that for a moment, loosely. And then he put the palm of his hand on her hip with just the right touch, the sort of gesture that says, *stay. Wait there.* She lay there next to him, not knowing what to say, do or feel. In a fortnight's time she would be gone and they would never see each other again. A fling. That was what everyone would call it. A fling – nothing more. In exactly the same way he'd put away his body, he would put this away from him too. But *she* couldn't, wouldn't ever be able to. For a brief, giddy moment when she'd held him in her arms, he'd yielded completely and she had the sense that she'd been allowed into that place in him that in every other circumstance he kept hidden, guarded against. It dazzled her, but it also left her famished for more.

43

JULIA
London, January 1997

'Well, well, well. If it isn't Little Miss Julia Burrows. Heard you were here.' The disembodied voice came from behind her. Julia stopped dead in her tracks. The sound of his voice sent a tremor of dislike rippling up her spine. *Little* Miss Julia Burrows! Aaron Keeler. Who else?

She turned carefully, holding on to her armful of books. 'Oh, it's you. Yes, I heard your mother had got you a job.' She saw from the way he flinched that she'd scored a point. 'Now, if you don't mind,' she said icily, 'I've got a lot to do.' She tried to step around him but her pile obscured her view.

'Oh, don't let me stop you.' His voice was equally icy.

'Don't worry, you won't,' Julia tossed out over her shoulder as she walked off down the corridor, resisting the temptation to turn around and fling a book at his head. Urgh! She clenched her jaw as she punched the lift button. Time had done nothing to diminish the tension between them. She prayed she would have next to nothing to do with him. She jabbed the lift button again impatiently, wishing it was his head. Or his eye. Either one, she wasn't fussy.

For the next few days it seemed as though her prayer had actually come true. Aside from catching the odd glimpse of him at the end of a corridor, they didn't run into each other again. Julia was relieved. By the end of the week, she was able to push open the front door without thinking about whether or not he'd be on the other side.

She was just beginning to relax when one Monday morning, Harriet Peters dropped a bombshell on her. She'd stopped by Julia's office to discuss their upcoming case review, which was scheduled to take place on Wednesday. Even though it was still technically Harriet's case, it would be the very first time Julia would present her own research and arguments. Aaron Keeler had been invited, Harriet informed her, along with Gerald Starkey and a couple of other senior partners. It would be a good opportunity for her to impress them.

'Aaron Keeler? What the hell for?' Julia asked, uncomfortably aware that her voice had risen to a squeak.

Harriet looked at her, surprised. 'It's perfectly routine,' she said, frowning. 'You'll be asked to do the same at some point in the next few months. We ask all the junior barristers to sit in on each other's cases. Besides, Keeler's a qualified solicitor . . . he'll bring a certain perspective to the case.'

Julia was silent. The thought of sitting opposite Aaron Keeler whilst she outlined her arguments was enough to make her ill. 'It's fine,' she muttered, as graciously as she possibly could. Harriet's brows lifted again but she said nothing. Julia bent her head back to her notes, cheeks flaming with outrage.

As soon as she entered the boardroom and saw him sitting there, a look of smug, self-satisfied boredom on his face, she knew the meeting wouldn't go well. She took her place at the end of the table, her heart thumping and her palms clammy with sweat. She hadn't been this nervous since Balliol. Harriet briefly outlined the case and then opened the floor to Julia. She tried not to look at Aaron as she spoke, but it was difficult. It struck her again just how much of a game it all was. Keeler *looked* the part; he *sounded* the part and therefore he *was* the part. He had all the right attributes: handsome, reasonably bright, or at least bright enough, and exceedingly well connected. It was enough; it was all he needed. The biggest difference between her and Aaron Keeler was confidence. He had too much of it; she too little.

'Julia?' Harriet was looking expectantly at her. She gave a little start. She felt her face go hot. 'Th . . . that's it,' she said lamely, losing her train of thought. She sat down abruptly, cursing herself. Now it was time for the others to speak.

'Thanks for that, Aaron. Very interesting. Well? What do you think, Julia?' Gerald Starkey leaned back in his chair as soon as Aaron had finished.

Julia had to bite down on her tongue. She was aware that her voice when she was angry had the tendency to turn shrill, and the last thing she wanted was to sound like a disgruntled housewife. She took a deep breath. Aaron was completely wrong. So what if their client's oldest daughter was emotionally involved? It was the mother who was on trial for the killing of her husband, not the daughter. It had absolutely no relevance here. From all accounts, he'd made the daughter's life hell – she would be the perfect witness. 'I think,' she said carefully, 'that Aaron is wrong. Mandy Taylor *is* emotional, it's true, but think of what she's been through. Gary Manning's abuse wasn't confined to his wife. Mandy's been through hell. I think she'll make a very strong witness.'

'Actually, I must say I think you're right, Julia.' One of the other barristers spoke up. 'I think it's a risk we can afford to take.' He looked at his colleagues.

Aaron shrugged. He smirked at Julia. '*Res ipsa loquitum.*' *The case speaks for itself.*

Julia's hackles rose. '*Qui habet aures, audiendi audiat.*' She delivered her rejoinder without batting an eyelid. *He who has ears, learn to listen.*

'Right, is there any other business?' Michael Parks broke in hurriedly. 'No? Good. Then I think that's it for this week's round-up.'

Julia left the room without looking at Aaron once. Arsehole. Just who did he think he was?

44

Her heels echoed loudly as she crossed the Great Hall on her way to the courtroom. Her stomach was churning with nerves. It would be her first audience in front of a judge. She'd spent the previous three days going over her argument, time and again. She'd practised in front of the mirror, in front of her flatmates, in front of her colleagues and friends – everyone was bored sick. She was ready. She paused just before entering the court and glanced up at the frieze above her head. *The Law of the Wise is the Fountain of Life.* Taking a deep breath, she pushed open the doors and walked in.

It began well enough. By the time Julia was ready to call Amanda Taylor as her primary witness, she was confident enough to risk a smile at the jury. But as soon as she saw Amanda's face, she began to have doubts. The girl entered the courtroom staring impassively ahead of her, as though she were afraid to look left or right. Julia glanced at her nervously. She ought to have made eye contact with her mother or with her two lawyers, surely? There was an obstinate set to Amanda's mouth that Julia hadn't noticed before. She tried to catch her eye but failed.

'Ms Taylor, if you please?' Judge Holmes looked down gravely from his position high above the proceedings. He began the familiar routine. 'Do you swear . . .'

Amanda's voice was flat and emotionless; she looked straight ahead, avoiding her mother's worried stare. Julia felt the beginnings of panic stir in her stomach. 'What's wrong with her?' whispered Chris Barnes, one of the other barristers on the case.

'I don't know,' Julia whispered back, glancing around the room. 'But something's not right.'

'She looks as though she's on drugs.'

'Shit, that's *all* I need,' Julia said grimly. She looked across the bench at the prosecution. Doug Rattery, her opposite number, appeared remarkably content. A slow burn of panic began to spread through her veins. Something was about to happen – she could feel it. She gathered her notes and approached the stand. As she did so, Amanda threw her mother a glance. Within minutes of beginning her questioning, Julia realised just what had happened. Amanda Taylor had conned her. She'd conned them all. Her expression as she looked across at her mother was one of triumph, not despair.

'I don't understand it,' Julia said when it was all over, grabbing her bag and her files and running for the doors. The press would be waiting outside – the last people in the world she felt like seeing. 'I just don't understand it!'

'When did you last speak to her?' Chris ran alongside, already out of breath.

'On Friday. There was nothing . . . *nothing*.' Julia's mind was racing. Amanda's testimony, far from being the crowning moment in her client's defence, had practically sealed the door on her fate. Her own *mother*? Julia couldn't believe it. Amanda's responses to the questions they'd rehearsed time and again were astounding. No, she'd never seen her stepfather hit her mother. No, there was no history of violence in the family. Her mother was a liar; always had been. She was cheating on her stepfather, too. She had a boyfriend. He was the one who'd hit her, more likely. Julia listened to the lies coming out of the young woman's mouth with a growing sense of incredulity and anger. It was rubbish! Utter rubbish! But *why*? Why now? Why hadn't she seen it coming? She had a brief, unwelcome glimpse of Aaron Keeler's face at the meeting that morning. *Don't mean to be a snob,* he'd said, pointing at the file Julia had laid out before them. *But these types . . . God knows what's been going on in that household. There's more to the stepfather and Amanda Taylor than meets the eye, I promise you.* She felt positively nauseous as she crossed the Great Hall in the opposite direction and headed for the barristers' entrance. With any luck the bulk of the press would be outside the main doors. Aaron had been right. But how the hell could he have known? And how had *she* missed it?

A few hours later, alone in the safety of chambers, Julia still didn't get it. She'd turned down all offers to join the rest of her team at the pub across the road from the Old Bailey and instead walked back to her office. She shut the door and leaned against it for a minute, fighting back the urge to cry. Three weeks' worth of work wasted. On a silly, immature young woman with a crush on her stepfather . . . or worse. The truth would eventually come out, Julia knew, but at that moment, she couldn't even bring herself to think about the reasons for Amanda Taylor's abrupt about-turn. She shrugged off her jacket and kicked off her shoes. She reached behind her desk for the bottle of Château Faugères that Dom had given her on his last visit and picked up a glass. She sank down into her chair and stared unseeing at the picture of her parents that sat to the left of her desk.

She was just about to take the first sip when there was a sharp knock at her door. She put the glass down, frowning. What *now?* It was probably Chris, in a last-ditch attempt to get her to come to the pub. She got up, crossed the room in her stockinged feet and yanked open the door. But it wasn't Chris. It was Aaron Keeler.

'Look,' he began without preamble, holding up his hands in front of his face in a mock gesture of defeat. Julia's blood pressure rose. He'd come to laugh at her. 'I know it's late—'

'What the hell do you want?' she snapped, annoyed that she'd lost the advantage of heels so that she was forced to look up at him even further.

'Nothing. I just came to see how you were. I bumped into the others in the Eagle and Chris said you were here.' He looked down at her with an expression that certainly wasn't mocking – he actually sounded sincere.

'I'm fine,' she said tightly. She pointed to the glass of wine on her desk. 'Absolutely fine. Glass of wine, crackers and cheese in the fridge.

A party, in fact. So you can trot back to the Eagle and report that to everyone, OK?'

There was a few seconds' silence as they stared at each other. 'Jesus, why are you so damned *defensive* all the time?' Aaron asked her suddenly.

Julia was momentarily taken aback. 'Defensive? *Me?*'

'Yes, you. You speak to me as if you'd rather stick a knife in me.'

'I . . . I do not.'

'Yes you do. You *know* you do. Look, if it's the whole Oxford thing you're still mad about—'

'I'm not,' Julia interrupted him quickly. She didn't like the path the conversation was taking. And she certainly didn't like standing in her almost bare feet, looking up at his hopelessly handsome face – she could have kicked herself for even *thinking* it, but there was absolutely no getting away from the fact. When he wasn't frowning or overtaken by pomposity, there was a sensual, almost feminine beauty in his face. She found herself staring at the blond hair that covered his forearms and the darker hair that escaped the collar of his shirt. He'd loosened his tie and rolled up his sleeves; standing there, one arm raised above his head, leaning against the door jamb, she almost had to put out a hand to steady herself. There was something so wonderfully reassuring about his phys-ical presence – an unexpected, sweet rush of longing to be held swept over her so forcefully that she had to turn away and walk back to her desk. Yes, he was handsome. He was also an arsehole.

'You know what I'm talking about.' To her consternation, he followed her into the room. 'I've forgotten all about it, don't worry.'

'*I* shouldn't worry?' Julia was speechless. The arrogance of the man!

'It was ages ago, Julia. Are you going to be mad at me for ever?'

The oddly plaintive note in his voice rendered her completely speech-less. She was suddenly aware of the blood pulsing in her veins, of the sound of her heart thudding as they stared at each other. Something had changed; there was a new tension in the air. He'd unsettled the space between them. She had to say something to break the silence. Some-thing. Anything. 'I . . . this isn't about Oxford,' she said quickly, her feet going to her shoes that lay beneath her desk. She slipped one foot in, then the other.

'So what *is* it all about? I *know* you can't stand me. Shit, Julia, everyone knows it. You've hardly kept it a secret.'

'I . . .' Julia's voice faltered suddenly. Now that the time had come to explain just what it was about him that set her teeth on edge, she'd lost her nerve. She who was afraid of nothing! 'It's . . .'

There was silence for a few seconds. He continued to stare at her with those deep blue, almost violet eyes. 'It's what?' he prompted gently.

To her horror, she felt the unfamiliar salty welling of tears in her throat and eyes. She put a hand up to her face, absolutely mortified at her response. She struggled to control her voice. 'I—' She stopped and turned away. She couldn't bear the thought of him seeing her cry.

It was too late. All of a sudden he was standing beside her. She sensed, rather than felt, the pressure of his hand on her shoulder. The temptation to turn and press her head against his chest was overwhelming. 'Hey,' he said quietly. 'So you lost the case. It won't be the last time, you know.' His voice was gentle. 'Even for someone like you.'

She shook her head, unable to speak. 'It's not the case,' she said at last in a strangled voice, hating herself for being so weak.

'Then what is it?' He still had a hand on her shoulder, but the touch was caring, not calculating, as if trying to gauge her mood. He turned her slowly until she was facing him. 'What is it, Julia?' he repeated, his voice sounding just above her ear. The question broke the surface of her thoughts. How could she explain? That no one had laid a hand on her shoulder in such a manner since her had father died? That she missed her parents more than she could ever put into words? That this – the office, her work, the case, her reputation – was all for the two people who would never see or hear of it? A small noise struggled in her throat. She tried to clear it, embarrassed. She was almost unable to breathe. In her confusion, she turned away from him.

He lifted his hand from her shoulder leaving an almost unbearable ache behind. 'Look, I'm sorry,' he said, also turning away. 'I didn't mean to impose—'

'It's fine,' Julia interrupted him, struggling to bring her voice under control. 'I'm fine. You're right. It was just . . . the case. Losing it like that.'

'It happens.'

She looked at him. He'd moved a few paces away. She was suddenly outside the dangerous orbit of his charm again. She nodded, trying desperately to bring her feelings back into line. He'd unleashed all sorts of unfamiliar longings in her and she had no idea how to control them, what to do. It was deeply unfamiliar territory; suddenly she was the one who was unprepared. 'I . . . I'm fine,' she stammered.

'If you say so.' His voice was neutral. He'd disappeared back into himself. He opened the door, gave her a brief, inscrutable look and then the door closed behind him. She put her hand up to her face. It was still hot and damp. She'd blown close to something she couldn't even name. She picked up her glass of wine and drained it in a single gulp.

PART FIVE

45

JULIA
London, February 1997

Just as before, in the days and weeks that followed her strange moment of intimacy with Aaron Keeler, Julia found herself inexplicably at sea. She couldn't explain it to anyone, least of all herself. Nothing had happened, yet everything had changed. She had suddenly become aware of him in the most unnerving way. Catching sight of him walking down the corridor or hearing his voice from across the table in a meeting, it felt as though the air around her had changed; a sudden drop in the barometric pressure or a temperature shift from hot to cold. He appeared oblivious, of course. He gave no indication whatsoever that anything was different. But for Julia, it was as though she'd been offered something rare and precious, only to have it snatched away again before she could take hold.

'It's awful,' she said to Dom over the phone when she simply couldn't bear thinking about it any longer. 'I don't know what's come over me. I'm being silly, I know I am. But I can't help it.'

'But you've always hated him,' Dom protested.

'I know. I still do. Well, I mean . . . I don't *hate* him, as such . . .'

'Oh come off it. You *do*. You've *always* loathed him.'

'I suppose so.'

'You *suppose* so? What the hell's come over you, Burrows? Wait, don't tell me . . . are you . . . ? Have you two . . . ?'

'Don't be silly! Of course I haven't. He just . . . we just talked the other week, after we lost the Taylor case. He stopped by my office and we just talked for a bit, that's all.'

'Burrows.' Dom's voice was firm. 'What aren't you telling me?'

'Nothing! I swear. It was just that he was different. I can't explain it.'

'Oh God. You *women*. Unbelievable. You're all the bloody same!'

'Oh, Dom,' Julia said weakly, inexplicably close to tears. 'It's not like that at all.' She reached for a tissue. She hated herself for even contemplating telling Dom – after all, *he'd* had the most monumental crush on Aaron himself for as long as she could remember. But Dom didn't seem to mind.

'Don't say I didn't warn you. Look, I've got to run. Some serf's waiting to see me about the bloody gardens. When are you coming?'

Julia suddenly longed for the expansive peace and space of Hayden Hall. 'C . . . could I come this weekend?' she asked, blowing her nose.

'You come any time you want, my love,' Dom said, his voice suddenly gentle. 'Shall I pick you up from the station?'

'Yes, please.'

'Consider it done. Come up on the early train. That way we'll have the whole of Saturday as well.'

'Th . . . thanks, Dom.'

'You look after yourself, Burrows. It's Hades you're about to enter. You know that, don't you?'

'Yes,' Julia said, her voice suddenly very small.

'Then you might as well go in prepared. You'd better talk to Mother. I'll see you on Saturday.'

'I always forget how beautiful it is here,' she said, the following Saturday, as they got out of Dom's car. She wrapped her arms around her and turned to face the gardens. 'I know I say it every time I come here, but I can't imagine what owning all of this must feel like.'

'A right pain in the arse,' Dom said, lifting her small overnight bag from the back seat. 'Come on. Mother's in residence. Father's down in London for the weekend. She's been looking forward to your visit all week.'

'Dearest Julia! How *lovely* to see you.' Lady Barrington-Browne rose as soon as they entered the drawing room. She gripped Julia's hands tightly. 'Dominic only told me you were coming on Monday. Very naughty of him. I'd have organised something, a dinner party or a luncheon at the very least.'

'Oh, Mother. That's the last thing this lovesick pup needs,' Dom said, looking at her fondly. 'And although I've told her she's allowed to speak to you, I intend to monopolise her all weekend. You can have an hour, no more, all right?' He looked at his watch. 'I'm just popping up to the cottages. I've got to see Mr McFayden about this film crew that are supposed to be coming.'

'Film crew?' Julia looked at him questioningly.

'Oh, it's too *dreadful* for words,' Lady Barrington-Browne interjected, rolling her eyes. 'Dominic seems to think it's worthwhile. Financially speaking, that is. I think it's a *dreadful* inconvenience. They're here for *weeks* on end. D'you remember the Americans last summer? My *dear*.'

'Mother.' Dom gave her a withering look. 'Do stop complaining. They pay the bills. Handsomely too, I might add. Now, I must dash. I'll be back to collect her in an hour. Make the most of it.' He winked at Julia and disappeared back through the impossibly high doorway.

Lady Barrington-Browne looked at Julia fondly. 'Do come and sit next to me, my dear. Tell me *all* about your life in London. Is it very exciting?'

Julia smiled. Lady Barrington-Browne was of the generation that regarded London as a necessary but annoying inconvenience. They had their sumptuous London townhouse, as did most of their aristocratic neighbours, but she genuinely disliked the hustle and noise of the big city. She was infinitely happier in the countryside. '*So* much more civilised, don't you think?' Julia never knew quite what to say. She'd never really been in the countryside until Dom started inviting her to Hayden. For her, it meant the occasional walk on the hills surrounding Newcastle or the odd day-trip to the beach. The idea of actually *living* in the countryside was about as foreign to Julia as Newcastle probably was to Lady Barrington-Browne. 'No, not very exciting, I'm afraid,' she said apologetically.

'No? What a shame! I was *so* looking forward to a bit of gossip. I can't stand the place myself, as you know, but one does like hearing all the tales.'

'It's mostly just work,' Julia said. 'There's no time for anything else.'

'Oh, you young things. That's all you do nowadays. Work, work, work. In my day, let me tell you, things were quite different. Shall we have tea? I'll ask Fowler to bring it up. And some scones? You look *dreadfully* peaky. Beautiful as ever, of course, but peaky. Oh my dear . . . whatever is the matter?'

To her absolute horror, Julia found she suddenly couldn't speak. Her throat was completely constricted. She put her hands to her face and shook her head. 'N-nothing,' she whispered, mortified beyond belief.

'Nothing? I think *not*. Come, my dear . . . tell me *all* about it. It's a man, isn't it? Oh dear. I thought so.'

The temptation to talk to someone – especially another woman – was overwhelming. At fifteen, Julia's relationship with her mother had just been on the cusp of changing when it had ended in the cruellest way possible. Now a fully grown woman, she missed her dreadfully. There'd been no one to turn to for advice or help, no one to share the pangs and pains of growing up, no one to talk to, and worst of all, no one to listen. Fortunately for both of them, Lady Barrington-Browne was both wise and experienced. She simply let Julia talk.

'It's quite simple, dear girl,' she said when she had finished. 'You're in love. Oh, I don't mean that you *love* him – how can you? You barely know him. But the attraction's there and that's what matters.'

'B . . . but I can't be,' Julia stammered. 'I've hated him for as long as I've known him.'

'Oh, fiddlesticks. Love, hate . . . practically the same thing if you ask me. I'm always mixing them up. No, the thing is, you've met your match. Very dangerous, especially for a woman. What you want, my dear girl, is someone considerably *weaker* than you. *If* you want an easy life. If you don't, well, that's another matter altogether . . .' She lifted her hands helplessly.

'What d'you mean?'

'Men are simple creatures, Julia. They'll try *endlessly* to persuade you otherwise, but the truth of it is, they're creatures of habit and instinct, I'm afraid. The problem lies with us. We're the ones who complicate everything. Especially your generation. The *demands*!' She put a hand to her throat. 'Impossible!'

'Wh . . . what demands?' Julia was truly bewildered.

'Oh, they've got to be *caring* as well as strong. Good at listening *and* good at talking. I read the magazines, you know, all the latest ones. The problem is, you can't have both. They're either talkers *or* listeners; very rarely will you meet a man who can do both. And yours – what's his name again? Aaron? Classic product of overachieving parents, if you ask me. Poor boy's struggling to live up to their expectations of him. What a strain. But give it time, dear girl. He'll come to his senses soon enough. All you have to do is sit tight and wait.'

'Wait? For what?'

'For him to make the next move, of course.' Lady Barrington-Browne seemed surprised at the question. 'You've got to give him time to work it out on his own. I know *you* know what's happening between the two of you. Of course you do. You're a very clever girl, Julia. But don't be *too* clever, there's a dear. Don't want to frighten him off.'

'But I'm not trying to catch him,' Julia protested.

'Of *course* you're not. What a dreadful thought. Still, from what you've said, men like Aaron don't pop up all the time, do they? Just sit tight, my dear. Now, shall I call about that tea?'

Despite laughing about the conversation later that afternoon with Dom, Julia did feel calmer after speaking to Lady Barrington-Browne.

'She's actually really perceptive,' she said to him as they walked down towards the lake at the bottom of the hill. The pale stone façade of the Great Hall dissolved in the late afternoon mist just as dusk began to waver away the cool blue surface of the lake. The air was chilly; she wound her scarf around her neck and tucked her arm into Dom's. 'I'm always surprised by her.'

'Yes, she is,' Dom agreed. 'I mean, I suspect she knew about me before even I did. Not that she'd ever say, of course.'

'Does she mind?'

Dom was quiet for a moment. 'I don't know, to be honest. I mean, yes, in the sense that she'd love to see me settle down with a nice Home Counties girl and produce tons of heirs . . . but she's always wanted me to be happy, too.'

'And are *they* happy, d'you think? Your parents?'

'Oh, they get along. I think Mother would say it's not a relevant question. She loves it here at Hayden. That's what makes her happy.'

'It all seems . . . I don't know, much simpler for them, somehow.'

'Don't you believe it. They have their problems. I just don't think they place such a premium on happiness, that's all. I mean, there's duty and responsibility and all that. Why d'you think I gave up the law? Does running Hayden House make me happy? No, not really. But it's my responsibility, and without sounding unbearably noble about it, there's some measure of satisfaction in that.'

Julia was silent. As often happened when she came to visit Dom, she felt the presence of the house and the weight of its history like someone standing behind her. She looked out across the lake to the trees beyond; the strange shyness of their friendship reasserted itself and she found herself unable to speak. Everything had turned over in the barrel of the world since her unexpected encounter with Aaron Keeler, but coming to Hayden had steadied it again. She gripped Dom's arm with a sudden uprush of affection. 'Come on. Race you to the bottom!'

46

NIELA
London, February 1997

'Mind how you go, love.' The shopkeeper smiled at her and handed over her groceries. 'Still raining, is it?'

Niela nodded. 'All day,' she said, pulling a face. 'It feels as though it'll never stop.'

'Oh, it will. Just when you think you've forgotten what the sun looks like, it'll pop up again. You'll see.'

'I hope so.' She paid for her groceries and left the shop. She opened her umbrella and hurried down the street. The shopkeeper was right, in one sense at least – she *had* forgotten what the sun looked like. It had been six weeks since her return from Djibouti and there'd been no word from Josh. Nothing. Not a single phone call or a message . . . nothing. It was as if they'd never met. As if it had never happened. Perhaps it never had? She thought with a mixture of disbelief and embarrassment of the three nights they'd spent together. Why had she imagined it would mean any more to him that that? Enjoyable, yes – his body had made that clear, even if his words hadn't. But memorable? It wasn't his fault that she'd had so little experience of the sensuality he'd managed to coax from her and that she would find it impossible to forget. 'You'd *better* forget it,' was Anna's grim advice when it became clear there would be no follow-up. 'This kind of thing can eat you up, believe me. I know. Just forget it. Forget him.' Niela had looked at her in a kind of numbed disbelief. *Forget* him? How could she? But as the days lengthened into weeks and the silence deepened, she had no choice but to conclude that Anna was right. Forget it. Forget Djibouti. Forget him.

She opened her front door. The smell of last night's meal still hung in the air. She took the groceries into the kitchen and opened the window. It was still light, despite the grey pall of rain. It was February; two more months of long nights and closed-in days. The damp, cold air curled around the windowpane. She unpacked the milk, bread and yoghurt, stowing them away in the small fridge. The flat was quiet; even the neighbours, whose noisy fights came through the walls as if they were there in the room with her, were silent. She folded the plastic bag, her movements neat and deliberate, and stowed it under the sink. She looked at the clock on the wall. It was nearly 8 p.m. Almost midnight in Djibouti. Her mind raced ahead to him out of habit. She wondered what he was doing at that very moment – was he still at the camp? She had no idea. He'd said so little about himself, where he would go or where he called home. She knew his parents lived in London but she had no idea where. After Djibouti he would probably take another contract somewhere in Africa or the Middle East. That was it. The slimmest, barest facts. Nothing to go on once he was no longer there.

She walked into the small living room and turned on the television. She needed something to distract her thoughts. It was ridiculous. She'd known him – if that was the right word – all of a month. Why should she care where he was, what he was doing, who he was doing it with? The latter thought slid into her mind unawares, making her wince. Was he with someone else? Someone new? She caught her lower lip in her teeth, nipping painfully down on the soft flesh, distracting her momentarily. She couldn't afford to start thinking about *that*. The television flickered dully in the corner; the newscaster's voice filled the room. A train accident somewhere in France. She gave herself up to his voice with relief. In a while she would get up and make herself something to eat. She'd had nothing since breakfast but her appetite had vanished. A line she'd read somewhere a long time ago suddenly came to her. *Eat without hunger, mate without desire.* That was her, now. She had no appetite for anything, least of all food. No, the sentence wasn't quite true, she thought to herself as she watched the news unfolding on the small screen in front of her. She was full of desire. Full. There were mornings when she woke almost choking on it. Come *on*, Niela, she whispered to herself, half in anger, half in despair. Three nights. That was all; that was nothing. What on earth had he said or done to make her think it could be anything more?

'Three bodies have been recovered from the wreckage of the carriage.' The disembodied voice of the presenter flowed over her. 'Although fears are growing that there may be many more.' That was her, she thought to herself. A body pulled from the wreckage of something she had yet to understand.

47

JULIA
London, March 1997

The venue for the Annual Law Society Spring dinner was the Great Hall at Gray's Inn. Julia walked down the gravel pathway, glad of her shrug. It was March but it was freezing. She was nervous. It had been over a month since her conversation with Lady Barrington-Browne – not that it had made the slightest bit of difference to her frosty relations with Aaron Keeler – but the annoying upshot of it was her increased awkwardness around him. If there was one thing she hated, it was women who made fools of themselves where men were concerned . . . and now she seemed in danger of doing the same. She pulled the shrug around her shoulders as if it might protect her from more than just the cold.

She walked into the hall. The magnificent hammer-beam roof soared way above her head; the buzz of several hundred lawyers, judges, academics and their invited guests floated all around. She wished with all her heart that Dom was there. He'd been invited but he'd gone off on an illicit holiday with someone he'd met in a London nightclub. 'Don't tell me,' Julia had protested, laughing in spite of her disappointment. 'I don't want to know.' Presumably Lady Barrington-Browne thought he was with her. She accepted a glass of champagne from one of the waiters and wound her way through the crowd to a corner where a couple of her colleagues stood, obviously and pointedly discussing everyone else.

'Gosh, you scrub up nicely!' James Harriman said as she approached. He raised his champagne glass.

'Lovely dress, Julia,' Katie Fitzsimmons agreed.

'Thanks,' Julia said, her cheeks reddening slightly. She hated being the centre of attention. 'Quite a do,' she added, looking round.

'Don't look now, but there's Banville's wife,' James said, pointing to the doorway with his champagne glass. 'D'you see her? The one with the concrete hairdo?'

Julia giggled. She liked James Harriman; he reminded her a little of Dom. The three of them spent a few minutes chatting about the various partners and significant others of their colleagues and then a loud gong announced the beginning of dinner.

'Who're you sitting next to?' Katie asked as they made their way to the Bernard, Bennison & Partners tables.

'I don't know. I hope it's someone I can talk to. Where's Daniel sitting?'

'I don't know. I told Liz to make sure I was next to James.'

Julia pulled a face. She hadn't thought of asking Liz. 'Oh well, so long as it's not John Doyle. I never know what to say to him.'

'Oh, no one does, don't worry.'

Julia was just about to say something when she saw Aaron Keeler cut across her line of vision, making his way towards them. She couldn't help staring. It was the first time since Balliol that she'd seen him in a dinner jacket.

'Weren't you two at Oxford together?' Katie said suddenly, as if she'd read Julia's mind.

'Er, yes. But we weren't friendly. In fact, we hated each other.'

'Oh yes, I remember someone saying something . . . didn't you chuck a bottle of champagne at him or something?'

'It was a glass,' Julia murmured, her cheeks scarlet. 'And he deserved it.'

'I'm sure he did. He's awfully dishy but he can be the most annoying prick. Watch out, he's coming this way. And he's alone.' She looked down at the place cards. 'Good Lord! He's sitting next to *you*.'

'Good evening, ladies,' Aaron said smoothly, sliding into the seat next to Julia. 'What rotten luck, Burrows,' he said. 'You'll have to put up with me for most of the evening.'

Julia couldn't think of a single even remotely witty thing to say. She shrugged and looked longingly at Katie's back. Aaron Keeler on one side, Graham Harvey on the other. It was going to be a long evening ahead.

All through dinner, Aaron was conscious of Julia's perfume – faint, tangy, delightfully sharp. Rather like her, he thought to himself as he tried unsuccessfully to make conversation with the wife of one of the senior counsel who was seated to his left. Across the hall on the High Table with all the other law lords and important personages he could just make out Diana. He caught her eye; she raised her glass to him in a silent toast and smiled. One day, she seemed to be saying, he too might be sitting up there amongst some of the finest legal brains in Britain. The thought pleased him. It occurred to him suddenly that he was already seated next to someone whose brain he admired, though he'd have sooner cut out his tongue than admit it. Julia was deep in conversation with Graham Harvey – a man with whom Aaron had never found much to talk about. From the snippets of conversation he overheard between them, it seemed Harvey had recently lost his wife. He was surprised to hear Julia sympathise with him. Beneath the prickly exterior and the acerbic tongue, there seemed to be some compassion. Her father had been a trade unionist, he remembered. That required a certain compassion, he supposed. Compassion for the common man.

'Are you quite finished?' Julia's low voice brought him back to himself.

'Sorry?'

'You've been staring at me for the past five minutes. I'm sorry you had the "rotten luck", as you yourself put it, to be sitting next to me all bloody night, but you don't have to stare. It's rude,' she hissed.

He was so taken aback that he began to laugh. 'Christ, Burrows . . . you don't let up, do you?'

'Me?' Her look was incredulous. 'You're the one—'

'Look,' he said quickly, pushing back his chair. 'Main course is over. Join me outside for a fag.'

She looked at him, confusion written all over her face. She was actually rather beautiful, he thought to himself, then regretted the thought.

'Outside where?' she asked finally.

'On the terrace. You're perfectly safe.'

To his surprise, she pushed back her own chair and stood up. 'All right. Come on then.' She marched off.

He hurried after her. The invitation to step outside had been his, and now he was running to keep up! Typical, bloody typical!

It was chilly outside. Julia wrapped her arms about herself as she strode on to the terrace that looked out over the formal gardens of the Inn. She could hardly believe what she was doing. She leaned against one of the stone balustrades and accepted a cigarette. 'I hardly ever smoke,' she said, coughing slightly as the smoke hit her lungs. 'Usually only when I've had a drink or two.'

'Me neither. I used to, though. When I went up to Balliol, it seemed to be the thing to do.'

'D'you always follow the herd?'

He smiled. She caught a glimpse of his teeth in the semi-darkness. Further down the terrace a couple were kissing, the man's hand running up and down the woman's bare back. 'I used to,' he repeated, and there was amusement in his voice. 'Not any more. And you? D'you always run in the opposite direction?'

It was Julia's turn to smile. 'Always.'

'Yeah. You don't strike me as the type to do what anyone else says.'

Julia's head was swimming. She'd had far too much to drink, she thought to herself, panicking slightly. The entire evening suddenly began to take on a surreal, strange quality. Not only were they chatting to one another, they were actually smiling. Laughing. Teasing. She felt the sudden tug of longing that had swept through her on their last encounter surface again. She put out a hand as if to steady herself and found it on his forearm instead – had *she* put it there? She felt the heat rise in her body like a blush; she lifted her hand from his arm to touch her face but he caught it halfway. Instead of releasing her, he drew her closer. Just as before, she was trapped between an almost unbearable desire and an equally unbearable fear. The distance that he maintained so rigidly when he was in her presence suddenly dissolved. His touch was both tender and strong. The sudden unexpected intimacy of him hollowed her out. She drew a deep breath as if to steady herself before a fall. That was exactly what it felt like, she thought to herself wildly in the seconds before his lips touched hers. A fall. Wild, abrupt, intoxicating. She felt her arms reach up and take hold of the soft, darker blond hair at the nape of his neck, drawing him down towards her as if she couldn't possibly get enough. *It's Hades you're about to enter, Burrows.* Dom's words came back to her. And then she couldn't think about anything else.

48

MADDY
New York/Iowa, March 1997

The chatter of the other diners in the crowded restaurant receded into the background. Maddy stared at the little black box. Across the table, Rafe waited, his handsome face full of nervous, expectant tension. She swallowed. Her thoughts began rushing over one another, tripping themselves up. It had been just over six months since Rafe Keeler had walked into her life. She loved him. Of course she did. Who wouldn't?

He was the kindest person she'd ever met. He was so solid and reliable; handsome, charming, talented . . . there were times when she still had to pinch herself to make sure it was real. Rafe Keeler loved *her*. He'd chosen *her*. He would always be there for her, always. He would never do to her what her father had done. The thought of Rafe simply not being there one morning was absurd. He would always be there. She could see it in his eyes, in his words, his actions . . . in his family. Aside from the tension that the younger brother, Josh, seemed to provoke in everyone, she'd never met a more tightly knit family. She'd been back to London twice since her first visit over Christmas, and whilst she hadn't managed to get any closer to his mother, Diana, she genuinely liked Harvey and Aaron. They seemed to like her, too. Rafe was offering her something she'd always lacked – a family, a place in the world . . . a home. With him she could start her own family – their family. The thought of it produced a funny, thrilling sensation inside her. Perhaps that was what fate or God or whoever it was who made such decisions had decided for her. Perhaps she *wasn't* destined to become the greatest stage actress ever. She knew it; her agent knew it. The only person who still seemed to believe in her was Rafe. He made no secret of the fact that he was fascinated by her, by what she did, the way she thought about things, the intensity that she brought to things, especially what he called her 'craft'. He'd gone along to see her perform in a small, off-Broadway production on his last trip over and couldn't stop talking about it for weeks. 'That was *you* up there,' he'd said to her over and over again. 'But it wasn't. It was someone else. Everything about you was different. I don't know how you do it. Even your *face* looked different.' Maddy squirmed, unused to hearing such praise. She'd tried so hard; she'd *worked* so hard . . . and in the end, it simply wasn't enough. Could she bear the thought of continuing to waitress at Sunshine's for the rest of her working life? She wasn't stupid – the older she got, the less likely her chances were of succeeding. Now Rafe had entered her life to present her with another set of options – marriage, a family, motherhood . . . a chance to make things right in a way that hadn't been given to her. She swallowed. Here they were, seated opposite one another in the French bistro on Park Avenue that Rafe had chosen. The little black box lay between them, unopened. Maddy looked up at him. His hair was ruffled. She was overcome with a sudden wave of tenderness. 'Your hair's all messed up,' she said shakily, her fingers coming to rest on the box. 'You must've slept on it.'

'Aren't you going to open it?' Rafe ignored her.

Maddy swallowed again. She prised open the lid. The diamond winked back at her. A simple solitaire set in a band of white gold. She felt her stomach turn over.

'I know it's a bit sudden . . . I should've said something . . . warned you. But I can't face the thought of going back to London without you. I just can't.'

'Rafe . . .' Maddy struggled to say something.

'Just tell me. Will you?' She drew the ring out of the box and held it in her fingers. Slowly she brought it up to her cheek. It was cold and hard against her skin. His face was a picture of conflicting emotions – hope, anxiety, worry, even fear. She didn't know whether to laugh or cry. 'Will you marry me?' he repeated, reaching across the table for her hand.

She could feel the cool rush of her future coming at her, a thousand questions trailing in its wake. She found herself unable to utter a single word, all feeling in her body concentrated on the third finger of her left hand. Marriage. *He'd asked her to marry him.* She looked down at the ring. 'Yes,' she whispered, barely audible to anyone but herself. 'Yes. Of course I will.'

49

'London?' Martha said, putting a hand to her throat. She stared at the ring Maddy displayed a touch self-consciously. 'You're moving to *London*?'

The guilt rippled through her. 'I know it's a bit of a shock, Mom,' she began hesitantly. 'I . . . we should have warned you, I'm sorry. I didn't know he was going to propose . . . it's a bit sudden.'

'A bit *sudden*?' Martha repeated incredulously.

Maddy looked anxiously at her. Martha's cheeks were flushed, the way Maddy's were when she was overcome with emotion. It was a week since Rafe's unexpected proposal. He'd gone back to London almost straight away, and in less than a month's time, Maddy was due to follow him. She slid a hand across the table and touched her mother's arm. 'I know we haven't known each other for very long, but it just feels right, Mom. I can't explain it. Of course it's a really long way away, but his whole family's there, his work is there . . . it's going to be easier for me to move, Mom. He can't. Say you're happy for me. Please.'

Martha stared at her for a second. Then she forced a smile to her face. 'Oh, Maddy . . . it's good news, really it is, and I *am* happy for you, honey. It's just . . . it's so far away, and what about your career and everything? You've worked so hard to get where you are . . . you can't just throw it all away.'

'I'll find something when I get there, Mom. London's the theatre capital of the world. I'll find an agent, do the rounds. It's not like there's anything here for me. I mean, it's been nearly three years and I haven't even bagged a commercial yet. There's too much competition in New York—'

'And there's no competition in London?' Martha couldn't stop herself.

'You'll come and visit, Mom.' Maddy tried to change the subject. 'And I'll come back often. London's hardly further than New York. It won't be so bad, will it?' Her voice sounded plaintive, even to her own ears.

Martha shook her head slowly. 'I just can't believe it,' was all she could say. 'I just can't believe it.'

That evening after supper, Maddy wandered out to the barns. The last time she'd been here there'd been snow on the ground, she realised with a pang of guilt. She hardly ever came home any more. There was something about the way the farm never changed that depressed her. Now, as she stood amongst the discarded milk pails and lumps of broken-down equipment, it came to her suddenly that she would miss it. There was no getting away from it. Iowa was home, perhaps not in the same way that Brooklyn was, but home nonetheless. She'd lived with the colours and contours of the landscape for practically her entire life. Now she was about to swap the pale blonde wheat fields and the flashes of silver where water had gathered in a gentle hollow to form a pond for a grey, cloudy city where the sun never shone.

She sighed and turned away from the barns. She pushed open the gate that separated the cows from the bulls and closed it behind her. She began to walk away from the house, across the fields to the small clump of trees that marked the edge of the farm. She shoved her hands in her pockets, conscious of the weight and feel of the ring on her left hand. A gust of wind whipped at her face; with the sun sinking fast below the horizon, it had suddenly turned colder. There was a dampness to the woods as she entered; the familiar musky scent of moss drifted up from the ground. She looked around her, seeking something out. There it was – the last tree before the fence. She walked up to it and put both hands out, feeling its girth as she'd done a thousand times before. The bark was rough and peeling, flaking away in places where the winter's frost had settled. She felt in her pocket for the small penknife she'd brought along. With one hand, she traced the last inscription she'd made. *21st July, 1982.* Her fingers danced lightly over the date. She bent closer and began carving another. Today's date. She brushed off the curled blonde shavings and slipped the knife back into her pocket. It had been a gift from her father. One of the last he'd given her. She peered at the tree. In a few months' time, the scars would have softened and dulled until the date would appear as natural as the toughened skin that made up its blackened husk. She walked through the woods, making her way back to the house. At the top of the slight incline, she turned her head to look back the way she'd come, in all likelihood for the very last time.

50

DIANA
London, April 1997

Diana paused in the act of chopping spring onions. Behind her, Rafe and Maddy stood, nervously awaiting her response. She withheld it deliberately until her voice was steady and she could trust herself to speak. Clearly. Naturally. 'A registry wedding,' she said at last. 'In a registry *office?*'

'The thing is, Mother . . . we talked about it. We don't want all the fuss of a big do, do we, darling?' He turned to Maddy. Who at least had enough sense to keep quiet. Diana thought to herself uncharitably. *We talked about it.* Who did? Who was 'we'?

Her hands were trembling. She pushed aside the small, neatly cut pile of green vegetables and turned slowly to face them. 'Well,' she said brightly. 'It *is* your decision, I suppose. I'd just never thought . . . I just didn't expect . . .'

'We could always . . . well, we haven't *totally* made up our minds . . . I guess it wasn't quite what you'd planned . . .'

That was Maddy, of course. Too eager to please. Waffling. Vacillating. Unable to take a stand. God, she was irritating! 'No, if that's what you've decided to do, Rafe, who am I to change your plans?' She was aware that her voice was colder than it should be, but she felt as though she'd been slapped. It was bad enough coming home one evening to find his message on the answering machine: 'Mother, it's me. I'm in New York. I've got some news . . . well, *we've* got some news. We're getting married! I'll be back on Sunday night . . . can't wait to see you and tell you everything. But she's accepted. We're getting married. I love you.' She'd replayed the message a dozen times. Who heard such news on an answering machine? She'd erased it before Harvey came home. And now here they were, standing behind her like two nervous children, telling her they'd made all the arrangements, made all the plans. He was her eldest son – and he was about to get married *in a registry office*? No, it bloody well wasn't what she'd planned!

'So what do you think of it all?' Diana asked Harvey later that evening when they'd gone and the house had returned to its usual quiet state. She kept her voice deliberately neutral. She finished brushing her hair and swivelled round to face him.

'She seems nice,' he said mildly. Harvey knew her too well to be fooled by her indifference.

'Nice?'

He put aside the journal he'd been studying and looked at her. 'We don't know her,' he said simply. 'Not yet, at any rate.'

'Don't you think it's odd?' Diana said, aware of a knot of tension slowly making its way up her spine.

'What? That it seems to have happened so quickly?' Harvey completed the question for her. 'Well, we always said we'd leave this sort of thing completely up to them,' he said after a moment. 'We always said we wouldn't interfere.'

'I just find it all so *odd*. I mean, he hardly knows her himself! How many times have they met? Four? Five?'

'Darling, Rafe's clearly over the moon about her . . . let's just leave things up to them, shall we?'

Diana said nothing. She felt her shoulders hunch of their own volition, and a tremor ran through her, her skin contracting like water under a shiver of wind.

51

MADDY
London, April 1997

'Just a sec . . . there . . . that's me finished. All done.' Claire, the hairdresser Diana had brought with her, finished making the last-minute adjustments and stepped away, admiring her handiwork. 'Looks lovely, don't you think?' She tilted Maddy's head towards Diana for confirmation.

Diana nodded. 'Indeed,' she said briskly. 'All set? I'm just going down to check on the caterers. Harvey's waiting to drive you over.'

Maddy nodded, not trusting herself to speak. It was her wedding day and she was completely alone. Sandy was on holiday in the Caribbean; she was the only one of her New York friends who would have been able to come. Martha couldn't leave the farm in calving season . . . it was their own fault; the decision to marry quickly had been theirs. 'We'll have another reception, later on in the year,' Rafe promised. 'And then we'll bring your mother over for a fortnight at least. Take her to Paris. If she's going to come all this way . . .' Maddy simply nodded. The whole thing still felt as though it were happening to someone else. She didn't feel able to make a decision on her own. About anything. Least of all the wedding. Luckily, once she'd recovered from the shock, Diana had taken charge. Of everything. From the wines and the flowers in the registry office to the caterers who were at that very moment setting up tables in the garden. She'd even organised the weather; it had poured with rain the previous day but today had dawned bright and sunny, not a cloud in sight.

Maddy got up carefully. Her hair cascaded over her shoulders and down her back in beautiful, perfect little ringlets. It had taken Claire the better part of the morning to wash and set them. Her dress was simple; an empire-line ivory silk number that fell from the tight, fitted bodice in a clean, straight line to the ground. In one hand she held the posy of tightly closed ivory roses, and in the other, the beautiful silk purse her mother had sent over as a gift. She took a final look at herself in the mirror and then followed Diana out of the room. It was almost 11 a.m. The entire Keeler–Pryce clan was waiting at the town hall, just up the road. When the short marriage ceremony was over, they would all come back to the family home, where the reception would take place. She'd seen the garden from the window. It had been transformed into a fairy tale of starched white linen, Baccarat crystal and trailing bunches of white roses and heavily scented lilies. She stood on the landing for a second. The house was quiet. There were three rooms up in the attic – the guest room where she'd slept the night before; a study that Harvey occasionally used and Josh's room, which no one went into. He'd always slept a floor away from the others, she remembered Aaron telling her once. She looked at the closed door across the landing. On an impulse she couldn't name, she reached out and tried the handle. The door swung open silently and she stepped inside.

It was a large room, dominated by the bed in the centre, a large peeling poster of Che Guevara on one wall and a stack of cardboard boxes against the other. There was a small bathroom leading off to one side and several suitcases piled up in the corner. She looked at the boxes curiously. They were all neatly labelled – *Bosnia. Smara. Gaza. Personal Effects. Files. Reports.* Whatever else Josh might or might not be, he was well organised. She'd never seen such neat handwriting. She was about to turn and leave when her eye was caught by a photograph stuck to the back of the door with Sellotape. She peered at it. It was Josh, standing with his arm around the shoulders of a girl whose face was partially obscured by her veil. One long strand of chestnut hair had escaped the veil; it cascaded in a thick, glossy tumble over his arm. She was laughing; he was not. She wondered who she was – a girlfriend, perhaps? Behind them, just visible in the frame, was an eclectic jumble of half-completed buildings, fluttering bits of plastic sheeting, corrugated iron and television aerials held aloft on spindly bamboo poles. A squatter camp of some sort. She wondered where the picture had been taken.

'Maddy?' Harvey's voice suddenly floated up the stairwell.

Maddy gave a guilty start. 'Coming,' she called back and quickly closed the door. She hurried down the stairs. Harvey was waiting for her on the bottom landing.

'You look lovely, my dear,' he said, looking up at her. 'Simply lovely.'

'Th . . . thank you,' Maddy stammered. As remote and unapproachable as he could sometimes be, there was something undeniably kind about Harvey. She felt the soft tug of tears in her throat again.

'You'll be fine,' he said, smiling down at her.

She nodded, drew a deep breath and walked down the stairs towards him. He offered her his arm. As she took it, his hand closed over hers. 'I'll be fine,' she repeated.

'Of course you will.'

Throughout the short ceremony she was conscious only of Rafe's hand in hers and the faint but discernible sounds of traffic on Upper Street. The window of the registrar's office, where they both signed the enormous leatherbound book, was partially open. The service – if that was the right word – was short and to the point. She signed with a hand that shook only a little. Then it was Rafe's turn. His handwriting was much like himself – strong, clear, steady. She kissed him; there was a good-natured, muted cheer from the friends and family who'd gathered to toast them and then, just as quickly as it had started, it was over. They made their way through the corridor to the front steps where still more friends and relatives were gathered. She was passed from one to another; introduced to this aunt, that friend, this colleague, that cousin. She would not remember a single name. By the time the party finally left the town hall and made their way slowly down Northampton Park Road to the house, her arm was numb and her cheeks ached from smiling.

Back at the house, she excused herself and quickly headed upstairs to change. Again, it was Diana who'd come to the rescue. Her after-ceremony dress was equally beautiful and equally simple – a soft rose-coloured linen shift with a pretty ivory silk and cashmere cardigan and simple black slingbacks. She unpinned her hair and fixed the black silk rose that she'd bought the day before just above her ear. The diamond on her finger caught the light; she stared at herself in the mirror. Mrs Rafe Keeler. She touched the rose again with trembling fingers, then turned and closed the door behind her.

In the garden, champagne flutes were handed round by long-haired girls in black skirts and crisp white shirts; music flowed from the living room; the laughter and chatter rose all around her. All was exactly as it should be. Rafe caught sight of her and hurried over; he tenderly tucked a strand of hair behind her ear with a smile and handed her a glass before he was dragged away again. She saw Diana moving regally through the crowd, stopping here and there to accept congratulations on the happy couple's behalf. Why do people congratulate the parents of the bride and groom? she mused, sipping her champagne and glad of the momentary lapse in everyone's attention.

'I hope you don't feel overwhelmed by all this.' Someone spoke just behind her. 'We're a bit of a clan.'

Maddy jumped and turned round. The man standing in front of her was tall and powerfully built with dark hair greying at the temples and deeply hooded dark eyes behind rimless glasses. 'I'm sorry?' she stammered.

'I was just saying I hope you don't find us all rather daunting – the whole clan, staring at you . . . but on second thoughts, you're probably managing just fine.'

'They're all . . . *you're* all very kind.'

'You look wonderful. Rafe's a lucky man.'

Maddy blushed. There was something strangely familiar about him; he reminded her of someone. 'Have we met?' she asked, trying to place him.

'Oh, I'm sorry.' He held out a hand. 'I'm Rufus. Harvey's brother. Rafe's uncle. And now yours, I suppose.'

'Oh.' She shook the hand he offered. She'd heard his name before – he and Diana didn't get along, apparently. She'd overheard Rafe and Aaron arguing about where to seat him at the wedding. But before she could say anything further, Rafe suddenly appeared. 'Uncle Rufus,' he said, grinning. 'When did you get here?'

'Half an hour ago. Nearly didn't make it.' He cocked his head towards Maddy. 'She's lovely. Lucky you.'

Maddy felt herself blushing under his gaze. 'Nice to meet you,' she said, touching his arm impulsively. He looked down at her hand but said nothing. She withdrew it hurriedly. Had she done the wrong thing? Again? Luckily there was no time to ponder the question. Someone else appeared, claiming their attention.

'Aunt Hermione,' Rafe duly intoned as Maddy felt herself being enveloped in yet another soft, perfumed embrace. When she managed to extract herself and look round, Uncle Rufus was gone.

'Rufus!' Diana heard Harvey's cry of surprise and almost dropped her glass. A ripple of fear ran lightly up and down her spine. She had to hold herself very still for a second to control the expression on her face before turning slowly around. 'Darling, look who's here!' Harvey's deep voice was tinged with delight.

'Rufus.' She forced a smile to her face. 'What a surprise. We didn't know you were coming.'

'I wasn't planning on it. I'm en route to the US – only just made it in time.' He bent down and kissed her on both cheeks. 'How are you?'

It was all she could do not to turn away. 'Fine,' she muttered. Her skin burned where he'd touched it.

'We did send you an invitation, you know,' Harvey said, draping an arm over Rufus's shoulder.

Rufus smiled. 'Yes, I did get it. Just wasn't sure where I'd be. She's lovely.' He inclined his head in Maddy's direction.

'Isn't she just? Lucky chap, Rafe. Now, what'll you have? No, don't tell me . . . a Bloody Mary.' Harvey grinned at him. 'I haven't forgotten.'

'Absolutely not. Double, if you don't mind.'

Harvey walked off in search of his drink and Diana was left alone with him. She bent her head, pretending to fiddle with a thread in her skirt.

'Where is he?' His voice was a tightly held thread in her ear.

She didn't lift her head. She knew to whom he referred. 'Djibouti. He was here just before Christmas.'

'How is he?'

'Fine,' she murmured. She kept her profile turned away from him, not trusting herself to meet his gaze. *Not now. We can't talk now.*

52

JULIA
London, April 1997

A fortnight after the dinner that had turned her completely upside down, Julia stood in front of a mirror in the sort of shop she wouldn't normally be seen dead in and fingered the silk dress indecisively. It was strapless, long and floaty – not the sort of dress she normally favoured, but it was beautiful. Plum, deepening to black at the hem, it had a fitted, fluted bodice and fell around her feet in loose, luxurious swirls. It came with a hefty price tag, too. She was standing in an agony of indecision, trying to picture herself in it, when the sales assistant suddenly appeared. Five minutes later, she was looking at her own reflection in the long triptych mirror in the changing room with anxious concentration.

'It's lovely,' the assistant breathed, her voice dripping with the desire to make a sale. 'Just lovely.'

'It's not too tight?' Julia asked anxiously, turning sideways.

'Not at all. You've got such a lovely figure. We've got the most adorable little shrugs just in, too. Let me get you one . . .' She disappeared before Julia could open her mouth to protest.

Half an hour later she walked out of the boutique with the dress, a shrug, a pair of shoes and a necklace in one of those oversized, expensive-looking bags and tried not to think about the small fortune she'd spent. It was worth it, she reasoned. She would wear the dress again and again – yes, it was an *investment*, not a purchase. She hurried along Fleet Street, the bag banging awkwardly against her legs. She'd spent her entire lunch break in the changing room full of the scent of other women's perfumes. *Most* unlike her. She hurried into her office and stowed the offending bag under her desk. She switched on her computer and tried to take her mind off the one thing that had been on it for almost two weeks. Aaron Keeler.

'Julia?' It was Katie Fitzsimmons. She popped her head round the door. 'Doyle's just asked if you'd sit in on the meeting with Aimée Sinclair. They're starting now.'

Julia came back down to earth with a bump. She made a small sound of impatience. 'Do I have to?'

'Absolutely. What Doyle wants, Doyle gets. Good luck. Tell us if she's had plastic surgery.'

Julia sighed and got up. 'Where are they?'

'Second floor. It's the big meeting room at the end.'

She picked up her notepad and followed Katie out of the room.

'Ah, Julia. Thank you for joining us.' John Doyle looked up as she entered. She slid into the nearest seat as quickly as she could. It was obviously an important meeting. Three senior partners, two heads of department, two barristers – nothing but the best. She tried to concentrate on the conversation taking place. She'd heard of Aimée Sinclair – who hadn't? A spoilt wannabe actress who had married an enormously wealthy music video producer in a blaze of publicity a few years earlier. She'd quickly produced two children, whom she paraded in front of the cameras at any and every opportunity – and now, of course, the children were pawns in what was turning out to be the most vicious divorce settlement the country had ever seen. Senior counsel were keen to take it on, she'd heard – the publicity and the fees it would generate would be good for the firm and, as they pointed out, would help subsidise other, less profitable sections of their practice. Julia listened to the arguments with half an ear. The divorce proceedings of rich couples bored her to tears – it wasn't the reason she'd chosen law. For the life of her she couldn't imagine why she'd been called to sit in on the meeting. She just hoped no one would ask for her opinion. She wondered why Aaron hadn't been asked, or Katie, or Daniel. Why her?

'What do you think, Julia?' Doyle asked suddenly, swivelling around in his chair to face her. 'Obviously the decision by Mrs Sinclair to spend more time in the south of France will impact on the case for joint custody . . .'

Julia blinked. The question had taken her by surprise. So did the sudden, unexpected rush of anger. She opened her mouth, knowing even as she did so that she'd probably regret it, but it was too late. The words were out before she could stop them. 'Look, we all know that children whose parents are going through a divorce have a hard time of it, no matter how we dress it up. Most of them spend half their lives going back and forth between homes when what they really should be doing is their homework, or playing with friends, forming their own relationships, which, if they're bloody lucky, will last them for the rest of their lives. In this case, these two kids are going to be on planes and trains for most of their childhood. Why?' She turned and looked directly at Aimée Sinclair, whose mouth had dropped open. 'Because you'll get a better year-round tan?' There was a stifled gasp from one end of the table. Doyle was looking at Julia in horror. He cleared his throat as if to interrupt, but there was no stopping her now. 'Everyone thinks children are resilient; isn't that what we all comfort ourselves with?' She looked round the table defiantly. 'Well, that's not what the latest research shows. Your kids will be feeling the pain of this ridiculous arrangement for the rest of their lives. Look, I'm not saying divorce is a bad thing. Christ, we've all been in situations we'd like to get out of. What I *am* saying is that there are two children here, and if the best reason you can come up with for wanting to dissolve your marriage is that you're *bored*, then I suggest you find a hobby. One that won't extract quite such a price from the only decent thing you've ever produced – your kids.' She got up, suddenly aware that the entire room had gone deathly quiet. She picked up her notes and walked out of the room.

*

After escorting a weeping Aimée Sinclair out of the building, Doyle returned to the meeting room. Everyone was still in shock. 'What on *earth* provoked *that*?' he asked dazedly of no one in particular. 'She's just lost us potentially our most lucrative client ever.'

'Good on her.' Mike Banville, QC, suddenly spoke up. 'Her timing's not great, but it's about time it was said. All these celebrity clients. It's absolutely ridiculous, if you ask me. They're just a distraction from the real business of the law.'

'Yes, but those distractions *pay* for the "real business", as you put it,' Nathaniel Peterson, Head of Litigation, remarked drily. 'They're the reason we can afford a department like that in the first place. In a sense, clients like Aimée Sinclair pay for barristers like Burrows.'

'I agree. All she does is take on controversial unwinnable cases that swallow up God knows how many hours of man time. It's practically pro bono.'

'But she's damned good at it. Granted, it's not the high-profile stuff your department brings in, but she's passionate about it and she brings a certain . . . integrity to this whole business. An integrity, I should say, that's wholly—'

'All right, all right, Ken, that's enough. I agree, she's a bit of loose cannon, but then again, some of the loosest cannons have gone on to become some of the biggest assets. I mean, I remember—'

'Oh, for Christ's sake, don't start waltzing down memory lane,' Alistair Kennedy groaned. 'We'll be here all day. Look, what are we discussing here? Are we going to sack her? Hardly. Might someone put in a word of caution? Good idea. Will she go on to do exceptional things in the future? Most undoubtedly. Let's leave it at that, shall we?'

Aaron listened to the buzz going around chambers with barely suppressed irritation. What the hell was it about Julia Burrows that seemed to provoke such passionate discussion? It had been exactly the same at Balliol. No one was capable of rousing emotions the way she was. As he picked up his notebook and papers, it came to him suddenly that he wasn't just annoyed – he was worried. Why wasn't he capable of generating anything other than a clap on the back, a hand on the shoulder, a brief nod of approval? Why didn't people wonder about him the way they seemed to wonder about Julia Burrows? Christ, he couldn't count on both hands the number of times her bloody name had come up in conversation – *every*body, it seemed, had an opinion on Julia Burrows, but no one had anything really to say about *him*. Other than what a credit he was, etc., etc. He was tired of being a credit, he realised irritably. Tenacious, passionate, stubborn, risky – the list of adjectives surrounding Julia Burrows was growing every day, and in direct proportion to the ways in which he *wasn't* being discussed. He had never upset the apple cart, had never delivered a verdict or penned a response that wasn't fully expected of him in some unidentifiable way that everyone seemed to understand – except him, of course. He conformed to everyone's expectations without even being aware of what those were. So why didn't she? And why the hell did it matter so much? Ever since the damned Law Society dinner she'd been on his mind. It wasn't that they'd kissed . . . Christ, a few glasses of wine and the interminable boredom of sitting next to Banville's wife and he'd have kissed anybody. Well, almost. Although . . . He stopped typing and looked out of the window, suddenly lost in thought. There *was* something about her . . . there'd been something special about her that night. Was it the dress? He tried to recall it. Her hair . . . had she done something different? She wasn't his type. Of course not. He liked women who looked – and acted – like women. Soft, feminine, willing . . . He didn't like her sharpness and her angularity. Although . . . he cocked his head to one side, pondering the thought. She wasn't *angular*, as such. Slim, almost boyish . . . but she was certainly pretty. He rather liked her hair, he realised . . . dark brown, glossy. He liked the way she smelled. And he liked the way she talked. Once you'd got used to the accent, of course. She had a way of putting things . . . she was quick, witty. He looked back down at his computer screen. Eleven minutes had passed since he'd last typed a word. Eleven minutes. All of them spent thinking about Julia Burrows. What the hell was going on?

Two storeys above him in the toilets adjacent to the library, Julia was dousing her burning face in cold water, wishing that the ground underneath her would open up and simply swallow her whole. What the hell had she done? She hadn't been herself since the night of the dinner. She and Aaron had kissed; nothing more. She would have liked more . . . but he'd pulled away, as he always did. He'd looked at her in the darkness, not saying anything. And then, in a gesture of unbearable tenderness, he'd kissed the tip of her nose and led her back inside. 'Before I do something we'll both regret,' he'd said. She'd been too hollowed out to answer. Regret? Why would he regret it? She realised she knew nothing about him. She knew nothing about his life. Was he with someone? Perhaps even a wife? She looked at her face in the mirror. Her eyes, normally so clear and bright, were dull, tinged with sadness. Her face seemed to her to be less of a face than an expression of a predicament. One that she seemed unable to solve. In the fortnight since they'd kissed, she'd seen Aaron twice. On both occasions he seemed to her as he'd always been. Aloof, unapproachable, remote. As if it hadn't happened. She gave herself a small, unhappy smile. Could it be that after all these years she and Dom were in the same situation? Both in love with Aaron Keeler, with no chance of it being returned? She let out a long, deep sigh. *Yes, admit it. Go on, say it. Say it out loud.* She mouthed the words against the silent mirror. She was in love. With a man who barely seemed to see her, and certainly not for herself.

53

JOSH
London, May 1997

The receptionist looked up at him. 'Niela Aden?' He nodded. 'I'll just check if she's in. Your name?'

'Josh Keeler.' He watched her dial an extension number with a long, polished fingernail. There was a wait of a few moments; he was uncomfortably aware of his heart beating steadily underneath the unfamiliar wool of his sweater.

'Sorry, she's not answering her phone. I'll just try the boardroom . . .'

The disappointment that burned over him was similar to the desolation he'd felt in the weeks and months following her departure: a desolation he'd fought against tooth and nail. He wasn't prepared for it. It had been years since he'd experienced anything like it – not since Rania, and he'd sworn then never to allow himself to go through it again. Never. No one else would ever get that close. But somehow, against the odds, Niela Aden had. She'd caught him completely unawares. He'd tried to do what he knew best – he'd buried her, forgotten about the brief time they'd spent together. He'd thrown himself into the job with renewed vigour, losing track of the number of units they'd built once she and her team were gone. He'd pushed the men until the point of near collapse – faster, quicker, faster. They were due to finish in June; he'd brought it in before time, on budget . . . something that had never been done before. A miracle. He'd been given a fortnight's vacation, as per usual, and the details of his next posting – and the next thing he knew he was booking a flight to London.

Now he stood in the reception of the office in which she worked, his heart thumping inside his chest like a teenager, steeling himself against the disappointment that flooded his senses as soon as it was clear she wasn't there.

'No, I don't know where she is.' The receptionist looked at him. 'She's usually in her office at this time. Would you like to leave a message?'

Josh shook his head. 'Thanks. I'll try back some other time.'

'No problem.'

He left the building and walked back up Rivington Road. The area had changed since he'd last been there. There were new buildings on almost every street corner: wine bars and small boutiques, a specialist book store and an organic greengrocer's. Yes, things had changed. As a student he'd come to more than his fair share of parties held in cavernous, unheated lofts along Charlotte Road. It was a desolate, forlorn part of London in those days. There'd been one memorable party . . . He stopped suddenly. Someone was staring at him from across the road. It took him a few seconds to work out who it was. A ripple of recognition ran lightly across her face, followed by a look of incredulity. He crossed the street quickly and walked up to her.

'Niela.'

'Josh?' She stopped. Her expression was one of astonishment. 'Wh . . . what are you doing here?'

He spread his hands out before him in a gesture of sudden help-lessness. 'I . . . I'm not sure, actually. I just stopped by your office . . . you weren't there.' He searched her face for signs of welcome or pleasure; there were none. She held herself exactly as he remembered. Still, calm, waiting. It moved him beyond words.

'When did you arrive?' she asked finally.

'Yesterday morning. I went to my parents' place. I would've come to yours but I didn't – I don't – know where you live.' He stopped, astounded at himself. It was so out of character – he was unsure of himself, unnerved, and by a woman at that – he felt as though he were watching someone else. He was not himself.

She was still looking at him with that mixture of wary disbelief that excited and frightened him simultaneously. 'Why?' she asked.

He lifted his shoulders. 'I wanted to see you.' There didn't seem to be any point in saying anything else.

'After all this time?'

He shook his head slowly. 'I don't know what to say. I . . . I didn't want to . . . It was . . .' He stopped suddenly. 'Look, is there somewhere we can go and talk? I mean, I feel a bit stupid standing in the middle of the road, and it's cold. Aren't you cold? You must be.' She wasn't even wearing a coat.

She stared at him. He was conscious only of the slow, steady beat of his heart, the feeling of anticipation as his eyes moved over her face. He couldn't believe he was seeing her again. Her features, which had remained in his mind's eye for almost three months, were both strange and familiar – sharper, more beautiful than he remembered, and yet more distant, too. He held his breath. The sound of traffic and pedestrians around him slowed suddenly; everything was still. And then she smiled. His relief was so great it broke over him like a wave. 'Why don't you meet me after work? There's a café at the end of the road. I'll see you there around five p.m.'

He nodded. 'I'll be there.' He hesitated. 'Thanks.'

She seemed to understand what he was saying. She gave him a small smile and continued on her way. He watched her for a moment or two, then shoved his hands in his pockets and walked off in the opposite direction. Five p.m. Two hours to kill. Easy. Or so he thought.

'Oh, Niela.' Jenny, the receptionist, looked up as she entered the building. 'Some bloke was just here looking for you. He didn't leave a message. Josh Keeler, I think he said his name was.'

'Thanks,' Niela said quickly and hurried to the lift before Jenny could ask anything further. Her cheeks were burning, despite the cold. She still couldn't believe it. Josh. Here. In London. She punched the number to her floor and stood back, allowing the lift to pull her stomach up behind her. She was trembling, she realised, as she got out and walked down the corridor to the office where all the translators worked. She gave Shaheeda and Ludmilla a quick wave and sat down behind her computer screen. Her stomach was in knots. She looked down at the brochure she'd been working on before she'd popped out. 'Some services and support are available to everyone, whilst others depend on your income. Your case owner . . .' She began to type the words in Arabic, her fingers flying over the keyboard as though she were trying to bury her own thoughts in amongst the wash of official jargon. It was nearly three. Another couple of hours to go. Josh. In London. What had he come for?

He was waiting when she entered the café, sitting alone in one of the booths by the window. He looked up as she came through the doorway, and the same tense hesitation that had characterised their every encounter back in the desert was there in London, amidst the noise and chatter of the café. He got up as she approached. His scarf was still wound tightly around his neck, although he'd taken off his jacket. He was wearing a dark green polo-neck sweater and his hair was longer than she'd last seen it. Amongst the other customers, whose skin had taken on the pale, lacklustre glow of winter, his dark, sun-ripened complexion jumped out. She was struck anew by just how energetically alive he seemed, as if he'd been stopped in mid-flight, his whole body attuned to some splendid physical activity that had only just ended. She had never met anyone with such a wonderfully strong sense of his own body and its limitless possibilities. Just thinking about when she'd last seen it brought a dark, bruised flush to her cheeks.

She stood in front of him, unsure whether to offer her hand or her cheek. He leaned forward; there was a second's hesitation and then she felt herself enveloped in the strangely familiar sense of his body. His arms were hard and muscled underneath his sweater. She let her own drop, alarmed by the immediacy of her body's reaction to him, as if the intervening three months of silence simply hadn't happened.

'Thanks for coming,' he said, his mouth very close to her ear. 'I wasn't sure you would.'

'Why wouldn't I?' She put a hand up to her face as if she'd been burned.

He held her a little away from him. 'Are you always like this?' he asked, a faint smile playing around the corners of his mouth.

'Like what?' She unwound her own scarf and pulled out the chair opposite.

'I don't know . . . so . . . *direct*? No, don't answer that. Yes, you are.'

It was different to how it had been in Djibouti. There, she'd been the one who was unsure, who'd waited to take her cues from him. She watched as he ran a hand through his hair, passing it over the faint stubble that showed up beneath the olive-toned grain of his skin. It was hard not to remember the touch and feel of his hair underneath her fingers. She sat down abruptly, unnerved. 'So why did you come?' she asked simply.

He slid into his own seat, his eyes still on her face. He placed his hands, palms facing downwards, on the wooden table before her. 'I don't know,' he said finally, shaking his head as if in disbelief at himself. 'We finished the project ahead of time . . . I had leave coming up . . . I . . . I just wanted to see you again.'

Niela looked at him. He seemed to be struggling with something, a deeper, somehow more difficult truth. She was struck again by the horizon that was always present in him, the distance he maintained that both drew her in and yet pushed her away. He seemed to be nursing something, a lost, buried secret, some emotion or experience he felt he couldn't share. There was a darkness in him that frightened her, and yet for all that, she understood it too. It was the same darkness that was in her, not as the result of her nature, but because of her past. Once or twice he would let something slip, like now. Turning up in London on the spur of the moment after months of silence was no accident, however offhand about it he tried to be. He wanted something, *needed* something, but he was unable to say what. His presence, she saw, was answer enough. At least for now. 'Come,' she said, finishing her coffee and standing up. 'Let's go. Let's get out of here.'

She lay slightly apart from him, dozing fitfully. The yellow glow of the hands of her alarm clock showed 1.49 a.m. The traffic outside had finally slowed to a halt; her tiny flat was just off the Goldhawk Road and the stream of trucks and lorries had lasted well beyond midnight. He was so used to the calm silence of Islington that he'd forgotten what other parts of London sounded like. His hand was buried in her hair; he stroked it gently, enjoying the weight and feel of it against his palm. The bedside lamp gave off a soft yellow glow, illuminating her dark skin as if from within. His eyes travelled down the length of her body. She slept with one leg thrown outside the cover, her arms curled tightly against her ribs. One full, rounded breast lolled against the other; there was a slight sheen to her skin that made him want to trace the contours of her body with his mouth, a saltiness on the tongue. He watched the gentle rise and fall of her stomach, admiring the smooth, clear line of her body all the way down past the tight whorl of her navel to the lovely hollow made by the muscles of her thighs. She was perfect, in almost every conceivable way. He pulled her towards him; now that he was here, with her, he found he just couldn't let her go.

54

MADDY
London, June 1997

It was exactly two weeks since the wedding. A fortnight. She corrected herself quickly, trying the word out on her tongue. 'Fortnight' wasn't a word that Americans used. She heard Rafe on the phone sometimes – 'Yes, it's been a fortnight already. I can't believe it.' She wondered who he was talking to. Sometimes he told her – 'Oh, that was so-and-so . . .' He seemed to have many friends. Or at least people who rang up and were keen to know who Maddy was. She didn't know the difference. It wouldn't have made one, she thought to herself with a wry smile. She knew no one. No one knew her. They hadn't had a honeymoon; Rafe was too busy at work. They would take a proper holiday later on in the year, after the big reception they were planning, when Martha and Sandy would come. He'd taken a couple of days off, which was all his team could afford. When he'd gone back to work, Maddy lay in bed every morning, long after he'd left the house, listening to the distant hum of traffic on the Euston Road, a few minutes away. She liked the area he lived in – Fitzrovia, he called it – a shabby-chic neighbourhood named after a developer called Fitzroy, whose house still stood somewhere along the streets that ran on either side of the square. The Post Office Tower loomed above them like a fat steel and glass finger – at night it was lit up in a dazzling array of colours. Students, tourists, office workers and the odd local inhabitant all came to Fitzroy Square at lunchtime; from the tall windows of the living room on the first floor, Maddy could see them, sitting in groups of two or three, tossing crusts to the pigeons who'd learned to gather in their wake. Rafe's flat covered the first and second floors of a handsome building on Cleveland Street, a minute's walk from the square. 'It's your flat too, darling.' The words sailed straight over Maddy's head. She couldn't comprehend it. The most expensive item she owned was the chocolate-brown leather coat she sometimes wore when she went for a stroll in Regent's Park. The flat was nice in an offhand, unlived-in sort of way. Diana's touch was everywhere – from the leather chesterfield sofa in the living room that was simply a smaller version of the one at the family home to the pale blue flowered bed sheets and the white bathroom towels with a black linen stripe. There was even a print in the dining room that she thought she recognised as a copy of the one in Diana's living room.

She traced out a pattern on the quilt with her fingertips. It was only nine o'clock. The whole day was in front of her. Rafe would be home late. A heavy caseload: two or three complicated operations that had been postponed until his return. She rolled on to her back, thinking about what he might be doing at that very moment. He sometimes explained things to her – anterior cervical discectomy; laminectomy; a stereotactic biopsy – a foreign language but one she was slowly getting used to. She loved the way his hands carefully traced the arc of his movements during an operation – cut, incision, probe; there was a delicacy and a lightness of touch that was at odds with someone so physically powerful.

She pushed aside the quilt impatiently and slid her legs out of bed. She had to get up. She walked to the windows and pulled back the curtains. She had a whole day in front of her. She ought to fill it with something useful. Give it some shape, some purpose. She couldn't lie around in the flat for ever. She had to find something to do. It was logical, she supposed, to start with what she knew. The theatre. She ought to find out what was going on, what was showing, who was playing . . . the usual stuff. Get a feel for the place, the players, the performers. Find an agent. Put herself forward. She stood in front of the bathroom mirror, mouthing the words to herself. She'd said something along those lines to Harvey at Sunday lunch. 'I might try and find an agent,' she'd said, hoping she didn't sound too full of herself. As usual, it was Diana who'd answered.

'Whatever for?'

Maddy blushed. 'If . . . if I want to find work,' she stammered.

'Work?' Diana's tone made it sound as if that possibility were simply too remote to even be worth considering.

Maddy found herself agreeing. 'Oh, I know it's kinda unlikely . . . I mean, you have so many fine actors here . . . such a great tradition of theatre . . . with Shakespeare and everything . . . I don't think I'd stand a chance . . . but you never know . . .' She was speaking too fast, and saying too much but she couldn't help herself. There was something about Diana that brought out the child in her, desperately seeking to please. Rafe had stepped in that time to save her. Remembering it brought the heat back into her cheeks. She had to find a way to deal with his mother. Nothing she did was right. Even the damn photograph. She blushed further. She'd been standing by the console in the living room, wondering what to do with her hands. Her eye had fallen on a silver-framed picture standing to one side. She'd picked it up, of course. A group of teenagers, huddled in the spray of a waterfall, sunlight catching the drops and pooling around their feet. She recognised Diana immediately. She was laughing, her face turned towards the camera. She was holding on to a young man; dark-haired and deeply tanned. 'Who's that?' Maddy asked, frowning. He looked strangely familiar.

'Who?' Rafe came up to her.

'Him.' She pointed with her finger.

'Oh, that's Uncle Rufus.'

Maddy stared at the photograph. Yes, it was . . . a much younger, much darker version. He reminded her a little of Josh, she thought to herself suddenly. Even though she'd only seen him once, there was a resemblance there. It was hardly surprising; Josh was Rufus's nephew after all.

'What're you two looking at?' It was Diana. She came to stand beside them, fingers curled protectively around her wine glass.

'Just these old photographs. That's the one of all of you in Crete, isn't it?'

'Oh, *that* one.'

'You look so young,' Maddy ventured shyly.

'Mmm. It was the summer I was seventeen. Our parents shared a villa there every summer.' She nodded in Harvey's direction.

Maddy was surprised. 'You've known Harvey since you were seventeen?'

'I've known him all my life.' Diana gave a small laugh. 'We were neighbours. They moved in when I was four. The boy next door.'

'That's . . . that's so *romantic*,' Maddy said, blushing as she said it.

'Is it?' Diana murmured. Her eyes lingered on Maddy for a second.

'It's funny. Your brother, Josh . . . he looks more like your Uncle Rufus than your father,' Maddy said, looking at Rafe. Diana's hand went out; she took hold of the frame and put it firmly back in its place. She'd offended her; that much was clear. Her mouth had tightened into a thin line. Maddy looked at her, momentarily confused. What had she said?

Diana turned away from the console. From the stiffness of her posture and the way she held on to Rafe's arm, quickly pulling him away, it was clear that the conversation was over. Maddy remained where she was, standing uncertainly by the door. She'd done it again – put her foot in it, said something she shouldn't have, spoken out of turn. She grimaced; that old, nervous feeling in the pit of her stomach was back. It seemed to follow every encounter with Diana but she'd no idea why.

She straightened the bed sheets, pulling the cover nice and tight and plumping the feather pillows up. She picked up their discarded clothing, setting the room to rights. It didn't take long. She'd come over from the States with all her possessions in two giant suitcases, pretty much the same way she'd come to New York. She'd given everything else away. A few pans, some plates, a chair or two . . . nothing that she couldn't replace. It was a strange feeling – in less than a day she'd uprooted herself, boarded a plane and was gone, just like that. There would be no trace of her in New York, just as there was little trace of her on the farm. In that way, she supposed, she was more like her father than she'd ever imagined. There one day, gone the next. Almost as if she'd never been. Aside from a weekly call to her mother, and two to Sandy, there was no one left behind who would miss her, or even notice that she was gone.

She walked out of the room and down the short flight of stairs to the kitchen and living room, which were on the floor below. She made herself a cup of coffee and carried it through to the living room. It too was tidy and silent. She wandered over to the window, absently touching the few ornaments that lay around the room. The wooden bowl from Swaziland that a friend had given him; the polished silver fruit bowl that lay empty of fruit . . . the television against the wall, a book on the coffee table. He didn't have much. She ought to go out and buy things, fill it up. Put her mark on it too. It was her home now. She sipped her coffee slowly, watching the signs of life on the street below. No rush, she thought to herself. No rush at all. She had time . . . more than she'd ever had. At that moment, it felt as though she had nothing but. All the time in the world and nothing to fill it with.

55

JULIA
London, June 1997

Julia hurried along Upper Street, her stomach churning with nerves. She was fifteen minutes late. She hated being late. Especially now. Tonight. She had a date. With Aaron. After nearly a fortnight of waiting in agonising indecision, he'd come up to her in the library one Wednesday afternoon and murmured something for her ears alone. 'Can I see you again? Apart from work, I mean?' The relief that flooded through her was so acute it almost brought tears to her eyes. *Idiot*, she hissed at herself under her breath. *Idiot. You're behaving like every woman you despise.* Well, despise herself she might, but the truth of it was, here she was hurrying along Upper Street to some restaurant he'd chosen, unable to think about anything other than the fact that she was late and that he'd barely spoken five words to her in the past two weeks. Yes, she was behaving like every single lovestruck woman she'd ever encountered, but what could she do? Overnight, it seemed, her feelings had changed and the strength of the dislike she'd felt for Aaron Keeler ever since she'd clapped eyes on him was matched only by the strength of attraction.

She saw him sitting to one side, his eyes fixed on her. She tried to slow her pace so as not to appear too eager. As always, his expression was difficult to read. 'Sorry I'm late,' she said, shaking her head as she approached. 'Katie caught me at the last minute.'

His smile was slow, but steady. 'No problem. I was enjoying waiting for you to walk in. I like watching you walk.'

She caught her breath; it wasn't the answer she'd been expecting. She sat down abruptly, aware of the heat slowly mounting in her cheeks. 'I walk like a duck,' she said, not sure why she'd said it as soon as the words escaped her lips. It wasn't even true.

'Funny sort of duck,' he said mildly. 'Definitely not a Regent's Park duck.'

She laughed. 'I don't know why I said that,' she said, shrugging off her coat. 'Nerves.'

'Are you nervous?'

'Aren't you?'

'I'm always nervous around you. You might pick up a bottle and throw it at me.'

'It was a *glass*,' Julia protested, smiling. 'Not a bottle. I don't know why everyone keeps talking about a bottle.'

'Everyone?' He raised an eyebrow.

'Well, not quite everyone,' Julia conceded, blushing. 'Just the odd . . . you know, person who brings it up.'

'And who might that be?' His voice was teasing.

Julia blushed even further. She certainly didn't want it to sound as though she was constantly talking about him. 'Oh, no one, really,' she said, as offhandedly as she could. 'Er . . . what're you drinking?'

'Whisky and soda.' He held up his glass. 'For my nerves.'

She couldn't help but laugh. 'You're full of it, Keeler,' she said, picking up the menu and pretending to study it.

'Full of . . . ?'

She felt the full weight of his blue eyes upon her. 'Shit,' she said calmly, putting down the menu and reaching across the table for his glass. She raised it to her lips and drained it in one fiery gulp. 'And don't pretend you don't know it.'

His expression changed; under the release of laughter he touched her arm. She looked down at his forearm, at the fine dark blond hairs and wide hands, skin sliding tightly over tendons, lightly tanned and freckled, a band of slightly paler skin showing at the edge of his thick black leather watch strap. She felt something inside her turn over.

The waiter came and went; a meal was ordered, a bottle of wine, coffee, some cheese . . . She ate and drank mechanically, her whole being concentrated fiercely on the man in front of her whom she'd hated for so long. Lady Barrington-Browne was right. Love/hate . . . *practically the same thing if you ask me*. She heard the words as if she'd spoken them out loud. Absurd. Love? How could she love Aaron Keeler? She barely knew him. But suddenly, she wanted to. Very much.

He was conscious of her hand tucked into his arm as they walked away from the restaurant towards his flat. It was June, though you wouldn't have guessed it. The brilliant blue skies of the previous weekend had given way almost overnight to a thick blanket of grey. At least it wasn't raining, he thought to himself as they turned off Upper Street and made their way towards Napier Terrace. There was a second's brief awkwardness as he unlocked the front door and stood back to let her pass. He stared at the back of her head as she made her way up the short flight of stairs in front of him. Her hair, which she usually kept pulled off her face, had come loose and swung glossily from side to side as she walked. He hadn't been joking; he did like watching her walk. In fact, he liked watching her, full stop. He'd often caught himself wondering at the body beneath the smart suits she wore to work. Nice legs, he'd noticed, more than once, it had to be said. She was tall and boyishly slender but the silk shirt she wore parted just enough to reveal the slight swell of her breasts. She was beautiful, he thought to himself, but in a restrained, controlled sort of way. All edge, corner, angle . . . hers wasn't the voluptuous softness of most of the women he found attractive. No, Julia Burrows's attraction was different – to do with the way she talked; the way she held herself, the distinct, hard-edged cadence of her accent . . . something a different sort of person would have been at pains to conceal. Not her. *Take me as I am.* Her pride in who she was had as much to do with who she wasn't trying to be – a far cry from most of the people he came across. She had more integrity – yes, that was the word! – than anyone he'd ever known. Without even trying, she impressed him. And who could he say that about?

'Nice flat,' she said as soon as she entered the living room. 'Not quite what I expected.'

'What did you expect?' he asked, taking her coat. It came to him suddenly that he very much wanted to know what she thought.

'Oh, I don't know . . . something a bit more traditional. You know. Chintz.'

'Chintz?' He smiled faintly. 'Me?'

'Mmm.' She touched the leather chair. 'Flowers. That sort of stuff. Who're these?' She'd picked up one of the framed pictures from the mantelpiece. 'I recognise your mum . . . is that the rest of your family?'

'Yeah, that's Rafe. And that's Harvey. My dad.'

'And who's that?' She pointed with her finger.

'Josh.' He hoped his voice was normal.

'Who's Josh?'

'My brother. My younger brother.'

'That's your brother?' She couldn't keep the note of surprise from her voice. 'You don't look anything alike. The two of you look just like your dad. But he looks so different.'

'He's overseas most of the time.' Aaron took the picture from her. 'Anyway, enough about my family. D'you want something to drink?'

She shook her head. 'I think I've probably had quite enough, thank you,' she said with a slow smile. 'Two glasses of wine . . . that's a lot for me, you know.'

'I thought you northern types could hold your liquor,' he said, and then held his breath to see how she took the quip.

She smiled – again, that slow, sexy smile that made his heart beat faster. 'Not this one,' she murmured. They looked at each other. Then, just as it had been the last time he'd kissed her, he wasn't sure who made the first move. Her mouth was soft and wonderfully warm. The feeling that this was only the beginning of something he'd waited for washed over him slowly. He felt his hands move of their own accord to the opening in the silk blouse she was wearing; he slid his hand, palm down, across the firm, tight flesh and felt her body tremble. He was taken aback by his own boldness – Julia Burrows wasn't the type to be rushed; he'd known that from the moment he first laid eyes on her, even if he hadn't understood it. But she was just as hungry. He could tell by the way her body arched towards him and by the willingness with which she allowed him into her mouth. The contrast between the cool aloofness of the woman he'd known for the past five years and the heat he seemed to generate in her now, in his arms, was enough to make him lose his head. 'Julia,' he whispered, his words lost in her hair. 'I don't mean to—'

But whatever it was he was going on to say was silenced by the touch of her hands on him, on his belt, sliding his trousers down over his hips, the way she turned him around until he was sitting on the armchair she'd teased him about. He couldn't think of a single thing other than the explosive longing to feel himself inside her. And then, of course, he couldn't think about anything at all.

56

DIANA
London, June 1997

Diana stared at Aaron as if she couldn't quite grasp what he was saying. He wanted to bring someone. A woman. To Mougins. With the family on their annual holiday. 'What woman?' she asked faintly.

He had the grace to blush. 'Her name's Julia, Mother. I . . . she works with me.'

'She's a lawyer?' Relief flowed over her.

'A barrister. Well, she's just about to finish her second six.'

'And how long have you . . . known each other?' she asked, as delicately as she could. She felt like slapping him. What the hell was wrong with her sons? Why was she always the last to know, presented with these . . . these *women* . . . as if they were unalterable facts. Fait accomplis.

'A while. Actually, she was at Balliol with me.'

'At Balliol? And you've never mentioned her before?'

He blushed further. 'Well, it's not quite like that. We . . . we didn't particularly get on. In fact, we sort of hated each other.'

'Oh. I see. Well, I suppose so. Rafe'll be there . . . with Maddy.' She tried not to let the disappointment show in her voice. In a way, she was forced to admit to herself, it was a bit of a relief. She'd been wondering what on earth she would do with Rafe's wife by her side for all of two weeks. Now at least there might be someone whose company she could at least tolerate, if not enjoy. A barrister. Better than an actress. A failed actress.

'You sure?' Aaron was apologetic.

'Yes, I'm sure. Of course.' Diana was gracious. 'I'm sure she'll enjoy it.' She watched as Aaron's face broke into a smile of relief. She suppressed the repeated urge to smack him. She hated surprises of that sort. First Rafe with his bombshell news of an impending marriage, now Aaron. What was the girl's name? Julia. Julia Burroughs? She wondered what she was like, which school she'd been to. At least she was Oxford-educated. That was a good sign, of the sort she liked. God, whatever next? She felt a sudden flicker of nervousness. Only Josh was left . . . and God only knew what *he'd* surprise her with. 'Well, you'd better bring her to lunch next week. We might as well get to meet her before we spend a fortnight together. Bring her on Sunday. She can meet Rafe as well.'

'And Maddy,' Aaron added quickly.

'Yes,' Diana said drily. 'And Maddy.'

'Mougins? Where the hell's that?' Julia asked him the following night.

'In France. South of France. We've got a home down there . . . it's lovely. You'd really enjoy it,' he said, echoing Diana.

'For two weeks? With you and your family?' Julia asked faintly.

'We wouldn't have to be with them all the time. It's huge . . . it's an old farmhouse. We've had it since I was born. We usually go down two or three times a year.'

Julia was silent. She and Aaron had been together – that old, tired euphemism – for nearly two months and every day there were things about him that surprised her. Like the invitation to join his family on holiday. Two weeks in the sun in the south of France. She'd never been anywhere on holiday before. 'It's very kind of them,' she began hesitantly. 'But I've never met them. Won't they think it a bit odd—'

'You're invited to lunch next Sunday,' Aaron interrupted her. 'It was Diana's idea, not mine,' he added hastily. 'She'd like to meet you.'

'Me?' Julia's mouth dropped open. Diana Pryce wanted to meet *her*? She swallowed nervously. 'That'd be lovely,' she said with a confidence she didn't feel. Her mind was already racing ahead. Sunday lunch at Diana's. What on earth would she wear?

57

Aaron's family home in north London was lovely in the way only old money can ever be, Julia noticed, as soon as they stopped outside the house. Tall, elegant, freshly painted but not garishly so; beautiful wooden sash windows, flower boxes and a neat, well-kept front lawn. There were stone-flagged steps leading down to a basement window and a tasteful arrangement of a rockery, a few cacti and flowering shrubs to lead and please the eye. The front door was stylishly black; a heavy, well-polished brass knocker . . . Julia took in the details with a sinking heart. It was light years away from the home in which she'd grown up. She held on to Aaron's hand as he led her up the steps. He opened the front door with his own key and they stepped inside. The house was cool and fragrant with the scent of cooking.

'Mother?' he called down the stairwell. There was no answer, but the sound of classical music floated up the stairs. He turned to Julia. 'We'll go downstairs. They're probably in the garden.'

The kitchen was as large as the entire ground floor of the Elswick house she'd called home. Stainless-steel worktops, a cool palette of colours and textures; paintings, African masks, a long row of cookery books and on the table, several bottles of opened red wine. She gulped. She looked down at her dress. Laura Ashley – clearly the wrong choice.

'Aaron!' Someone was coming towards them. Julia squinted through the sliding glass door. She'd taken off her glasses. The figure emerged into clarity. It was Diana Pryce. 'Darling, you're here. At last.' She came into the kitchen, holding her arms out to her son. She lifted her face to be kissed.

'Yes, sorry we're a bit late.'

'My fault,' Julia said quickly. 'I was late getting to his.'

Diana looked at her, her eyes widening a fraction at the sound of her voice. Julia recognised the look straight away. *Good God*, she seemed to be saying, *what have we here?* She held out a hand. Julia took it. A limp, brief handshake, a wan smile and a quick sweep up and down the length of her, assessing her clothes, hair, shoes . . . Julia's fate was sealed. A working-class girl. Oh, dear.

'Come and meet Rafe,' Aaron said, putting a hand on hers. 'Is Dad here?'

'He's upstairs. He went to get a record . . . something he wanted Maddy to hear.' Diana turned and led the way. She hadn't said a word to Julia. There was a couple sitting in the shade of the leafy oak tree. The woman, a slender redhead, was all smiles. The man looked up. Julia's eyes widened. He and Aaron were so alike it was uncanny. It was like looking into Aaron's face, but with a few details either missing or altered very, very slightly. A mole above the left corner of his lip; blue eyes a shade darker than Aaron's; his hair was shorter, messier. Julia hung back as the brothers embraced but the woman turned her head expectantly towards her and got up. Julia didn't know whether to offer her cheek or her hand. The redhead solved the problem.

'It's so *great* to meet you,' she exclaimed, jumping up and kissing Julia on both cheeks. 'I've heard so much about you!'

Julia recoiled immediately. She knew Aaron hadn't said a thing about her to anyone, least of all this loud red-headed American with a smile that showed far too many teeth. She felt Aaron's hand on the small of her back, guiding her towards his brother. Rafe's welcome was more guarded.

'Hello,' he said, extending a hand. 'I'm Rafe. Nice to meet you.'

'Same here,' Julia said faintly.

'Here, have a seat . . . I'll get another one.' Rafe offered her his own. She sat down carefully, tucking her bare legs underneath her. In her floral summer dress and plimsolls she felt childish and overdressed. Diana was wearing white linen pants and a light blue kaftan. Simple, understated elegance of the sort Julia desired but never quite managed. Even Rafe's wife looked interesting – large gold hoop earrings and a long, swirling gypsy skirt. Julia accepted a drink from Aaron and concentrated on finishing it in silence, nodding politely whenever something was said.

Lunch was served inside. The food was delicious – *bouillabaisse*, Diana said in a clearly perfect French accent. In honour of their upcoming holiday. Julia sat next to Aaron, answering questions when they were directed at her. She liked Harvey, his father, immediately. He had an old-fashioned charm, a way of talking to you that put you straight away at ease. His questions were thoughtful and to her surprise, she found herself volunteering more information than she normally would. He asked about her family, her parents . . . were they still in Newcastle? She felt Aaron stiffen beside her but she was able to answer, quite naturally, 'No, they're both dead. Car accident.'

'Oh, my dear. I'm so sorry to hear that. Not recently, I hope?' Harvey's kind blue eyes were on her.

She shook her head. 'No, it happened when I was fifteen.'

Maddy piped up suddenly. 'Your parents *died*? *Both* of them? Oh my *God*!' She stared at Julia. Julia flinched as if she'd been slapped. *It's my loss, not yours*, she wanted to snap at her. She nodded coolly but it did nothing to stop Maddy's gushing enquiries. 'But how did you cope? I mean, how *old* were you? Fifteen? You poor *thing*. That is just the *worst* thing ever.'

Julia was speechless. She set her wine glass carefully to one side and hurriedly excused herself from the table. Her eyes were full of tears – but of rage, not sadness. How *dare* she? What had happened to her parents wasn't the plot of a play. It was life – *her* life! Not Maddy's, to be appropriated in some over-the-top performance. It took her fifteen minutes alone in the toilet to calm down. When she returned to the table, Maddy was subdued. Clearly she'd understood the message: a step too far.

Three hours later, the ordeal was over. Julia and Aaron walked up Northumberland Park Road together, hand in hand. It was a beautiful afternoon but Julia wasn't in the mood to appreciate the sunlight. Her mind kept drifting back to the lunch. She didn't care for Maddy. Not in the slightest. There was something about her that set Julia's teeth on edge. She tried too hard. She was too eager, too desperate to please. She laughed at jokes that weren't funny and empathised to the point of absurdity. But at least she'd had the sense to shut up after her silly little outburst over Julia's parents. Julia wasn't sure she could have taken much more. As for Diana . . . well, she wasn't what Julia had expected. Not at all. She was ice-cold, controlled and controlling. She sat at the head of the table, her boys ranged alongside her, claiming them all. The two women present were a minor and irritating distraction. Julia knew the type; Diana was a man's woman. The sort of woman who loved her sons and viewed their wives and girlfriends as nothing more than silly threats. She shivered suddenly, despite the warmth of the afternoon. No, Diana Pryce wasn't at all what she'd expected, but now that they'd met, she was somehow not surprised. She could sense Diana's presence in both Aaron and Rafe. There was a softness in them that was also a weakness – the effort, no doubt, of living up to her and her exacting, painful demands.

As if on cue, Aaron turned to her suddenly. 'What did you think of Diana?' he asked, and the anxiety was back in his voice.

'She's . . . she's lovely,' Julia lied. 'Quite formidable. I . . . I'm not sure she liked me much,' she said after a moment.

'Oh, she'll warm up,' Aaron said happily, relieved. 'It takes her a while, you'll see.'

Me too, Julia wanted to say, but didn't. For the moment, she was happy her answer had pleased him. She began to think about what to take to Mougins. In spite of her reservations about both Diana and Maddy, she was excited. In fact, she couldn't bloody wait. A two-week holiday in the south of France! 'I've never been abroad before,' she'd said to Diana over lunch.

Diana raised a perfect brow – just the one. 'Never?'

Julia shook her head. 'Nope. Not unless you count Scotland. And we drove.'

'You've never been in an aeroplane?' Aaron couldn't keep the surprise from his voice.

Julia shook her head again, but before she could answer, Maddy leapt in. 'Me neither,' she said cheerfully. 'The first time I came to London, I was so excited I couldn't sleep . . . I remember every minute of that plane ride, I promise you!'

Julia risked a quick glance at Diana's face. Not one but *two* women in her house who were so clearly unsuitable it was laughable. Diana murmured something inaudible and the moment passed.

And now Diana would be forced to spend a fortnight with them. Two women who'd never been abroad, never been to private schools, never had horse-riding lessons and couldn't play the piano; doubtless neither of them could swim, pick a fine wine or say *bouillabaisse* in a way that wouldn't make you wince. Despite it all, Julia had to smile. It just went to show . . . clearly Diana had spent a lifetime controlling everything around her. She'd planned it all, right down to the last detail. The right schools, the right homes, the right jobs . . . and then, at the eleventh hour, just when everything should have come together, both her boys had turned around and done something else. An out-of-work American actress and a girl from Up North. You had to laugh.

I've done it again, thought Maddy to herself miserably as the door closed behind Aaron and his girlfriend. *Over-the-top. Too loud, too friendly, too American.* She'd sensed Julia's withdrawal as soon as she opened her mouth. Would she never get the balance right? With Diana she was too reserved, too uptight, too sharp. With Julia she'd been too friendly, too effusive. She was no match for Diana's cool, offhand charm and she was convinced Harvey thought her dull. Even Aaron appeared to have forgotten her as soon as he turned away. She seemed unable to hold anyone's attention – ironic, given the fact that she was an actress. She'd studied Julia as discreetly as she could. Glossy dark shoulder-length hair; straight thick eyebrows, pale, flawless skin. She was attractive – even beautiful – but in a rather prickly, defensive sort of way. Her accent was very different to Rafe's and Aaron's – broader and flatter, and harder for Maddy to understand. She said very little; occasionally her eyes settled upon Maddy. *What in heaven's name is Rafe doing with someone like you?* she seemed to be asking. Maddy had none of the poise and sophistication that the English women she'd met seemed to have. Julia's flowered frock and white plimsolls seemed to Maddy to be the epitome of European chic. Her own full, gathered skirt in a patchwork of contrasting patterns, her peasant-style blouse with its frilled, embroidered neckline and her gold hoop earrings suddenly seemed cheap and silly. She slid a little further down in her seat. She found herself in awe of Julia, even though she'd barely opened her mouth. She was also a barrister . . . she'd been to Oxford, of course – a younger, even more reserved version of Diana, in other words. She would fit in perfectly, thought Maddy enviously, whereas she simply never would. Never.

58

JULIA
Mougins, July 1997

The car wound its way through the pine and olive groves, each bend a fraction sharper and tighter than the last. They were climbing steadily into the hills above Cannes. She and Aaron would be the first to arrive. 'Nearly there,' Aaron said, taking a hand off the steering wheel and placing it on her thigh. 'You'll love it, I promise.'

Julia was speechless. She sat beside him, unable to tear her eyes away from the landscape. Mile after mile of thickly carpeted dark green foliage, broken every now and then by the upright index finger of a cypress or a village spire. The soft stone-walled farmhouses and villas were nestled into the hills, an escape from both the sun and prying eyes. At the top of a hill where the road forked, Aaron turned down a narrow lane. 'Just down here,' he said, steering the car over the rutted tracks. 'Look – there's the oak tree we used to swing on when we were young. It belongs to old Cassoux, the neighbour. Dad built a sleeping platform one summer, and when we came back the next, he'd pulled it down. He can't stand us. Never could.'

'How long have you been coming here?' Julia asked, craning her head to take in the view. It was more peaceful than anything she'd ever seen.

'We've had it for ever. Since I was two, I think. My grandparents used to have a villa here . . . Harvey and Diana used to come here as kids. Diana's always doing something to it . . . new bathrooms, new kitchen . . . she loves it.'

'It's gorgeous,' Julia said, leaning out of the window and taking the scent of pine and the lemony tang of citrus groves down into her lungs. 'I'd never want to leave. Ooh . . . is that it? That little white gate?' she exclaimed suddenly.

'Yep. That's it.'

She almost pounded her knees in childish excitement. She opened the door as soon as Aaron pulled the car to a halt and got out. A white gate set into a thick yellow stone wall. Huge bunches of pink oleanders, a row of pale green olive trees, a gnarled old cedar – she pushed open the gate and ran ahead of Aaron. The farmhouse at the end of the short track had ochre-coloured walls and pale blue shutters; one side was covered entirely in ivy mixed with a yellow flowering plant of some description. It was August and everything was in flower. She slowed to a halt as she approached the front door. She and Aaron were the first to arrive. They would have the place to themselves for a night; Diana and Harvey were due to arrive the following afternoon, and then Rafe and Maddy were flying into Cannes that evening. She stopped in front of the door, over-come with a sudden shyness. What wouldn't her mother have given to come somewhere like this?

The entrance hall was cool and dark; the shutters were still drawn against the late afternoon sun. There was a partially open door to her left. She pushed it open and found herself in an enormous kitchen. A huge wooden table dominated the room – hanging above it, Provence-style, were scores of copper pans and utensils. A jug of freshly cut flowers stood in the centre of the table, releasing the sweet scent of lilacs and roses into the air. She stood in the middle of the room, looking dazedly around her. It looked like something out of a magazine. She wandered back into the hallway. The stone floor was covered with a beautifully intricate pale yellow and cream rug that ran the length of the hall. Diana's hand was everywhere – interesting-looking paintings on the walls, a piece of exquisite pottery here, a small carving there . . . to her left was an African mask that stood proud of the wall, a densely patterned riot of lines and deeply scored grooves. It was beautiful. Everything was beautiful.

'We're upstairs.' Aaron came through the front door, dragging suit-cases behind him. 'I'll bring these up. It's the top room, second flight of stairs.'

She climbed ahead of him, past the first landing and then up the narrow flight of stairs to what must once have been the attic. There was a single door at the top. She pushed it open slowly and stood in the doorway. It was a long, wide room with windows on both sides. The quality of light changed as it brimmed against the ceiling, casting dancing patterns against the smooth white walls. The bed was large and low with a white embroidered counterpane and a profusion of richly coloured pillows. A bowl of scented peaches stood on the dressing table, slowly releasing their heavy perfume into the air. An intense feeling of well-being flooded through her just as Aaron entered the room. She turned to him and put her hand on his arm. 'It's perfect, Aaron. Absolutely perfect.' The bag he was carrying slid slowly from his grasp and landed with a gentle thud on the floor. He kissed her.

'I'm glad you like it.'

'I do.'

She put a hand on his chest and laid her head against his shoulder. His body was warm. He kissed her, hard, and his grip tightened suddenly. She could feel his heart racing underneath her fingertips as he began to unbutton her shirt. They sat down together on the bed and turned to each other. Through the furry sweep of her lashes she caught a glimpse of his face, dreamily diverted as his body began seeking its own pleasure. He ran a hand down her stomach, fingers sensitive to the trembling his touch produced, stopping every now and then as if to check her reaction before sliding into the sweet wetness in a move that brought a sudden gasp from her throat.

'Aaron,' she whispered, 'I—'

'Shhh.' He moved inside her, his eyes closed, hands reaching for hers. He held her steady, pinned underneath him, increasing the tempo until he too exploded, an inarticulate sound coming from his own chest. 'Julia.' Slowly his whole body relaxed, becoming heavier by the second until the even, uninterrupted sound of his breathing told her he'd fallen asleep.

The sounds of unfamiliar birds pulled her slowly out of sleep. She lay beside Aaron, listening to the soft warbling call of a cuckoo and the answering sing-song of a bird she couldn't name. From somewhere over the hill came the distant sounds of construction – a mechanical drill and the whine of machinery – but even they failed to break the bubble of peace and tranquillity that surrounded the farmhouse. She got out of bed and surveyed the room. Their clothes lay scattered around – Aaron's jeans flung comically over the end of the bed, one leg still attached to his ankle under the bedspread. She slid it carefully off and picked up the rest. She pulled on her own jeans and slipped her shirt, still half unbuttoned, over her head. The floorboards creaked as she walked but Aaron slept on, undisturbed.

She walked downstairs and into the kitchen, her toes curling up under the cold flagstone surface. Someone had clearly been into the house that morning – there was a basket on one of the counters covered with a bright red-and-white checked cloth. She lifted it – inside were half a dozen fresh eggs, a white butter dish, and a brown paper bag of tomatoes. There was a jug of fresh milk on the table and two long, thin baguettes. She was suddenly hungry. She pulled off the tip of one of the baguettes and ate it whilst looking for a pot to make coffee. There was one in the cupboard – a silver stove-top affair like the one Diana used in London. She fiddled about with the flame on the enormous cooker before getting it right. She set it to boil and walked over to the window. The garden was wild and lush, extravagant bursts of colour and texture, different from the manicured lawn in Islington. A flock of birds – swallows? – cut across her line of vision and disappeared beyond the distant grey-blue line of the hills. She turned on the tap and slowly filled a glass with water. She drank dreamily, a part of her still left behind in the low bed where Aaron slept. There was a collection of photographs on the large French farmhouse dresser by the door. She wandered over and picked one up. She'd noticed the same silver frames at Diana's house but lacked the courage to look at them. She studied the photograph – there was Diana, and Harvey . . . and the three brothers. She couldn't get over how different Josh was. He was glowering into the camera, his body partially turned away from everyone, as if marking his distance. A sudden sound behind her made her jump. She nearly dropped the photograph.

'What're you doing? I woke up and you weren't there.' It was Aaron. There was a hint of sulkiness in his voice.

'Nothing. I just came down to make coffee. D'you want some?' She put the picture down carefully.

'What're you looking at?'

'Just a photograph. I was just thinking about how different you are . . . you know, from him.' She pointed to the picture. 'Josh. Did . . . did something happen between you,' she asked delicately. 'You never talk about him.'

'No.' Aaron's voice was flat. 'He's abroad.'

'You never talk about him.'

'Can we drop it? I've no intention of ruining the first day of the holiday talking about him.'

Julia looked at him in surprise. She'd never seen his face so tight and closed. 'Of course,' she murmured, putting the picture down. She walked to the stove. 'Coffee?' she asked, as lightly as she could.

He nodded. There was a strange look on his face. He held the expression for a moment, then all of a sudden it was gone. He came over to where she stood and buried his face in her hair. She put up a hand to touch his face. They stood like that for a moment, both breathing deeply. It was the first discordant moment since their relationship had begun. Slowly Julia felt his body relax against her. Something wasn't quite right, she thought to herself as she caressed his face, but she had no idea what. A falling-out, a deeply buried fight, an estrangement in the family? But wasn't that just the way of families? Some childish fuss that had refused to die? She was an only child; she had nothing to compare it with, nothing to offer Aaron except her embrace.

59

DIANA
Mougins, July 1997

Harvey braked suddenly and stopped the car. Diana was dozing – she felt the sudden lull as he switched off the engine and woke up, but he was already gone. A few minutes later, he pushed several thin batons belted in tissue paper through the back window. The car was immediately full of the yeasty scent of freshly baked bread. Diana's stomach was rumbling. It had been a while since lunch. She reached behind her and pulled one of the flour-dusty *ficelles* towards her. The crust crackled under the pressure of her hand. She brought the stick to her nose like a flower and carefully broke off a piece. She handed it silently to Harvey and broke another one for herself, chewing it slowly. She looked out of the window. Children in school uniform – the red and white check pinafores she remembered from childhood – were being dragged reluctantly along the street by young mothers in impossibly high heels and miniskirts, the firm, tanned flesh showing in glimpses as Harvey changed lanes and sped up. Tables outside bars were small islands around which old men in singlets clustered, clutching glasses of pale yellow *pastis*.

Sunlight pricked through the trees that bordered the highway – as they drove into the hills away from the town, the forest grew thicker and denser until they were finally driving under a canopy of green. She gazed out of the window at a day without landmarks. They rounded one bend after another; quick flashes of roadside flowers, some turned ashy with dust. Behind them, the blue tent of the sea tilted from side to side. They crested one hill and a lavender-blue valley, still shrouded in mist, spread out before them. 'It's spectacular, isn't it, darling?' she murmured to Harvey. 'Doesn't matter how often we come, I always forget how beautiful it is.' He laid a hand on her thigh without speaking; it was often his way of responding to a question that didn't need an answer.

The tyres crunched gravel underfoot as they rolled slowly down the track towards the house. At the gate, Diana got out, enjoying the feel of sun on her face and the chance to finally stretch her legs. Harvey drove through; she closed the gate behind him and walked slowly down the driveway, her arms wrapped around her waist. There was a white car parked under the shade; Aaron and that girlfriend of his were already there. Rafe and Maddy would arrive later that evening. She walked into the kitchen; Mme Poulenc had already been in that morning. The place was spotless, as usual, and the fridge was stocked. A large casserole dish of something delicious was on the stove, gently cooling. She picked up the kettle and took it to the sink. First things first – a cup of tea. *Oh, les Anglais* . . . she could practically hear Mme Poulenc's voice. She waited for it to boil and brought out two mugs from the dresser.

'Cup of tea, darling?' She turned as Harvey walked into the kitchen. His head practically touched the low ceiling, she noted with amusement. It was the same with all the boys. She could remember the summer when Rafe had suddenly shot up – he'd spent most of it holding his head in his hands. All the old dimensions had suddenly changed. Every room he went into, he'd had to duck. The following year it was Aaron's turn, and then a couple of years later, Josh's. She felt a peculiar lurch in the pit of her stomach when she thought of Josh. How afraid she'd been that he wouldn't grow to be as tall as the others. Silly fear – he was now an inch or two above even Harvey.

Harvey came to stand beside her whilst they waited for the kettle to boil. For a few moments, there was no sound in the house except their own breathing. Then she heard the gate creak open and the heavy tread of Mme Poulenc's feet on the gravel. She always insisted on coming to greet them in their first hour in the house. Diana slipped out of Harvey's arms and turned towards the door. Mme Poulenc stood in the doorway, her face beaming in welcome. It was a ritual that hadn't changed in twenty years.

Harvey was in the shower; she could hear his deep baritone as he hummed a few bars of the Chopin they'd been listening to on the way down. The two suitcases lay slack-jawed on the bed by the window; clothes and hangers in hand, she walked back and forth to the small dressing room that led off the bedroom, putting away clothes so that the suitcases could be stowed in the attic. She finished hanging up the last of them and was just about to close the sliding door to the dressing room when her eye fell upon the trunk pushed to the back of the rack of clothes against the wall. Her fingers went automatically to the thin gold chain that she'd worn around her neck for more than thirty years. The key to the trunk was one of the four gold charms strung on it. She touched it lightly, as if to remind herself of its presence. It had been a few years since she'd opened the trunk; she was suddenly overcome with a longing to delve inside it again, but the sound of the shower being turned off and the bathroom door being opened stopped her. Harvey had once asked her, years ago, what was inside it. 'Oh, just the usual childish stuff. You know, letters, trinkets, postcards, that sort of thing.' Dear Harvey – he'd taken her word for it, of course, and had never asked again. She'd had a copy of the original brass key made for her a few months after she'd bought it, and since then, it had never been off her person, not once. Not even when she'd been admitted to hospital with a ruptured appendix. She'd made such a fuss about having to remove all her jewellery that Harvey had arranged for her to keep it on. The colleague who'd done the operation was a friend after all.

But there was really no need to be so paranoid. Neither Harvey nor Mme Poulenc, the only two people who, so far as she knew, were aware of the trunk's existence, would ever dream of trying to open it. No, her things were safe. Only she knew what was inside it; only she would ever know.

60

MADDY
Mougins, July 1997

Brushing aside the thick, cloying flowers and leaves that jumped out on either side of her, Maddy made her way down the overgrown path to the pool. She'd been at the villa all of three days and this was the first day she'd had entirely to herself. She sighed luxuriously. A whole day free of the demands of others, free of Diana and her acerbic wit, of Julia's sharp tongue, free of everything except her own thoughts. She pushed through the last branch and came upon the pool. She gasped. It was beautiful. A slick turquoise skin, rolling in on itself gently in the breeze. Someone – Diana, in all likelihood – had organised for the sunloungers to be laid out. She put the large pannier down; in it was a novel, some sun cream and a chilled bottle of white wine. She sat down, slipped her sunglasses on and turned her face up to the August sunshine. Slowly, the tension of the previous three days began to dissolve around her. She picked up her novel, turned to the page she'd bookmarked and began to read. It was wonderful and hot. The air was a warm, soft lick against her skin. In the hazy spell of warmth, her pulse slackened; her hand lazily brushed at the insects that flecked the page. She pushed a strand of hair away from her face. The faint wasp-like stutter of a nearby motorcycle drifted through the air; a minute or two later it was gone. She lifted a hand to shade her eyes as she read, but the print danced and blurred and her mind ran free of the text. She dozed.

She woke with a start. Someone's hand was on her knee, slowly making its way up her thigh. She pushed herself upright; in those blank few moments between waking and sleep, she struggled to remember where she was, who she was . . . and who the man sitting on the edge of the sunlounger with his hand halfway up her bare leg was. 'Rafe,' she murmured weakly, happily, as it all came flooding back. *I'm Maddy. I'm on holiday in Mougins. This is my husband.* 'You scared me.'

'Why's that?' His hand did not stop at her thigh. It floated higher, sliding a finger underneath the thin stretchy fabric of her bikini.

'I . . . I thought you'd gone to town with the others.'

'I did. I came back early. No, don't move.'

She drew in her breath sharply. His fingers were marking out a light, teasing dance across her skin. She looked down and saw the muscles of her stomach quiver. 'Rafe . . .' she protested weakly. 'Someone might see . . .'

'Yeah? Who? There's no one here.' He slid a finger inside her; she had to bite down on the urge to pull her legs up underneath her and draw him in. 'Sshh.' His finger continued its slow, teasing stroke, turning her insides to jelly. She watched in fascination as he began building her gently but firmly towards a climax. He was in total and perfect command of her body. Her abdomen began its slow rhythmic shaking; her nipples were hard, standing firm against the skimpy fabric . . . she took in a deep breath, and then another, and then the delicious, slow shuddering began. She closed her eyes, utterly content to let him orchestrate things – to build her up, slow her down, bring her to the edge of pleasure and then hold back suddenly, letting the whole symphony begin again. He was teasing her; taking his time. She opened her eyes. He was watching her, the hint of a smile playing around his lips. She tried to resist, pulling herself back to show him that he wasn't the only one capable of control. 'Why don't you guys ever talk about Josh?' she asked suddenly. The question had been on her lips for days.

She felt his hand move away from her as if she'd physically pushed him away. He stood up abruptly, withdrawing himself. He looked as if he'd been slapped. His face was suddenly dark. He glanced down at her, as if he was about to say something, and then turned on his heel. 'Rafe!' she called out as he strode away from her. 'Rafe!' She stared after him. The bushes parted to let him in and just as suddenly as he'd appeared, he was gone. She lay back, stunned. Her right breast had pushed itself clear of her bikini cup and her bottoms were half undone. She struggled upright, hurriedly readjusting strings and straps, covering herself as quickly as she could. She felt naked and horribly alone. She'd done it again, she thought to herself as a tear began to slide its way down her cheek. She'd said something wrong. Made the wrong comment. Spoken out of turn. But how would she ever work out what was the right thing to say and when to say it when she didn't understand the problem? She'd asked about Josh . . . what on earth was wrong with that? What the hell had happened in this family to cause everyone such pain?

61

NIELA
London/Paris, August 1997

Niela woke first, dragged out of sleep by the unfamiliar presence of someone else in her bed. In her flat. She turned her head to look at Josh; he slept deeply, as if he might never wake. Her gaze slid past him to the room beyond. Her jeans lay discarded on the floor – a boot here, her sweater there, his shirt crumpled into a ball and flung across the chair. Reminders of the haste with which he'd pulled off her clothing the night before, presenting himself to her with such tremendous need that the tears formed thickly in her throat the minute he touched her. If he noticed, he said nothing. There was tension in him, like oil under the earth, welling constantly. She'd seen the evidence of it – and his temper – more often than she cared to admit. But there was another side to him; a half-buried, half-suppressed spirit of generosity, a lightness and charm that others often sensed and responded to . . . but as soon as he began to reach out, he withdrew, like a child who has received one too many blows and dare not risk another. She had never met anyone like him. Something had happened to make him turn from what she guessed was his true nature – easy, light, generous – into something else, more guarded, closed down and sealed off. Josh revealed himself agonisingly slowly, layer by layer, incident by incident, fact by isolated fact. It would take her a while to piece it all together, she saw, to fully understand him. Everything about him – the quicksilver moods, the flashes of anger, the sudden laughter, his enormous wit and his withdrawals – these were his weapons that kept the world at bay. She recognised it in him because she knew something of it in herself. He nursed a secret, just as she did, though she had no idea what. As she lay in the growing light beside him, listening to the slow, steady sound of his breathing, feeling the rise and fall of his chest against her arm, it came to her slowly, very slowly, that perhaps healing him might be her own healing as well.

She was making breakfast a couple of hours later, expertly cracking eggs into a bowl and whisking them in preparation for an omelette, when she heard him enter the kitchen and come to stand behind her. He wrapped his arms around her, burying his face in her hair. It was moments like these she would miss, she thought to herself, her throat suddenly aching. He'd been in London all of a fortnight; in a few days' time, he would leave. His next assignment had come through – Yemen. He would be gone for almost three months. She tried not to think about it or what it would mean. He would be gone – would he come back? They seldom spoke about the future, as if by some private silent admission that it was too precious to risk. His arms tightened about her. She smiled. 'I'm trying to make breakfast,' she murmured, pointing with her spoon to the open flame. 'You said you were hungry.' She felt his lips move against the curly mass of her hair. He said something indistinct. 'What?' she asked, turning down the flame.

'I said, this works, doesn't it?' There was a note of surprise in his voice.

'What does?' She switched off the flame and turned in his arms.

'This. You and me.' He made a small movement with his head that seemed to encompass not just their own presence in the room but something beyond.

'I . . . I suppose so,' she said hesitantly. Josh's quicksilver changes in mood were often precipitated by a question that wasn't really a question at all, more a statement of intent.

'You don't sound sure.' He pulled back from her for a moment. 'Any regrets?' He looked down into her eyes. His were dark and unreadable. His tone was light but he was anything but – she knew that about him now.

'No. No regrets.'

'So . . .' He paused, carefully pushing a strand of curls away from her cheek. 'How about it?'

'How about what?'

'How about we do this properly.'

She looked up at him, the breath catching in her throat. What was he asking her? She studied his lovely profile – the long, straight nose, tapering to two finely etched points above his lips; the sharply bevelled edge of his mouth and the strong jaw line in which the faint tremor of a muscle could always be seen, moving in secret time to some emotion he struggled to keep in check. She was amazed at the speed with which he had become familiar to her – she knew every shadow, every hollow, every surface of his body and face in a way she'd never known anyone before. 'Do what properly?' she asked.

'This. Us. You and me.'

257

She gave a short, almost embarrassed laugh. 'What are you talking about, Josh?' There was a moment's carefully held silence. 'You're not . . . ? Are . . . are you asking me to *marry* you?' she asked incredulously. She stared into his coal-black eyes, plumbing some unfathomable depth. His expression was neutral, but she could feel the tension in his whole body concentrated in his grip. His lips moved; he gave a wry, sardonic smile that didn't quite reach his eyes. His hand moved; it plunged into the thick dark tangle of his hair. 'Christ,' he murmured, his whole face breaking into a perplexed grin. 'I suppose I am.'

'Ma'am, is your seat belt fastened?' The flight attendant moved smoothly down the aisle, her blonde ponytail bobbing from side to side as she performed the usual last-minute rites before descent. Niela sat next to Josh, conscious of his hand on her thigh, the fingers tightening every once in a while in response to some private thought, his concentration elsewhere, only peripherally on her. She looked out of the convex bulge of the window. Beneath them, spreading in tight, neat circles towards the distant horizon, she could see the city of Paris unfolding, mile after mile, boulevard after boulevard, the occasional flash and patch of green. She felt her stomach lurch and not just in time with the turbulence. Her palms were sweating, despite the cool of the plane's interior. It had been a week since his proposal, which had seemed to surprise him as much as it had surprised her. In another, he would leave for Yemen. An old friend from university had given them the run of his Paris flat; it was Josh's idea. 'Let's get married in Paris. Let's not do it here.' That was the moment in which she ought to have said *I can't. I can't marry you anywhere, Josh, because I'm already married.* She didn't. She kept silent and the words she'd never uttered to anyone, ever, remained where they were – locked up, hidden from view, even her own. Her silence he took for consent. Before she properly understood what was happening, he'd taken charge.

And now here they were, descending through a grey, windy sky, huge swathes of angry cloud dissipating as they were reached to reveal flashes of summer sun. A series of bumps and shudders, a sideways lurch and then they were upon the ground once more. In a few hours' time she would be married. Again. She followed him out of the terminal building, her whole body flooded with a mixture of anticipation and dread. The last time she had been in Paris she'd been in flight, on the run from a future she'd done her best to forget. Now she was heading towards something, another kind of future, and one she desperately wanted. But the dread coursing through her veins couldn't be quite as easily dismissed. She would be found out. There would be some record, somewhere . . . someone would know. A letter would be sent; a phone call, an interruption in the happy event. Something official to say that Ms Niela Aden couldn't possibly become Mrs Josh Keeler because she was Mrs Hamid Osman. *Look. Do you see? Here it is. The* Heiratsurkunde. *Certificate of marriage. Here's the date, the place, the time. She signed it. See?* Her heart flipped back and forth between her mouth and her stomach as she waited beside Josh for their bags. Any moment now she would be found out. Any moment now.

The white onion-shaped domes of Sacré-Coeur dominated the landscape from every angle. Niela, Josh, Antonio and his girlfriend, Jeanne, who were their witnesses, walked into the city hall in the 18th Arrondissement. The three of them were laughing; Niela was not. Every second seemed an eternity – every fibre of her being attuned to the moment when someone would cough, interrupt the proceedings, cast a quick, puzzled look at her and then the whole thing would grind to a halt. But the moment had not yet come. The list of formalities was endless – *justificatifes de domicile, l'attestation d'hébergement sur l'honneur, l'extrait d'acte de naissance.* Niela looked on in bewilderment as Josh produced the necessary documents. Where had he found the time? His hand on her arm was a quiet, steady reassurance. They passed through one office after another; papers were produced, stamped, signed . . . no one even glanced at her. At last they were presented before the mayor, a tall, elegant woman who performed the simple ceremony in minutes. No one questioned her. The ceremony that had taken place earlier in Vienna was forgotten, buried under stacks of paperwork and computer files that no one would ever find or see. For the second time in her life, she held out her hand. Josh hadn't even had time to find an engagement ring. The simple silver band was all. It was done. They were married.

Jeanne knew of a restaurant a few blocks away. They hurried down the street. A summer storm was threatening. Niela was sweating, but with relief. It was humid; the close, thick air hung over the city, waiting to be cleared. The four of them entered the cool air of the restaurant, Antonio shouting for champagne as they walked in. The owner, a short, balding Algerian, was delighted. '*Un mariage? Très bon!*' Champagne was brought to the table in four delicate flutes. They drank just as the first drops of rain began to fall, fat and steady against the ground. The tension that had been building up in Niela for over a week had peaked; now it began to fall. Under the sweet intoxication of champagne, she found herself beginning to unwind. It helped that the two ceremonies were so dissimilar as to be two completely separate things. She had almost no recollection of the marriage that had taken place in Meidling. She remembered it in snatches – the sea of faces, the *nikkah*, the scratchy, starchy feel of the fabric of her pale lilac *dirac*, one of three, she remembered. She looked down at the pale blue linen shift Anna had helped her choose in Top Shop the previous Saturday. It was very simple – a pretty piece of white lace embroidery at the neck and on the single front pocket, 'Very Sharon Stone,' Anna had murmured, holding it against her. 'In *Casino*,' she added helpfully. Unfortunately Niela didn't know either. 'Yes, it's a little bit fifties,' Anna said. 'But that's a good thing.' It was hard to tell who was more surprised about the wedding, Anna or Niela herself. Anna had met Josh once, though she'd been the shoulder on whom Niela leaned after her return from Djibouti. She was darkly suspicious. 'I can see why you like him,' she said on the telephone the following morning. 'He's gorgeous. He reminds me a little of my brother, you know. But . . . be careful, Niela. Please be careful. A man like that . . . he doesn't need anyone, least of all you.' But Anna was wrong. She didn't know Josh the way Niela did. Few people, she was beginning to understand, did. She looked at Josh; now, in Antonio's presence, he was animated and expansive. They were arguing fiercely, but there was laughter too. Antonio was the first person she'd met from the unknown depths of his past. They'd studied architecture together; somehow they'd bucked the trend and wound up doing almost the same thing – building camps rather than luxury homes, travelling to places most people would rather not see, living a life far removed from the sorts of comforts their family backgrounds could so easily have provided. It was funny, she thought to herself with a slight, wry smile – Anna often said she was an enigma no one could ever hope to solve; it occurred to her now that she had married someone whose depths were perhaps even more hidden than her own.

PART SIX

62

JULIA
Hayden Hall, November, 1997

The air in the little chapel at Hayden Hall was thick with the scent of lilies. The florists were putting the finishing touches to the displays. Lady Barrington-Browne walked around with the two assistants, making sure that everything was perfect, just so. Across the courtyard, in the bedroom where she'd stayed the previous night, Julia pulled back the curtains and looked out of the window. The morning mist had lifted and the red and gold oak trees that lined the view all the way to the horizon were slowly emerging into view. Through the patchy, misty sky, she could see flashes of blue. Somewhere in the distance, a border of clouds was hovering, massing thickly. Lady Barrington-Browne, who never left anything to chance, had been listening to the weather forecast all week. A thirty per cent possibility of rain, she'd announced cheerfully the evening before. As a result, there were enough umbrellas on hand in the hallway of the house to shelter every single guest. Quite how or where one got a hundred and fifty umbrellas from was anybody's guess, but that was just the way things were done at Hayden.

She turned from the window and looked down at her dress. Her fingers trailed over the delicate roses at the waistband. It still felt like a dream and not just because she'd never expected to get married in a place like Hayden Hall. She'd never really expected to get married at all – and certainly not to Aaron. She thought back to the conversation she'd had with Lady Barrington-Browne, almost a year ago. *Love, hate . . . practically the same thing if you ask me. I'm always mixing them up.* Was it true? She tried to remember what she'd seen in him the night he'd come round to her office and that fragile line between love and hate had slowly and subtly been crossed. Most women looked at Aaron and saw only the exterior – six feet two of rugged, blond good looks. Julia saw that too, was deeply attracted to it, but it was the other, hidden stuff that was the real pull. For all his confidence and self-assured exuberance, there was a quieter, more troubled Aaron lurking within – that was what she loved. She sometimes wondered what he saw in her. He admired her – he'd said so often enough. When good food and wine had loosened his tongue, he'd let slip the fact that he thought her much cleverer than him. That she'd go further than he ever would; that she was the brilliant one, not him. Listening to him, despite the embarrassment she felt whenever someone praised her too loudly or too long, she'd experienced a deep thrill of pride. There was no one else to share her achievements with, no matter how small. Aaron was all she had. There was a sudden lump in her throat, and for a moment the room lurched in tears. Harvey would give her away. *And you, Dad,* she whispered to herself. *And Mum.* She had to steady herself; it was her wedding day, she kept reminding herself sternly. Not a good time to cry.

'Julia?' Diana's voice interrupted her. She rapped on the door and walked in without waiting for an answer. 'Ah, there you are. Harvey was wondering where you'd got to. Did you have something to eat?'

Julia shook her head. 'I'm fine. Just not . . . not very hungry.'

'Whatever's the matter?' Diana regarded her in alarm.

Julia shook her head clumsily. Her throat was thick with emotion. 'N . . . nothing,' she said, tilting her head backwards so that the tears wouldn't spill. Diana's hairdresser had spent an hour doing her make-up that morning. The last thing she wanted was to walk into the chapel on Harvey's arm looking like a raccoon.

'You'll be fine,' Diana said briskly. There was a moment's awkwardness. 'I'll leave you alone for a few minutes, shall I?' she said, turning to go. 'I'll send someone up to get you. Everyone's beginning to make their way across.' She hesitated for a second. 'You look lovely, Julia,' she said, her voice suddenly gentle. She was gone before Julia could blink.

It was cool inside the chapel. As they walked slowly up the aisle, Julia was only dimly conscious of the muted sounds of conversation and people getting to their feet. Harvey's arm was a solid, reassuring presence. Ahead of her, turning nervously every few seconds to check on their progress, was Aaron. She saw Dom turn and smile at her. There was a swell of music and the sound of chatter falling away. She felt herself being passed from Harvey to Aaron as they reached the altar. The priest's voice broke the silence; the smooth, mellifluous baritone held everyone's attention as the service began. Julia heard very little. 'You may kiss the bride,' she heard the priest say, smiling at them both indulgently. There was the brief pressure of Aaron's lips and then a loud burst of applause as they both turned. Through a blurry double veil of tears and lace, she could see a few of her old school friends dabbing their eyes. In the front row, Dom's grin threatened to split his face. To his left sat his mother, resplendent in a glorious hat that obscured everyone on either side. She felt Aaron nudge her towards his parents. There was a kiss on either cheek from Diana, a hug from Harvey . . . and then everyone came forward, crowding round. There were a dozen people from work, various aunts and uncles and one or two others whose names she would not remember. One of the bridesmaids tripped over her train – she was led, howling, from the chapel. The other three kept running up to touch her dress or hide shyly behind their mothers. The photographer, a young woman with a thick wad of gum wedged somewhere at the back of her mouth, came and went, snapping away. Julia kept catching sight of Aaron's head as he too was passed from one set of congratulations to another. Rafe and Maddy were there, Rafe's blond head towering over most of the other guests. It all unfolded dreamily in front of her; as though it were happening to someone else.

At last they were summoned from the chapel to the Great Hall for the wedding lunch. She held Aaron's hand tightly as they walked across the yard. No sign yet of rain, she overheard Lady Barrington-Browne say. The gardens shimmered in the late morning sunlight. It seemed to her that she was the only one who saw the beauty of the early winter light, the pale gold of leaves and the green grass that was slowly fading to silver. She disappeared along with the others under the archway, smelled the damp mossy air of the short passage before emerging into the light. Gold, silver, incense and light – that was how she would remember it always, the most important day of her life.

Across the spectacular foyer where the guests had gathered for a pre-lunch drink, Maddy watched Julia being passed from one set of relatives to another, just as she'd been a few months earlier. Julia and Aaron's wedding was altogether a very different affair. Julia looked lovely, Maddy thought enviously. She was wearing a slim-fitting ivory dress and elegant heels; her dark hair had been smoothed off her face and swept up into an sleek chignon. The high emotion of the day was caught in her normally reserved face. Yes, she looked lovely. Maddy, on the other hand, looked terrible. She held a glass of sparkling water in her hand. She was four months pregnant and felt like a whale. 'I look fat, don't I?' she'd asked Rafe as she struggled with the zip on her dress earlier that morning.

'No, you don't.' It was Rafe's standard response. He didn't look up from the newspaper he was reading.

'I *do*,' she hissed, annoyed at his lack of interest. She was being childish but she couldn't stop.

'Champagne, ma'am?' A waitress suddenly appeared at her elbow, breaking into her thoughts. Maddy looked at her – a teenager, a tiny slip of a girl – and felt the slow burn of panic begin to set in. She had once been that slim – but not any more.

She shook her head. 'Oh, I'd love to, honey, but I can't.' The girl looked at her, puzzled, but said nothing and passed on to the next guest instead. Maddy looked around the room. Rafe was over in one corner, talking animatedly with Aaron and two older, distinguished-looking men whom she assumed were Aaron's colleagues. She watched Aaron and Julia exchange a private, loving glance. No one had so much as looked in her direction. She felt out of place and out of sorts. She looked around for the toilets. They were across the room. She put down her glass and walked towards them, passing Rafe on the way.

'Hello, darling,' he said, putting out a hand absently. 'Where're you off to?'

'Nowhere. The toilet, I mean.' She crossed the room quickly, her high-heeled shoes marking out a quick staccato on the parquet flooring. She opened the door and locked it behind her. It beckoned to her – gleaming white porcelain, shiny taps, fluffy white towels . . . everything she needed to make herself clean again. She tucked her hair behind her ears and knelt down. It took her a few attempts to get started, but once she did, it was over in seconds. She leaned back on her haunches, dizzy with effort. Her eyes were smarting and there was a soft ringing in her ears. But she felt lighter, free of the nervous worry that was beginning to plague her. She stood up, rinsed her mouth and flushed away the evidence of her distress. It was all over. Everything nice and calm. Everything under control. For now.

63

It wasn't in her nature to be impressed by such things but now, looking around the exquisite interior of Hayden Hall, Diana grudgingly had to admit she was impressed. With Julia. She thought back to the conversation they'd had after coming back from Mougins in the summer. Although she shouldn't have been surprised when Aaron announced it, the news that he and Julia were engaged had still come as a shock. She'd barely recovered her breath when Julia followed up with the news that they intended to have the ceremony at Hayden Hall. 'In November,' she'd added.

'Hayden Hall? Are you sure?' Diana asked her, surprised. Yes, of course she knew the girl was friendly with Dominic Barrington-Browne . . . but to *that* extent?

'Of course I'm sure,' Julia said shortly. 'Dom's my best friend. It was his idea.'

Diana's eyes narrowed. 'Oh. Well. It's a beautiful setting. It's very generous of them.'

'Very.' Julia's chin lifted a fraction. They'd stared at each other, but it was Diana who was forced to drop her gaze first. She'd been forced to admit there was more to the girl than the accent that jumped out at you like a barking dog and the quiet watchfulness with which she seemed to endure the world around her. She'd never quite grasped what it was that Aaron saw in her – now she realised that underneath the quiet exterior there was something altogether tougher to be had. Julia was obviously no fool; one didn't get to Oxford on a wing and a prayer, certainly not from a background like hers. It was clearly not the privileged upbringing that Diana's own sons had had. But she'd never given Diana much of a chance to see beyond the prickly defensiveness. Now Diana wondered if it hadn't been a ruse all along. The girl was smarter and more ambitious than she'd guessed.

And now here she was, married to Aaron, her son. Diana shook her head in disbelief. She still couldn't get over the speed at which everything had happened. In the space of a few months, two of her boys were married. Taken from her. Just like that. Worst of all, she hadn't even had a chance to get to know the women they'd chosen beforehand. Maddy had been a fait accompli, practically presented after the fact. Now Julia was, too. That only left Josh. Her stomach gave a sudden, horrid lurch. She looked around her, almost furtively. No, Josh hadn't come, not to this wedding either. Nor, thank God, had Rufus. It had been over a decade since she'd seen the two of them together; she wasn't sure she had the stomach for it, not now.

64

DIANA
London, Christmas Day, 1997

Diana walked around the dining table putting the finishing touches to the place settings, then stood back to admire her work. The table was beautiful. There were sprigs of holly at each place, a huge wreath of Christmas flowers in white, red and green at the centre; sparkling crystal wine and champagne glasses off which the light bounced and scattered in every direction; starched white linen napkins and the beautifully embroidered tablecloth she'd received from her mother on her wedding day, almost thirty-five years earlier. She folded her arms suddenly and ran her hands up and down them, hugging the memory to herself. What was it her mother had said? Something about gifts often outlasting their recipients or the occasions for which they'd been bought . . . exactly the sort of bizarre, straight out of left-field thing her mother could be counted upon to say. She shook her head slightly. What a time to be thinking about her mother, she thought to herself with a frown. She hardly ever did that, least of all at Christmas. It was one of her small triumphs to have conquered the ghost of Christmases past. Christmas in the Pryce household had always been an unhappy time, fraught with tears and tension. There was something about the forced jocularity of the festive season that brought out the worst in her parents and therefore in herself. If it hadn't been for Harvey and Rufus next door, she didn't know what she'd have done.

There'd been that one Christmas, the worst she could remember . . . her mother sitting in her bedroom upstairs, drinking herself into oblivion as quickly as possible; her father preoccupied in his surgery at the end of the road with last-minute patients, delaying the moment when he had to come home to a drunk wife and a silent, tearful daughter. She'd gone round to the Keelers' as soon as she could, taking with her the single present that her mother had somehow managed to buy. She was still in her nightie, she remembered. Dot, Harvey and Rufus's mother, opened the door. If Dot had ever found it strange that the girl who lived next door spent more time in their home than in her own, she never said a word. She treated Diana as if she were simply one of the family. 'Come on in, darling,' she'd said, giving Diana a hug. Diana could still remember the warm, faintly perfumed feel of Dot's arms, more comforting and familiar to her than her own mother's. 'Boys are upstairs, pet. Cocoa or milk?' It was a ritual that they performed nearly every holiday.

'Cocoa, please.' She'd gone upstairs and knocked on Rufus's door. She very much wanted to open her present in front of him. Of the two of them, Harvey was by far the nicer . . . but it was Rufus whose approval she longed for. It was Rufus whom she adored. Not Harvey.

'Go away,' Rufus had growled. Diana held her breath. 'I'm busy.'

'It's me. Diana,' she whispered into the keyhole. Across the landing, Harvey was still asleep. She was ten at the time. Harvey was eleven and Rufus was an age away, thirteen. Grown up, at least to her eyes, aloof and utterly unapproachable. He hadn't always been that way. She'd lived next door to them in London since she was two; as long as she could remember, the Keelers had always been there. Later, to her delight, Dot and Jim had bought the old villa at the end of the lane in Mougins, in the south of France, where her parents had a holiday home. Their lives had a perfect symmetry that reassured and sustained her. She would live next door to them for ever. Dot was the perfect mother; Jim the perfect father. And Rufus and Harvey were the perfect brothers she didn't have but desperately longed for. Only sometimes she wasn't sure that what she felt for them, especially Rufus, was entirely right. She didn't think of him as a brother, at least not in the way her friends at school seemed to feel about their brothers. Those relationships seemed to be about mutual hatred, buffered occasionally by reluctant tolerance. Diana *loved* Rufus; she couldn't wait to get home from school so that she could go round and show him what she'd been doing all day, what she did in those painful hours when she wasn't with him. At first Rufus appeared to like it; he seemed flattered by her devotion. She couldn't say when it changed; when he became different. Meaner. Colder. More demanding. At first she was bewildered, then devastated. There were days when she went home in tears; being rejected by Rufus was worse than anything she could have imagined. No amount of explanation on Dot or Harvey's part could comfort her. She was inconsolable. She would come round, day after day, begging him to talk to her. He refused. He went out, ignored her, sometimes he even taunted her. Then, when it appeared as though he would never speak to her again, he'd suddenly change tack. He would notice her again and the sunshine would be returned to her world; all was well. So long as Rufus liked her, everything would be fine.

That morning, she bent down to the keyhole, her heart in her mouth. She wasn't sure she could bear the thought of being sent away again, not on Christmas Day. 'It's me,' she whispered. 'Can I come in?'

There was another second's agonising pause, then, reluctantly, 'Oh, all right. But make it quick. I'm busy.'

She opened the door. Rufus was lying in bed, his knees drawn up to his chest. He was reading something. A comic book. 'Wh . . . what are you reading, Rufus?' she asked, advancing into the room, her unopened present still in her hands.

He lowered the comic book to look at her. There was a funny expression on his face. 'Come here,' he said softly. 'Look.'

She clambered on to the bed beside him. He had one hand underneath the duvet cover and the other hand held the comic book open across his bent knees. She looked at the page and swallowed. It wasn't a comic book at all. She struggled to take in what he was showing her. Naked women, their bare breasts jumping out at her at all sorts of strange, contorted angles. Wide, open mouths; eyes all with the same vacant, glossy stare. Other things, too. Things she knew about, somehow, but had never seen. There was a horrible leaden feeling in the pit of her stomach as he turned the page with his free hand, the other moving rapidly up and down beneath the covers, touching himself. He too had a funny, glassy stare and his breathing had suddenly gone very rough and shallow. She sat very still next to him, not knowing what to do or say. Slowly, without taking his jet-black eyes off her, he peeled back the covers and—

'Diana?' A voice broke through the fog of memory. She almost jumped out of her skin. Harvey had come upon her in the doorway. 'All set?' He bent his head and kissed the back of her neck. It took every ounce of self-control not to twist herself away. 'You smell lovely,' he said against her ear. 'New, is it?' She shook her head, not trusting herself to speak.

'They'll start arriving any minute now.' He gave her shoulders a small squeeze. 'Glass of wine, my love?'

She nodded. Wine. Champagne. Anything. Anything to take the edge off. Damn him, she thought to herself furiously, accepting a glass a few moments later. *Damn* him.

Maddy turned her attention away from the bowls of snacks and plates of small, mouth-wateringly delicious canapés and focused on the conversation unfolding around her instead. It was safer that way. She was nearly six months pregnant; she had no business stuffing her face and then escaping to the bathroom shortly afterwards. There was no telling what sort of damage she was doing to the child she was carrying inside her. But she couldn't help it. Pregnancy just didn't suit her, physically or emotionally. She was swollen from head to toe; she was tearful and irritable and she'd long ago stopped thinking of herself as anything other than a whale, a hippopotamus or a cow, depending. She'd been dreading the Christmas lunch, from the food to the conversation. But it seemed to be going . . . well, OK. She'd managed to limit herself to a small triangle of toasted rye thickly spread with caviar – she'd cut it into three and eaten each piece slowly, concentrating on the flavour and texture and resisting the urge to cram the whole thing into her mouth and reach for another one, and another. So that was good. She'd resisted sneaking a quick gulp of champagne, which also helped. She'd even managed a bit of light-hearted banter with Aaron, whom she'd never found particularly easy . . . All in all, it was a good, safe start.

She looked around her. The whole family was there – Diana, Harvey, Aaron, Julia, Rafe and herself . . . a proper family Christmas. The day was carefully planned – presents wouldn't be opened until much later. That was the way Diana liked it. Lunch first, then the Queen's speech, which Maddy thought hilarious. They would all sit in the upstairs living room, the heavily decorated tree twinkling beautifully in one corner . . . Harvey would bring in wine and port and cheeses and only then, after another hour or so of conversation, would the presents be brought out and opened. Maddy was used to sneaking downstairs before dawn; not in this household, clearly. Diana spent weeks preparing for the Christmas lunch, or so she'd heard. Maddy allowed herself a small smile. Actually, the *housekeeper* would have spent weeks preparing it, not Diana. She'd been busy – she'd been on television a couple of times in the past week. Maddy had been at home, doing something boring and mechanical like the ironing or folding towels, when Diana's face popped up on the screen. She'd only just managed to resist the temptation to hurl a shoe at the screen. 'I saw you on television the other day,' she said to Diana as she got up to open a bottle of red wine. 'You were really impressive. How do you manage to stay so calm with all those microphones in your face?'

Diana's eyes narrowed suspiciously, as if trying to work out whether Maddy was being facetious or not. 'You get used to it,' she said shortly.

'I don't think *I* could.' Maddy smiled. 'I mean, it's one thing to remember to smile but it's a whole different ball game when you've got to give an opinion, too. I mean, I know you must rehearse what you're going to say, but you make it seem so effortless.'

Diana paused. She seemed to be struggling between disbelief and flattery. Maddy saw it and was pleased. 'Well,' she said after a moment, 'it's not as difficult as it seems. You generally know what they're going to ask . . . it's all a bit of a game, to be honest.'

It was the most Diana had ever said to her, Maddy realised with a growing sense of wonder. She glanced quickly at Rafe. He smiled back encouragingly. Maddy felt a warm glow of satisfaction slowly start to spread within her. Why hadn't she thought of it before? Flattery will get you everywhere, as someone once famously said – and if anyone could act the part of flattering sincerity, she could. 'Game or not,' she said, warming to her role, 'you play the part really well.'

'Why, thank you, Maddy.' Diana picked up the bottle she'd been aiming for. 'That's sweet of you to say. Can we tempt you with just one little glass? I know you're not supposed to, but *I* did . . . didn't seem to—' She stopped suddenly, a reddish blush spreading over her face. She seemed about to say something, then changed her mind. 'Will you?' she asked again, her voice unnaturally loud.

Maddy quickly held out her glass. 'Just one,' she said, smiling at her. She caught sight of Julia's faintly sneering glance. *I can see right through you*, Julia seemed to be saying. *Oh, fuck you*, Maddy thought to herself, suddenly defiant. Who cares what *you* think?

All of a sudden, the doorbell rang. Diana frowned. It was almost four o'clock and they were just about to start lunch. 'Now, who on earth could that be?' she said, putting her napkin aside and getting up. 'It's Christmas Day. Hang on, let me just go and see who it is.'

65

NIELA
London, Christmas Day, 1997

As they turned into Northumberland Park Road and the houses began to flash past, a sense of panic suddenly swept over Niela and she reached out to grip Josh's hand. 'Are you sure this is a good idea?' she asked nervously.

'We won't stay long. It's Christmas.'

'But you haven't told them anything. I mean, they don't know about . . . they're not expecting us. They're certainly not expecting *me*.'

'Niela, stop worrying about it. It's fine.' His voice carried with it the impatient warning tone she'd come to recognise.

She sighed but did not let go of his hand. Her heart was thumping loudly in her chest. 'Which one is it?' she asked. They all looked the same. Tall, elegant, wealthy. Where she lived in Shepherd's Bush, such houses had long since been chopped up, divided, scaled back. Here the opposite seemed to be true.

'Here we go.' He pulled up in front of one such house. 'Stop worrying. Nothing's going to happen.'

She said nothing. It didn't seem right to her that her first introduction to his family would be *after* the fact of their marriage, not before. She didn't care what he said – or, rather, *didn't* say – about his tense relationship with them. She followed him up the short path to the front door, her stomach churning with nerves. He rang the bell and looked down at her, a strange expression on his face. Someone turned the handle on the other side and flung open the door. She blinked. Standing in the doorway, framed by the soft glow of light spilling out from behind her, was a woman whose face she immediately recognised. Niela stared at her in confusion. It was Diana Pryce. The lawyer. She knew who she was. She'd seen her on television, many times. What on earth were they doing at Diana Pryce's house?

'Josh?' There was a look of stunned incredulity on the woman's face. 'Wh . . . what are you doing here? When did you come? When did you arrive?'

'Hello, Mother.' Josh bent down and kissed her on both cheeks. 'I only just got here. A couple of days ago. I thought it would be a nice surprise. Where's Dad?'

'He's in the living room. They're all here . . . Rafe and Aaron and everyone.' She looked behind Josh to Niela. 'Who . . . who's this?'

Niela had to resist the urge to turn and flee. Her mind was whirling. Josh had called Diana Pryce 'Mother' – she looked from one to the other, struggling to remember what Josh had said to her about his parents. Yes, he'd said his mother was a lawyer. Why hadn't he mentioned who she really was? 'I . . . I'm . . .' she began, looking nervously at Josh. He drew her towards him. There was a brief pause; Diana looked at him expectantly. Out of the corner of her eye, Niela saw a small black cat pick its way delicately across the thickly carpeted floor and curl its tail around the banister, staring at them. 'I probably should have warned you, I know . . .' Josh spoke suddenly, putting out a hand to catch Niela's. He put an arm round her, giving her a small squeeze. 'Mother, this is Niela. My wife.'

They all looked up expectantly as the sound of footsteps carried down the stairs. Julia could hear a man's voice, deep and resonant. Harvey stopped slicing; he put the knife down and looked towards the doorway, his face breaking out into a smile. 'Josh?' he called out in the instant before a man appeared, his frame and presence filling the doorway.

'Josh? What the fuck's *he* doing here?' The expletive was ripped from Aaron's lips.

'Aaron!' Harvey frowned at him as he moved towards the door. 'Josh! What a surprise! What . . . when did you arrive?' Harvey was laughing; he caught hold of Josh around the neck and pulled him close. 'What a wonderful surprise!' Behind them, Diana stood, an expression of absolute joy on her face.

Julia looked at Josh. Her breath caught and held. She could feel the anger burning off Aaron sitting next to her. Across the table, Rafe was similarly smouldering; Maddy too appeared dumbstruck. She turned her eyes back to the man in the doorway. So this was Josh. A secret thrill ran through her. The wayward, difficult brother. The rebel. The outcast. She almost smiled – the biblical references seemed hilariously out of place. It wasn't that he was taller or bigger than anyone else, but she had never in her life seen anyone who looked quite so alive. Diana cleared her throat suddenly, like a bird about to sing, breaking the spell. Her face had the bright, carefully prepared look of authority upon it.

'Well, everyone . . . it seems there's a bit of an announcement to be made.' She turned. There was someone standing behind her. She drew the young woman in. 'This is Niela.' She said the word carefully, glancing at the girl as if for confirmation. 'Josh's wife.' She pressed her lips together until the flesh whitened to a cleft on either side of her nose. Julia looked on in amazement. Diana was crying! She put a hand up to her cheek as if she too were surprised by her own tears and then turned and walked quickly out of the room. There was another pained silence as Aaron and Rafe looked uneasily at one another, then at Harvey, as if, in his capacity as head of the household, there should be something from him. There wasn't. Harvey got up, mumbled an apology and hurriedly left the room.

Niela sat with her knees pressed together, acutely aware of everyone's stares. Someone had hurriedly produced a glass of red wine, which she held in her hand, not sure whether to drink it or not. Josh was sitting opposite her, his attention momentarily claimed by the red-haired woman whose name she'd already forgotten – Mary? Marie? She seemed to be married to the older brother, Rafe. Next to her, having got up to make room for herself and Josh, was the other wife – Julia? She was married to Aaron, who sat on her left. All three were silent. No one knew quite what to say. There were plates of half-served food congealing on the table. They'd arrived in the middle of Christmas lunch and swiftly put an end to it. It was strange. Back home in Mogadishu, everyone would just continue eating; it didn't matter when people arrived or who they were . . . all were welcome, at all times. Here in England, it was different. You had to be invited, anticipated, prepared for. To do what she and Josh had done was, quite simply, rude. She took another sip of wine and stole a quick look across the table, where Josh sat drinking his wine in silence. The redhead had obviously given up trying to coax a conversation out of him.

'Sorry, where did you say you were from?' The older brother addressed her suddenly.

'Somalia.'

'Somalia?' Julia looked at her, surprised. 'You're a long way from home.'

Niela met her gaze. Julia was dark-haired and quite coldly beautiful – ice-blue eyes, a porcelain complexion and a rather harsh voice that was at odds with her appearance. 'Yes,' she said simply, refusing to be drawn.

'D'you miss it?' It was the redhead. She was American; Niela caught the accent on the back of her tongue.

'Yes, I do. Don't you?'

She saw from the way a faint blush spread across the woman's features that she'd made her point. She was also away from home.

'D'you go back often to visit?' Rafe asked.

'There's a war on, in case you hadn't noticed.' Josh's voice was terse.

'Where did you two meet?' the other brother asked suddenly.

'None of your business,' Josh broke in. His eyes flickered over his brother with a look Niela couldn't fathom. There was another short, embarrassed silence. 'Right.' Josh stood up suddenly. 'We're off. Say goodbye to Mother.'

Niela put down her wine glass and scrambled to her feet. They'd been in the house all of ten minutes. She was bewildered. They'd come all the way across London on Christmas Day for this? She followed Josh up the stairs, something close to anger surging in her chest. No wonder he wanted nothing to do with them. What kind of a family had he brought her into?

Diana stood by the bedroom window, looking down on to the garden. But it wasn't the garden she saw – it was Josh. Josh as a baby, staring up at her from the cocoon of blankets the day she'd brought him home from the hospital. He was a June baby; the weather that year had been warm. She'd taken him outside on the second or third day, laying him gently down on the grass, swaddled in blankets, Rafe and Aaron hovering nearby, already entranced with this tiny, perfect baby brother she'd brought. Things were so different back then. They couldn't stop staring at him, peering into the crib that had been theirs before his. Even then the differences were marked – Josh's olive-skinned face and dark hair and eyes a stark contrast to their fairness. She couldn't remember when their fascination turned to irritation. It was the crying, then the screaming. Josh was unable to settle. No sooner had she put him down to sleep than he began wailing; no sooner had she fed him that his angry screams began again. He seemed consumed with a rage that no one could understand. It began to take its toll on them, all of them. She remembered Harvey's face, numb with exhaustion as he stumbled from the operating theatre to the house and the sound of crying that never stopped. The boys too were affected. 'Why's he always crying?' Rafe would ask her, only a hundred times a day. 'What've *we* done?' She couldn't answer; she didn't

276

understand it herself. She tried everything. She and Harvey began to quarrel – she was over-attentive; she wasn't attentive enough. She fussed over him and ignored the other two. She put Josh's needs before everyone else's – no wonder the child was becoming unmanageable. She ought to put her foot down. *Leave him alone. He'll stop screaming soon enough, you'll see.* He didn't. She couldn't stand it any longer. After that last argument with Harvey, she'd taken Josh and driven down to Mougins alone – that long, miserable drive, and then the shock and terror that had followed. A kaleidoscope more dreadful than anything anyone could possibly imagine. Her mind skirted dangerously around the territory she avoided every single second of every single day. Stop it. She drew in deep, shuddering breaths. It took all of her formidable control to stop herself from entering into the dark cave of her memory. It was that girl. Josh's wife. When she opened the door and saw her standing there, half hidden by her son, she'd been unable to stop the thought running through her mind: he's not so dark after all. Next to her, the dark, rich colour she'd always feared in Josh paled; he became more like her, like the others. Like her son. Stop. *Stop.* She clutched at the material of her dress, as if she could somehow physically push the thought away. The rest of the family were waiting downstairs for the lunch to proceed. She had to go back down; she *had* to. Behind her, she heard the toilet flush and the sound of the tap being turned on. Harvey would come out of the bathroom any minute now, cross the floor and wrap his arms around her as he always did when what he called her 'dark moods' came on. She heard the door open.

'Are you all right, my love?' He came to stand behind her. 'I know it's a bit of a shock.' She leaned back into his embrace as if he might shield her from herself. How narrow the gap was between the balance of their lives and its complete destruction. A wrong word, a slip of the tongue, a gesture made out of place . . . and the whole thing would come crashing down around her. She thought back to the last time she'd seen Rufus. *We can't talk now.* No, we can't.

66

MADDY
London, Christmas Day, 1997

Christmas lunch had not been a success; an unqualified disaster would have been closer to the mark. In fact, the only good thing to be said about the whole tortuous afternoon was that she'd caught a glimpse of a smile on Julia's face when Diana had come back downstairs and asked where everyone was. Maddy couldn't help herself. The words were out before she could stop them. 'They've fucked off and gone home. I would've too, to be honest. You didn't make them feel very welcome.' As soon as she spoke, she saw from Diana's shocked expression that she'd overstepped the mark – by a *very* long shot. Diana said nothing, but the thin, angry line of her mouth spoke volumes. Rafe stared at Maddy as if she'd temporarily lost her mind. And then she'd looked quickly at Julia. Had she imagined it? The faintest hint of a smile, a ghostly flicker of solidarity? Despite her own embarrassment, Maddy was touched.

'Harvey, would you be a dear and fetch the turkey?' Diana asked icily, her eyes sweeping coldly over Maddy, then moving away. She'd been dismissed. 'I do hope it won't be all dried out.' And that was that. The case, such as it was, was closed. The rest of the Christmas lunch proceeded uneasily but smoothly.

Now, sitting next to an uncharacteristically silent Rafe as they drove back home, going back over the events of the afternoon in her mind, she recalled again the look Julia had flashed her. What had she meant by it? *Well done? Good for you?* It was hard to tell, but the warmth it generated stayed with Maddy all afternoon. She'd almost been on the verge of asking Julia if she wanted to meet up or have a coffee perhaps, but she'd stopped herself just in time. No need to make an even greater fool of herself. Yes, she was lonely, and yes, it would have been nice to have someone to talk to other than Rafe and the few shopkeepers she'd struck up a passing acquaintance with, but there'd been no indication that Julia felt the same way. In fact, aside from Diana, Maddy had never met anyone quite as self-contained as Julia . . . she didn't need anyone, least of all an overeager, desperate American with an eating disorder. She stopped herself just in time. Her thoughts had a nasty habit of running away with her. That was the problem with not having anyone to talk to. She *didn't* have an eating disorder. A little difficulty around food, perhaps, every once in a while. Certainly not a *disorder*.

'You OK?' She turned to Rafe, anxious to break her sudden strange train of thought.

'Mmm.' Rafe was distracted.

'What did you think of her?'

'Who?'

'Josh's wife.'

He made a small face. 'With Josh you never know.'

She glanced at him. 'What do you mean? What on earth happened between you guys?'

'Nothing,' Rafe said shortly. 'He's just . . . he's just difficult, that's all.'

'Come on. There's more to it than that, surely?'

He shook his head. 'There isn't. Can we drop it, please? I don't feel like talking about Josh right now.'

'But you never want to talk about him. I'm just curious—'

'Maddy. Please. Just drop it, will you?'

Maddy sighed. She turned her head to look out of the window. She could feel the resurgence of her old, familiar panic. How was she ever supposed to get a handle on things when everyone around her refused to talk? She thought of Niela, sitting there at the end of the table, so still and beautiful and composed, her face giving nothing away. And Josh. She'd seen something in him that first time, a few months back. He was strong and remarkably self-assured, but he was watchful too, as if for all his solidity and confidence he could be hurt. She'd seen it in him again that afternoon, when he'd stepped into the dining room and seen them all ranged against him. Looking into his face, she'd had the impression she was looking into a mask. His expression was one of someone who was so deep inside himself that he was no longer aware of what he might have to conceal. She'd recognised it because it was the look she herself wore when she was on stage. He was acting out a part, she realised. But which one?

Aaron and Julia left shortly after Maddy and Rafe. Diana was withdrawn all afternoon. She kissed them both – much to Julia's surprise – and stood at the door waving until the taxi was out of sight.

'God, what a lunch,' Julia murmured against Aaron's jacket as they sped off. She'd had rather too much to drink after Josh and Niela's departure – she could feel the beginning of a headache coming on. 'I felt a bit sorry for her, you know.'

'I know. Poor Mother. Trust Josh to ruin things.'

'I wasn't talking about your mother,' Julia replied, a touch impatiently. 'I was talking about Niela. It must've been hard.'

'What?' Aaron's voice held a note of scorn.

'You know . . . being introduced to the family like that. What is it with you lot anyway?' Aaron didn't reply. He yawned, slowly and deliberately, and turned his face to the window. 'No, I'm serious,' Julia went on. 'What happened between you and Josh? Why'd you all take against him like that?'

'Can we stop talking about Josh for once?' Aaron's voice was tetchy.

Julia felt her own temper begin to rise. 'What d'you mean, "for once"? We never talk about him. *You* never talk about him. I just don't understand it. Why—'

'Jules, just drop it, please. It's been a long day and I'm tired. Josh has already ruined lunch, I don't want him to ruin my night as well.'

'But—'

'Drop it, will you?' Aaron's voice rose a notch.

Julia's lips tightened. 'Fine,' she muttered, turning her own head in the opposite direction. 'If that's your answer . . .'

'It is.' Aaron didn't speak again until the cab pulled up in front of their flat. They walked upstairs to the front door in silence.

Some Christmas this has turned out to be, Julia thought to herself angrily as she took off her silk blouse and trousers, folding them neatly and hanging them up. She walked into the bathroom and shut the door firmly behind her. Sod Aaron. Sod them all. Couldn't they see how lucky they were to have one another? She'd never met a family more careless of each other's feelings. None of them knew what it was like to be without, that was the problem. She felt the unmistakable tug of tears in her throat as she turned on the tap and began brushing her teeth. She thought of Maddy suddenly. There'd been a moment at the table when she'd almost laughed out loud. She hadn't thought Maddy capable of the sharp, stinging kind of comment that ran around perpetually in her own brain. *They've fucked off and gone home. I would've too, to be honest. You didn't make them feel very welcome.* She smiled, in spite of her tears. She'd almost been too afraid to look at Diana's face, but of course Diana had affected not to notice. She blew her nose, taken aback by the unexpected warmth she'd suddenly discovered for Maddy. Perhaps she'd misjudged her? No, she thought to herself firmly. She hadn't.

67

NIELA/JOSH
London, Christmas Day, 1997

Josh was silent all evening. As soon as they came through the door, he'd switched on the television. He sat on the couch, watching the news. Niela knew better than to press him for an explanation of the day's events, but she saw, as she quietly went about the task of folding laundry and setting up the ironing board, that his mind was elsewhere, not on the television or even in the room where she was at all. She said nothing, but after a while became aware of a change in the atmosphere between them. He looked up once or twice, but she kept her gaze averted, concentrating on the smooth, clean hiss of the iron and the smell of fresh linen as she pressed the sheets. She understood him in more ways than he perhaps knew. He was waiting until the anger in him had died down. Staying quiet until he knew where things stood, inside him, was the only way he could cope. She'd seen that in him in Djibouti; here in London, the understanding served her just as well.

'Sorry about that,' he said after a while, so quietly she thought she might have misheard it.

'Nothing to be sorry about,' she said softly.

'No, there is. I don't know why I even bothered to go there.'

'Why did you?' She lifted the heavy coverlet and turned it over. The iron gave off a satisfying puff of steam.

He shrugged, his eyes on the television again. 'I don't know . . . I'd promised Diana I'd go round if I was here over Christmas.'

'Why didn't you tell me who she was?'

He was quiet for a moment. 'It didn't seem relevant, to be honest. I don't know . . . back there in Djibouti, it seemed much simpler, somehow. Just you and me.'

'What happened between you, Josh? Between you and your brothers, I mean.'

He shrugged nonchalantly, but there was a great tension in his shoulders. 'Childhood stuff. Long time ago.'

'What sort of childhood stuff?'

Again, it took him a while to answer. He was struggling with something, something he couldn't bring himself to say out loud. She could feel the energy of it like a new kind of heat in the room. She continued with the slow, unhurried lift and press of her task, waiting for him to answer. Whatever was smouldering inside him would need to burn itself out, she saw, before he could bring himself to speak. She waited. And at last he began to talk.

He couldn't say when he first knew. It seemed to him somehow that he'd always known. It wasn't just that he looked different – he *was* different. In every way, not just physically. Rafe and Aaron were like Harvey . . . simple, straightforward, uncomplicated. They knew what they liked and why. There was nothing in either of them that hinted at the kind of slippery, dark territory he inhabited, even back then. His dreams were full of mystery and secrecy, things he could only guess at but couldn't explain. He would wake in the morning exhausted from the effort of trying to understand what was being told to him in the silent dark hours between Diana putting out the light last thing at night and waking in the morning to a world that was so utterly different from the one he inhabited in his sleep that he sometimes had difficulty distinguishing between them – which was the dream and which was real? Diana understood. She would be there in the morning, already dressed for chambers, that far-off place where she worked and which took up almost every second of her waking time, but the slow, special smile she had just for him made him realise that she understood. Not Harvey, not his brothers – only Diana.

'Tell me about your dreams,' she would say to him on a Sunday morning when the others were at rugby practice or out somewhere in the garden, which was their second home. 'Tell me about the one you had on Tuesday.' That she remembered exactly which day it was, which precise dream, sent a warm glow coursing through him. Diana understood everything. 'How utterly marvellous,' she would say, listening to him recount whatever it was that had come to him in the early hours of Tuesday morning. 'Imagine that. And all of that came out of that little head. What a wonderful imagination you have.' She often caught hold of his head, squeezing him to her and tousling the short, thick black curls which were like hers but not theirs. 'Good Lord, where'd he come from?' people would often ask when presented with the Keeler brothers all at once and for the first time. He hated hearing it and yet he loved it too. It marked him out as different. Special, as Diana would always whisper to him. *You're special because you're mine.* The others felt it too. Or did he feel it because they showed it first? He didn't know; couldn't say. All he could say for sure was that when it happened, there was no surprise involved. He'd looked at the scene unfolding in front of him and his only thought had been, *Yes. This is how it is. This is how it's always been. This is why.*

'Why what?' Niela interrupted him softly. She was sitting opposite him, her knees drawn up against her chest.

They were in Mougins, his favourite place in the whole world. He was ten at the time. In those days, there was a wonderful pattern to their summer holidays. Diana's chambers always closed exactly to the day when they came home from school. Rafe and Aaron were at boarding school; Josh was still at home. The following year he too would go to Eton, the draughty, forbidding school that his brothers loved. He was dreading it. Not because he couldn't hold his own – at ten he was already nearly as tall as Aaron, who was four years older, and his lean, tough physique meant that he'd never been bullied at school, not once. He was more than capable of looking after himself. It wasn't the bullying that he was afraid of – it was being away from Diana. That summer, his last before the dreaded lonely years of boarding school began, the four of them, Diana, Rafe, Aaron and himself, had gone ahead to Mougins; Harvey was due to follow them in a couple of weeks.

They drove down from London in the Volvo estate with Buster in the back, yapping excitedly all the way. The ferry crossing was magical. It was windy and the clouds were giant, shape-shifting puffs of white chasing each other across the sky. He stood on the upper deck gazing mesmerised at the creamy white foam thrown up behind them by the ferry's engines as they ploughed through the dark green sea, marking out their progress. At Calais, Diana took them to a café, where they all had *café au lait* and paper-thin croissants stuffed with almond paste and chocolate.

They stopped overnight in Lyon at the small *pension* they always stayed at – the owner and his wife, M. and Mme Santos, made the usual ex-clamations at how much they'd grown, how their French had improved, how wonderful Diana looked . . . where was M'sieur Keeler? Ah, working. Such an important job, saving lives. Rafe looked particularly pleased when they said that. He wanted to be a surgeon, just like Dad. Aaron wanted to be a lawyer, just like *Maman*. And you? Mme Santos looked at Josh indulgently. He felt the tips of his ears reddening as he answered. He wanted to be a cook. No, a chef. A cook was a lady. The roar of laughter sent the pigeons scattering in fright. A chef! 'Darling, whatever do you mean?' Diana's hand was on the back of his neck, affectionately stroking the soft curls that fell over his collar when his hair had grown too long. 'A chef?' Rafe and Aaron threw him sidelong looks of such smug satisfaction that he was taken aback. What was wrong with wanting to be a chef? Mme Santos was a chef, wasn't she? He *liked* cooking. 'Of course you do, darling,' Diana murmured, silencing the other two with a look. 'Of course you do.'

'Tosser,' Aaron murmured under his breath so that no one would hear it. 'Stupid, silly tosser.' It was his favourite insult that year.

The farmhouse was just as he remembered. The big oak tree was in full and splendid bloom; the oleanders, roses and hyacinths that Diana had painstakingly transplanted from London were out in colourful force. They pulled up as the shadows were already beginning to lengthen and the sun was slipping out of the sky. He rushed ahead with Buster to open the gate. There was a car in the driveway. He stopped in confusion, turning his head to look enquiringly at Diana. 'There's someone here, Mum,' he shouted. 'Someone's here.'

'It's all right, darling, I know. It's only Uncle Rufus.'

Josh looked uncertainly ahead. His uncle Rufus – his dad's only brother – was strange. It had been a few years since he'd seen him. He dropped in and out of their lives at random. Sometimes he'd be around in London for a few weeks; there'd be a dinner at the house and some presents . . . he'd be there in the morning for breakfast and lunch and then he would disappear, sometimes for a couple of years. In between there'd be no word, not even a postcard from all those exotic places he went to . . . South America, Asia, Japan, Africa. He couldn't say exactly what it was that Uncle Rufus did . . . something with the word 'development' in it, but he had no idea what that really meant. He came back to the house in Islington with stories of meetings with presidents and con-men, being shot at in places with unpronounceable names and narrow escapes that always seemed to involve guns and being smuggled in the boot of a car. Josh didn't know why he didn't like him. It wasn't that the stories were implausible – no, one look at Uncle Rufus and you could see that it was all true. He was tall, like Dad, but much more powerfully built . . . thick dark brown hair, dark brown eyes, a curved, Romanesque nose (he'd had to ask Diana what that meant) and a deep, booming laugh. He was nothing like Harvey, in the same way Josh was nothing like Aaron or Rafe. But Diana seemed to like him. She was different when he was around; livelier, somehow, less guarded and less reserved. He didn't like her like that. He preferred the quieter Diana whose attention wasn't claimed by the man who, however temporarily, seemed to him to have usurped his father's place.

'Uncle Rufus is staying for a few days,' Diana said to him out of the window as she manoeuvred the car into the driveway. 'Just until Dad gets here.'

Josh stood in the doorway of the farmhouse, curiously unwilling to go in. There was music playing in the background – deep, flowing music that washed over the whole house, stealing around the doors and windows, entering every room. He didn't like it. Dad never played music so loudly.

'You're here!' Uncle Rufus emerged from the living room at the end of the long corridor and stood there, his hands in his pockets as he surveyed them coming through the doorway. 'At last. Thought you'd never arrive.'

'Sorry, sorry . . .' Diana came through into the hallway struggling to hold on to Buster and a large suitcase at the same time. 'We left a bit late this morning. When did you get in?'

'Last night.' Uncle Rufus made no move to help her, Josh noticed. His dad would never have let Diana struggle with a suitcase.

'Here, Mum . . . give me that.' He took the case from her and threw his uncle what he hoped was a suitably murderous look. Uncle Rufus affected not to notice. Josh took the case – it wasn't *that* heavy – and marched upstairs with it. His earlier good mood was completely soured. It wasn't even the first day of their holiday and it was already ruined.

It was on their third night that it happened. They'd all gone into the living room after supper, each preoccupied in their own way – Aaron and Rafe were playing a card game; Diana was reading a thick stack of files; Uncle Rufus was listening to the stereo with his headphones on and Josh was lying on his stomach, his eyes closed, going over the events of the day – eating, swimming, more eating, more swimming – thinking of how he would tell his friends at school what he'd done during the holiday. Uncle Rufus suddenly stood up, took off the earphones and announced that it was time to play a game. Hide and seek. Aaron and Rafe jumped up enthusiastically; it was exactly the sort of rowdy game they loved to play. Diana looked up, an expression of indulgent cheerfulness on her face. 'A game? Oh, Rufus . . . really? You *really* want to? You're as bad as these three.' Josh didn't like that. He didn't want to play; he was nothing like Uncle Rufus or the other two.

'Come on, then . . . who's going to be the catcher?' Uncle Rufus shouted cheerfully. 'You, Rafe? You're the oldest. Count to a hundred and then come and find us. Come on, everyone. Let's scram!'

Josh found himself being swept along in the rush to get out of the living room. Even Diana had joined in enthusiastically. Rafe stood in the corner, his face turned away from them as he counted slowly and loudly. 'Twenty-six, twenty-seven, twenty-eight . . .' Aaron had opened the front door as soundlessly as he could and slipped out. Ahead of him, going up the stairs, Josh could see Diana and Uncle Rufus. He waited for a second, his hand on the banister, trying to think of the one place in the house where Rafe would never look. Ah, he had it. He grinned, in spite of himself. If he was lucky, he could hide out there all evening, away from the others and their stupid, silly games. Maybe even until morning.

He ran up the second flight of stairs, wriggled easily into the space at the end of the corridor and then up the short flight of wooden stairs to the attic. It ran the entire length of the farmhouse and had always been a junkyard storage room for all the things they'd inherited from Diana's parents' farmhouse just down the road when her father died. Diana didn't want anything that had been left to her. Josh thought he could vaguely remember the removals people one year lugging huge, ugly pieces of furniture up into the roof, where they'd stayed ever since, buried out of sight.

He moved through the dark, his feet remembering the loose floorboards, his hands judging the distance between objects with ease. It had been a year since he'd been in the attic space but he knew every square inch. Outside he could hear the trees in motion; a light wind had blown up since that afternoon, setting the garden in gentle movement, trees whispering to one another and the birds chattering in reply. He found the spot where the mattress had been slung and lay down, cracks of light appearing as his face was laid close to the ground and his eyes and ears attuned themselves properly to the dark. He could hear someone moving about in the room below – through the floorboards he could see that it was Diana. He was directly above the spare bedroom at the end of the corridor. She opened the door and the movement sent the curtains blowing. The crack of light widened; he put his face closer to the ground and peered downwards. There was a figure standing in the doorway, lit from behind. It was Uncle Rufus. Across the room the curtain rose and fell like a veil. Diana was standing by the window, looking out into the inky darkness of the garden. Uncle Rufus closed the door behind him and turned the key, locking it. Josh felt a sudden tightness in his chest, as if he knew what was about to happen next. In a way, he did. He'd dreamed it, he realised, many times. He heard his mother sigh, a soft, tense little sound that rose up from her throat. He wanted desperately not to look, but he couldn't turn away. Uncle Rufus came up behind her. The tips of his fingers came to rest on her face. His own skin tingled uncomfortably as he watched the next moves in an act that he knew he shouldn't be witnessing. He lay there, his face close to the floorboards, with the curtains lifting and falling in time to the lifting and falling of Uncle Rufus's back, on top of his mother, squashing the breath out of her. Only the sounds coming from them both didn't suggest an ending of life – rather the opposite. A beginning. Something new. Something that shouldn't have been seen, especially not by him.

He couldn't remember how long he stayed there, or how it ended. He remembered getting up and tiptoeing out of the attic, not wanting to be seen or heard. He went first to his own room, unaware that his hands were still pressed against his ears. He caught sight of himself in the mirror that hung on the wall of the landing. He sat on the edge of the bed for what seemed like a very long time. Then he got up and did the only thing he could think of to do . . . he went downstairs to tell his brothers. He wanted Rafe to make Uncle Rufus leave. He was the oldest; he could do it. They'd given up playing hide and seek and were lying in front of the empty fireplace, playing some silly card game that they wouldn't teach him. 'Rafe,' he said, and he realised as soon as he spoke that he was crying. He could feel his lip quivering though he desperately wished it would stop.

Rafe and Aaron looked up. It was Aaron who began laughing first. 'Cry-baby . . . did you get scared? Were you all alone? In the dark. Look at him! God, you're such a baby . . .'

He blurted it out. Everything. He couldn't hold it back. *Make him stop*, he remembered begging Rafe. *He's hurting her. Make him leave.* He didn't know who hit him first. What he did remember was the taste of blood in his mouth and the thundering in his ears that was the sound of his own heart. They took it in turns to push and shove and slap him. He was a liar. A sneaky, dirty little liar. And a cry-baby. You couldn't get much worse than that. If he didn't shut up and take it all back – those nasty, filthy, ugly lies – they would jolly well see to it that his life from then on was hell. He didn't. They did. And that was the beginning of the animosity between them that had lasted for almost twenty years. It wasn't the end, though. He'd got his own back.

'How?' Niela whispered, though the answer was already there between them.

He shrugged, unable to meet her eyes. He was the difficult one; the wild charmer, the one no one could tame. It had its . . . attractions. He recognised it, early on. He'd taken away everything he could from them, whenever he could. Especially girls. Women. He'd lost count of the number of times he'd seduced one or other of their girlfriends and then chucked them immediately aside. It had started out almost as a game – just to see if he could, that was all. Meaningless, quick revenge. And then he found he couldn't stop. The more they pushed him away, the more he pursued what they loved. The last had been Rafe's fiancée, a silly, simpering girl called Amy. The night they announced their engagement, he'd kissed her in the upstairs bathroom; a couple of days later he took her to his bed. She told Rafe; a few days later the engagement was off and Josh left for Burma. That was the last time. There was no pleasure in it; he wasn't sure there ever had been. And now he didn't know how to make amends.

There was absolute silence in the room when he finished speaking. He sat very still. She had seen something in him that he'd never shown anyone, not even Rania. No one had ever seen him like that, open and completely exposed. It put you at risk, he thought to himself, but with Niela it was different. She would not let him down. He reached across and took her hand, very gently at first, then he tightened his grip. She responded with a gesture that had become familiar to him, though he'd never really thought about it. She reached up with her free hand and lightly brushed the top of his head, her fingers barely touching his hair. She had to look up at him to do it and her lovely long throat was bared, turned towards him, giving away so much of herself to anyone who'd care to look. He found himself inexplicably choked. All the anger and hot, uncomfortable pain he'd felt in the retelling of the story suddenly went right out of him. An ordinary little gesture, of the sort that could – and probably did – mean nothing. She looked at him in that clear, candid way of hers that tried to see what there was behind his aloofness; something she'd glimpsed, long ago, and had been looking for ever since. He took in the smooth dark skin of her face, the neat, beautifully drawn eyebrows and the dark eyes, and understood that what mattered to her the most was also hidden in her, and that if he intended to find it, he would have to do as she had done with him, discovering it slowly, bit by shy, hesitant bit.

PART SEVEN

68

MADDY
London, April 2000

'Do we *have* to go?' Maddy turned round to look at her backside in the mirror. 'Does this look all right?' she asked anxiously.

Rafe looked as though he wasn't sure which question to answer first. 'Yes. To both,' he said, adjusting the ribbon in Darcy's hair. 'There. All done, darling.'

'Why don't you and Darcy just go instead?' Maddy murmured. 'I'm sure Diana won't mind if I don't come.'

'Maddy, stop being difficult. Come on, we haven't been out in ages.'

It was on the tip of Maddy's tongue to say that going round to Diana's for lunch was hardly going out, but she managed – not without effort – to hold herself back. 'All right, all right. Are you sure this looks OK? It's kinda tight.'

'It's fine, darling,' Rafe said, without looking up. Darcy had pulled the ribbon out of her hair for the fifth or sixth time and was now demanding that he put it back.

'Darcy, will you *stop* it?' Maddy couldn't help herself. 'Either leave the damned thing in or take it out. Your choice.'

Darcy looked at her mutinously. They stared at each other for a second, a battle of wills. Ridiculous, Maddy thought to herself. Darcy was three. How could you battle with a three-year-old? How? Darcy's lower lip began to tremble. Maddy rolled her eyes and turned away. She couldn't bear to watch what would surely follow. Tears. Naughty Mummy. Poor Darcy. She could almost hear Rafe's thoughts. She was being silly. She knew exactly where Darcy's appetite for performance came from. Bang on cue, Darcy began to cry. Rafe shook his head in exasperation and bent down to console her. Maddy walked out of the room.

She sat down on the edge of the bed. Her hands were trembling. Why did it always wind up that way? Where had she gone wrong with Darcy?

293

She could hear Rafe's soothing voice through the door – within seconds, Darcy had stopped wailing. With her, it was a different story. From the moment Darcy opened her eyes every morning to the realisation that Daddy wasn't there, it was downhill all the way. Tears, tantrums, screams, shouts . . . those twelve long hours each day between Rafe's departure and return home were nothing short of torture. For both of them. The minute Darcy was born, Maddy knew something was wrong. In her more despairing moments, she wondered if it had anything to do with the fuss she'd kicked up over her name. Diana had wanted to call her Elizabeth. Maddy had looked at him from the protection of her hospital bed.

'You're joking, right?' she'd said, holding her baby tightly to her.

'No. It's my grandmother's name. It's a nice name.' Rafe ran a hand through his hair. She recognised it as a gesture he made when agitated. A tremor of fear ran through her. 'We could shorten it to Liz,' he suggested hopefully.

'No fucking way.'

'Maddy!' Rafe stared at her. 'It's my grandmother's name.'

'And she's *my* daughter.'

They'd stared at each other, both taken aback by the sudden and hostile turn in the conversation. And at that moment, the baby had begun to scream. She hadn't stopped since.

'Maddy?' Rafe tapped on the door. 'Ready?'

'Coming,' she said, quickly averting her head. She didn't want him to see her reddened eyes and nose. 'Just going to the bathroom. I'll be out in a second.'

She stared at her face in the mirror. She looked all right. Her eyes were wide and bright but she'd managed to avoid smudging her mascara. She turned her head sideways, considered her profile and quickly pinned up her hair. A last squirt of perfume, a dash of lipstick and she was ready. She squared her shoulders. Darcy would have her three favourite people in the world all doting on her today. With any luck she'd fall asleep soon after her early lunch and Maddy would be free to enjoy the conversation at lunch – or not.

'It's just us today, isn't it?' Maddy asked Rafe as they pulled away from the kerb. She wasn't sure she could stand the thought of a large Keeler gathering.

'I think so. Aaron and Julia are away.'

Maddy was silent. It had been three years since she and Julia had been thrown together by the accident of marriage. It seemed like a lifetime and yet she still hadn't warmed to her. She'd *wanted* to like her, but there seemed to be no such desire on Julia's part. She was always so terrifyingly *busy*. It unnerved Maddy. They met at Diana's on Sundays; they met in Mougins – they were perfectly polite to one another, but it was clear that Julia thought Maddy a complete dolt, and Maddy . . . well, secretly she was terrified of Julia. At the last lunch they'd all had a little too much to drink – you had to, there was no other way of getting through the afternoon – and she'd made some comment about being bored in London . . . she wasn't moaning or complaining – just stating a fact. Julia had suddenly opened her mouth and attacked her.

'Why don't you just get a job?' she'd asked.

'A job?' Maddy could feel her face turning red. She saw Rafe looking at her strangely.

'Yes, a job. Work. Like the rest of us.'

'I'm an actress,' Maddy said haltingly. 'It's really difficult. There aren't many parts out there.'

'Well, do something else. Volunteer. Whatever.' Her cool grey-blue eyes flickered over Maddy; there was no mistaking the contempt she felt. Maddy wished desperately she'd never brought the subject up.

'Dessert, anyone? More wine?' Diana's smooth voice quickly closed the matter. Maddy excused herself from the table and went into the bathroom to throw up. Another successful lunch *chez* Diana.

Oh well . . . win some, lose some. People always accused Americans of being overfriendly, too eager. What was wrong with being friendly? Maddy always thought. What was the harm in spreading a little charm?

She turned her head to look at Darcy, who, as soon as she'd been strapped in, had fallen asleep. Her heart suddenly and unexpectedly turned over. She looked positively angelic. She took after Rafe, that much was obvious, but there was a reddish tint to her strawberry blonde hair that was very much Maddy. Her temper was Maddy's too, though few would suspect it. After her father disappeared, there just didn't seem to be any point in getting angry or throwing the sort of tantrums she once had. The stunned look of loss on her mother's face was enough to squash even the smallest hints of rage. She'd learned to keep her emotions well in check – it was only in acting, and in that other thing that she did from time to time, that they spilled out. Thinking about that 'other thing', she felt herself blush in the darkened interior of the car. She'd started again.

Not every day, of course, but at least once a week. It was being alone with Darcy all day that did it. And then there was the time Darcy had wandered into the bathroom and caught her in the act. That was exactly what it felt like – she'd been caught out. Ridiculous. How could a child who wasn't quite three catch her out? She'd stood there in the doorway for a few minutes, as quiet as a mouse. Maddy hadn't noticed her. She'd lifted her head, her eyes streaming and her stomach still heaving, and turned to get a tissue – and then she'd seen her. Darcy had her thumb in her mouth, but her huge blue-green eyes were fixed accusingly on Maddy. 'Mom's not very well,' she'd gasped, embarrassment flooding through her veins. 'Go on up to your room, honey. I'll come by in a minute. I'll read you a story, would you like that?' Darcy said nothing. Just turned and trotted off. Maddy was left with the sour taste of vomit in her mouth, only now it was mixed with guilt.

Fortunately, lunch looked as though it would be a quiet affair. Aaron and Julia had gone on holiday somewhere to celebrate the fact that she'd been offered a junior partnership in the law firm where she worked. From Diana's guarded, barbed comments, Maddy was led to understand that Julia's career was beginning to take off – and Aaron's wasn't. He was older than Julia, and more experienced. He'd worked as a solicitor before becoming a barrister, so he ought to have been much further along in his career. He wasn't and it was clearly one thing Diana couldn't solve for him. It puzzled Maddy; she was forever hearing about how brilliant Diana's boys were – clearly, things weren't going according to Diana's plan. She could see how much it annoyed Diana to have to talk about Julia, not Aaron. As for her other sister-in-law . . . it had been over a year since she'd seen Josh or Niela. They were both on assignment – Josh somewhere in the Far East and Niela a little closer to home, Jordan or Syria . . . somewhere remote and unimaginable like that. She couldn't imagine their lives. Niela was now a full-time interpreter, travelling all over the place. Maddy liked Niela, insofar as you could like someone you'd only met twice.

The wines were excellent, as usual. Maddy nursed a large glass of white and watched Diana fuss over Darcy as she gave her an early lunch. Harvey kept her brilliantly amused with anecdotes about his day. Maddy tried to attune her performance to suit the occasion – not too loud, not too funny, not too brash. It was the only chance she got these days to act. Darcy was the centre of attention for thirty minutes and then, holding tightly on to Rafe on one side and Diana on the other, she was led upstairs to the room that Diana had redecorated *just for her*. Maddy hated it – pastel-coloured walls covered in stencils from children's books she'd never heard of and windows swathed in yards of pink silk. Pink *silk*? For a three-year-old? Darcy loved it, of course. *My fairy-tale room*. Or some such.

'So what have you been up to lately?' Harvey asked, removing a large casserole pot from the oven. He placed it carefully on one side and lifted the lid. A wonderful, rich aroma of fish and herbs immediately filled the room. 'Smells good, doesn't it?' he asked conversationally, replacing the lid.

'Oh, nothing much.' Maddy perched on one of the swivel stools at the breakfast bar, watching him prepare the table. His movements were neat and precise, just like his son's. Surgeons, she supposed. She remembered the first time she and Rafe had talked – properly talked – in New York. She'd been fascinated then by his hands; almost more expressive than his words. Harvey was the same. She took another sip of wine. 'The weeks just seem to fly by, don't they?' she said, trying to find the right level of banter to match his tone.

Harvey paused in his preparations. 'Did you ever hear back from that agent? The one you were going to see the last time we saw you?'

Maddy shook her head slowly from side to side. 'Nope. Not a thing. Not even a return phone call. I don't know . . . I don't think I expected it to be quite this hard.'

'You mustn't give up.'

Maddy looked at him quickly. As was often the way with Harvey, something more was being said. She liked him enormously. He was kind, with the sort of gentle manner she'd always associated with English actors of a certain generation. He had a way of looking you directly in the eye, head cocked to one side whilst listening, as if you were the most important person in the room. 'I . . . I won't,' she said uncertainly.

'Won't what?' Rafe's voice sounded just behind her ear. Maddy jumped guiltily, as if she'd been caught out.

'Give up.' Harvey handed his son a glass. 'We're looking forward to seeing you on the stage, my dear. Now . . . where's your mother? We're almost ready to eat.'

'She'll be down in a minute. Darcy's almost asleep.' Rafe's hand came to rest on the nape of Maddy's neck. She felt a sudden tremor of apprehension run through her, instantly skimming away. Across the table

Harvey was looking at her with an expression she preferred not to meet. For a moment, when it was just the two of them talking, she'd felt a warmth from him that disarmed her. She didn't want to spoil it. She took another cautious sip of wine and felt their attention slowly slip away. She was relieved, in both senses of the word.

69

JULIA
London, May 2000

Julia slipped out of bed, taking care not to wake Aaron, and hurried across the floor to the bathroom. She closed the door as quietly as she could, slid the bolt and opened the medicine cabinet. She fumbled around in her little washbag until she found the small white carton she'd been looking for. She pulled it out and looked at it, her heart thudding. Clearblue. Results in less than a minute.

She perched herself awkwardly on the edge of the toilet, pulled off the wrapping and positioned the stick to catch the flow of urine. She waited for a full minute as instructed, held her breath and then withdrew it slowly. She drew a deep breath and looked down. Nothing. The little window was clear. No blue line. The hot flush of disappointment was physical. She bent over, wrapping her arms around herself, trying desperately not to burst into tears. She waited a few moments, then got up, flushed the toilet and dropped the useless stick in the waste-basket. It was the third time she'd taken the test and the results were always the same: negative. She'd told no one – not her friends, not Dom and certainly not Aaron. She wasn't sure how he would react. After their return from Mougins at Christmas that year, a strange fear had begun slowly to creep over her. Until that point, she'd been happy, content. For the first time in years, her first waking moments were ones of pleasure, sometimes even joy. It had been so long since she'd experienced it. Little things. The feel of Aaron's bare sole against hers or the way he held her as he slept, a hand always touching some part of her as if he were afraid to let her go. The way he called out to her as soon as he came through the front door. 'Jules?' It was her father's nickname for her. Aaron didn't know that – how could he? The first time he'd said it she'd stopped dead in her tracks, a ripple of emotion running up and down her back. 'My dad used to call me that,' she'd said to him softly, turning round.

'Suits you.' He'd grinned at her, unaware of its impact. 'C'mere, Jules.' He'd held out his arms. A small gesture of the sort he made every day. Nothing special, but in its simplicity there was absolution. He'd begun to take the hurt away.

There'd been a short period of bliss, and then the fears began to creep in – of a different kind, perhaps, but they terrified her nonetheless. It would all disappear. There would be an accident. Aaron would find someone else. She would lose her job. The scenarios were endless and unfounded but she was unable to stop. She found herself thinking up ever more intricate ways to bind herself more fully into the life she'd found herself in – which essentially meant *his* life – except that it wasn't in her nature to depend on anyone, least of all a man. She'd always been a loner, content with one or two close friends, never looking to be the life and soul of the party. She hated that side of her that sat up at night waiting for him to come home after a night out with his friends. It was bad enough that they worked in the same office – to her horror, she found herself suggesting they lunch together or wait for one another to go home. For a few weeks the twin urges inside her fought for control, and then, one morning, it came to her suddenly, literally out of the blue. A child. A child would seal the gaps, heal the pain that losing any part of her new-found happiness would bring. She loved Aaron; he loved her. What more perfect way to put the panic to rest?

Except that nothing was happening. It's only been three months, she told herself, splashing cold water over her face. She looked anxiously at her reddened nose in the bathroom mirror. Three months is nothing. She picked up the face cloth and passed it over her burning cheeks. It'll happen soon. Of course it will. She switched off the light and opened the door. Aaron was still fast asleep. It was a Sunday. The weather outside was cold and rainy. Diana had rung that morning to complain they hadn't been round for lunch in ages. They'd been away the month before; why didn't they come round that afternoon? Julia wasn't sure she could bear it. She'd somehow managed to persuade Aaron to decline. Maddy and Rafe would be there with Darcy, the very picture of family bliss that Julia so badly craved. That it should find expression in that vacuous, overfriendly American and Aaron's older, slightly pompous brother was hard to take. She slipped back into bed beside Aaron and thought back to the last

Sunday lunch, which was the last time she'd seen them. Maddy had been moaning about being bored in London and Julia just couldn't stop herself.

'Why don't you just get a job?' she'd asked. She saw Rafe's head jerk upwards and she wondered if she'd spoken out of turn.

'A job?' Maddy echoed, as if it were the most novel idea she'd ever heard.

'Yes, a job. Work.'

'I'm an actress,' Maddy said haltingly. 'It's really difficult. There aren't many parts . . .' Her voice trailed off. Julia saw her look at Rafe.

'Well, do something else. I'm sure there's loads of other things you can do.'

'Julia,' Aaron interrupted her, a look of gentle warning in his eyes.

'Dessert, anyone? More wine?' Diana quickly cut short the conversation.

'Did you have to?' Aaron had asked her afterwards as they'd walked back home.

Julia's face immediately reddened. 'Sorry,' she muttered. 'I didn't mean to. But she doesn't half get on my nerves.'

'I know. But you didn't have to attack her like that, you know. After all, what do you care?'

'I didn't! I only asked her if she ever intended to get a job, that's all.'

'Jules—'

'All right, all right,' she said sulkily. 'I know. Me and my big mouth.'

'Just take it easy. We can't all be geniuses like you.'

The comment hit home; Julia flushed. Ever since she'd been made a partner at work, there'd been an undercurrent of tension in almost everything Aaron did or said. She knew what was wrong: that terrible, gnawing combination of envy and fear. Fear that he wasn't good enough, or worse, that his wife was better. She saw it in his eyes and read it in his voice, but this time she didn't know how to help him. It wasn't her fault the family unit under Harriet had gone from strength to strength. Or that her refusal to join the corporate division of the firm would pay such dividends, and so soon. She'd done it out of principle, nothing else. Corporate law bored her to death. She certainly wasn't doing what she did for the glory; that wasn't why she'd chosen to work for three years in the basement, lugging Harriet's files around, taking on cases that no one else would. It was just luck that they'd had one or two high-profile suits where Julia had been caught on camera with a comment that had made people sit up and notice her. She was young, articulate, dedicated . . . a working-class girl made good. She wasn't stupid; for the first time in her professional life, her profile had become something worth showing. She was in the right place at the right time, that was all. Aaron's chance would come. In the meantime, she wished he would just carry on with whatever aspect of tax law it was he'd chosen to specialise in and leave her the hell alone.

The following day, sitting at her desk, the comment still rankled. She looked with irritation at the enormous stack of papers that had been placed there since Friday. She'd spent the whole of Friday afternoon clearing out stuff – what the hell was this? She tossed her briefcase to one side and picked up the memo that was on top of the pile. *Please give this your undivided attention. See me when you're done. Rgds, Harriet.* She frowned. In a week that was already full to the brim with meetings, client briefings, court appearances and research requirements, why on earth had Harriet chosen to drop this on her? She pulled the stack towards her, exasperated.

An hour and a half later, she was no clearer as to why Harriet had sent it to her. It was interesting, certainly – the transcripts of the enormous conference on women's rights that had taken place in Beijing a few years earlier. Julia had heard of it – who hadn't? But what did it have to do with her?

A few minutes later, she stared at Harriet as if she couldn't quite believe her ears. 'Me?' she asked incredulously. 'You want *me* to go?'

'Why not?'

Julia struggled for a reply. 'Because I've never done anything like this before,' she said eventually.

'And since when has that ever stopped you? Question is, do you *want* to go? No point in discussing this any further if you've no interest.'

'No, no . . . I *am* interested. Very interested . . . it's just a bit of a surprise, that's all. Wh-what would I be expected to do?'

'Deliver a paper, of course. But that's the easy bit. This conference is supposed to be the follow-up to Beijing. From our perspective, what we're most interested in is getting our name out there as a practice that doesn't only deal in corporate law and taxation issues, but tackles the other stuff – the stuff that you and I do. The family unit's young, granted,

but we've done some really interesting work. It's a fantastic PR opportunity, in a nutshell. And you're good at it.'

'But why don't you want to go?' Julia couldn't help herself. 'The family
unit's yours, really. Not mine.'

'I don't like flying,' Harriet said briskly. There was a short pause.
'Look, I happen to think you're better suited to the policy side of things,
Julia. I'm not saying for a moment that you're not a good barrister. But
leave that sort of mundane stuff to people like your husband. Policy's
your natural home. Just don't waste the opportunity.'

Julia stared at her. Harriet had already bent her head back to her
work. It was clear that the short interlude was over. She got to her feet.
'Thanks, Harriet,' she said as she headed to the door. 'I won't let you
down.'

'I should hope not.' Harriet looked up briefly as Julia closed the door.

She was an odd person, Julia thought to herself as she walked back
down the corridor to her office. Beneath the prickly, professional exterior,
there was someone actually very kind. Not that she went out of her way
to show it – but still . . . asking Julia to go to the conference in her place
was a touching measure of her faith in her. It had been a while since
anyone had done anything like that, Julia realised suddenly.

'What did the old battleaxe want?' One of the other barristers with
whom she shared an office looked up as she walked in.

'Oh, just some conference she wanted to talk about.'

'Conference?' Martin, the third barrister in the office, looked up too.

Julia felt herself blush. 'Yes, there's a UN conference on women's
rights next month. She just wondered if I wanted to go, that's all.' She
was aware the conference literature had been lying on her desk whilst
she'd been out.

'So how come *you* get to go?' George asked, a trifle sharply.

Martin snorted. 'Oh, easy enough. She's a Keeler now, remember?'

Julia flushed deeper. 'What d'you mean?' she asked, turning to face
them both. 'This has nothing to do with Aaron.'

'Yeah, right,' Martin muttered.

'Have you got something you want to say to me?' Julia demanded
angrily. She could feel her temper rising. She'd never particularly cared
for either George Forrester or Martin Griffiths but she'd managed to
maintain a reasonable enough working relationship with them both. Not
any more.

'No,' George muttered, throwing Martin a sideways look.

'Good. Because if you do, at least have the guts to say it to my face.' There was an uncomfortable silence. Then George mumbled something about having to go to the library and walked out. A few minutes later, Martin followed suit.

Julia sat alone in the office, contemplating their screen savers, trying not to give vent to her anger. How *dare* they? Was that what everyone else thought? That she was given special treatment because of whom she'd married? She swallowed, aware of the need to keep a fierce grip on her emotions. Nothing upset her as much as an injustice – she was only just beginning to discover how much more upsetting it was when it was aimed at her.

If she'd expected sympathy from Aaron that evening, she was sorely mistaken. 'So what?' was his response.

Julia stood in the kitchen and gaped, open-mouthed, at him. 'So *what?*' she repeated, her voice rising of its own accord.

'Who gives a shit what George Forrester thinks? He's a little turd.'

'I do.'

'Why?'

'Because it's not true!' she protested. 'I'd never use your . . . my . . . *our* contacts to get ahead,' she stammered. 'Besides, what contacts do we have?'

'Oh, come *on*, Julia.' Aaron rolled his eyes at her. 'Diana spoke at the Beijing conference. She was one of the keynote speakers. It's not a coincidence, you know.'

'This has nothing to do with Diana,' Julia said angrily, unable to keep the sharpness from her voice. 'Not everything's about you and your bloody family—' She stopped herself just in time. They glared at each other. Then she turned round and quickly left the room. Aaron in pompous mode could be – and was frequently – unbearable. And she didn't feel like having an argument. Not tonight. Lately, she and Aaron had been having a few too many arguments. Small things, minor dis-agreements; nothing that resulted in anything other than a slight cooling towards each other for the day or so it took to regain equilibrium. Aaron wasn't the type to shout or have things out. Withdrawal was his preferred method of conflict resolution; something which, much as it infuriated Julia, seemed impossible to change. For someone who had spent most of her working life seeking to improve conflicts, Julia thought to herself grimly, Diana had done a spectacularly bad job with her own sons.

She walked into the bedroom and sat down on the edge of the bed. She kicked off her shoes and lay back, tracing the pattern of the embroidered duvet cover with her hand. There was an angry tightness in her chest that refused to quit. And yet underneath it, below the surface of her irritation with Aaron and her colleagues, was a bubbling sense of excitement, of something new and potentially life-changing coming into play. It had been a while since she'd felt so alive, she suddenly thought to herself. The Fifth International World Conference on Women. Just saying the name out loud brought on a rush of pleasurable anticipation of the kind she hadn't felt in a while. She lay there in the slowly darkening room, listening with half an ear to the muted sound of the television coming through the walls and the faint, stuttering sounds of traffic along the main road, thinking about the challenges that had suddenly presented themselves, seemingly out of the blue.

70

DIANA
London, May 2000

Diana put down the phone and had to bite down hard on the temptation to scream. She looked at her face in the mirror. There was an angry vertical line between her eyebrows; the result of the five-minute phone call she'd just had. She reached up a finger and tried to smooth it away. She felt the beginnings of a headache coming on. She gave a short, mirthless laugh. It was absurd! Aaron had phoned looking for a bit of sympathy, but she'd given him short shrift and had wound up with a pain between her own ears instead. Julia was going to Maputo, to the Fifth International World Conference on Women . . . and *she*, Diana Pryce, QC, founder of Libertas, board member of half a dozen prestigious charities whose names she couldn't always remember, keynote speaker at Beijing, the Fourth International World Conference on Women . . . was not? She was 'too expensive, unfortunately', the young woman from UNIFEM had told her earlier in the week. Too *expensive*? She'd waived her speaker fee, naturally. But if they thought she was about to fly to Mozambique in economy class and stay in some crappy little hotel next to the airport . . . they ought to think again. Well, clearly, they had – and as a result, Julia Burrows, her daughter-in-law, was going . . . *and she was not*. She couldn't believe it.

'Is . . . is she actually speaking?' she had forced herself to ask.

'Yeah . . . one of the plenary sessions. Some report on what they've been doing in the family unit. Why aren't you going?'

'I . . . I'm too busy. I've got so much on at the moment . . . I just can't take that sort of time off.'

'It's only five days. She leaves on Monday morning and she's back by Saturday.'

'Well, I've got far too much on at the moment,' Diana snapped. 'These conferences are a complete waste of time—'

'That's not what you said about Beijing,' Aaron interrupted her. 'You said—'

'I'm well aware of what I said,' Diana said shortly. 'That was then. Look, I've got to go. Someone's waiting to see me.'

'But I wanted to talk to you about—'

'Some other time, I'm afraid.' And she'd put the phone down without another word. She turned away from the mirror and walked upstairs to her study. She closed the door and leaned against it, breathing deeply. A niggling worry had lodged itself somewhere in her gut. Was she . . . ? She hesitated, afraid to even *think* it to herself. No, she had to. Was she past it? Was she out of touch? Seen as too old, not current enough? She was fifty-four, for crying out loud, not sixty-four. At the peak of her faculties and her career. She'd done so much, but there was still so much more to do. She was one of the youngest Queen's Counsels in chambers. Christ, Douglas Haller-Lane was in his eighties and still going strong. She was one of the very few women in her position in the UK – a force to be reckoned with, respected and often feared. How *dare* UNIFEM write her out of the script? She crossed the carpeted room to her desk and sat down. She ran her hands across its gleaming, polished surface. How many hours had she spent at this very desk penning the arguments and judgements that had catapulted her to such early fame? She looked around the study at the rows of books, the paintings, the beautiful *objets* that she'd brought back from the places she'd been . . . everything carefully, tastefully arranged. She brought her hands up to her cheeks and was shocked to find them wet. She wiped them hurriedly, furtively.

Harvey was downstairs in the kitchen; the last thing she wanted was for him to come upon her crying. She opened one of the drawers and pulled out a notebook. It was Harvey's sixtieth birthday party in a few weeks. She paused for a second to look down on the garden. Spring had been late in arriving; the trees had only just lost their bare, unfettered air and the garden was thrumming with new life. In Mougins, where they would have the party, summer would already be there. Mougins in June. She swallowed suddenly. It would be the first time she'd been back there in June for over thirty years.

She turned her attention quickly back to the birthday party. Would Josh come? It would be his birthday in a few weeks' time, too. She desperately hoped so. It had been years since they'd all been together down there. Eight members of their immediate family; a nice round number. She put her pen down again and stared at the names. There was one person missing. When was the last time she'd seen him? At Rafe's wedding, of course. He'd shown up, unannounced. Just as he always did. And the time before that? She put a hand to her cheek again – burning hot, as always, when she thought about him. She struggled to turn her mind elsewhere, but it was no use. Mougins in June. In that way that only memory can move back and forth in time and place, she was there again, the summer she turned sixteen, reliving it as if for the first time.

He was the first man she'd ever seen naked, and the thought of him even after all these years was enough to make her catch her breath. Back then, as now, there was something splendidly indolent about Rufus, the way his body was so carelessly and beautifully put together. She lay beside him that first morning when everyone had disappeared and traced her name across his chest with her fingertips. She wasn't afraid; on the contrary. Rufus was leading her in the way he'd always done: carefully, intently. He slipped her clothing off, piece by piece, until she was lying beside him in only her thin cotton panties. He teased the waistband a little, producing sweet rills of feeling, her whole body being turned over and over like the light, empty shells in the clear water down on the beaches at Cannes and Juan-les-Pins. He took them off and his hand moved down to stroke her, softly at first, preparing her for something that she knew about but had never experienced. The feeling inside her intensified until she thought she might just pass out with the sheer pleasure of it all. Her breath quickened to keep pace with his and then he moved on top of her. She was amazed at the way her whole body arched to meet his, as if it belonged to someone else. She kept her eyes open the whole time, as if she didn't want to miss a single second of it; all she could remember of the extraordinary pain when he pushed his way inside her was the frown of utter concentration on his face and the depthless black of his eyes, now half-closed, only half-seeing. The Rufus who hung supported by his arms above her bore no resemblance to the Rufus she knew. Something inside her turned, dissolved. She belonged to him now. Now and always.

71

NIELA
London, May 2000

There was a pile of unopened letters lying on the floor. Niela dragged her small suitcase in behind her, kicked them out of the way and shut the door. She leaned against it for a moment. It was just after eight in the morning; she'd landed at dawn and already the day felt as though it should be over. She'd just spent three weeks in Amman on assignment and was glad to be home. Home. She gave a small, rueful smile. In the past year, she and Josh had spent a total of two months in the tiny flat off Goldhawk Road. At this very moment, Josh was somewhere in southern Africa, finishing up construction of a camp that should have been completed three months ago but for the rains. What was it he'd said when he managed to get through to her on the phone the other night? He couldn't remember what it felt like to be dry. She left her case in the hallway and walked through into the living room. It was exactly as she'd left it almost a month ago. Everything was neat and tidy; chairs pushed in to the table, all the surfaces wiped clean. There was a thin film of dust on the dining table. She brushed a finger lightly across it as she walked past. In an hour's time she would unpack, but for now, a coffee and a shower, though not in that order.

By noon she'd squared away the last of her belongings, sorted out the laundry and dry-cleaning and made herself a small salad for lunch. She carried her plate over to the couch and sat down, idly sorting through the mail as she ate. There was an invitation card amongst the bills and circulars. She slid a finger underneath the flap – it was from Diana. It was Harvey's birthday in a few weeks' time. She and Josh were cordially invited to celebrate it with them at 11, Chemin du Fassum, Mougins, on 14th June. She raised her eyebrows. Mougins. She'd never been. She turned the thick, heavy card over in her hand. She wondered whether Josh would go. It would be his birthday shortly afterwards – would he want to spend it with them? As much as she understood his aversion to the place, there was a part of her that was curious to see it. And although she'd never much cared for Diana, on the few occasions she'd met Harvey, she liked him very much indeed. It was his birthday; it was only right and proper that they should all attend. She made a mental note to tell Josh so. It would take time to bring him round, she knew. She finished the rest of her salad and switched on the news. It always took her a few hours to unwind from the cycle of arrival and departure that had once been Josh's terrain, and was now, for better or for worse, hers as well.

72

MADDY
London, May 2000

Maddy's hand hovered over the telephone. Twice she dialled the number, and twice she hung up before she heard the first ring. Her palms were sweating; ridiculous, really. She couldn't have said why she'd suddenly decided to ring Julia, now after all these years. It was something Rafe had said the other night – 'You don't make much of an effort. I don't blame her.' She'd been stung by his words but afterwards wondered if there wasn't a grain of truth in them. She'd always been afraid of Julia, but once or twice there'd been a tiny spark of something other than the habitual expression of bored uninterest on her face that made her stop and think. Perhaps Rafe was right: she hadn't made much of an effort beyond their meetings at Diana's on Sundays . . . perhaps it was time to change that.

On the third attempt, steeling herself, she waited until the line was answered. And then it was too late. 'Julia? Hi, it's Maddy. Hi . . . I hope . . . I'm not disturbing you, am I? Oh, good. Um, I was just wondering . . . if you're not too busy, that is . . . well, what I was thinking was . . .' She swallowed nervously, and then it all came out in a rush. 'Would you like to have a drink sometime? Or lunch? Or maybe a coffee, if you're too busy, or we could even have dinner, or not, if you prefer, or—' She stopped. Julia had said something. She'd been so busy anticipating her refusal that she'd ceased listening. 'Sorry? Oh, you *would*? Oh, that's great. That's terrific. That's—' She stopped herself again, just in time. 'Wh . . . when would suit you? Saturday? This Saturday? Lunch? That would be lovely. I'll . . . I'll give you a ring in the morning. We can go somewhere near you, if you like? No? OK, well, I'll think of somewhere. See you on Saturday, then.' She put down the phone and didn't know whether to laugh or cry.

The flat was quiet. She wandered into the living room. Darcy was at her thrice-weekly playgroup. Maddy had been sceptical of the idea at first – she didn't work, she was at home all day long . . . why should she drop her child off three times a week to be in the care of others? But Rafe insisted; Diana was behind it, Maddy was sure of it. But she lacked the will to argue. Deep down, she was partly relieved. The problem was less to do with Darcy than it was with her. After three years, she still had no real friends in London to speak of. A few wives of colleagues of Rafe's; Marie, the hairdresser she'd been going to for a couple of years; one or two mothers from Darcy's playschool group whom she met every other week for coffee, but she hadn't made a single good friend, at least not in the way Sandy had been. She missed her like hell. It was that that had propelled her to make the phone call that morning. Reaching out to Julia was an act of desperation. She thought she'd seen something in Julia's eyes at the last lunch that hinted at something *slightly* less frosty, *marginally* more welcoming than usual, or so she hoped. Well, only one way to find out, and that was exactly what she'd done. Rafe found the whole thing amusingly silly. 'Just give her a ring,' he'd said the night before, exaggeratedly patient. 'After all, what's the worst that can happen? She'll say no, that's all.'

Well, she hadn't. She'd said yes. To lunch. Maddy felt the unexpected, giddy pull of pleasure. Silly, wasn't it? She was hardly a teenager, for crying out loud, but she certainly felt like one. In a flash she was fourteen again, standing off to one side at the Christmas prom, wondering why no one had asked her to dance. There, huddled together in a corner, laughing at her, were Lindy Myerson and Andrea Halgren. Lindy tossed back her long, blonde hair, rolled her baby-blue eyes to heaven and shook her head at Maddy's shoes. Or her dress. Or her hair. Whatever. It didn't matter what she wore, how she fixed her hair or how many sandwiches she threw up . . . she wasn't part of the cool crowd and never would be. Her friends were like her – misfits, the odd ones out, the 'artistic' types, a code word in Iowa for downright *weird*. She'd been lucky in New York, that was all. Amongst all the weirdness contained in several hundred drama students, Maddy Stiller was hardly the type to stand out. Aside from her hair and her Midwestern accent, which she'd quickly learned to tame. But here in London, it was as though she'd reverted to type. She hadn't moved on; she hadn't found a close-knit crowd to replace the one she'd left – not that one or two people really constituted a crowd, but it was part of the myth about herself that she'd created, unwittingly or otherwise, when she met Rafe, and now it was too late. If he sometimes missed the cheerful, carefree New Yorker she'd purported to be, he never said. Like so many other things about her, he seemed to accept the slow changes without comment or care. It hurt, she admitted with a small shrug. Being yourself, she'd realised since coming to London, was as much about how *you* saw yourself as it was about how others saw you. Without the mirror of her friends, she'd lost herself almost straight away. It didn't help that the image Rafe saw when he met her wasn't quite the whole truth. Not a lie, granted, but certainly not the whole truth. She was no longer sure what the truth was. Who was she now? Rafe's wife? Darcy's mother? Dare she even think it out loud . . . Julia's *friend*?

She stood by the sink, waiting for the kettle to boil, unnerved by the pleasure that the simple thought of being someone's friend had wrought. What had happened to the old Maddy? The one who'd got on a bus without telling anyone and travelled alone to Chicago to perform on a stage in front of strangers? The one who'd nailed her final-year perform-ance, causing Julie McMahon to write, 'only Madison Stiller consistently breaks through the rote quality that pervades the evening. It's not that she gets better lines, it's that she delivers them with such spectacular vehemence.' She'd memorised the entire review. Where had she put all those things – the clippings from her various performances, the emails and letters from her agent, the tickets she'd bought Rafe to watch her perform? It wasn't just that she'd stowed them in a box and slipped it into some forgotten corner of the flat – it was that she'd put those things away from *herself*. It was time to bring them out again. It was time to return herself to who she really was, hard as that might be to decipher.

Maddy was already seated when Julia came through the restaurant door. She spotted her immediately and gave a quick, hesitant wave. It was hard to miss her hair. Today she'd pulled it back off her face but it still spilled over her shoulders, cascading down her back. She hardly ever looked at Maddy properly, Julia realised as she walked towards her. She was one of those people who gave off a general, rather than detailed, impression. Theatrical, the wide smile showing those perfect teeth that only Americans ever had, the laugh and those dramatic hand gestures . . . all distractions that deflected the attention away from her, rather than towards her. Maddy was nervous.

'Hi, is this OK? By the window? I wasn't sure . . . we could change, if you prefer? I didn't know—'

'It's fine, honestly,' Julia assured her, sliding into the seat opposite. 'I like windows. I like sitting by the window just watching the world go by.'

'Really? Me too.' Maddy stared at her as if she'd said something extraordinary.

'What's so funny about that?' Julia asked, smiling.

Maddy's smile of relief was instant and pure. 'I don't know . . . I just find it funny. I mean, you don't strike me as the type of person who sits in a restaurant on their own watching—' She stopped herself suddenly, as if aware she'd given away too much. 'Not that *I* do that,' she added hastily. 'It . . . it was just a manner of speaking.'

Julia looked at her, uncomfortably aware that something more was being said. 'How about a drink?' she asked, guessing that whatever they would go on to talk about would be made infinitely easier with a glass of wine. Maddy nodded her head vigorously. 'White? It's a sunny day.'

Maddy nodded again. 'White would be lovely,' she said faintly.

'Cheers,' Julia said when their glasses had been poured. She hesitated for a second. 'I'm glad you rang, actually.'

Maddy blushed bright pink. 'I didn't know if I should,' she said, taking a large gulp. 'I mean, I'd always wanted to, but . . . I don't know, you always seem so busy, you and Aaron.'

Julia had to laugh. 'With work, you mean. That's all we ever do. I always think your life must be much more exciting . . . all those crazy theatre people and all that.'

311

'Theatre people? Which theatre people?' Maddy looked genuinely surprised.

'Oh, the people you hang out with . . . your friends.'

'I . . . I don't really have any,' Maddy said slowly. The smile had gone from her face. 'I used to, back in New York. Well, a couple, anyway. But not here.'

Julia took a slow sip of wine. Again, something more was being said. She looked at Maddy more closely. Her face was an open book, she was surprised to notice, on which every single emotion was registered. At that very moment her expression was a finely nuanced mixture of lone-liness and a strangely hopeful quality that tore straight into Julia – it was the precise expression she'd worn at Balliol for most of her time there, she recognised dimly. That awful, aching out-of-placeness that had never quite left her. She was shocked to find it in Maddy, sitting opposite her in a restaurant on Upper Street looking for all the world as though she utterly belonged there in her midnight-blue woollen dress and knee-high patent leather boots. She looked down at her own clothes and wished she'd dressed with more care – as usual, she'd thrown on a polo-neck sweater over a pair of black jeans, tied a scarf around her neck and found her most comfortable pair of walking boots. Next to Maddy, she felt positively dowdy. Plain. 'Do you like living in London?' she asked hesitantly.

Maddy waited a moment before replying. She turned her head towards the window, and when she turned it back again, there were tears in her eyes. 'I hate it sometimes,' she said, her voice suddenly small. 'I mean, there's Rafe and Darcy and everything. But I find . . . it's hard, you know. It's hard when you don't know anyone and no one seems in any hurry to get to know you. I know I come across badly . . . too loud, too friendly, too *American* . . . all of that. But I don't know any other way to be. I wish I wasn't. I'd love to be like you, or Diana, you know . . . the way you English are. But I can't.'

Julia stared at her. There was genuine anguish in Maddy's voice. She'd never imagined that there was so much going on behind the friendly, eager mask. 'Is everything all right with you and Rafe?' she asked guardedly.

Maddy nodded. 'Rafe's not the problem. It's me. It's just as you said, remember?'

Julia blushed. 'I was probably way out of line,' she said with a grimace. 'Sorry. I've got a bit of a gob on me.'

'Don't apologise. I needed to hear it. Like I need to hear it now. It's exactly as you said. Just do it.'

'Isn't that what Nike's always exhorting us to do?' Julia said with a smile. 'Just do it?'

Maddy smiled. 'Feel the fear and do it anyway, isn't that another one?'

'So why don't you?'

'You want to know something?' Maddy lifted her glass. 'This year, I will. I don't know how yet, but I will. I can't bear the thought of another Christmas lunch with Diana looking at me like that. She thinks I'm a complete dunce.'

'She thinks that about everyone, not just you,' Julia said drily.

'Did you get an invitation?'

'Harvey's birthday? Yes . . . are you going?'

'Of course. We can't *not* go. But I'm dreading it.'

'D'you think *he'll* come?' Julia asked suddenly.

'Who?'

'Josh.'

Maddy looked at her quickly, almost furtively. 'Well, that'd make the trip worthwhile,' she said with a sudden giggle.

Julia found herself smiling in response. 'He's gorgeous, don't you think?' she said suddenly, lowering her voice.

Maddy nodded emphatically. 'His wife's beautiful, too.'

'What d'you think happened?' Julia asked after a moment. 'Between them, I mean.'

Maddy shook her head. 'I don't know. Rafe won't talk about it.'

'Aaron neither. Every time I bring it up, he just about takes my head off.'

'Same here. I'm curious, though.'

Julia smiled at her. 'Well, if you find out, tell me.'

Maddy laughed. 'Let's hope they do come. I'm not sure I can stomach a whole week down there with Diana on my own.'

'You won't be,' Julia said, smiling a little. 'We'll be there.'

Maddy looked at her uncertainly, as if she wasn't sure how to respond. Julia felt again a sudden pang of guilt. Why hadn't she seen the loneliness that was so apparent on Maddy's face? She was off to Mozambique on Monday; when she came back, she resolved to make much more of an effort. She was surprised to find she actually liked Maddy. It took guts to reveal yourself that completely, she realised. She herself had spent most of her life hiding what she really felt, concealing her feelings behind a mask of self-assurance that in reality was anything but. What she'd mistaken in Maddy for silliness, eagerness, was much deeper than that. Mixed in with the confusion and loneliness was something Julia recognised because she longed for it in herself – courage.

73

JOSH
Maputo, May 2000

The heat was a wet gag placed over his mouth and skin. He fought his way out of the din of the arrivals hall and saw to his relief that the agency had indeed sent someone to collect him. His name was roughly scrawled across a piece of cardboard that still bore the imprint of the last person's name. He gave a quick wave and was answered in turn. The driver, a short, squat man with a dark, almost midnight-blue sheen to his skin, took his bags, overriding Josh's protests. They walked out into the blinding sunlight; despite the long journey and the strange mood he'd found himself in, it was a relief to be away from London and the discomfort his last visit had provoked. He would wait until he'd got to the hotel room where he was due to spend one night before heading off on the long, arduous journey north to the camp before he rang Niela. The thought of her produced a small ache of loss in his side, which he noted with surprise – it had been years since he'd actually missed anyone, least of all a woman.

He jumped into the pick-up next to João and they began to thread their way out of the chaos of the parking lot. The airport, like much of the city, was under construction and there were tall, disjointed cranes everywhere. The roads were also half-built, with giant concrete boulders and huge mounds of red earth in massed piles at the sides of the roads – a good sign, Josh knew from experience. International investors weren't stupid; they followed each other like packs of dogs, sniffing out opportunities for profit wherever they could, and Mozambique was clearly on the rise. His job was never quite as straightforward. For the next four weeks, he would be dealing with the human misery that the pull-out of those very same investors had helped create. His briefing notes were scant

– some 1.7 million refugees had begun pouring back into Mozambique from the neighbouring countries after the decades-long civil war finally drew to a close – his task, as always, was to try and house them. Some of them. The camp in Cabo Delgado, right up in the north of the country, close to the border with Tanzania, couldn't hold more than a couple of hundred thousand. It was the same story wherever he went. House those he could, forget about those he couldn't.

The sun was at a level that struck him right in the eye as they drove towards the hotel. It was nearly five in the afternoon; the long flight down from Lisbon had worn him out, but he'd been unable to sleep. They drove through the city centre, streets clogged with traffic and hawkers, the same makeshift kiosks and colourful displays of wares he'd seen all over the continent. There was something jubilant in the stances and gazes of the pedestrians they passed at a crawl – the war was over, trade was returning, the markets were full. Scraps of white and light grey clouds drifted past the buildings above their heads; like everywhere in the tropics, the threat of rainfall after a particularly hot day was always present. The sky was intensely blue, despite the rapid approach of night. He gave himself up to the lurch and roll of the vehicle as João expertly negotiated the potholes, dogs and hawkers all jostling for space.

The hotel was much like international five-star hotels the world over. After calling Niela, he stood under the shower, enjoying what would be his last taste of luxury for quite some time. The irony of the move from the Intercontinental to the camp at Mueda wasn't lost on him. He towelled his hair dry, pulled on a clean T-shirt and a pair of jeans and walked down the air-conditioned corridor to the restaurant, where he would probably eat his last decent meal. Between the gracefully swaying palms and over the soft tinkling sounds of a piano, he could make out the faces of the international businessmen and their local contacts and counterparts – the same plump, sweaty, shiny faces, full of eager greed. Up north, a twelve- or fourteen-hour drive away, a very different sort of face would present itself. He squared his shoulders and drew a deep breath, preparing himself for the sudden, shocking descent.

74

JULIA
Maputo, May 2000

They landed in Johannesburg on a cool, misty morning. It was autumn in the southern hemisphere. Julia emerged bleary-eyed but excited into the early morning neon glow of cafés and shops, only just beginning to stir. The same duty-free goods were on sale as they were everywhere in the world. If she'd been looking forward with impatience to her first glimpse of Africa, Johannesburg wasn't quite what she'd expected. Through the enormous frosted-glass windows she could just make out the landscape around the airport. Low grey clouds, construction cranes, a flat, dusty plain. It looked almost exactly as Heathrow had done, twelve hours earlier.

At 11.05 a.m. on the dot, the flight to Maputo was called. There were two other women who had been on the flight from London. They smiled tentatively at each other; introductions were made. Susan and Jean, both Americans and veterans of the development circuit. They picked up their bags and laptops and followed the small group of tourists on to the plane. Julia was too excited to feel properly tired. Her itinerary showed time for an afternoon nap before the opening session of the conference that evening and the post-lecture dinner. She almost hugged herself as she took her seat in the small plane. All of a sudden, London and everything in it, including Aaron, seemed a very long way away.

Her first glimpse of Maputo was the long, golden arc of sandy beach that separated the city from its southern suburbs. The plane banked gracefully over red-tiled roofs, occasional splashes of swimming-pool blue and larger dark green patches that looked like parks. The houses were densely packed together; she could just make out the long black tongues of roads before everything disappeared under the thin layer of cloud that hung suspended above the city. It was the rainy season; she'd been told to expect high, humid temperatures during the day but cooler breezes at night. The conference was due to last three days – there was an extra day added on at the end for sightseeing, then it was a late afternoon flight back to Johannesburg, an overnight stay at the airport hotel and the early morning flight back to London.

She followed Susan and Jean off the plane and walked down the rickety steps on to the tarmac. After the dim interior of the plane, the sunlight was almost blinding. The breeze lifted; palm trees stirred; she caught the whiff of woodsmoke at the back of her throat, the scent of carbon monoxide and the sound of car horns . . . the sensations rushed at her, one by one. They were shepherded quickly by the ground staff into the air-conditioned terminal building, where everything disappeared once more into the same cold, arid plasticity of airports. There was a young man in a startlingly white shirt and beautifully pressed khaki trousers bearing a sign with their names creatively misspelt. The three women nodded and smiled as they came through the doors.

'*Bom día,*' he said, flashing a dizzyingly brilliant smile. 'Welcome to Maputo.'

The radiance of water and the radiance of sky; two elements endlessly flashing out there on the horizon, whichever way you turned. On the last day of the conference, Julia declined the invitation of a guided bus tour and went instead with Susan and Jean to the edge of the city, the shore. A tongue's lick of hot, humid air hit them as soon as they stepped outside the air-conditioned lobby and emerged on to the street. Laughing and chatting excitedly at their release, they hailed a cab and piled in. Julia's shirt opened patches of damp under the arms as she clambered into the back seat. The thin trickle of sweat between her shoulder blades thickened, slowly making its way down her back. The driver drove slowly along Avenida 25 de Setembre, explaining local landmarks to them in his sing-song broken English. *The police station. The bus terminal. The international school. Another police station.* Julia listened to him with half an ear, gazing instead at the horizon, now reduced to a single, unbroken white line against the diminishing contrast between water and air. It was three o'clock in the afternoon and the heat was intense. They wound their way around the peninsula and found themselves on Avenida Julius Nyerere. Next along was Avenida Mao Tse-tung, then Avenida Kenneth Kaunda. They swung right on to Vladimir Lenin . . . all ghosts of the socialist past, engraved in the streets and avenues of the capital city. How her father would have thrilled to see this, Julia thought to herself suddenly.

At a junction crowded with cars and vans and jostling pedestrians, Jean recognised the signs for *mercato*, the central market, and shouted for the driver to stop. They got out and were immediately swallowed up in the throng. Julia bought a cup of crushed ice and watermelon juice from a roadside vendor, marvelling at the bicycle-with-a-cooler contraption from which he extracted plastic cups and bright red juice with ease. The cold, sugary drink was a physical release from the sticky heat – she gulped it down and asked for another. They strolled through the *mercato*, picking up souvenirs for those back home, a postcard or two, a small roasted plantain with a handful of peanuts . . . It seemed to Julia, haggling amicably over the price of a pair of silver-and-ebony cufflinks that she thought Aaron would like, that the real purpose of the conference she'd just attended was out here, in broad daylight, in the voices and gestures of the market women in whose name they had all come. Underneath the fierce sun, gesticulating and smiling in the manner of those who had no common language, it was hard to believe in the grim statistics they'd spent three days hearing – a life expectancy of forty-one years for women; infant mortality rates of 289 per thousand births; fifty-four per cent of women enrolled in primary education . . . she'd sat with hundreds of others in the same overcooled rooms, listening to the same voices with growing despair. Yet there was very little despair in the open-air market around her. The women were resplendent in brightly coloured swathes of patterned cloth; some turbaned, others – the younger ones – with braids that fell to their waists and swirled about their faces as they deftly slipped produce into a bag or counted out change. The contrast between the earnest, painfully politically correct academics and politicians and the vibrant, exuberant market women who laughed and joked with their customers was hard to comprehend. Inside the conference hall, African women were portrayed as submissive, passive victims of circumstances far beyond their control. Out here in the city and in real life, it seemed to be the opposite. There was nothing remotely passive about these confident, laughing women. In the little shared language available to them, they asked about children, husbands, lives . . . they knew about produce, prices, making money, births, marriages and deaths – pretty much the same as women everywhere. Julia turned away from them in confusion and collided with someone. For a brief second she was brought cheek to damp, sweaty cheek with one of the market queens. There was a guffaw of laughter and a chorus of voices, '*Desculpé, desculpé!*' as everyone around her laughingly apologised for something that was actually her own fault. It was all so different from the irritated 'tut-tutting' that would have gone on in a London department store if she'd bumped into someone by mistake. She gathered her postcards and gifts and with a last smile and a wave hurried to join the others.

'We're thinking of having a quick drink at one of the roadside bars before we have to leave,' Susan said to her as she drew level with them. 'Jean and I don't much fancy the thought of meeting everyone in the hotel again – not on our last night. I've had enough, to be honest.'

Julia smiled, relieved. It had been her good fortune to meet up with Jean and Susan. 'Same here,' she agreed. 'I'm all for skipping it.'

'Fabulous. Our kind of girl.' They began to thread their way through the crowd. Roadside bars were the one thing Maputo didn't appear to lack. They were everywhere. Susan marched boldly towards one nestled between what appeared to be two makeshift bus stops. There was a free table covered in a red-and-green-checked plastic cloth. A small boy hurried over with two extra plastic chairs. They sank down gratefully – a second later, three already sweating bottles of ice-cold beer had been produced. 'Cheers,' Susan said, lifting her beer. The bottles made a satisfying 'clink'.

'Cheers,' Julia murmured. 'Welcome to the *real* Maputo.'

'You did *what*?' Aaron's voice carried with it all the outrage that could possibly be corralled into a single word thrust down a crackling international phone line.

Julia rolled her eyes – at her own reflection in the mirror. 'It's perfectly all right, Aaron. I was with Susan and Jean.'

'And who the hell are Susan and Jean?'

'I told you the other night. They're the two other women from the conference I've been hanging out with. They're very nice. They're both Americans. Susan's an economist and Jean's a historian.'

'I don't care what they do. They led you off to some . . . some underground *bar* in a *slum*?'

Julia had to laugh. 'It wasn't an underground bar. And it certainly wasn't in a slum. It was in the central market.'

'Julia, it's no laughing matter,' Aaron said sternly. 'You weren't supposed to leave the hotel. That's what it said in the conference pack, remember?'

'Oh, Aaron! It's perfectly safe. People are amazingly friendly and—'

'Don't be so naïve, Julia. You're in Africa, for God's sake. There are wars on. Anything could happen. You've got to be more careful. You can't just wander off on your own like that. You could've been mugged, or worse.'

'Aaron, I'm in Mozambique, not Sierra Leone. There's no war going on here. You're being ridiculous.'

'*I'm* the one being ridiculous?' Aaron's voice rose in indignation.

Julia sighed. 'Look, let's not argue. This phone call's costing me a fortune. I'll ring you when I get to the hotel in Johannesburg tomorrow, all right?'

'All right.' Aaron's tone was sulky. Julia made a few further conciliatory remarks and then put the phone down before he could irritate her any further. A sudden uneasiness at the thought of returning to London stole over her. She'd been away for almost a week – she ought to be pleased to be going back home. To Aaron, if nothing else. But she wasn't, and she couldn't say why.

75

JOSH
Johannesburg, May 2000

Josh strode impatiently through the arrivals hall. After seven weeks in the bush, the smell of coffee wafting from the small Café e Vida stand located halfway down the corridor was unsettling. He had one night in the Intercontinental located just across the road from arrivals and then it was the long eleven-hour flight back to London – and to Niela. At the thought of her, his pulse quickened. He'd been away almost two months. There had been times out there in the thick humidity of the bush around them when it was almost impossible to believe in her, or her small, neat flat in London . . . or in London itself. It was the end of May; he'd seen on the news the night before that it was still cold. That too was hard to believe in, although Johannesburg was certainly cooler than Cabo Delgado.

He crossed the road and walked quickly up to the check-in desk. Ten minutes later, he was walking down a thickly carpeted hallway, his single rucksack swinging from side to side on the back of the young man in uniform who was escorting him to his room. 'Here you are, sir,' the young man said, sliding the plastic card into the slot. He opened the door and quickly ran through the checklist of amenities – minibar, TV, shower, patio doors . . . Josh had been through it all a million times before. 'Can I get you anything, sir?' He paused at the door.

'No thanks,' Josh said, sliding over the obligatory ten-rand note. The young man's grin was thanks enough and he slid silently from the room.

Josh walked over to the window and drew back the drapes. The material felt luxuriously soft in his hands, which, for two months, had held nothing but nylon rope and coarse sheets that were always damp with sweat . . . yes, a night spent in luxury was probably a good thing before he touched down in London once more. He walked over to the shower, stripped off his dusty, tired clothing and stepped in.

Half an hour later, his hand still going to his freshly shaved jaw-line as if in disbelief, he walked into the lobby and made his way towards the bar. The tinkle of a piano came to him from behind the potted palms and the Japanese-style screens; the room had the soft lighting and neutral, fashionable decor of hotel lobbies everywhere. He pulled out one of the leather bar stools and slid on to it. 'Gin and tonic,' he said to the barman. 'Double.'

'Very good, sir. Ice and lemon?'

He nodded; a few seconds later, an expertly mixed drink was slid across the marble top towards him. He took a sip, feeling it burn its way down his throat pleasurably. There were a few men sitting alongside him; their eyes were fixed either on the drink in front of them or on the doorway. Josh recognised the stares: men who had either seen too much or too little. All they were able to focus on was the half-empty glass a hand's reach away or the young prostitutes with their tight, round backsides and long fake tresses who sauntered in and out of the lobby under the watchful eye of management. He watched the man next to him eyeing one of the girls further down the counter as she preened beside a customer; her sequinned skirt was split from ankle to thigh. The ridiculously firm flesh shone blue-black in the soft lighting, a slick, polished surface like marble. Her companion's fat hand was stamped proprietorially on it; he looked as though he might bite the head off anyone who so much as looked at her. Josh turned his head wearily. He'd seen it all before. The next night she would be in with someone else. For the price of a handbag, a cell phone or a month's supply of corrugated roofing sheet – depending on your preferences and most pressing needs – the girl's undivided attention was yours.

'Josh?' A woman's voice suddenly cut across his thoughts. He turned. A young woman was standing to his left, eyes wide with surprise. She looked familiar but he couldn't place her at first. 'Josh Keeler?' He nodded, wondering where the hell he'd seen her before. She was smiling at him, her face breaking open in welcome. 'Julia! I'm Aaron's wife.' The confusion that ran through him was so great he almost dropped his drink. Aaron's wife? What the hell was she doing in Johannesburg, of all places? Her own surprise seemed to equal his. 'I can't believe it! What a coincidence . . . this is incredible!' She turned to the small group who were standing some way behind her. 'This is my brother-in-law,' she said, gesturing towards him. 'I can't believe it! What are you doing here?'

Introductions were made: Susan, Jean, Alison, Khadija. He shook hands with them in turn. A conference – they'd been at a conference. Explanations were offered; this one was the head of such-and-such programme at the World Bank; that one was the director of this and that . . . He nodded at each, wishing only that they would hurry up and leave him alone. It was on the tip of his tongue to ask Julia what she was doing in such company, but not only would it have seemed rude, perhaps, but it occurred to him that he didn't really care. The last thing he felt like doing was making small talk with the wife of one of his brothers. Especially this one. What was it Diana had said about her? 'That *accent*. Jumps out at you like a barking dog.' He felt the ghost of a smile cross his lips but he suppressed it just in time. It wasn't her accent that bothered him – on the contrary, he found it rather refreshing. It was so at odds with her cool, polished appearance. No, it was the way he'd seen her looking at Niela that one time they'd met, her cold blue eyes passing judgement on someone whose life and circumstances she couldn't possibly even imagine. He slid off the bar stool. 'Sorry, ladies . . . if you'll excuse me. I've had a long day.' And with that and without so much as a backward glance or a goodbye, he strode off.

Julia's cheeks were flaming as they watched him walk out of the bar. 'Sorry about that,' she muttered, lifting her glass to hide her face. 'I've only met him once. He wasn't quite as rude the first time but he was close. No bloody wonder they don't get on.'

'Mmm. Well, he didn't seem *especially* thrilled to see us,' Susan said diplomatically. 'But perhaps he really did have a long day. Oh well. Drink, anyone?'

'Hell of a good-looking guy, though,' Jean mused. 'Ooh, yes please. I'll have a very large whisky, thanks.'

They carried their drinks off like prizes and found a table underneath the palms. 'Cigarette?' Susan pulled out a packet.

Julia shook her head. Then she changed her mind. 'Oh, I'll have one. I tell you, he doesn't half get my goat.' She lit up, savouring the taste at the back of her throat. It had been years since she'd smoked, and although she rarely missed it, there were times, like now, when she craved one.

'Gets your goat?' Jean asked, frowning.

Julia laughed wryly. 'It's a northern term. He gets on my nerves.'

'Oh, ignore him. We've had a great conference, we got to meet each other . . . forget about him,' Jean said with a smile.

Julia nodded. Jean was right. She took one last puff on her cigarette, stubbed it out and banished Josh Keeler from her thoughts.

By 10 p.m. the restaurant was almost empty. Julia sat alone for a few minutes after the others had gone to bed, toying with the remains of her drink. She too was tired but she found herself curiously unwilling to go upstairs to her room. She wanted to savour every last minute of what had been the most interesting week of her life. She'd been transported straight back to the heady days of the Pro Bono Publico at Oxford. Curiously, too, the whole conference and the conversations it had generated brought her mother-in-law to mind. This was what she'd dreamed about as a young girl watching Diana on TV and thinking about the power and grace of the law. She couldn't believe she'd been gone for only six and a half days; it felt like a lifetime, as though everything about her life had changed. In a way, it had. She'd discovered a whole world outside the narrow confines of the law as she'd understood it − six days in the company of passionate, articulate and fiercely intelligent women had given her another perspective. She'd been one of the youngest presenters in Maputo, but to her great surprise, it hadn't made a jot of difference. At Bernard, Bennison & Partners she'd become so used to the double disadvantage of age and gender that the realisation in Maputo that neither meant anything to anyone had come as a complete shock. In six days she'd discovered there were multiple ways to be a professional woman, from the Diana types, brisk, brusque, rake-thin and stylish, to the homely, motherly ones, often dressed in ethnic clothing, to the serious intellectuals from places like Princeton and Oxford with their short haircuts and always dressed in black. There were others, too; women from places as far afield as Bangladesh and Bahrain, the latter in their long black gowns with beautifully composed faces partially hidden by their veils. She'd had lunch on one of the days with a group of Nigerian women who were simultaneously wives, mothers, policy-makers and activists. She'd come away awed by the complexity and richness of their lives. She'd met lawyers in Maputo, but what really struck her was the way they adapted the law to suit the demands of working for and on behalf of women worldwide. For someone like her to become a successful barrister would mean she would have to work twice as hard and twice as long as anyone else. She was painfully aware that her accent and her background worked against her and that her marriage to Aaron Keeler had provoked more jealousy than anything else. Diana would never lift a finger to help or advise her and—

She looked up suddenly. Something had interrupted her thoughts – a man had come into the empty room. It was Josh. He was walking towards the bar, his back turned towards her. She felt the heat rise in her cheeks as she looked at him. He was ordering something, a drink – any second now he would turn around. She ought to get up and make her way across the floor to the lifts before he saw her. She wanted nothing further to do with him. She ought to get up . . . but she didn't. He turned slowly, drink in hand, and then, of course, he spotted her. There was a moment's awkwardness, before he lifted his glass, acknowledging her. She hesitated, then lifted hers in return. He began to walk towards her. It struck her as he approached that she felt the same way about Josh as she had about Aaron, all those years ago. Despite their obvious differences, there was something remarkably similar about them. She wondered whether she'd misjudged Josh, just as she had Aaron.

'Hi,' he said, setting his glass down on the table and pulling out the seat opposite her. Julia was too surprised to answer. It hadn't occurred to her that he might actually *join* her.

'Hi,' she muttered, not wishing to appear ungracious but not relishing the thought of his surly company either.

'That looks empty,' he said, pointing to her glass. 'What're you drinking?'

Julia hesitated. 'Whisky and soda.'

Josh seemed to be considering something. 'Tell you what,' he said suddenly. 'How about a proper drink? In a proper place. Not here . . .' He let his hand drop disparagingly.

'What d'you mean?' Julia asked, further taken aback.

'D'you know Jo'burg?'

She shook her head. 'No. It's only the second time I've been abroad,' she said ruefully, expecting him to laugh.

He didn't. 'There's a bar in Braamfontein that I've been to a couple of times . . .' He glanced at his watch. 'It's quarter to eleven – they should just about be opening up. Come on. Let's get a cab.' He drained his own glass and put it down on the table. He stood up, looking down at her. 'Well? Coming?'

Julia scrambled to her feet. It was the last thing she'd expected, but there was something thrilling and compelling about Josh just the same. She couldn't imagine Aaron doing anything even remotely like this, she thought to herself wildly as she followed him out of the lobby and waited as he organised a cab. Aaron would sooner have *died* than gone out at midnight to a bar in a city he hardly knew. Getting into the back of the cab after Josh, it occurred to her that it was hardly the sort of thing she did, either. When was the last time she'd done anything remotely like this? Never, was the answer. Never.

All the life was withdrawn from the city streets as they drove towards the address Josh had given the driver. There were few streetlights, a couple of abandoned cars; no one was about. 'You sure?' was all the driver had said on hearing the street name. 'You been there before?' Josh nodded. 'Well, if you're sure . . .' The driver lifted his shoulders. Julia bit her lower lip. Suddenly all the stories she'd ever heard about Johannesburg came flooding back.

'Isn't it very dangerous?' she whispered to Josh as they plunged down one deserted street after another.

He shrugged. 'No more dangerous than anywhere else,' he said cryptically. Julia's pulse began to race again. What was she doing? The car suddenly came to an abrupt halt.

'This it is, sir.' The driver turned his head disbelievingly.

Josh peered out into the darkness. 'Yeah, this is it. Thanks.' He pushed a note through the glass and got out. 'Well?' He looked down at Julia for the second time that evening. She got out with some difficulty and stood beside him as the cab pulled away, faster than it had arrived, she noticed, as if the driver couldn't wait to get away. She looked up at the building in front of them. It was tall, almost entirely blacked out, with thin strips of light showing here and there as if the darkness had worn thin. There was a buzzer on the door in front of them. Josh stepped forward and pressed it; after a wait of a few seconds, the door swung open. The hallway was dark, but there was the unmistakable sound of laughter and music coming from behind the door at the far end of the room. It opened to release a surge of activity. Someone was standing in the doorway. From his stance, Julia understood he was carrying a gun. She swallowed nervously.

'Hi,' Josh said, making no move towards him. 'I'm a friend of Tumi's.'

The man looked them over once or twice, then nodded, standing aside to let them pass. Like Alice plunging after the White Rabbit, Julia followed Josh in. They went down three or four steps into a basement space. It was dark, but there were candles and tea lights strung up everywhere. The sound of laugher and music was a warm, thick blanket covering them. In contrast to the cool night outside, it was hot inside; the smells of alcohol, perfume, cigarette smoke and the occasional whiff of a joint filled her nostrils pleasurably. A band was playing in the far corner of the room. Josh turned and pulled her forward by the wrist towards the bar. 'What'll you have?' he shouted above the noise.

'Rum and Coke,' Julia shouted back. Despite her nervousness, she was beginning to enjoy herself. She looked at him, his body half-turned towards the bar, chatting animatedly with the barman. His face glowed under the soft neon lights. She found herself staring at him, unable to tear her eyes away. The whole evening had suddenly taken on an unreal, otherworldly aspect. He passed her a drink over the head of a young woman who stood in between them. Her smile, as the drink sailed above her, was both sweet and flirtatious; Julia felt something inside her lift. She smiled back and took a sip. The alcohol flowed thick and strong through her veins. The band began to play again. Julia had never heard music like it. It was strong and soft at the same time, intensely lyrical but with a pulsing, driving beat. The singer, an extraordinarily beautiful young woman with an enormous, theatrical Afro, came out on to the makeshift stage to roars of applause. The crowd was almost totally mixed, Julia noticed, sipping her drink and looking around with interest. Black, white, Indian . . . students, young professionals, workers . . . it was un-like any bar or club she'd ever been to. Not that she'd been to many, she reminded herself. She took another mouthful of her drink. Someone asked her to dance; she shook her head, laughing: *no, no* . . . He smiled regretfully and turned his attention elsewhere, singling someone else out.

It was almost three in the morning by the time they finally left, but for Julia, it felt as though it had been only a few minutes. Dancing, talking, drinking, laughing . . . the man beside her was almost unrelated to the surly, withdrawn person she'd met. She followed him outside. The same bouncer who'd let them in opened the door for them on to the beginnings of a storm. Fat drops of rain were falling from the inky black sky. 'Summer storms,' Josh said, looking up. 'It always rains early in the morning.'

Julia lifted her jacket above her head and they ran towards the waiting cab. Squalls of wind gusted at their backs and a small tornado of leaves whipped up just as Josh opened the door. They clambered in, wet and giggling, and the car pulled away. Josh gave instructions to the driver. 'Well, did you enjoy that?' he asked, turning his head to look at Julia. She nodded vigorously. A sudden intimacy had sprung up between them in the darkened interior of the cab. The steady drumbeat of rain on the roof turned into a soft, enclosing rhythm, drawing them into its sound. Julia was acutely, uncomfortably aware of Josh's thigh pressed close to hers. She shivered, suddenly cold, and moved away as imperceptibly as she could. It was only the second time she'd met him and already she was aware of the danger she was in. He was like Aaron; and yet he was not. There was both familiarity at work here, and the erotic pull of a stranger. She turned to look unseeingly out of the window at the darkened streets through which they passed. She put a hand up to her face. It was hot with fear, but also with desire. There was the same distance in Josh that had first annoyed her in Aaron, then intrigued her. That same quality of something else lying just beneath the surface, if only you could reach it. She suddenly felt herself close to tears. She was tired, drunk and overwhelmed. She was alone in a very foreign country, all sorts of strange and unfathomable thoughts spiralling around in her head. She longed for home and the comforting security of Aaron's embrace.

76

MADDY
London, June 2000

Maddy shook off the drops of water from her umbrella and propped it against the wall. The flat was lovely and quiet: Darcy was at playschool. She took off her raincoat and walked into the living room. The cleaner had been in the day before and everything was spotless. Just looking at it made her feel calmer. She kicked off her shoes and walked over to the couch. It seemed almost a pity to destroy its soft, plumped-up comfort. She sat down, picked up the pad and pen that were lying neatly aligned on the coffee table and opened to the page she'd been working on the night before.

She ran a finger down the list on one side of the page. Those were all the possible agents, listed alphabetically. Next to them were the smaller theatre companies – occasionally, very occasionally, an actor might be hired on the strength of a tape or an interview. It was a long shot, but definitely worth trying. Finally, next to them she'd drawn up a list of cooperatives, tightly knit groups of anything between two and twenty actors who worked and sometimes lived together, putting on their own productions and performances, taking care of the business end of things themselves. She would try every single avenue; she wasn't fussy. She couldn't afford to be, that was the point. She'd wasted four years here in London; she couldn't afford to waste another four minutes. Christ, if Julia could get herself invited halfway round the world to speak, surely she could manage to get herself the tiniest, most insignificant part? She had to lift the cloud of hopelessness that seemed to have descended permanently on her. Rafe couldn't do it for her, neither could Julia. Only she could. Alone. Armed with her new-found determination and a long list of numbers, she picked up the phone and began to dial.

Two hours later, she'd gone through the long list of agents and was halfway down the theatre companies without a single spark of hope. The responses were always the same. 'Sorry, we're not taking on anyone new at present,' or 'Do send in a tape and a CV. We'll be in touch.' All she wanted was the chance to *see* someone – she didn't care who – an agent, a casting director, a producer, a talent scout . . . anyone! How would she ever persuade anyone she was any good if they weren't prepared to see her? An old tape of a performance in a play none of them had ever heard of, directed by a young American whom they'd never read and reviewed by American critics whose opinions meant nothing to them was hardly likely to persuade anyone on this side of the pond to hire her. No, she'd have to do it on the strength of her personality and talent . . . and how to convince anyone she had either when she was on the other disembodied end of a telephone was anyone's guess.

Wearily she picked up the phone again. The London Theatre Company was a small set-up known for its experimental, cutting-edge performances. Maddy had actually sent them a tape when she first arrived in London. She steeled herself for disappointment as soon as the phone was picked up, but to her great surprise, the voice on the other end of the phone was warm. 'Madison Stiller. Gosh, I remember the name. It's unusual. Didn't you send us something a few years back?'

'Y-yes, yes I did. About four years ago. I . . . I can't believe you'd remember that,' Maddy stammered, her face immediately going bright red with pleasure. She was glad the woman on the other end of the phone couldn't see her.

'I remember your name. Why don't you come in and see me?'

Maddy almost dropped the phone. 'When? Now? I mean, what would be a good time for you?' The words came tumbling out, one after the other.

Stephanie Whyte chuckled. 'How about next week? We're running a production of *Hedda Gabler* at the moment. Tonight's the last perform- ance. Do come – I think you'll enjoy it.'

It was all Maddy could do to stay standing upright. 'Oh, I'd *love* to but I've got a young daughter . . . No, yes, I'll come. *Thank* you.' She managed to stop herself just in time. Her childcare arrangements were hardly likely to interest the director of the London Theatre Company. Stammering another round of thanks, she put down the phone, her pulse racing. Whom could she leave Darcy with for all of four hours that evening? There was only one person – and much as it killed her to ask Diana for help, there was nothing else for it. She wouldn't have missed the performance for anything.

Enjoyment was too mild a term for the rush of emotions that swept through her as the play unfolded. Maddy sat in the back row, entranced.

She felt a chasm open up inside her and for the next ninety minutes nothing in the world existed save the performance in front of her and Ibsen's timeless, poetic suggestion that the key to the future lay in embracing the past, not rejecting it. It was as if the message were directed at her alone; the words spoken for her.

'It's a very small part, I warn you. But it's a start.' A week after she'd gone along to see them, the London Theatre Company had good news – she'd been asked to audition for a part. Maddy sat opposite Stef Whyte, almost too stunned to speak. Stef peered at her over the top of the multicoloured rim of her glasses. 'We're inundated with Americans at the moment, unfortunately. And even more unfortunately for you, they tend to be famous. That's the draw. In your case . . . well, let's just say you'll be starting at the other end of the spectrum.'

Maddy nodded her head vigorously. She didn't care where she started . . . the fact that she was starting at all was gift enough. She looked at the script in her hand and felt her toes begin to curl with excitement. The opening description brought out the hairs along the back of her neck. *Flames perceptible through ice. Mishima believed that this quality was found in classical Japanese poetry and in the Noh plays, where the passion is shielded under polished surfaces.* 'Th . . . thank you,' she said fervently. '*Thank* you.'

'Don't thank me,' Stef laughed. 'You haven't got the part yet!'

She practically ran all the way down Upper Street, still clutching the script to her chest, and got on the bus at Newington Green. She made her way upstairs and sat right at the back, oblivious to the sounds and noise around her. The bus lurched its way past the Angel, past King's Cross and Euston and was winding its way slowly down Oxford Street before Maddy realised she'd missed her stop – by about a mile. She jumped off and ran all the way home. She couldn't wait to read the rest.

She was still full of excitement when Rafe came home that evening. 'OK, OK, just let me get my coat off,' he protested, when she tried to describe the play to him in the hallway. 'So what's the part?'

'Oh, it's a tiny part. If I get it, I'll have about three lines, I promise you . . . nothing big. But you'll never guess who's playing the lead.'

'Who?' Rafe unwound his scarf.

She could feel the smile stretching across her face. 'Judi Dench. And Maggie Smith's in it, too. It's by this Japanese playwright, Yukio

Mishima,' she went on. 'It's an adaptation of the story of Marquis de Sade, told through the eyes of the women. It's amazing, Rafe . . . just amazing. You *have* to read it.' She only just managed to suppress a smile. Rafe hadn't read anything non-medical in a decade, as far as she knew. 'Or I'll read it to you. D'you want to hear my part?'

Rafe made a quick grimace. 'Look, d'you mind if you read it to me some other time? There's cricket on tonight and I've had a hellish day.'

Maddy stared at him. She could feel her enthusiasm slowly seeping out of her pores. Cricket? 'No, you go right ahead. I'll just do the washing-up.' She turned on her heel and walked through to the kitchen, her eyes smarting. *Cricket?*

77

NIELA/JULIA/MADDY
London, June 2000

'We can't *not* go,' Niela said calmly, clearing the dishes from the table and taking them through to the kitchen. 'It's your father's birthday. It's disrespectful.'

'Christ, Niela . . . a whole *week?*'

'We don't have to stay for the whole week,' she said, coming back into the living room. 'We could go for the party, stay a day or two and then come back.'

He sighed but she knew the argument had already been won. She breathed a sigh of relief. He'd been back from Mozambique for over a week, and although she was overjoyed to have him home again, the distance that she often sensed in him when he first returned was still there. He'd said very little beyond the usual comments about what they'd managed or failed to accomplish. She was due to leave at the end of June for a two-week assignment in Yemen; there was no word yet on where Josh would go next. But at least they would have some time off in Mougins together. She was curious about the place; it seemed to hold the key to so much of who Josh was and what he'd become. She found herself thinking ahead to the party and to the daunting prospect of spending a week with the people he seemed to both love and despise. She knew, even if he didn't, that the situation was in no way as simple as he made it seem.

Julia stepped out of the doctor's office just off Harley Street and made her way down the Marylebone Road towards Baker Street. It was raining lightly, but she didn't notice. The doctor's words still reverberated in her ears. 'Well, the good news is, there's absolutely nothing wrong with you. No reason at all why you shouldn't be able to conceive. We've run all the tests; everything's come back well within normal ranges . . . no, there's no medical reason that *I* can see that's preventing it from happening.' She'd looked at him, almost afraid to ask the next question. But she had to.

'So if the problem's not with me . . .' she'd said hesitantly. 'You're saying there may be a problem with my husband?'

'It's possible. He'll need to come in for us to run a few tests. You can make an appointment with my secretary. I'm fairly sure we can fit him in reasonably quickly.' Julia said nothing. Her heart sank. She and Aaron had had one conversation – just one – about the issue and she'd never dared bring it up again. 'There's nothing wrong with me,' he'd said coldly, putting down his paper and glaring at her with such hostility that she regretted opening her mouth.

'Of course there isn't,' she'd hastened to assure him. 'But there might be something the matter with *me*. It's always better to check these things out. It might be something really simple.'

'Yeah, well, if you feel like having someone prod about inside you, fine. *I* don't. And I don't want to discuss it either.' And that was that. She hadn't dared bring it up again.

'Is there something the matter?' the doctor asked kindly, noticing her silence.

'It's just . . . I don't know . . . my husband's a little . . . er, reluctant.'

The doctor regarded her thoughtfully. 'Infertility's a difficult thing for many men to accept, quite frankly. People – especially men – tend to think of it as primarily a woman's problem; completely erroneously, of course. But you've done the right thing and had yourself checked out – now your husband needs to come in. That way we can get to the cause of the problem and see what sort of help we can offer. We can't do that until we know what's wrong.'

Julia was silent. She had the sinking feeling that this was going to be harder than she thought. 'I'll . . . I'll try,' she said, sliding down from the examination table. 'But he's pretty set against the whole thing.'

'Once he hears there's nothing wrong with you, he'll change his mind. Trust me, I've seen it many times before.'

'I hope so,' Julia said, pulling on her coat. 'I really hope so.'

Now, walking down the escalators towards the Tube, she was again assailed by doubt. Perhaps she should wait until they'd gone on holiday to bring it up. He'd be more relaxed then. He was under a lot of pressure at work – something to do with the taxation and corporation section having lost a few cases recently . . . nothing to do with Aaron personally, or so it seemed, but the pressure was on nonetheless. Not for the first time, Julia was glad of the relative anonymity of her department. After her trip, she'd been thinking long and hard about where her future might lie – did she want to continue where she was, or was she brave enough to make a break? It didn't seem the right time to bring it up with Aaron . . . plus there was the awkward little detail that she'd said nothing about meeting Josh in Johannesburg. She couldn't explain why she hadn't mentioned it – there just didn't seem to be a right moment, that was all. And it wasn't as if anything had happened – well, that depended on how you defined it, she thought to herself wryly. No, they'd barely talked; he'd made no move to touch her, nor she him . . . aside from the strange invitation to come along to Braamfontein that night, it was almost as if they hadn't met. So why hadn't she mentioned it to Aaron? And why, if nothing had happened, did she feel as guilty as if it had?

78

'Julia?' Aaron's voice floated up the stairwell. 'Come *on* . . . where the hell are you?'

'Coming,' Julia shouted back. She took one last look around her, picked up her small suitcase and shut the bedroom door. 'Sorry,' she said as she walked down the stairs, the suitcase banging awkwardly against her legs. 'I forgot something.'

'Christ, anyone'd think we were going for a month,' Aaron grumbled, locking the front door behind them. 'We're late.'

'No, we're not. There's loads of time. Train's not until one o'clock . . . we've got hours yet.'

'You know I hate being late.' Aaron stowed the cases in the boot of the rented car.

Julia sighed but said nothing. The last thing she wanted or felt like was an argument before they'd even begun the journey down to Mougins. She was looking forward to it; would Josh be there? She'd been unable to ask Diana directly, and Maddy didn't seem to know, or care. She'd been forced to miss an audition for a part in a play because of the birthday party – when she rang Julia the week before, she'd been in tears. Rafe wouldn't hear of her missing the party; she had no option but to turn the part down. Poor Maddy, Julia thought to herself, unable to come up with anything even remotely comforting to say. The thought of not being able to do exactly what she wanted, when she wanted and how she wanted was so alien to her that she didn't even know where to begin. What could she say? Nothing, it seemed. Maddy's life was so different from her own that she had difficulty imagining her pain.

Sitting stiffly beside Rafe on the long journey down to Mougins, Maddy was no longer tearful; she was seething. Stef had just looked blankly at her when she'd mumbled something about not being available. 'Not available? It's potentially a really good role, Maddy. I've a feeling Chris Meyerson'll really like you.'

'I'm really, really sorry . . . I'm going to be away on holiday for those two weeks. Is there . . . is there any chance I could audition before the second? Or after?'

Stef shook her head. 'He's flying in from New York on the Friday and auditions begin on Saturday morning. I'll show him your tape, but . . . you know how it is. There'll be hundreds of actresses lining up to see him. Shame . . . he's a great director and it'd be a fantastic opportunity to meet him, even if you don't get the part. You're sure you can't change your holiday dates?'

Maddy shook her head glumly. She and Rafe had already had one of the biggest rows of their marriage over the issue. 'No,' she said sadly. 'I can't.'

And that was that. She'd left Stef's office in tears. A few hours later Stef rang to say the part had gone to someone else. So now here she was, sitting in the car beside her husband, whom she hadn't talked to for well over two hours, having driven almost the whole day to get to Lyon with another day's drive ahead of them. Darcy was thankfully fast asleep on the back seat. Maddy turned her head to look out of the window at the kaleidoscope of green and yellow fields, tall, unwavering lines of poplar trees, creamy brick farmhouses and narrow country lanes that was the French countryside, but saw nothing other than the dark chasm of her future. Just when things had started looking up – that was the irony of it all. How would she ever get her career off the ground when the obligations of the Keeler family always came first?

Josh and Niela left at dawn. They would spend a night in Paris with Antonio and then do the Paris–Cannes leg of the journey in one go. Niela was quiet on the drive down through France, content to look out of the window at the countryside sliding past. The further south they went, the sunnier and more Mediterranean the landscape became. Lyon, Montelimar, Aix-en-Provence, Vidauban and finally Cannes. There was heavy traffic heading out of the city. As they stopped at a set of lights, bursts of conversation from other cars came through the open window; she was dimly aware of swaying palm trees, the whiff of a bakery against the carbon monoxide, shop signs and the rat-tat-tat of small motorscooters darting in and out of the traffic lanes. The hills were dark green and shady; the air was cooler, fresher. Mougins sat perched on top of a hillside, its medieval walls still visible for miles around. They wound their way towards the top in a series of never-ending bends until they came to a small junction. Josh turned right into the olive groves, and they bumped their way gently down a single-lane gravel track until they reached a white gate and he turned to her. 'Well, this is it,' he said wryly, the corner of his mouth lifting in a mocking smile. 'Home, I suppose.'

79

DIANA
Mougins, June 2000

Diana watched the small white car make its way slowly down the gravel path. Her face broke into a smile as the door opened and Niela got out. Josh. Josh was here. At last. He and Niela were the last of the family members to arrive. She leaned out of the open window, resting her arms on the sill, and resisted the temptation to call down to him. He was so handsome, she thought to herself, watching him take the cases out of the boot and lock the doors. So very handsome. And kind, too. She saw how he took the case from Niela, shaking his head at her very slightly as she went to pick it up. He said something to her and they both laughed. There was an ease between them that she hadn't seen before. How would she? she thought to herself suddenly. She rarely saw them, and certainly not together. The pattern over the past couple of years had been dinner with Josh whenever he was in town, which was seldom, and twice, perhaps three times in as many years, the two of them had come for lunch. She knew so little about the girl — from the few conversations she'd had with her, it was clear she was no ordinary refugee. She thought back to the first time they'd met — Christmas Day, three and a half years earlier. She'd been unable to handle the news that the last of her sons had gone ahead and made what was potentially the most important decision of his life without telling her — not even a hint of a warning. He'd just shown up that day with Niela in tow. *Mother, this is Niela. My wife.* She could feel the pain of those words as if it were yesterday. She'd been so afraid . . . Who was she? What was she, other than some girl he'd picked up somewhere on his travels? What sort of a person had he brought into their home? Well, she'd been wrong, she'd been forced to admit. Niela wasn't what she'd feared — the contrary, in fact. But she still was none the wiser about who she really was. She knew the facts — Niela was an interpreter; she'd done a part-time degree at one of the London colleges; she spoke three or four languages. She had fled Somalia with her family, with whom she seemed to have little or no contact . . . but beyond that, the girl was a complete mystery. What irked Diana was her quiet self-possession. On the few occasions she and Josh had been invited to the house, she'd made it clear that the weapons Diana had assembled — the tasteful house, the good food, good wines, the family photographs and the anecdotes — meant little to her. She was not impressed. She had a way of holding her head slightly to one side, not arrogantly — she was far too polite for that — but in a manner that let Diana know she was no pushover. She too came from a home in which good food was served, there was fine linen on the table and framed pictures on the walls. Well, Diana thought to herself as she pulled the window up and prepared to go downstairs, they would be here for a week — during which she might learn more about the girl who seemed to have captured Josh's heart.

80

NIELA/JULIA/MADDY
Mougins, June 2000

Diana came towards them, arms outstretched. She was wearing white; a long, sheer kaftan over wide-legged trousers. Her toenails were painted dark ruby-red and she wore a floppy straw hat over her pale, lightly made-up face. She kissed Josh and then it was Niela's turn. A brief, light touch on either cheek . . . the faint trace of her perfume left behind, a smile of welcome fixed firmly on her face. Enquiries were made – how was the drive down? The overnight stay in Paris . . . had they eaten? A glass of wine or *pastis*, perhaps?

'You're in your old room, at the top of the stairs,' Diana called out as they began to take their bags upstairs. 'I've put Aaron and Julia on the floor below. Just put your bags away and come and join us. Dad's on the patio. The . . . er, others are at the pool.'

Niela followed Josh up the second flight of stairs to the landing at the top. He pushed open the door and she stepped inside. A beautiful room; a low ceiling, exposed wooden beams, a gleaming polished floor and rich patterned rugs. The bed was wide and low with a pretty white lace coverlet. A bowl of freshly picked flowers stood on the dresser, slowly releasing their perfume into the air. Niela walked into the room as if into a dream. It was cool at the top of the house. The shuttered windows opened on to a view that went on for ever – right across the valley to the dark green forest beyond. She gave a sigh of pure pleasure. 'It's lovely,' she said, going over to the bed and sitting down. 'You didn't tell me how beautiful it was.' Josh paused in the act of opening one of the suitcases. His expression was wary. She realised immediately what she'd said and what it was he couldn't. She got up and went to stand beside him, laying a hand on his arm. They stood like that for a moment, neither saying anything. Then he touched her lightly on the cheek and went out of the room. It would take more than a tiny caress to bring him back to himself, but she could see, even if he couldn't, that the mere fact that they'd come was in itself a sign of sorts. A good one, she hoped.

She walked to the window and leaned out. The garden was full of colour: thick flashes of pink, blushing roses, climbing their way across the

337

yellowed stone wall and exploding in a riot of petals at the top; dark olive trees, their hard fruit not yet ripened by the sun, and overhead, the brilliantly blue sky now fading towards dusk with hardly a wisp of a cloud in sight. She could hear someone coming up the garden path. She leaned out a little further. It was Maddy, her red hair bobbing in and out of view as she walked. Rafe swam into view, holding their little girl by the hand, then Aaron and finally Julia. She watched them cross the forecourt to the house, their feet crunching loudly on the gravel. They looked happy, she thought to herself. Julia's face was pink; she wore a pretty light blue sundress and flip-flops. Maddy was wearing a bikini top and a sarong tied loosely around her waist. As she passed underneath, Niela was surprised to see how thin she was. Had she always been that thin? She couldn't remember. She pulled herself back in and closed the window. She wondered where Josh had gone. She could hear voices downstairs. It was time to go down and join the gang.

She really was the most exquisite creature, Maddy thought to herself as Niela came into the kitchen. She wore a dark green summer dress that fell to just below the knee. Her dark, beautifully burnished skin shone against its rich colour and her hair was loose, falling in great swathes of black almost down to the small of her back. It had been nearly two years since she'd seen her, she realised. There was something different about her – she'd lost that slightly wary, defensive air she'd had about her when they first met. Now the young woman who kissed each of them in turn was coolly self-possessed, totally relaxed and open. Maddy wished she too could be like that; Niela looked as though nothing could touch her, least of all Diana and her small, stinging barbs. She stole a look around her on the patio – finally, and for the first time in years, the entire family was gathered. Aaron and Rafe stood together at one end, glasses in hand. Diana was moving back and forth between the kitchen and the patio, bringing more wine, more delicious snacks that the housekeeper had prepared, a glass of juice for Darcy, who, for once, was sitting quietly next to Harvey, swinging her legs and behaving herself. Niela and Josh stood together; Maddy looked at them from behind her wine glass. They were the most extraordinary couple – for all their differences, they were uncannily alike. Both had the same sleek, taut beauty and a quiet watchfulness . . . like cats. But not the domestic variety. Big cats. Game. The thought suddenly made her smile. She stopped, aware of Rafe's questioning glance on her. But it was true. They resembled nothing so much as a pair of beautiful panthers. Suddenly, impulsively, she moved to stand next to Niela. She ignored Josh's questioning glance and smiled at her. She was rewarded with an open, friendly smile in return.

'Did you have a good journey down?' she asked, emboldened by the smile.

Niela nodded. 'We stayed overnight in Paris but it's a long drive. And you?'

Maddy looked across to where Darcy was chattering to Harvey. She shrugged. 'Well, with a three-year-old in tow . . . you know how it is,' she began, then stopped. How would Niela know? She and Josh had no children. But to her complete surprise, Niela agreed. Within minutes, she began talking about her younger brothers and the long car journeys they'd made back in Somalia. Maddy was taken aback. She'd expected the conversation to be hard work – it was anything but. Niela had a light, generous sense of humour and a ready smile. She was so different from the girl she'd met on previous occasions – had she totally misjudged her? After a few minutes, Julia came over; Josh was claimed by Diana, leaving the three of them to chat alone. Outside, across the valley, the sky flickered eyelids of lightning somewhere in the distance; a summer storm was on its way. The large lanterns that stood at the edge of the patio had been lit; golden candlelight danced around in the breeze. Suddenly, from somewhere in the deepening twilight, a sound emerged, breaking into their conversations.

'Listen,' Harvey murmured, putting up a hand. 'It's the nightingales.' All around them a piercing sweet ringing was just audible. They all stopped talking and stared out into the fading light.

'Nightingales?' Maddy asked, a note of wonder in her voice. 'I've never heard a nightingale before.'

'Every summer. Once or twice they've gone on all night. It's the most ravishing sound. Wait, wait.' Harvey's head was cocked. The song intensified, warbling around them. It rose, dizzyingly, higher and higher . . . a ring of waves whose centre couldn't be reached. They all stood there; no one spoke. The song tipped and sailed, twirled upwards, again and again. And then, just as slowly as it had started, it began to lose its pitch, dying away as the bird – or birds? – moved on, flew off and the garden slowly returned to its purple-fading-to-black silence. It took a while for them to start speaking again. Maddy felt herself inexplicably close to tears. There was something extraordinary about Mougins, she thought to herself, and not for the first time, either. It wasn't just the beauty all around them – there was something else in the air . . . an intensity of emotion that drew her in and seduced her, but frightened her at the same time. She found herself standing a little closer to Niela, as though the quiet strength she detected in her might rub off on her. She looked over to where Diana stood with Josh. They were talking quietly, Diana's dark head tilted upwards to meet her son's. She was gazing at him, frowning in concentration at something he said. She glanced at Maddy, and for a second or two, their eyes met and held. A line suddenly came back to Maddy, though she couldn't have said where from. 'His was less a face than the expression of a predicament.' Such was Diana's face, though the predicament couldn't clearly be read. Diana's glance fell away and the moment was gone. Maddy turned back to Julia and Niela. Julia was making plans for the following afternoon. 'Let's all go, just us,' she was saying. 'You can leave Darcy with Rafe, can't you?'

Maddy's mind was still claimed by the nightingale's song. 'What're we doing?' she asked, forcing herself to concentrate.

'Going for lunch tomorrow. Just the three of us. We could go to l'Amandine. It's up the hill, just by the Mairie. Aaron and I went the last time we were here – it's lovely.'

'Sounds good,' Maddy said absently. She looked over again at Rafe. The tension between them hadn't quite dissipated. She was aware of a thin crust of resignation in her that kept the resentment at bay. Of the four women in the Keeler family, only she had no role other than that of wife and mother . . . she was nobody's friend. She felt the crust break; the resentment flooded in. She drained the last of her wine quickly and turned to go. She needed the toilet. She needed to escape.

81

Mougins, June 2000

The restaurant spread itself under pretty yellow and white striped awnings across a stone patio, tumbling in a series of smaller terraces to the road. Blood-red geraniums in terracotta pots stood sentinel at the edges; the table to which the waiter led them was a leafy shelf of sunlight dappling through the potted olives. '*C'est bon?*' he asked, anxious to please the three young women whose entrance had caused heads to turn.

'*Oui*,' Niela said, looking at the others for confirmation. '*Merci.*'

'Oh, I wish I could speak another language,' Maddy said enviously as they sat down. 'I can speak about ten words of Spanish and that's it.'

'How many languages do you speak?' Julia asked Niela curiously.

'A couple,' Niela said, embarrassed.

'A couple? That's not what I've heard.' Julia smiled. 'Josh said you spoke about six.' She coloured immediately. It was one of the things he'd said in passing in Johannesburg. How was she to explain that? But Niela didn't appear to notice and the moment passed. The waiter appeared again and there was a flurry of explanations and orders, and yet again the opportunity to say something – anything – floated away.

The food was simple but delicious – long, thick red tongues of chargrilled sweet peppers, still hot to the touch and drizzled with olive oil; artichoke hearts the size of small cabbages in a tangy brine; plump, glossy black olives and thick slices of wonderfully crusty bread that they dipped into tiny bowls of peppery olive oil and sweet balsamic vinegar. The conversation flowed with the aid of a bottle of crisp white wine. On the terrace immediately below them, the sun marked out the advance of the afternoon in stripes of sunlight. Waiters moved around in a slow dance; Niela felt the wonderfully slow, heavy lassitude of the afternoon steal over her. They talked about everything and nothing; every so often a burst of laughter would cause the people around them to turn and look, smiling in indulgent conspiracy with whatever had been said.

They were on their second bottle of wine when someone at the table next to them suddenly leaned over, putting out a wrinkled, tanned hand. 'I'm so sorry to interrupt,' she said apologetically and in an almost absurdly posh English voice. 'But I couldn't help overhearing . . . did you just say the name Rafe?'

Maddy looked at her, slightly taken aback. 'Yes, Rafe Keeler. I'm his wife. Why?'

'You're married to Rafe Keeler?' The woman's voice rose in surprised delight. She was in her early seventies, an Englishwoman in every sense of the word, dressed in a summer frock that belonged on someone twenty years younger but with a chiffon scarf and gloves that gave her the air of a bygone era. 'Goodness me, George! Did you hear that?' She turned to the man sitting in companionable silence beside her. 'She's married to Rafe Keeler! What a lovely, lovely surprise! How are they all?'

'They're fine,' Maddy said, smiling tentatively.

'Oh, we used to be *such* dear friends. It's been thirty years, hasn't it, George? We used to live at the bottom of the hill, a few houses down. We spent the summers here back then, like everyone. How *are* they? Aaron? And the little one . . . Joshua?'

'Ask them,' Maddy said, laughing and pointing to Niela and Julia. 'They're married to them. We're all sisters-in-law.'

'Well I *never*! Did you hear that, George? They're married to the Keeler boys! All three of them! How *utterly* marvellous! D'you know, we haven't been back in almost thirty years, and to think we just bump into you, just like that! Who's married to whom? No, no, don't tell me. Let me guess!' She said it with an air of delight. She pointed at Julia, pursing her lips and tilting her head to one side as she considered her. 'Aaron, am I right?' She beamed as Julia nodded. 'I *thought* so, don't ask me why. You just seem like his type. From what I remember, he was always a serious little one. And that only leaves you,' she said, looking at Niela. 'You must be Joshua's wife. How marvellous!' she repeated. 'Isn't it, George?' George grunted.

'Josh*ua*?' Maddy smiled. 'We only know him as Josh.'

'Oh, well, it's been thirty-odd years, you know. I only saw him the once, must've been a few months after he was born. Dark-haired, I seem to remember. Not blond, like the other two. More like Diana, I suppose. How *is* she? And Harvey? Thirty years! After all that unpleasant business with the gardener, it rather ruined things for us, I'm afraid. We must tell the children, mustn't we, George?'

George grunted again. He seemed more interested in polishing off the contents of his glass than reminiscing about the Keelers.

'What business?' Julia couldn't help herself.

'Oh, it was terrible.' The woman's voice dropped an octave immediately. 'A *terrible* affair. Quite ruined the place for a lot of us ex-pats, I don't mind telling you.'

'Leonora, I'm sure they don't want to hear about all of that,' George protested mildly, signalling to the waiter for another bottle almost simultaneously.

'Oh, *George* . . . why ever not? It was dreadful. *Dreadful.* Diana was the only one to defend him, you know. She was like a bulldog, wouldn't let go. And then he just disappeared, just like that. They never caught him.'

'Who?' All three of them stared at her.

Leonora looked at them, then quickly glanced around the terrace. There was only one other couple present; young and in love, they were looking into each other's eyes, certainly not at them. 'The gardener. Mohammed. It was pretty obvious. *I* think he killed her, if you ask me. What other explanation could there be? How could both of them just disappear? Mother *and* baby? It didn't make sense. He kept saying they'd gone back to Algeria, or wherever it was he came from, but the police didn't believe him. There'd been a spate of them, you see. What do they call them? Honour killings? Though quite where the honour is in killing your own daughters is beyond me. D'you remember, George? That terrible affair in Valbonne? So they were on to him, you see. And when he disappeared it was all the proof they needed. Except they never found him, did they?'

'Leonora,' George said again, more forcefully this time. 'I do think that's enough.'

'When did all this happen?'

'Thirty years ago, almost to the month.' Leonora said it almost triumphantly. 'It was the summer of '69. That was it, wasn't it, George? That was the last year we were here.'

'It was a long time ago,' George said with the weary tone of one who's heard the story too many times to count. 'A *very* long time ago.'

'Well, it was good of Diana to defend him,' Julia said faintly.

'Oh, that's not what some of the ex-pats said,' Leonora chuckled. The four of them looked at her. Niela was aware of something else having entered her voice. From somewhere long ago and buried in the memories of their first few months in Vienna, a hackle of disquiet rose in her. She'd heard the tone before. Leonora leaned forward conspiratorially. 'There were even some who said—'

'That's quite enough, Leonora.' George had suddenly risen from his stupor. 'That's quite enough.'

Niela stood up abruptly. The others looked at her. 'I . . . I'd better go,' she stammered. 'I've just remembered I left something back at the house . . .' She pushed back her chair, grabbed her bag and quickly threaded her way through the chairs and tables until she reached the exit. She was breathing fast – she could hear the blood pumping steadily through her veins. The woman's talk – and her tone – had triggered something in her. She needed somewhere quiet to be able to think. A shiver ran through her again. Something wasn't right.

The house was deserted; she pushed open the front door cautiously, half expecting to see Diana in front of her, but there was no one. Just the hum of the refrigerator coming through the half-open kitchen door and the faint but steady background chatter of birds that never seemed to stop. She stood for a moment in the hallway. After the heat and the buzz of the restaurant terrace, the farmhouse was cool and silent. It was a welcome respite. She put a hand up to her face. It was hot, and her fingers trembled a little. Something had come over her, hollowing her out, all through her body, her limbs and hands. It was like waking from a bad dream. Sometimes, putting out a hand as if to catch it or ward it off, all she grasped was the empty air. There'd been a part of her that was shocked by what Josh had told her, but equally, she'd understood it before the words were even out. She thought of Josh, aged ten, sitting crouched above an act that he should never have seen, and her heart almost broke. She knew, even without him saying it, that he'd learned about power from that moment on. It was there in the way he and Diana skirted around each other; Diana flattering him a little, he resisting . . . the deadly game of push-and-pull between two people who have a secret to keep. Niela too had a secret – her marriage and her flight from it; that was why and how she recognised it. But there was something else. Another feeling had come over her in the restaurant; the sort that took her straight back to childhood, into her grandmother's house just outside Mogadishu. She had few memories of her father's mother. She was her grandfather's second wife, who, after bearing him three children, had divorced him for reasons no one ever spoke about. She lived alone in her own house on the outskirts of the city with half a dozen servants and retainers who attended to her every whim. She was a difficult woman; Niela had grown up hearing all about Umm Hassan, as she was known to everyone, and her 'ways'. It was claimed she spoke to the dead, Niela remembered her own mother saying, touching the amulet she wore around her neck as if to protect her from the very words. Umm Hassan believed in the *djinn*, those otherworldly creatures who lived in a parallel world to their own. Niela was too young to understand the significance of the stories, and by the time she was twelve, Umm Hassan was dead. She remembered very little about her – all that remained was a faint memory of the scent of her home, that mixture of cardamom and coffee and the

perfumed incense of the rooms surrounding the courtyard, and occasionally, like now, a sudden fearful tremor would run through her that
brought Umm Hassan to mind. There was an English expression, *someone's walking over my grave* . . . it wasn't quite that – her feeling wasn't
as strong as a premonition, but rather the sense that she was in a place
or space where something that shouldn't have happened, had. In fact,
she thought to herself wonderingly, the last time she'd felt it had been
in Diana's presence, the afternoon they'd first met. She shook her head,
both puzzled and unnerved. Whatever it was she'd sensed, Diana's shadow
was upon it.

82

RUFUS
London, June 2000

He pulled up outside the white house on Northumberland Park Road
and killed the engine. The house was in darkness. He opened the car
door and got out, stretching his arms above his head. It had been a very
long journey – LA to New York on Thursday night; a day and a night in
New York and then a morning flight from JFK that put him on the
ground at Heathrow at 9 p.m. He'd toyed with the idea of the hotel room
that his PA had booked, but on the spur of the moment he'd decided
against it. It was Harvey's birthday on Saturday; it would be a nice
surprise for him. Not quite as nice for Diana, perhaps – his presence
always upset her – but Harvey was his brother, regardless of everything
else.

   He took his case out of the trunk and walked up the steps. He rang the
bell, just in case, but when there was no answer, he selected the right key
on his bunch and opened the door. He switched off the alarm and stood
for a moment in the dark hallway, his nostrils taking in the strangely
familiar scent of his brother's home. It had been a while since he'd been
there – a couple of years, at least. Not since Rafe's wedding. He put down
his bag and groped for the light. He switched it on and the hallway was
flooded with light. There was a small, neat pile of mail on the console; he
picked up a couple of letters . . . they were dated from earlier in the week.

The housekeeper must have put them there. Clearly, they were away. He made a small sound of impatience – he hadn't anticipated that. In Mougins, in all likelihood. He walked downstairs to the kitchen, pondering what to do next. As always, the fridge was full of food – wine, some good cheese, sliced meats, home-made chutney. He found an unopened packet of oatcake biscuits in the pantry and made himself a small plate. He turned on the radio – it was set to the classical music station Diana liked. He walked over to the table and pulled out a chair, Handel's *Messiah* washing over him. He ate quickly and decided against calling Mougins. He would ring Diana's office in the morning. It was Thursday – if he was lucky, his PA could get him on an afternoon flight to Cannes on Saturday morning and from there he'd pick up a rental car. It was only an hour's drive from the airport . . . with any luck, he'd make it in plenty of time for the party. He wondered if any of his nephews would be there. Rafe, Aaron, perhaps even Josh? He was married. Harvey had written to tell him. To some young Somalian or Sudanese refugee, Harvey had written to him, ages ago. He'd chuckled when he read it. A refugee. It would doubtless have irked Diana no end. She hated being upstaged.

He took his glass of wine upstairs to the sitting room and sank into the comfortably soft upholstery of one of the couches. It was wonderfully quiet after the bustle of the previous two weeks in LA. These days, he reflected, his life was mostly a succession of airports, aeroplanes and hotel rooms – not that he wished it any other way. The cosy domesticity of Harvey's life was not for him, thank you very much. He liked the fact that he had no real fixed address. Aside from the Paris flat, which he rarely went to these days, he lived out of a suitcase. His career, of course, made it all possible – he was in such demand as a conference speaker and lecturer that there was no point in even attempting to settle anywhere. In fact, the small break he'd managed to take in between conferences would be his last for a while. The following week he'd be in Beijing for a fortnight; then Saigon for a week and then Tokyo for almost a month. He loved it: the constant buzz and thrust of new-yet-familiar places; new people, new ideas, new experiences. Although, he gave a short, wry laugh, at nearly sixty, 'new' wasn't what most men his age sought. Or perhaps they did, but were too circumspect to admit it. Certainly amongst his colleagues, once they'd had a few drinks and were in cities away from home, wherever or whatever that was, there was a streak of wild abandon that never ceased to surprise him. Sometimes the most unlikely of them, too. He recalled a particularly debauched evening in Bangkok several months earlier with the two finance directors of a large multinational – he could no longer remember which one. Their appetites had amazed even him. Girls, drink, drugs . . . they'd been insatiable and unstoppable. He, Rufus, knew where to draw the line, but perhaps that was because he'd never fooled himself – marriage, kids, a house in the suburbs . . . no, that was not for him. He'd always been honest with himself and that was the difference between him and most others he knew. Granted, there were exceptions – his brother was one. But it would have killed Harvey to know that his wife wasn't. He smiled to himself. Diana. How long had it been going on? Forty years, probably more if you counted those silly childish games they played. Cowboys and Indians. Hide and seek. Doctors and nurses. Thinking about Diana could still produce an erection in him almost spontaneously. What was it about her? She was pretty, certainly . . . and as she'd grown older, and especially after marrying Harvey, her prettiness had matured into a cold, aloof beauty that he found difficult to resist. The more successful she became, the more pleasurable it was to unmask her. He'd lost count of the number of hotel rooms they'd been in where the cool, unflappable barrister had transformed herself into a wanton, screaming, panting bitch in heat. He shifted uncomfortably. Blast it. His erection was digging into his thigh. He gave a short, rueful laugh. There would certainly be no pornography in *this* house that he could use for relief. And it was too late to call any one of the girls whose numbers he'd memorised . . . or was it? He glanced at his watch. It was almost eleven. Would any of the neighbours notice? He didn't care if they told Diana, but he would hate to have to explain himself to Harvey. Fuck it, he was tired. He had a long journey ahead of him. He was nearly sixty, for crying out loud. Surely he could use the rest.

83

DIANA
Mougins, June 2000

The green silk dress fitted her perfectly, like a shimmering second skin. Diana sat in front of the mirror in her dressing room, listening to the sounds of preparation downstairs, her stomach tightening pleasurably at the thought of the decor, the food, the wine, and the family she'd managed to bring together. She'd asked one of the girls from La Mas Candille, the wonderful hotel up the hill, to help Mme Poulenc with the dishes and with serving the food. The garden had been strung with tiny paper lanterns; there were giant citronella candles in bamboo spikes to keep the insects at bay. The glass hurricane lanterns that she and Harvey had bought in a little shop in Antibes and transported in four separate trips were all lit, casting beautiful dancing patterns across the patio. The living room had been turned into a dining room with two long tables, elegantly dressed in linen; wine in heavy crystal decanters on the sideboard; champagne in the fridge; roses from the garden in every room and those wonderfully pungent giant white lilies that Harvey liked in the hallway, gently releasing their fragrance into the house. Yes, everything was well under control; it would be beautiful and lovely in the way only she knew how to ensure. It was Harvey's sixtieth – it ought to be special. She was suddenly overcome with a wave of tenderness for her husband. She'd never known anyone with greater integrity and compassion. Oh, that wasn't to say he was a saint – far from it at times. He could be moody and grumpy and impatient, just as she could. He didn't suffer fools lightly. There was a growing list of junior doctors and nurses who could attest to that! But he possessed some other, keener sense of justice that awed and humbled her. She could only shake her head at it. He had an inner moral compass like no one she'd ever come across. Ironic, really. She, the barrister, the guardian of the law . . . she was rotten to the core. She looked down at her shaking hands. She didn't know what it was this time that was causing so much introspection and anguish. Perhaps it was the fact of the birthday? Or the fact that they were all here together in a way they hadn't been for more years than she could remember? Or the fact of that blasted interfering old cow, Leonora Simmonds, who'd suddenly appeared out of the blue and set all sorts of questions in motion. Damn it, she mouthed at herself in the mirror. She had half an hour to get ready – the last thing she needed was a moment of weak, self-pitying self-analysis. She picked up her blusher brush and began to apply powder in strong, regular strokes.

In the room above Diana, Niela was also getting ready. She stood up and walked over to the wardrobe; inside was a full-length mirror. She looked at her reflection. The long white evening dress she and Anna had seen in the window of Next on Oxford Street had been a good buy. She'd

348

thought it a little plain but Anna, as always, was full of practical advice. 'You'll never have as much money to spend as the rest of them,' she'd advised. 'So keep it simple.' She was still looking at herself when the bathroom door opened and Josh walked into the room. He'd just come out of the shower; he wore a towel wrapped around his waist and was still dripping water over the floor. Niela looked at him in the mirror. She could never quite get used to the sight of his naked body, despite its growing familiarity. *She* would certainly never walk around in front of him like that, she thought to herself, trying not to stare. Josh, of course, was oblivious. He was as comfortable in his nudity as he was fully dressed. 'Boarding school,' he'd once told her, smiling. 'You get used to it.' Well, she never would.

He came up behind her, his body still damp from the shower. She felt her own body begin to flush with that peculiar mixture of desire and embarrassment that looking at Josh always produced. He smiled at her, resting his hands lightly on her shoulders. 'You'd better get dressed,' she said, wriggling out of his damp embrace. 'We're supposed to be downstairs in ten minutes.'

He rolled his eyes. 'Pity. You know, I was sort of hoping . . .' He reached for her suddenly and pulled her towards him.

'Josh! No . . . I'll wrinkle my dress,' Niela half-squealed. 'And you're still wet. No . . . look out! You're dripping all over me!'

'Take it off,' he murmured against her ear. 'Or it really will get wrinkled.'

'Josh . . . no . . . don't . . .'

But it was pointless and too late. She stood still whilst he unzipped the dress and let it fall to the ground. He picked it up, one hand still on her waist, and with the other tossed it on the bed, straightening it out quickly before turning back to her. 'Is the door locked?' she whispered as his lips made a snail's trail of light kisses across her neck and shoulder blades. He shook his head but didn't break his stride or his concentration. 'Should I lock it?' He shook his head again.

'No one's going to come in,' he murmured. 'Stop worrying. We've got ten minutes. I'll be quick. And I know you will be.' Niela suppressed a smile. It was something of a joke between them. He only had to touch her and she was ready, and the ease with which he coaxed pleasure out of her was astonishing to them both. She turned until she was fully in his arms. It took him less than a second to expertly dispose of her bra and for her to step out of her panties . . . he pushed her back gently until she was lying on the bed. Her whole body was flushed with desire. He laced the fingers of one hand through hers, pinning her arm above her head. He let his other hand trail down the trembling line of her stomach, touching her lightly, stroking the soft wetness between her legs. He lay beside her for a moment, then turned her body towards him until she was lying on top of him. He knew it embarrassed her to be on top, but he seemed to delight in her shyness. She shook her head in half-hearted protest but he was insistent. She slid on top of him easily; he closed his eyes and the sight of his face almost brought her to the edge of her own pleasure. He thrust into her slowly, his fingers never letting go. She let her body lean towards him, her nipples barely grazing his stomach, and was rewarded by a groan. 'Niela . . .' His voice hung in the air as his breathing grew deeper and stronger. He thrust again, once, twice . . . She felt a cool rush of air against her back as he exploded inside her, but her eyes were closed, and when she opened them again, the coolness had disappeared.

Julia shut the door as quietly as she could with her eyes tightly closed. Her heart was thumping. She backed away from it, almost too afraid to turn around in case someone had seen her. She could hear footsteps coming up the first flight of stairs; she remained where she was, frozen with embarrassment and fear, until they'd died away. She wanted to run from what she'd just seen. She'd come up to Niela's room just to see if she was ready, or if there was anything she needed . . . no, that wasn't quite true. She'd come to see what Niela was wearing and to check her own outfit against hers. Aaron had gone downstairs to help Diana, so she'd nipped upstairs in her bare feet, hoping for a quick look at Niela's dress. She'd opened the door and it took her a second to work out what she was looking at. Josh. His face looking directly at her over Niela's unseeing form. She'd taken in the smooth, dark brown line of Niela's back, her perfectly rounded buttocks and thighs, and realised – too late – that she'd walked in on them having sex. She'd backed out so quickly and quietly that Josh didn't even have time to register that it was her, or so she hoped. But the sight of his beautiful face contorted in its own secret lust was enough to send a corresponding red-hot flash of desire through her that almost completely hollowed her out. That was why she'd backed away so quickly. *That* was why her heart was racing and her palms were clammy. Josh . . . She gave a small groan of despair and fled as quietly as she could back down the stairs. To her horror, Aaron was coming up the first flight directly towards her.

'What's wrong?' he asked as he gained the landing. 'What's the matter?'

'N-nothing . . . I . . . I just needed a . . . a safety pin,' she lied. 'I just went to see if . . . if Niela had one, that's all.'

'Oh. You look awfully hot,' Aaron said, looking at her with a puzzled expression. 'Have you been running or something? Your face is bright red.'

'Must be the shower . . . it was boiling.' Julia hated herself for lying, but what could she say? 'I'll be back in a minute.' And before Aaron could ask anything further, she ran past him and into the bathroom as fast as her dress would allow.

Diana was on her way to the kitchen to make sure Eloise was ready with the silver trays of canapés when she heard Harvey's great shout of surprise. 'Rufus!' She almost dropped the two bottles of wine she was carrying. She caught herself just in time, dumped them on the sideboard and practically ran to the front door. No – it couldn't be! Rufus? What the *hell* was he doing here? She saw him walking towards the house holding a small overnight bag in one hand and a bottle of champagne in the other. Harvey was standing in the doorway, his arms outstretched in welcome. She watched in horror as the brothers embraced. She wanted to turn and flee, but Rufus had already caught sight of her.

'Diana.' He turned from Harvey and opened his arms to her. 'Why didn't you tell me you were coming here for his birthday? I had to track you down!'

She struggled to keep her voice even. 'Rufus,' she murmured, hating the sweep of familiar desire and anger that his presence always provoked. 'We didn't know where you were.'

'I can't believe you're here!' Harvey's pleasure was genuine. 'How bloody fantastic!'

'Wouldn't have missed it for anything,' Rufus said smoothly, releasing her. 'Didn't have time to get you a present, I'm afraid, old boy.'

'Oh, don't be ridiculous. Just the fact that you're here is marvellous. Come in, come in . . . the boys'll be thrilled to see you. They're all here.'

'Even Josh?'

'Yes, even Josh, can you believe it? I can't remember the last time they were all here together. And only one little disagreement so far!'

'So far,' Rufus echoed, smiling. 'There's always tonight.'

'God, I hope not.' Harvey smiled back. 'Come on, let's get you a drink.

I'll take your bag upstairs . . . the small bedroom at the end's still free, I think.'

The two brothers walked in ahead of her, arms still on each other's shoulders. Diana followed them into the hallway, her mind racing. She felt physically ill. How was she going to get through an entire evening with Harvey on one side and Rufus on the other? She burst into the kitchen and barked out a string of orders – another place setting at the table; fresh sheets and towels to be taken upstairs to the remaining spare bedroom. Damn him, damn him, damn him.

84

To Niela, the whole evening had an air of unreality about it. In the soft, balmy candlelight, they all looked like actors on the set of a spectacularly beautiful film. Rufus's arrival had set Diana on edge, and no wonder. It was hard to tell whether the incident Josh had witnessed all those years ago had happened only once, or if it was part of a longer-term affair. Whatever it was, or had been, it was clear that Rufus still held some sort of power over her. Niela found herself studying him intently, watching for signs that might give her a clue. There was none; he gave absolutely nothing away. On the other side of the nervous Diana, Harvey was his usual charming self. It was hard not to like Harvey. He was that unusual blend of brilliance and kindness – his humour had none of the calculated edge of Diana's, nor the sullenness of Josh and Aaron either. Did he know what had taken place between his wife and his brother all those years ago? No. It wasn't possible. He couldn't have sat between the two people who should have been his closest allies and contemplate the fact that he'd been betrayed at least once, if not repeatedly. No one could have that depth of understanding or forgiveness, not even Harvey. As Niela watched them, she was slowly aware of a lump rising in her throat. She was used to the unexpected ways in which the things she had to hide sometimes came to the surface of her thoughts without warning, but this was different. She lifted her glass and tried to swallow the threat of tears. It was thinking about forgiveness that had done it. The idea that Harvey might possibly be the person to whom one could confess something was suddenly overwhelming. It had been so long since she'd had the need to speak . . . to say out loud what she normally kept hidden and buried . . . why *now*, of all times and of all places? But she knew why. She was sitting halfway down the table in the bosom of her adopted family, listening to them talk, swap stories, watching them play to the audience of invited guests . . . doing just what families everywhere did, every day. The family gatherings in Mogadishu were of a different order – the parents rarely spoke to the children, or vice versa, and there was none of the gentle ribbing in front of guests that everyone seemed to enjoy. There was no alcohol at the table and her mother would never have dared sit in between her father and Uncle Raageh, but the sense of belonging somewhere, to people whose blood and history she shared, had been missing from her life for a long time. She'd shut out so completely the pain and loss she felt when she ran away from them all that she'd thought there was nothing to go back to. Now, sitting there in the midst of this family, sensing the poison that had slowly seeped its way through that very same love, she found herself mourning what she'd lost, and afraid of what they all might one day lose if any of it came to light.

Next to her, Josh was quiet. His position in the family was precarious – she could see that; she could also see that he knew it, and for all his sullen anger, was hurt by it. Whenever a joke or an anecdote was directed at him, she could see in him a spirit of generosity that broke something in him that he knew needed to be broken . . . but as soon as he began to reach out, he backed off. It moved Niela greatly, and over and over again, it broke her heart.

Maddy had drunk too much; she could feel it in the way her words kept sliding around in her mouth as though she couldn't quite handle them. She could feel it too in the way her gaze was drawn to Niela and Josh, who were sitting opposite her. She slid a hand underneath the table and placed it provocatively on Rafe's thigh, but he moved away in irritation. He was in the middle of telling a long, complicated story about an operation and she could sense he was trying to impress Harvey – the last thing he wanted was the distraction of her fingertips caressing him through the wool of his trousers. She moved her hand away, rebuked. She took another sip of wine. Dangerous. Wine made her bold; it loosened her tongue and heightened her emotions. In this state, who knew what might pop into her head and then come straight out of her mouth? She tried to con- centrate on Rafe's story. 'When we saw the blood, we thought we were bloody done for . . . it wasn't quite tight enough . . . you know how it is, Dad, when you've opened up the arterials . . . you just can't tell, can you? Luckily for us, Martins had given her a triple dose of nembuthal . . .' *Stop trying to please your father*, Maddy wanted to whisper to him. *Stop trying to impress him. Just be yourself.* She caught Niela's eye on hers and quickly looked away. Was her impatience written all over her face? She took another sip, and then another. She was drinking too fast but she couldn't stop. There was someone else watching her – it was Rufus, Rafe's uncle. He was staring at her. He was very quick; she could see from the way he was studying her that he'd caught the look in her eyes. He was sitting next to Harvey; there was a disturbing quality of sameness about them both, although Rufus was dark where Harvey was fair. It was like looking into a mirror where the reflection was just slightly out of focus – the features were the same but the cast was different. She shifted uncomfortably in her seat. There was something very slightly off-kilter about the whole evening. It was a birthday party, a celebration . . . and yet it was not. It had a tenor and climate all of its own. She felt a light goosepimpling all over her skin. She shivered, though it wasn't cold.

Sitting three spaces down from Maddy and sandwiched between Aaron and Harvey, Julia was also struggling to keep hold of her thoughts. She too had had too much to drink, but where Maddy's attention seemed fixed on the company around her, Julia's was anywhere but. She kept returning to Africa, not just to her chance meeting with Josh in Johannesburg, but to the trip as a whole and the chain of emotions it had set off in her. She was restless; without ever having put it into words, she'd been steadily growing away from the path that Bernard, Bennison & Partners had set her upon. The fact that Aaron seemed so content to follow it had become a greater source of irritation than she could ever dare admit. The trip had changed her utterly; it had moved her to what could become the centre of her own life – everything that had previously lain dormant had suddenly come to attention. She felt as though she'd stepped into something she'd always intended to do, and the fact that Aaron seemed unable to understand what had happened to her was putting a strain on what had once been easy between them. In a strange and not so pleasant way, Aaron was slowing coming full circle. When she met him at Bernard, Bennison & Partners, he seemed to have abandoned the arrogance that had characterised him at Balliol and allowed her to see something else inside him . . . *that* was what she'd fallen in love with. The night after she'd lost her first case, it was the note of uncertainty in his voice that had made her see him differently. She could still remember every detail – the way he'd leaned against the door jamb, his shirt sleeves rolled up, the desire that had swept over her to be held by him . . . all of that. But as time went on and he grew more confident in the role that everyone else seemed to have mapped out for him, the Aaron she'd fallen in love with slowly began to fade. Now he was returning to who he'd always been all along. Conventional to the core. And in that, they were diametrically opposed. For Julia, especially after what she'd just experienced in Maputo, the law wasn't simply a means to a particular kind of lifestyle; it was as much a moral as a material means, and to her distress, it was becoming increasingly clear that in this, as in so many other things, she and Aaron were worlds apart. To compare him to Josh was an unfair comparison – chalk and cheese, those two, as her father would have said. In some ways, not dissimilar to Harvey and his brother, Rufus, she suddenly thought. She stole a quick glance down the table. They were talking to one another, their heads bent close. Rufus's darker head, with its smattering of grey hair, and Harvey's, so fair that he appeared silver – and next to them, sitting with all the upright tension of someone on a bed of nails, was Diana. Her eyes darted this way and that, never still. She seemed to be measuring the evening according to some criteria other than her own enjoyment. Something else was being said underneath the laugher and the anecdotes and the good wine and food, but Julia was damned if she could work out what.

85

The house was deathly quiet. After the din of the evening's celebrations, the silence that had descended like a blanket once everyone had gone to bed was unnerving. Diana lay stiffly awake beside Harvey, unable to sleep. She'd hardly touched a drop of alcohol all evening, unlike everyone else. She'd been too nervous. The evening had dragged on and on; all she could remember was the longing for it to be over, for Rufus to leave, for things to return to normal. She gave a small, stifled groan. Normal? There was nothing normal about her situation; nothing normal about anything any more. Next to her, Harvey snored softly. For him, at least, the evening had been a great success. If he'd noticed the fact that she was quieter than usual, he'd made no comment. Every now and then, during the course of the dinner party, he'd touched her lightly on the shoulder or her arm – small, thoughtful gestures that kept him in touch with her, as he liked to say. Harvey was good at that sort of thing. Rufus was not. For almost fifty years she'd pondered the question – why?

She turned carefully on to her side, not wanting to disturb Harvey. She tried to relax, to breathe deeply and evenly in the hope of drifting off to sleep, but it was no use. The sleep she so desperately craved simply wouldn't come. She turned back the covers and slid quietly from the bed. The floorboards made a single squeaking sound as she walked across the room in her bare feet, but Harvey didn't wake. She pulled her silk dressing gown from its hook and opened the door carefully. All down the corridor, doors were closed; behind them, her entire family was asleep. She walked downstairs, wrapping her dressing gown around her more tightly. She went into the kitchen; all was quiet except for the refrigerator humming reassuringly in the corner. She walked over to the sink and opened the window; the sweet night air rushed in, bathing her in its familiar fragrance, a combination of pine and lavender, the smell of Mougins. She looked out over the driveway, now bathed in silvery moonlight. Everything was still and perfectly calm. She turned on the tap and slowly poured herself a glass of water. She drank it standing, her gaze resting on the spot where she'd stood thirty years ago, waiting. There was a creak behind her; the kitchen door opened and closed again with a soft thud. She could just make out footsteps coming up behind her. She knew without turning round just who it would be.

'Do you ever think about it, Rufus?' she asked in a low voice, holding the cold glass of water to her burning face. 'Do you?'

'No.' He caught hold of her shoulder and turned her round to face him. 'No, I don't.'

'Never? Not even—' She stopped, unable to complete the sentence. In the dark, she couldn't make out his features; was he frowning?

'Your son is asleep upstairs with his wife. That's all you need to know.'

'But Rufus—'

'Stop it, Diana. There's no point. It's over and done with. The whole thing's buried—'

'Buried?' Diana gave a short laugh. 'Yes, you could say that. In fact—'

'Stop it.' His grip on her shoulders tightened. 'This isn't like you, Diana. What's the matter?'

There was silence for a few seconds as she struggled to bring her voice under control. 'I don't know,' she whispered finally. 'I can't seem to stop thinking about it. About him.'

'Don't. Josh is safe. He's alive. That's all there is to it.'

'But—'

'Stop it.' His hand slid from her shoulder down the small of her back. He pressed her close to him.

'No,' she whispered, 'not here. Please.' He held her loosely for a second, his hand sliding further down to hold her buttocks. She felt the surge of customary desire and it took all her strength to push him away. 'No,' she repeated, hoping her voice was steady.

He sighed and held his hands up in mock defeat. 'OK. I'll be gone first thing in the morning, Diana.' His tone held a touch of mock regret. 'You win.' He touched her very lightly on the chin and moved off into the darkness. She heard the kitchen door shut quietly behind him. She could breathe again. She turned back to the window, staring out into the night. This time there was no stopping the memories as they flooded out, one after the other, a waterfall of pain.

DIANA
London/Mougins, June 1969

She woke up feeling as though she'd only just shut her eyes. She struggled upright in the narrow hospital bed and looked around, as if forgetting for a second why she was there. The room was empty. Harvey couldn't stay, he'd told her so the night before – he had a long list scheduled for that morning but he'd promised to pop in whenever he could. In the small cot next to the bed lay her newborn son, her third. Josh. Joshua Alexander Keeler. She shifted uncomfortably in the bed and leaned over to look at him again. He was sleeping. His tiny, delicately painted features were relaxed; she felt the same surge of emotion that she'd had after the births of both her older children. So perfectly made, so perfectly formed. She couldn't stop staring at him. The other two had both come out resolutely blonde, like Harvey. Josh was barely a few days old, but already his hair was darker, and darkening by the day. She resisted the temptation to insert a finger in one of his tiny little hands; she didn't want to wake him. He was a screamer, it seemed. 'Right pair of lungs on him,' one of the nurses had commented the night before. 'Once he gets started . . .' She'd smiled good-naturedly at Diana, who was too exhausted to reply.

She swung her legs out of bed and carefully stood up. Her lower body was still heavy from the epidural; it would take her a while to get back on her feet. She was still shocked by how difficult the birth had been. The first two had been easy by comparison. With Rafe she'd been in labour for only a few hours before he made his rushed appearance into the world; he'd almost been born in the back of the car on the way over. Aaron too . . . an easy delivery . . . she'd gone home the very same morning. But Josh was different. Almost twenty-four hours' worth of contractions followed by another four of pushing against the most excruciating pain she'd ever known . . . until she thought she couldn't possibly stand another second . . . and then he'd arrived, kicking and scream-ing, and he hadn't stopped since. She'd stared at him, too drained to even see properly but she'd known, right there and then, that this one would be special.

She'd had to have an episiotomy and several tiny stitches; it took a few days for it all to heal, and although Harvey brought the boys in every day to see their new brother, it felt strange returning to the house after almost a week. For some reason, she couldn't settle into the routine she'd so carefully built up with Rafe and Aaron. Josh's cries kept the rest of the house awake, day and night. As soon as she put him down, he would begin again. Nothing seemed to placate him. Rafe and Aaron were resentful; who wouldn't be? Rafe was five and Aaron was a year younger – for four years they'd shared Diana equally. They were as close as it was possible for two boys to be, everyone remarked fondly. They gave her no trouble at all. Rafe was fiercely protective of Aaron and Aaron absolutely worshipped his older brother. The arrival of a screaming new baby in the house turned everything upside down. 'Why's he always crying?' Rafe asked Diana, only a hundred times a day. Diana was tired and irritable – she ought to have been more patient with him, with them all . . . but she wasn't. She couldn't be. Harvey did his best, of course, but he was a junior surgeon in one of London's busiest hospitals . . . he couldn't afford to be kept up, night after night.

It was his suggestion. She'd moved with Josh to the attic at first, hoping to give everyone else a break from the noise. But it seemed to make little difference. Josh's screams penetrated the walls; on the third morning Harvey had come down to breakfast with bloodshot eyes and a temper to match. 'Why don't you take him down to Mougins for a couple of weeks?' he'd asked, lifting his

358

shoulders helplessly. 'Maybe a bit of time alone together? Mrs Pitcher and I can manage the boys. I'm not sure I can go on like this, Diana.'

Diana looked at him, her brows knitted together in worry, and nodded. She wouldn't dare admit it, but the thought of spending some time alone with Josh thrilled her. She hesitated, for fear of appearing too eager. 'No, I couldn't do that,' she said slowly, the idea beginning to take root.

'Why not? Rufus is down there already. It's summer, the weather'll be lovely and hot. He'll meet you at the airport, give you a hand for a couple of days. Actually, darling, I must confess, it was his suggestion. He's in between assignments at the moment, said it would be no trouble at all.'

Diana felt the flush start in the pit of her stomach and travel slowly up her body. At the same time, two floors above them, Josh began to wail again. In seconds, his screams had intensified.

'That settles it,' Harvey said, rolling his eyes. 'You're going down, even if I have to take you there myself.'

'No, no . . . it's fine. You're right. I'll take Josh. Just for a couple of weeks.'

'Just for a couple of weeks,' Harvey repeated, already looking relieved. 'I'll phone Rufus in the morning. He'll be pleased. He's been on his own with only Mohammed and Khadija for company for almost a fortnight.'

Diana said nothing. She nodded slowly and then turned and hurried back upstairs. Relief, guilt, joy, fear . . . the familiar treadmill of her emotions began again.

The BOAC flight to Nice was a nightmare. Josh screamed practically the entire way. She disembarked into the brilliant blue late afternoon sunshine almost weeping with relief. Rufus was there to meet them; she saw his dark head rising head and shoulders above the waiting crowds of mothers, fathers, lovers and grandparents who were there to welcome their loved ones. 'Rufus,' she murmured weakly, allowing herself to be folded into his embrace. Miraculously, Josh was silent.

'So this is the little tyke who's been causing all the problems,' was Rufus's only comment as he led them away from the arrivals hall towards the car park. Children were not his strong suit, as he liked to put it. She stowed the sleeping Josh in the back seat, praying that he wouldn't wake up. They drove out of the airport and joined the traffic on the E80 heading west towards Cannes. She was too tired to talk; she tucked her feet underneath her and gave herself up to watching the hot summer landscape slide silently by.

It was just past six in the evening when Rufus turned the car down the *track towards the farmhouse. She woke with a start; she'd dozed off somewhere along the journey and her face was stiff with fatigue.*

'I'll get it.' Rufus pulled the handbrake up and opened the door. He unlatched the gate and got back in. 'Mohammed's gone home for the afternoon. Khadija's just had a baby. Boy, like Josh.'

'Khadija? Little Khadija?' Diana was momentarily shocked into wakefulness. Khadija was Mohammed's only daughter. His wife, Doha, had died when Khadija was very young. She was the absolute centre of his universe. 'How old is she?'

Rufus shrugged. 'Sixteen, seventeen . . . something like that.'

'She can't be, Rufus. She's only just started high school. She can't be more than fifteen.'

Rufus shrugged again. He brought the car to a halt in front of the farmhouse and Diana fell silent. The sight of it never failed to soothe her. She got out of the car and stood for a second in the driveway, her eyes roaming over the yellowed brickwork, the stain of ivy spreading itself up the wall, the roses still in bloom, despite the lateness of the year . . . it was beautiful still. She turned and opened the back door, taking care not to wake Josh. She carried him into the house; there was the warm, yeasty smell of freshly baked bread and coffee, two scents she would always associate with Mougins. 'I'll just pop him in the living room,' she mouthed to Rufus, who was carrying her bags. 'He'll wake up soon, I should imagine. He'll be hungry.' Rufus didn't reply. He took their bags upstairs, the floorboards creaking overhead as he walked.

She was feeding Josh when he came back downstairs half an hour later. She was sitting in the easy chair over by the window. The evening sunlight was streaming in through the French doors; in the misty light created by the shaft, tiny dust particles were suspended, floating dreamily around them. Josh was quiet; he'd fallen off the breast and was snoring gently. For the first time in the ten days since the birth, he seemed peaceful, almost content. She was tired but it was a different kind of tiredness this time. She watched the light dappling and brimming against the walls and ceiling, not even bothering to cover herself up again, enjoying the feeling of air and sunlight on her bare skin. The summer sun could be fierce and relentless in Mougins, but here in the valley, halfway down the hill, it was always cool inside the house. She turned to Rufus as he walked in and put a finger to her lips. 'He likes it here,' she whispered.

Rufus looked at her but said nothing. There was a bottle of wine standing on the sideboard. He poured two glasses; a small one for Diana and a more generous one for himself. He walked over and handed it to her, brushing aside her protests. 'It's good for them,' he said brusquely. 'Isn't that what they say?'

Diana laid the sleeping Josh down in the wicker bassinet, tucking the blanket carefully under his chin. He slept on, undisturbed. She was about to rearrange her clothing when Rufus's hand stopped hers. He reached for her nipple, still wet and engorged, rubbing it lightly between his fingers. Diana nearly spilled her wine. The electric shock of desire was so strong she had to close her eyes. It had always been that way – the merest touch of his hand on her skin and her head would begin to swim. She shook her head in protest. 'I can't, Rufus . . . not now. Not yet.'

'Shhh.' He set his own glass on the floor and knelt down in front of her. He pushed aside her blouse and unfastened the ungainly brassiere. Her breasts, almost twice their usual size, spilled forward. He took first one nipple in his mouth, then the other, his tongue sliding expertly around the nubs of hardened flesh. She had to clench her fists to stop herself from crying out loud. Her newborn son slept beside them whilst her husband's brother skilfully drew the silken, guilty threads of pleasure from her, one after the other, as only he could.

Over the next couple of days, an easy rhythm developed between the three of them. Rufus always slept late; Diana rose early and took Josh down to the pool every morning to sit on the sun-warmed flagstones, watching the light dance across the surface of the water, listening to the sounds of the garden and the valley beyond. She was right; the very air seemed to calm Josh down. It was wonderfully warm and sunny in the mornings. At lunchtime, she would pick up the bassinet and walk back up the path to the farmhouse to prepare lunch. Occasionally she would stroll with Josh up to the village to the open-air market, wandering slowly amongst the stalls, taking in the weak, sweet perfume of flowers and fruits, the sharp odour of cheeses and the smell of still slippery fish. She showed off Josh to the market women; they pulled back the white shawl protecting his face from the sun and made the appropriate coos and sounds of delight. She sometimes sat with him at the tiny espresso bar just by the place, eating a piece of spinach tart or a slice of tarte aux pommes.

One morning, about three days after their arrival, she was lying on the sunlounger by the pool, soaking up the sun. She turned her head lazily to look at Josh lying next to her in his little bassinet. He was looking up at her with an expression of such intense concentration that she had to laugh out loud. 'Ça va?' she cooed at him in French. 'Ça va?' She bent down and slipped her

*forefinger into his palm; he clutched it tightly. A thought moved across his face
– he was still too young to smile, but he looked so contented just lying there in
the sun that she couldn't stop smiling herself. She let the book she was holding
in one hand drop to the ground. With Josh still holding tightly on to the other,
she turned her face towards the sun. She was suddenly drowsy; within
minutes, she slipped into sleep.*

*A sudden shift in temperature woke her. A passing cloud had obscured
the sun and sent a momentary chill across her skin. She sat up with a start.
Someone had come down the garden path with a wheelbarrow of tools. It was
Mohammed. 'Oh, it's you, Mohammed,' she called out, shading her eyes. 'Ça
va? Tout va bien?' There was someone with him, half hidden by the
wheelbarrow. It was his daughter. 'Khadija? C'est toi?' Diana smiled at her.*

*'Oui, madame.' Khadija smiled back shyly. She was holding something – a
bundle wrapped in white. Her baby! Of course . . . Rufus had mentioned it
the day they'd arrived.*

*'Ah, c'est ton bébé, Khadija. Félicitations!' Was it the right thing to say?
She didn't know. Khadija was barely out of her teens. She stood up, holding
out her arms to take the little bundle from her. Beside her, Mohammed looked
on. It was hard to tell from the expression on his face what he thought of it all.
Should she ask after the father? Khadija gingerly passed the baby to her,
reluctant to let go of him, even for a second. Diana peeled back the shawl and
took a peep at the sleeping infant. There was a sudden shock of recognition – a
physical shudder that ran through her as she registered the baby's features. He
was the spitting image of Rufus, of Harvey . . . and even more bizarrely, of
Josh. She looked up; the knowledge of what she'd recognised was there in
Khadija's face. And in Mohammed's. She looked from one to the other. There
was a moment of stunned silence as they all took in what could not be said.*

*'How could you?' Diana's voice was a muffled shriek. 'She's a child, Rufus! A
fucking child!'*

'Don't be ridiculous! She's no more a child than you are.'

'Have you lost your mind?'

'Will you just shut up?'

*They stood there in the bedroom, glaring at one another, Rufus's face dark
with anger. Diana couldn't stop shaking. It wasn't the fact that Rufus had
slept with someone else – Jesus Christ . . . if that were the issue, she'd never
have a moment's peace of mind. No, it was the fact that he'd done it with
Mohammed's daughter, Khadija. She was the apple of his eye, the daughter
he'd been so proud of. She was a good student; she'd had dreams of going to*

university . . . What the hell had Rufus gone and done? 'She's a child,' Diana repeated, her breaths turning to sobs. 'Now you've gone and got her pregnant . . . what the hell is she supposed to do?'

'Oh, for fuck's sake . . . you and your bloody moralising! She wanted it as much as I did, you stupid cow! Why do you women always make such a bloody fuss?'

'We women?' Diana was speechless. 'Who the hell are you talking about?'

'You, her mother . . . Listen, she wanted the fucking child, not me!'

'Of course she wanted it! They're from a different culture, Rufus! She had no choice, can't you see that?'

Rufus slowly clenched and unclenched his fists. He was climbing into his anger. 'Look, I'm not discussing this any further. It's pointless. She's had the child, it's over . . . that's all there is to it.'

'And are you going to support it? Your child, I mean?'

'Of course I am. Christ, what sort of a person d'you think I am?'

Diana was suddenly silent. She couldn't bring herself to answer. She knew exactly what sort of person he was – she knew it because she was the same. She lifted her hand wearily. 'It doesn't matter,' she said finally. 'What matters is that you've ruined that girl's life whether you pay for the child or not.' Rufus glowered at her. There was a tense, angry silence as they faced one another, and then he turned on his heel and walked out of the room, slamming the door behind him.

Josh gave a small cry; he'd been lying quietly, listening to the argument going on around him without a sound. Now that there was silence, he threatened to fill it. Diana hurried over and picked him up, holding him to her. She still couldn't get over the sight of Khadija's baby – she didn't even know its name – lying there in her arms, the spitting image of Josh. A bit darker, perhaps . . . that was Khadija's North African blood . . . but the features were essentially the same. The Keeler genes. Even though Josh was dark-haired, like she was, he took after Harvey, not her. She looked at Josh's tiny face; the delicately scrolled nostrils and mouth and the fine, downy dark-brown hair that had already grown since the birth. He was an extraordinarily beautiful child, she thought to herself proudly. Both Rafe and Aaron had been so fair at birth that their features were vague, almost smudged. There was nothing vague about Josh. Everything about him was clear and precise. She looked into his eyes; they were dark, aubergine-coloured, with a film that reflected the light the way oil sometimes reflects the rainbow. What did he see? she wondered, as the expression on his face changed again. She put out a hand and touched him lightly on the cheek. He turned his head towards her, seeing her outline. His face broke into a tentative smile, so fleeting that she thought she might have imagined it. She felt her heart lift ridiculously. Impossible; he was a fortnight old. It had taken both his brothers twice that time! She pressed him to her, suddenly, thinking of all she had and could offer him. The best schools, the best homes, holidays all over the world, his older brothers to look after him . . . Poor Khadija. Poor Mohammed. Most of all, she thought, as she unbuttoned her blouse to feed Josh, that poor child. Would he ever know who his father was? She doubted it. She'd known Rufus all her life – even she couldn't tell who he really was.

It took Rufus the better part of the day to return. He strode in at dinner, a bottle of wine in one hand and a joint in the other. He'd been smoking; his eyes were slightly reddened. 'Want a drag?' He offered it to Diana.

'Don't be ridiculous,' she said, annoyed. 'I'm breast-feeding, remember?'

He shrugged. 'Suit yourself.'

'Have you eaten?' she asked, more out of habit than anything else.

He shook his head. 'I'm not hungry.'

Diana bit her lip. He was sulking. She knew how the rest of the evening would unfold. He would continue to sulk; she would begin to cajole him. Eventually, with enough persuasion on her part, his mood would lift, they would drink a glass of wine . . . and then he would lead her upstairs and into the large, soft bed that she and Harvey shared when they were on holiday together. She couldn't make love properly – it was too soon for that – but it didn't seem to bother Rufus in the slightest. He took and gave his pleasure in other ways, ways that he still delighted in showing her. Just thinking about it now brought on a flush of excitement that she hated herself for but couldn't control.

'Have some anyway,' she said, spooning a generous helping of the stew she'd cooked that afternoon on to a plate. He looked at it for a mutinous second, then pulled it towards him. She breathed a sigh of relief. Once he'd started to sulk, there would be no stopping him. He could be unbearable. She passed him the salt and pepper and he began to eat. By the time he'd finished, the tension had almost completely gone. They drank together in more or less companionable silence in the kitchen, the only sound the radio playing quietly in the background. Josh slept deeply, induced no doubt by the single glass of wine she'd had and the spirit of calm that had descended on the farmhouse once again.

She'd just finished tucking the white blanket tenderly around Josh when Rufus came into the room. He was smoking another joint. She could smell its

364

pungent, acrid scent. 'Oh, Rufus.' She frowned and shook her head at him. 'Not in here. Not in front of the baby.'

'Christ, Diana. Relax, will you? He's fast asleep — can't smell a thing. What's the matter with you? You're no bloody fun any more.'

'I just don't think it's good for him,' Diana began hesitantly. She looked at Josh; Rufus was right. He was fast asleep.

'He'll sleep through the night. You had enough wine at dinner — it's knocked him out. Go on, have a puff. You need to chill out. I hate seeing you like this. It's not like you.'

'Oh, Rufus . . .' Diana murmured weakly. He was smiling at her. That dangerous, complicit smile.

'Go on. Be a good girl. Actually, on second thoughts . . . don't. You know I don't like good girls.' Rufus's smile deepened as she took a drag. 'That's it. And another one. I want you to properly relax.' He reached out a hand and caught hold of her arm, pulling her close to him. They kissed; his tongue was a warm, wet intrusion in her mouth. She put her arms around his neck, nuzzling her face into his shoulder. Rufus's arm tightened around her waist and his hands slid up the still soft length of her stomach to touch her heavy breasts. He pushed her down until they were both lying on the bed. Diana pulled him towards her, away from Josh. She took another drag, and then another, under Rufus's approving eye. He began to kiss her, his hands working their magic on those parts of her he knew to be especially sensitive — the hollow at the base of her neck; the soft, delicate skin under her breasts, now heavy with milk; the length of her forearm, turned inwards. She was shivering with a combination of cold and desire. Her pulse quickened and her breathing changed; her senses began to swim as he traced a snake-like pattern over her skin, down her stomach, between her legs, taking care to touch her so gently she thought she might have imagined it. He grabbed hold of her hand and placed it firmly on his cock, sliding it up and down until he came in great shuddering spurts, his semen leaking all over her hand. In seconds he was hard again. It was something she'd never got used to — Rufus was truly insatiable. He rolled her over on to her back, pinning her arms above her head with one hand. He took a deep drag on the joint with the other, then passed it to her, inserting it between her lips. She was swimming now, her senses folding in on themselves in a combination of pot and desire. She couldn't focus properly; whatever it was Rufus was smoking, it was strong. Her tongue felt thick and heavy in her mouth, as if she couldn't speak. She felt his knees part her own, felt him push his way inside her, impatient and rough. She could feel herself responding, but it was as if she wasn't really there. His thrusts were deep and strong; she was pushed this way and that, her hands clawing wildly at his back. A thick, dark fog descended on her, blunting her senses, making her limbs heavy with sleep. She caught a glimpse of his face; his teeth were bared. She couldn't say why, but it frightened her. She reached out to gently touch the sleeping bundle on the other side of her. Josh. He'd slept all the way through it, thank God. It was her last conscious thought before sliding into sleep.

It seemed to her afterwards that she knew what had happened even before she'd opened her eyes. She put out a hand and touched something. Not someone. Not a warm, sleepy baby, but something cold and hard. She began to tremble. A wave of fear ran straight through her. She sat upright and tried to lift him, but he was heavy, much heavier than usual. And stiff. She was conscious of the sound of her own heartbeat thudding thunderously in her ears. She must have screamed; Rufus was suddenly awake. She couldn't really remember what happened next. All of a sudden he was on his knees beside her, taking the lifeless bundle from her arms.

'Shit, shit . . . Jesus Christ. Shit. Diana . . . don't scream. I'm going to breathe into him . . . hold him.'

She watched him, every nerve ending in her body tight and alive with fear, opening his own mouth very wide before laying his face over Josh's still one. She couldn't speak; she couldn't think. Head up, breathe in; head down, breathe out. Head up, breathe in; head down, breathe out. He repeated it over and over again. Time seemed to slow down and speed up simultaneously – she pressed her arms against her face and bent her head to the ground. She was no longer aware of anything other than the nauseous fear coursing through her veins and the desperation on Rufus's face. She had never, ever seen Rufus afraid. She'd smothered Josh. She'd smothered her own child. And then the screaming inside her head began and nothing could shut her up.

'Drink this.' Rufus handed her something. A glass, filled with a pale gold liquid. 'All of it.' His voice was terse.

She took the glass but couldn't hold it properly. Her hands were shaking so badly she nearly dropped it. He held it to her lips and forced the liquid down her throat. There was a wrenching upheaval inside her at the taste of the brandy, but he was insistent. 'R-Rufus . . .' she stammered, her whole body revolting against it. 'I c-c-can't . . .'

'Yes, you can. Finish it.' He tipped the glass against her lips once more. She gagged, but managed to swallow it.

'Wh-what are we going to do?' she whispered, watching him pour her a

366

second glass. 'Wh-wh-what am I going to tell H-Harvey?' Her chest was heaving small, hard breaths that became sobs. 'Wh-what am I going to say?'

'Nothing. Not yet. Give me some time to think. Don't do anything. Don't call anyone, d'you hear me?'

'I . . . I ha-have to c-c-call Harvey,' Diana ground out, her teeth chattering.

'Don't. I'll be back in half an hour.'

'D-d-don't leave me, Rufus,' Diana implored. 'P-p-please don't leave me.'

'Diana . . . look at me.' Rufus put a hand under her chin and lifted her face to meet his. His eyes were cold. 'Don't do anything. Nothing, d'you hear me? This was an accident . . . it wasn't your fault. It was an accident.' He forced her chin upwards again. 'But it could get nasty, Diana. D'you understand? If the police get involved. So I want you to finish that glass and lie down. I'll be back in half an hour.'

'Wh-where is . . . h-he? Wh-where is J-Josh?'

'Don't worry about that now. Just finish that drink.' He got to his feet. 'I'll be back as soon as I can.' And then he was gone.

Mougins, June 2000

'Were you having a bad dream, darling?' Harvey's voice was a thread pulling her out of sleep.

She struggled awake to some awful interruption. 'Wh-what time is it?' she whispered thickly.

He pushed back the covers and pulled out his arm to look at his watch. 'Just gone nine. I thought I heard Darcy a few minutes ago. You were whimpering in your sleep. You haven't done that in years. Was it a bad dream?'

Diana couldn't speak for a few moments. Yes, it was. More terrible than anything her imagination could have produced. But it was no dream. She had the sensation of terrible discovery, but Harvey's hand on her arm was a warm, reassuring presence. His breathing was the passing of time, a steady in and out, slowly bringing her back to herself. 'Yes,' she whispered, turning her head away from him so that her voice was muffled by the pillow. 'But I can't remember it now.'

'Poor love. It must've been all the wine. And the stress. The whole thing went beautifully, darling. Thank you.' He leaned across and planted a kiss on her forehead. 'Now, what about a cup of coffee? Shall I bring you one? In one of those bowls that you like?'

She nodded, not trusting herself to speak just yet. He kissed the top of her head and got out of bed. She watched him slip on his dressing gown. He was in his fifties, and nothing about him had changed in forty years. His hair was grey now, of course, and there were deep lines in his face made deeper by the reading he did every night, a frown of concentration between the brows that would never disappear. But his waist measurement − like hers − hadn't gone up by so much as an inch. She knew because she measured the elastic in his favourite pyjamas every year. He opened the door and closed it gently behind him. She was alone again. She clenched and unclenched her fists under the covers. It was Rufus. It was his presence that had done it. She hadn't been this upset in years. She shook her head, trying to clear it. Their holiday still had a few more days to run . . . she couldn't risk another night like the last. Thank God he was leaving. It was the first time she'd been back in Mougins with him since it happened. The first and last time. She couldn't go through another night like last night. She simply didn't have the strength.

86

It was cool and quiet inside the hall of the Mairie. Niela walked over to the clerk's desk, her footsteps echoing loudly across the tiles. The clerk looked up as she approached. '*Oui?*' she asked pleasantly enough. '*Vous cherchez?*' It took Niela a few minutes to explain her request. 'Ah, you'll need public records. When did you say it happened?'

'The summer of 1969, I think,' Niela said. 'In July, possibly August.'

'Those records would be kept in the archives. They'll be on microfiche, I should imagine. There's a small charge for using the facilities here, but if you're looking for the newspaper reports, which are usually more detailed, you'll have to go into Cannes, I'm afraid. We don't keep those cuttings here. If it was a very big case, it would probably have been covered by the nationals.'

Niela hesitated. 'I don't actually know if it was a case or not. I *think* someone was arrested . . . the gardener. Apparently he worked for a few of the English families who lived here at the time.'

The woman frowned. 'Oh, you're talking about the Ben Ahmed case.

Mohammed Ben Ahmed. I was a teenager when it happened. Yes, there *was* a case. The records will be in the archives. Who did you say you were?'

'I . . . I'm a journalist,' Niela lied. 'I'm doing an article on honour killings and someone mentioned the case. I thought I'd just come up and see what I could find.'

'Oh. Well, it's such a long time ago. I don't really remember the details, except that it never came to court. He vanished, just like his daughter and the child. Anyhow, the archives are down those stairs over there.' She pointed to the archway at the end of the corridor. 'It's a six-euro fee for three hours . . . no, you can pay the woman downstairs. She'll give you a receipt. Good luck. I hope you find what you're looking for.'

Ten minutes later, she was seated behind a microfiche screen with a little box of transparent slides, all neatly identified and stacked in chronological order. The friendly clerk showed her how to operate the machine, gave her a receipt and left her to it.

Niela carefully slid the first plastic sheet on to the metal plate. Her heart was racing. She looked at the monitor and began to read. She sat there, hardly moving except to slide on one film after another, for the better part of three hours. When she was finished, she picked up her bag, walked back up the stairs and out into the sunlight, her vision blinded by tears.

She had gone almost halfway down the hill when she noticed a familiar figure coming towards her. It was Josh. He stopped as they drew level. She was still crying but there was nothing she could do. It was too late; he'd seen her.

'What's the matter?' he asked, looking at her face with a frown of concern. 'What happened?'

'N . . . nothing,' Niela stammered.

'You're crying. What's wrong?'

Niela looked away from him. She wasn't sure how to even begin. The silence between them deepened. She was conscious of his eyes searching her face. 'I . . . I was in the Mairie,' she said finally. 'In the archives.'

She could feel Josh stiffen. 'What d'you mean? What were you doing there?'

Niela hesitated. 'I . . . I just felt I had to.'

'Had to what?' His voice had suddenly turned sharp.

'I . . . I was looking for something . . . for some old records.'

'Why?'

She could feel the tension emanating from him like heat. She looked away again. 'It was just something someone said,' she began hesitantly.

'Who?'

'Josh . . . do you remember someone called Leonora? Leonora Simmonds?'

Josh's eyes narrowed immediately. 'Niela, what have you been doing? What were you looking for?' His voice was cold.

Niela shivered, despite the midday heat. 'She said something about a gardener . . . Mohammed Ben Ahmed?'

'What about him?'

Niela hunched her shoulders. 'Did you know about him?' she asked finally. 'About what happened to his daughter?' She could feel the hostility emanating from him like a fever. It was time to stop, but something drove her on. 'What do *you* think?' she asked, spreading her hands outwards in front of her. 'D'you really think he did it? Killed his own daughter and his grandson?'

The expression on Josh's face was one of such pain and anger that she instinctively took a step backwards. 'Leave it alone, Niela,' he said in a low, tight voice. 'Don't go any further with this.'

'Wh . . . what d'you mean?'

'This is none of your business,' Josh said angrily. 'Just leave it alone.'

'But—'

'Listen to me.' Josh grabbed hold of her arm, his fingers digging painfully into her skin. 'I'm warning you, Niela. Stay out of this. Stay the hell out of things that don't concern you.'

'But this *does* concern me,' Niela burst out, shocked at his reaction. 'Of course it concerns me. I'm your wife!'

'I'm warning you, Niela. Drop it, d'you hear me?' he snarled, his fingers still tightly embedded in her arm.

She tried to shake it loose. 'You're hurting me,' she protested. 'Let go.'

'Not until you promise me you'll drop whatever the hell it is you're doing. This is *my* life, Niela. Not yours.'

'I know it's your life! I'm just trying to help—'

'I don't *need* your fucking help! Did I ask you for help?' His voice was tight with anger. 'Just stay the hell out of my life!' He let go of her arm abruptly. She stumbled backwards, catching her heel on a stone and almost falling to the ground. She put out a hand to stop herself; by the time she'd regained her balance and straightened up, Josh was already gone. She started to shout something after him, but the rigid set of his back and shoulders told her what she already knew – he was past hearing or caring. Her fingers went automatically to where his own had dug into her arm, rubbing the tender skin. She looked around her to see if anyone had seen what had just passed between them. There was no one. The country lane that led to the main road was empty. A bird flew overhead, uttering a cry – the only witness to the scene. She pulled her hair into a knot with shaking fingers. Thank God no one else had seen them. What on earth had she just touched upon?

Josh strode up the hill towards the village, his breath coming in fast, angry spurts. He was trembling; he couldn't stop himself. He hadn't intended to shout at Niela, but the sense of betrayal that swept through him as soon as she opened her mouth about where she'd been all morning had blotted everything else out. She'd gone snooping into the past – why? What would she do with the information she found? The resentment and fear in his throat rose up as if it would choke him. He had to get away.

He pushed open the doors to the brasserie that stood at one end of the *place*, opposite the Mairie. He walked straight to the bar and ordered a cognac. He took the glass and tipped the entire contents down his throat. If the *proprietaire* thought there was anything unusual about it, he said nothing, simply poured him a second measure. It was one thing Josh liked about the French – discreet to a fault. If he'd been in London, there'd have been some sort of conversation to strike up and follow, remarks to be made and answered, questions asked . . . Here, no one seemed to feel the need to pretend. If a man wanted to drink himself to oblivion, so be it. It was his choice, his business. He picked up the glass, muttered his thanks and proceeded to drink a little more slowly this time. He fished a packet of cigarettes out of his pocket and lit one. Another thing he liked about France. He could smoke wherever he pleased. He took his drink and his cigarette and found himself an empty booth towards the rear of the room. He needed to be alone, and to think.

L'Aubrevoir de Mougins. Julia looked up at the sign, hesitant to go in. Should she . . . ? Dare she . . . ? She'd been coming up the hill towards the village, a few hundred yards behind Josh, when she saw him stop, saw Niela coming down the lane towards him. She too stopped; she overheard the beginning of the conversation, which made it difficult for her to continue up the path. She'd looked around for somewhere to hide and had moved behind one of the oak trees that lined the path. After a few minutes, she'd seen him storm off up the hill. Niela walked past her without even noticing, tears running down her face. She'd waited a good ten minutes before continuing up the hill, not even sure what she was doing.

She put out a hand; the door opened suddenly. '*Merde, pardon, excusez-moi . . .*' A man almost fell on top of her as he came out. '*Excusez-moi,*' he apologised again, straightening up. He hurried off across the square. She looked around her. The bar was dim and smoky; there was a handful of men standing by the counter, but no Josh. She scanned the bar – she saw him, sitting alone towards the rear of the room. She swallowed nervously. What the hell was she *doing*? She walked over, ignoring the voice in her head.

'Hi.' She stood in front of him. He looked up. Neither spoke for a moment. 'I . . . I saw you come in,' she said finally. 'I just wondered . . .'

'What?' His voice was calm.

She couldn't stop herself. 'Just wondered if you wanted a bit of company,' she said, sliding uninvited into the seat opposite him.

He shrugged. 'Suit yourself. I'm not really in the mood to chat.'

'Well, I don't recall you ever being chatty,' she said, surprising even herself. Where on earth had this breezy manner suddenly come from? 'I've spent an evening in a bar with you before, remember?'

'Yeah. So you have.'

'So what're you drinking?'

'Cognac. It's my third.'

'I'll join you. Want another one?'

'Sure. Why the hell not?'

The cognac was strong and fiery. It burned a pleasurable trail down her throat, settling and spreading its warmth throughout her belly. She hadn't eaten; it was almost noon and the events of the morning were beginning to feel like a dream. They sat facing one another. Julia was trying unsuccessfully not to stare at him; at the dark brown skin of his forearm, toughened and touched by the sun. He wore a silver bracelet – a simple, plain band – and no wedding ring, she noticed. Come to think of it, neither did Niela. She shifted uncomfortably in her seat. Once again the image of Niela's bare back rising and falling slid into her head and she couldn't shake it. She'd seen him, too . . . just glimpses . . . slivers of images she'd rather not remember. She took another sip of her drink, wondering if and when he would deign to speak. There was some emotion burning inside him but she didn't dare ask herself what it might be. They went on sipping their drinks quietly, not speaking. It came to her slowly that that in itself was communication of a kind, just not the kind she wanted.

What the hell was she doing there? Josh sat opposite Julia, watching her through half-lowered lids. The anger that had blown up so bewilderingly inside him earlier was slowly trickling through his veins, mingling with the fiery cognac. He'd never been much of a talker; he preferred the safety of his own thoughts. Niela had changed all that – her own silences were stronger and more profound than his, and as a result, he'd felt himself drawn to express what he'd always kept hidden, almost against his will. That, he thought to himself, taking another fiery sip, was what angered him the most. He'd trusted her with something he barely trusted in himself. His anger rose and fell, like his breathing, until he couldn't stand it any more.

'Come,' he said abruptly. He got up, only dimly aware of what he was doing. Julia looked up at him. He'd never thought of her as beautiful – far too cold and aloof for that – but facing her now, watching the expression of wary confidence on her face, he could feel his opinion change, some old form of behaviour surfacing in him, leading him on. 'Come,' he repeated, draining his glass and setting it down carefully on the table. She got up without saying a word and followed suit.

He walked out into the bright sunlight, his eyes rapidly adjusting to the change. He said nothing to her, just started down the hill away from the *place*. At the bottom, he turned left instead of right, plunging into a lane overgrown with bushes and thick weeds; she simply followed. It was the back route to the farmhouse; the track petered out after a few minutes before opening on to the back wall of the property. He pushed his way through the overgrowth until he found the small latch. It was stiff and rusty but it eventually gave way. He pushed open the wooden door and stepped through. He turned to her, holding out his hand. He felt the cool pressure of her fingers in his palm. The door to the pool house was unlocked, as always. Still holding hands, they stepped into the cool, damp-smelling space full of old tools and pieces of abandoned furniture.

There was an old sofa pushed up against one corner of the room. He experienced a strange sense of falling backwards in time and space as he sat down on it, pulling the woman he'd brought with him into his embrace. He'd lost count of the number of times he'd come here as a teenager, sometimes with a girl, sometimes not. Sometimes he'd come just to escape the house with all its undercurrents and the knowledge of what had gone on, what continued to go on. It infuriated him; why had *he* been chosen to bear witness to what Diana had done? Why couldn't it have been Rafe or Aaron? They wouldn't have been tormented by it the way he was. They had each other; he had no one.

His hands went around her waist in the all-too-familiar game. His mind was elsewhere as he slid them under her shirt, his fingers sliding over her skin, stopping here and there, touching, teasing. She responded eagerly and quickly. Within seconds, or so it seemed to him, she was lying underneath him. He'd grown used to the dense cloud of Niela's hair; Julia's was very different. Like Rania, it fell about her shoulders in soft, slippery strands. He gathered it in his hands but he couldn't hold it, not the way he could bury his whole being in Niela's. He tried to hold on to her, gripping her hips and legs, gathering her to him, but there was a fury in him that wouldn't cease. He was dimly aware he might be hurting her, but he didn't care; there was a part of him that simply wasn't there. He pushed himself roughly into her, not knowing whether she was ready or not. She must want it – why else would she have followed him? The cognac and the anger and the hurt swirled round and round in his head, each chasing the other, until all he could think about was Niela's face when he'd shouted at her that morning and then, just before his body raced away from him and he lost it altogether, Diana's face and his uncle's, contorted together in violent, angry lust . . . and then all of a sudden, much sooner than he would have liked, there was a tremendous surge in him and he couldn't think about anything at all.

Julia's heart was racing. Her legs were trembling underneath her. Josh's head was turned away from hers; his eyes were closed and she could feel his whole body slacken, withdrawing from her. She couldn't believe what had just happened. What had she done? She tried to sit up, but Josh was still pinning her down. Her mouth was dry and her tongue felt like lead.

'S-sorry,' she mumbled, struggling to get out from underneath him. He shifted slightly and she was able to withdraw first one leg, then the other. Her skirt was rucked up around her waist and her shirt was undone. Shame flooded her senses, spreading across her face and neck like a stain. She staggered backwards clumsily, but Josh's eyes were closed. She pulled down her skirt, looked around for her underwear but couldn't see anything in the dim half-light. She slipped her feet back into her shoes and tried to smooth down her hair. She needn't have bothered, at least not on Josh's account. His eyes remained firmly closed. She opened her mouth to say something, but nothing came out. Her last glimpse of him was of his semi-clothed body lying on the old sofa as if he would never wake. She opened the door and slipped out, distress rising and falling in her chest, like breath. What in God's name had she just done?

PART EIGHT

87

JULIA
London, August 2000

It was very quiet in the bathroom. Halfway down the corridor, Julia could hear Aaron moving around the kitchen, looking for things. He'd offered to cook dinner. It was the third time that week that she'd not been feeling well and his concern was touching. 'I'll do it,' he'd said when he came home that evening from work to find her lying, pale and wan, on the couch. 'What d'you feel like eating?'

She'd looked up at him, unable to think clearly. Food was the last thing on her mind. 'Anything, I'm not fussy. I'm not actually very hungry.'

'Right. Well, I'll think of something. Just stay where you are.' He'd disappeared into the kitchen. She got up slowly, her heart in her mouth, and went along the corridor to the bathroom. She couldn't put it off any longer.

She opened the packet she'd been carrying around all day with trembling hands and took out the instructions. 99.87% accurate, or so the manufacturers claimed. She peeled back the rest of the wrapping and dropped it in the waste-paper basket. She sat down on the toilet and looked up at the corner of the ceiling. There was a faint spider's web tucked away where the housekeeper's brush had failed to reach. A few seconds later she withdrew the white plastic stick, but she couldn't quite bring herself to look at it. A minute ticked by, then another. *Come on, Julia*, she whispered to herself. She swallowed hard and forced herself to look down. Two thin blue lines stared back up at her. Fuzzy at the edges, but unmistakably blue. Positive. Just as it said on the packet. She stared at it, aware of a slow burning sensation in the pit of her stomach and of the sudden build-up of tears behind her eyes. Suddenly a car horn punctured the air. Seconds later a woman's sharp staccato laugh floated upwards. She turned her head to the window. Outside, on a late summer's evening, people were going about their business, blissfully unaware of the drama unfolding several storeys above them. She wrapped the test stick in toilet paper and stowed it carefully in her bag. She stood up and washed her hands, her mind racing. She had to talk to someone . . . *any*one. She couldn't keep the secret to herself any longer.

She opened the door and stepped out into the corridor. She could hear Aaron setting the table, opening and closing drawers, the soft 'pop' of a wine bottle being uncorked. Here, too, life continued as usual, moving along its normal course. Small talk, a chat about his or her cases, office gossip. She would push the food around on her plate, decline a glass of wine . . . business as usual. Only it wasn't, of course. It was anything but. She was pregnant. She was carrying her husband's brother's child. It didn't make sense. Nothing about her life made sense any more. She wanted only to turn her face to the wall and weep.

Three days later, she sat opposite Dom in the upstairs drawing room at Hayden Hall, overlooking the grounds where she'd married Aaron. She couldn't bring herself to look out of the window so she concentrated on Dom instead. The look on his face would have been comical if Julia had had the capacity within herself to laugh.

'You did *what*?' Dom said faintly, passing a hand over his face.

Julia looked at her own hands. 'I . . . I can't explain it. It just . . . sort of happened.'

'Julia, things like that don't just happen. How the hell did it start? *When* did it start?'

'That's the thing . . . nothing started. I mean, we barely speak to one another. I met him that time in Johannesburg, and—'

'What time in Johannesburg?' Dom interrupted, looking even more alarmed. 'You met him in Johannesburg? Julia, what's going on?'

Julia blushed. 'Nothing. Nothing at all. Well, nothing was going on . . . it's just that now . . . oh, shit, Dom . . . what've I done?'

'What've *you* done? I hate to point out the obvious, my dear, but it takes two, you know.'

'I know.' Julia's voice was suddenly a whisper. 'I can't explain it. I saw him and Niela . . . they'd had an argument and he stormed off. I went after him to talk to him and then it just sort of happened. It was just the once. You've got to believe me, Dom. I'll never do it again. Never.'

Dom whistled softly and then slowly let the air out of his cheeks. 'That's all well and good, Burrows. But what about this child?'

Julia felt something inside her turn with his words. 'I don't know what

380

to do,' she said, twisting her hands nervously together. 'The thing is . . .
Aaron and I . . . we've actually been trying for a while. There's nothing
wrong with *me*,' she said, her voice barely above a whisper. 'At least that's
what the doctor says. And now . . . well, I suppose it looks as if he's
right. But Aaron wouldn't even hear of going to get tested. I don't think
he can bear the thought that something might be wrong with him.'

'Not surprising. Most men can't.' Dom finished off his tea and pressed
the bell. 'I think it's time to have something a bit stronger, don't you?'

Julia shook her head. 'I can't. Not now, anyway.'

'Sorry, I forgot. Well, forgive me, my love, but *I* need something. I'll
have a G and T, if you don't mind.' Julia shook her head. Seconds later, a
uniformed maid appeared and took his order. 'So . . . what *are* you going
to do?' Dom asked as soon as she'd gone again.

Julia was quiet for a moment. 'I don't know,' she said, spreading her
hands helplessly before her. 'I just don't know.'

'Does Aaron know?'

'No, of course not!' Julia looked shocked. 'I can't tell him, Dom. I just
can't.'

'Well, you know him best, I suppose. You'd better make sure he never
finds out you got rid of it.'

Julia lifted her eyes slowly. 'That's the thing, though, Dom,' she began
hesitantly. 'I'm not sure I can. Have an abortion, I mean.'

'What're you talking about? No . . . you're actually thinking of *having*
it?' Dom's expression was again comical. 'You can't be serious, Jules. You
mean have it and not tell him it's not his? How's *that* going to work?'

'I don't know.' Julia shook her head miserably. 'I . . . I haven't really
thought it through.'

'*I'll* say. Jesus, Burrows. Ah, thank you, Mary.' Dom's G & T had
arrived. 'You sure you don't want a sip?'

She shook her head and turned to look out of the window. The lawns
stretched all the way to the horizon. It was August, and the grounds
were slowly turning yellow. The line of oaks that led the eye away from
the house and over the gently rolling hills towards the lake had lost their
summer freshness. By her own calculations, she was nearly six weeks
pregnant. She had, at the most, another couple of weeks to make a
decision. It felt like a lifetime. 'I don't know what to do, Dom,' she said,
turning back to him, the tears falling straight down her cheeks. 'I just
don't know what to do.'

Dom was quiet for a moment. He lifted his glass and drained it in a single gulp. Julia watched him, listening for the reproach that didn't come. 'If you keep it, Julia, you'd better make sure Aaron never finds out. That's the sort of secret that can tear a family apart. Are you prepared for that? To keep it a secret for the rest of your life?'

Julia shook her head numbly. She couldn't answer, let alone speak.

88

'Will you hold my calls, please, Liz?' Julia shrugged on her coat and picked up an umbrella. 'I should be back within an hour.'

'Sure.' Liz smiled briefly at her. 'I'll hold the fort.'

She opened the heavy wooden door that led to the quadrangle at the Inns and opened her brolly. It was raining again. It was a week since she'd been to Hayden and she couldn't put it off any longer. She crossed the quadrangle and went through the archway, heading for Gray's Inn Road. The church tower ahead of her chimed 4.30 p.m. She quickened her pace. She'd asked Josh to meet her at four thirty on the dot. Traffic surged slowly up and down the main road as usual. She threaded her way through and reached the café, five minutes ahead of time. She pushed open the door and looked around. He was already there, sitting with his back to the window. She folded her umbrella and stowed it away before crossing the floor.

'Josh.' She looked down at him warily. He looked up at her, his expression carefully unreadable. His skin hadn't yet lost the sunny glow of Mougins. In the dreary, wet London light he looked impossibly alive. There was a sudden, dreadful surge of elation inside her that both shocked and surprised her. Her heart was racing. 'Look, thanks for coming to meet me,' she said quickly, sitting down opposite him. 'I know you're busy, so I'll be quick.' She'd heard from Diana that he would be off soon, but she had no idea where. She *had* to talk to him; she'd no idea how long he'd be gone for. 'D'you want something to drink?' she asked hesitantly. He shook his head and pulled out a packet of cigarettes instead. 'Diana said you'll be leaving again soon,' Julia began hesitantly. Now that she was seated opposite him, she found it almost impossible to begin.

'Yep.' He lit a cigarette but didn't elaborate further.

Julia took a deep breath. The chatter in the café receded into the distance. She opened her mouth to begin. 'Look, there's no other way to say this. I'm pregnant, Josh. I'm nearly seven weeks pregnant.' She folded her hands in her lap to stop them shaking and tried to look anywhere but at him.

'When did you find out?' he asked after a moment, stubbing out his cigarette.

'A couple of weeks ago.' She swallowed. 'I did the test at home.'

'How d'you know it's mine?'

She felt a sharp stab of pain. She waited for a second before answering. 'I . . . haven't been with Aaron since . . . since Mougins. We . . . we've been trying for a while. Look, I didn't want to have to tell you all this . . . you don't need to know. And it's not fair on Aaron. But I don't know what to do, and—'

'You can't keep it.' Josh's tone was flat.

Julia stared at him. 'That's up to me,' she said sharply, stung by the hostility in his voice.

'You can't keep it,' he repeated.

'My choice, not yours,' she repeated.

He picked up the packet of cigarettes that lay on the table and got to his feet. 'You can't keep it, Julia, you can't. It'll . . . it'll destroy everything. Everyone. Trust me, I know what I'm talking about.' He ran a hand through his hair. There was a strange, hunted look on his face. 'I . . . I've got to go.'

She was too surprised to speak. She watched him pull on his leather jacket and walk quickly to the door. It banged shut behind him and she was suddenly alone.

Josh stumbled out of the café and into the fine drizzle of rain. There was a sharp, gusting wind that turned umbrellas inside out and blew the skirts of women up and around their legs. He didn't see any of that. He turned the collar of his jacket up against his ears and made his way down Gray's Inn Road, though he had no clear idea of where he was headed. *I'm pregnant.* Julia's words reverberated in his skull. *I'm pregnant.*

There was a bus coming towards him. He had no idea where it was going; he climbed on board. He took a seat at the rear, crammed in between two generously proportioned Turkish women and their grocery bags who talked over his head as if he simply weren't there. He was grateful for their disregard – he couldn't think, let alone think straight. He tried to reconstruct the day's events in his head. He'd been at home, lying on the couch watching afternoon television, when the phone rang. It was Julia. 'Niela's at work,' he said flicking through the channels, wondering what the hell she wanted. He had another week of enforced holiday before his next assignment. He couldn't wait to be gone.

'No, I'm not phoning for Niela. I . . . I really need to talk to you.'

'Talk to *me*? What for?' He was both surprised and annoyed. He'd tried to put what had happened in Mougins out of his head.

'Can we just meet? I'd rather not say it over the phone.'

A feeling of panic had swept over him, settling on his skin. 'When?'

'Could you meet me this afternoon? Around four thirty or so?'

'Fine. Where.' She named a café along Gray's Inn Road. He put down the phone, uncomfortably aware of everything he'd tried to suppress over the past couple of months rising slowly to the surface.

Now here he was, sitting on a bus heading God alone knew where, squashed between the two women, who talked incessantly across him in a language that washed over him like rain. How had it happened? He shook his head in irritation. Stupid question. He knew exactly how. Why it had happened was another question altogether. He now understood the expression 'temporary insanity' – it was as if a momentary madness had come over him that day. He shook his head again, this time more forcefully. Who was he kidding? What was it Rania had said to him? The memory of those last few months with her, when they'd both done all they could to hurt each other, burned over him, reaching down into every part of him. *What you have done once you will do again.* She was right; he'd cheated on her, just as she'd cheated on him. It was the way he'd always done things, and at the time it seemed the only thing to do. Tit for tat, an eye for an eye, burning for burning. He knew his sense of justice was warped, and he knew why – not that it helped. When he found out about Rania, it seemed to be the only thing to do. Do unto her . . . and that was exactly what he'd done. Not once, not twice, but over and over again until she couldn't stand it any longer and neither could he. He'd packed his bags then, leaving the flat they'd shared in Amman, and that was the last home he'd had – until now, until Niela. And now he'd done it again. Only this time, the person he'd done it with wasn't some insignificant young NGO worker whom he could fuck once and leave behind. This time, it was different. Julia was pregnant. The child was his. He believed her, in spite of himself. There was something clear and straightforward about her expression; she'd looked at him without a trace of coquetry or guile. No, whatever else Aaron's wife was, she wasn't a liar – that much was obvious, even to him. What the hell was he supposed to do now? He ran a hand through his hair in agitation. Christ. What a mess. History endlessly repeating itself. Chickens coming home to roost. Apples and trees. The clichés came at him, thick and fast.

89

NIELA
London, August 2000

Niela stared down at her hands. Anna was looking at her expectantly, waiting for her to continue. 'I . . . I don't know,' she said finally. 'I tried to talk to Josh about it. That same morning when I went to the archives. But he got so angry . . . he just stormed off.' She stopped, as if she was aware she'd already said too much. She hesitated, clearly torn. 'The thing is . . .' She stopped again. It didn't seem right to her to be telling Anna what Josh had told her about Diana and Rufus, but she had to tell someone. She took a deep breath. 'Diana had an affair,' she said slowly. 'Only I don't think it's actually over. I think it's still going on. It's Harvey's brother. Rufus. Josh's uncle.' She stopped again.

Anna's eyes were wide, round saucers. 'Go on,' she said, her voice almost a whisper.

'There's something else.'

'What?'

'There's a gardener. His names is . . . was . . . Mohammed. He disappeared about thirty years ago. There was this case . . . I found it in the archives.' She began to tell Anna the story.

Anna was silent for a long time after she'd finished. Niela watched her, not saying anything. It was such a relief to spell it out, to put into words what she'd been too afraid to even think. 'What do *you* think?' she asked Anna finally, when she couldn't stand the silence any longer. 'D'you think I'm mad?'

Anna lifted her coffee cup and took a sip. She shook her head. 'No, you're not mad. But there are too many secrets in that family. Too many secrets. You can't go on like this. You've got to tell Josh what you just told me. You've got to help him find out who he really is.'

Niela nodded slowly. Anna was right. It was time to end the cycle of silence. Josh was leaving in a few days' time. She had to do it now.

'Thanks,' she said to Anna, getting up and putting on her coat. 'Thanks for listening.'

'Good luck,' Anna said, hugging her. 'Call me if you need to. I'm here. Remember that.'

Niela smiled wanly. 'How can I ever forget? You've always been there for me, Anna. Always.' She picked up her umbrella and left Anna's flat. She was on the verge of heading for the Tube when she changed her mind and hopped on the bus coming towards her instead. It was a Friday. She'd taken a couple of days off work to spend with Josh. It was nearly five and she didn't relish the thought of the Friday rush-hour chaos on the Underground.

She saw him almost as soon as the bus rounded the corner. He came out of the café, walking fast, perhaps a hundred yards or so in front of the bus. She stared down at him, wondering if she was mistaken. He hadn't said anything about coming into the West End that afternoon. He seemed to be in a hurry. The bus drew level with the café. She wondered whether to get off at the next stop – she half-stood up, looked down at the street and then she saw her. Julia came out of the very same café Josh had left. Niela turned her head and looked backwards in disbelief. Julia was hurrying down the street in the opposite direction, clutching her coat. Niela's heart began to beat faster. Something wasn't right. The bus gave a sudden lurch, bumping her back down into her seat. There was a queer feeling in the pit of her stomach. She clutched her umbrella tightly, aware of a slow, horrid build-up of dread.

It was almost 8 p.m. by the time Josh returned. Niela was in the kitchen, half-heartedly preparing dinner. Ever since she'd seen them, the questions had gone round and round in her head. Why was Josh meeting Julia? What business could the two of them possibly have together? Was she overreacting? She sliced onions, dropped a few tomatoes in a pan of boiling water, put a frying pan on the hob . . . her movements were automatic; she wasn't even sure what she was cooking. Perhaps it was nothing. Perhaps they'd met to talk about Aaron. Julia had mentioned they were having problems, though she'd been careful not to say anything else. Perhaps that was it – a bit of brotherly advice, nothing more. She looked at the gently browning onions and saw that her vision was blurred. She knew. She knew it was more than that.

By the time she finally heard his key in the lock, she couldn't think straight. The fear that blew up inside her was stark and pure and it broke over her like sweat. She was terrified, by the thought both of what he might say and what he wouldn't.

'Hi.' He stood in the kitchen doorway. He looked tense, as if he might speak.

'Hi.' She waited, holding her breath.

'Did you have a good day?' he asked, his voice sounding strained. He lifted his arms above his head, resting them on the architrave around the door. Niela stared at him.

'I . . . I went round to a friend's,' she said slowly. 'I had the day off, remember?'

'Oh, yeah, right. I forgot.' He brought his arms down and walked into the tiny space. He reached out suddenly; his hand brushed her face. She flinched. He removed an offending curl, tucking it tenderly behind her ear. The gesture disarmed her, and in her confusion, tears came to her eyes. She turned away before he could see and busied herself with a pot. Neither of them was able to speak.

He lay awake long after she'd gone to sleep, measuring the passing of time by the rhythm of her breathing. He was due to fly back out to Tanzania in a few days. It was a three-month assignment – by the time he returned, everything would have changed. Julia would be nearly five months pregnant by then. Impossible to conceal. He rolled over on to his side, facing the wall. He lay there in the dark, facing the long, endless tunnel of the night that he had no idea how to get through. It wasn't just that he'd done the unthinkable and cheated on Niela – there was more to it, and worse. He, more than anyone, knew the sort of damage a secret could wreak. Secrets were like poison, slipping in unseen, spreading themselves silently until everything was tainted and nothing was true or pure. That was what he'd been attracted to in Niela – a sense of pureness. She'd seemed to him to be so open and clear . . . he'd been drawn to her, to her lightness, her purity, her strength. And now he'd gone and spread his own kind of darkness all over her and the one thing he seemed to have done right. He closed his eyes, trying at the same time to close himself against the pain.

90

DIANA
London, August 2000

Dr Geoffrey Laing stopped talking. His voice fell away into the deepening silence. Outside, barely visible through the grey-blue of the Venetian blinds that hung at every window, a slow, steady rain was falling. It was almost the end of August. It felt as though it had been raining for months. Diana took a deep breath and forced herself to concentrate.

'How long?' she asked, her voice sounding unnaturally loud in her ears. She brought a finger to her mouth, absently tracing the fine line of her lips. Although she hadn't smoked in forty years, she suddenly longed for a cigarette. She needed something to do with her hands. The clock on the wall chimed suddenly. It was 11 a.m. The whole morning felt unreal. She'd known from the moment her secretary took the call, asking her to come in, that the news wouldn't be good. In some hard-to-define way, she'd been expecting it for longer than she could remember.

'It's very difficult to say, Diana.' Geoffrey was a colleague of Harvey's and a friend. The results for which she'd come into his clinic that morning were as difficult for him to divulge as they were for her to hear. There was barely muted distress in his voice. 'There's new, experimental treatment available, which we could quite easily put you on. We don't yet have all the results of the clinical trials, but early indications are that it's looking—'

'How long?' Diana interrupted him, repeating the question. She raised her head to look him squarely in the face.

He lifted his shoulders and let them drop. 'Six months? A year. It's almost impossible to say.'

'And if I don't agree? To this new treatment?'

He shook his head slowly. 'Then we're looking at something greatly reduced.'

'What? Weeks? Months?'

'A few months. Not much more. It's unusually aggressive, Diana . . . I haven't seen a case like this in a while.'

'Does Harvey know?'

He looked shocked. 'Goodness, no. I wouldn't . . . no, this is between you and me. It's up to you when and what you tell him. I'm available to you both, of course, you know that.'

'Thank you, Geoffrey.' Diana was conscious of the formal note that had crept into her tone. She'd known Geoffrey Laing for years. He and Harvey had been at medical school together. When she'd first discovered the small, hard lump under her left arm, just at the point where her breast separated from the muscle, a couple of weeks after coming back from Mougins, there'd been no question of going to anyone else. She'd told no one, not even Harvey. Judith, her secretary, made the appointment. She'd gone along to Geoffrey's consulting rooms just off Harley Street. He'd come out into the waiting room as soon as he'd seen her name. He'd held up a hand and quietly flagged her in. No need for her to wait. Under a few raised brows, she'd passed through the doorway and into the quiet sanctuary of his office. He'd kissed her on both cheeks – she caught the oddly familiar scent of his aftershave as he showed her to a seat. She'd last smelled it in the context of a dinner party, or at one official function or another of the sort she and Harvey had once attended when their careers were younger and there'd been more time. It had been a while since she'd been to any of the annual Medical Society dinners or the various fund-raising events. Cancer research, usually. The irony of it didn't escape her.

Now, almost ten days later, with the results of the tests he'd done spread in front of him, the moment of truth had finally arrived. *A moment of truth.* The oddly biblical tone of the phrase struck her anew. She, more than anyone, knew just how many of those moments were now to be had. As she sat there in the comfortable chair opposite Geoffrey's desk, the realisation that *this was it* – this was the definitive moment of her life, forget everything that had gone on before – was slowly breaking over her in waves.

'Thank you,' she said at last, getting to her feet. She picked up her bag and turned to face him. 'I'd like to have some time to think this over, Geoffrey. I'll be in touch again very soon. I . . . I'd appreciate it if you didn't say anything to Harvey. Not just yet.'

'Of course, Diana. I—' He hesitated for a second, his professional mask momentarily giving way. 'I'm dreadfully sorry. I don't know what to say. You, of all people. I'm sorry. It just doesn't seem fair, somehow.'

'Thank you, Geoffrey.' She nodded her head gravely. 'Who's to say what's fair?' She touched him briefly on the arm and left the room before either he or she could say another word.

There was a cab waiting for her as soon as she stepped outside the door; Judith would have organised it. 'Primrose Hill, please,' she directed the driver. She couldn't return to chambers just yet. There was a tea shop on Chalcott Crescent that she hadn't been to in years. It was just the sort of place she needed to go right now. She needed to be alone. There were things she had to think through first.

'There we go.' The smiling waitress put down a cup of tea and a slice of home-made cake in front of her. 'Can I get you anything else?'

Diana shook her head. She looked at the pretty cup with its pattern of pink and red roses and smiled faintly. It was the sort of cup her mother would have appreciated. Bone china, hand-painted, delicate – just the sort of old-fashioned English aesthetic that she had liked. She lifted it to her lips. It had been a long time since she'd thought about her mother. It felt as though she'd been gone far longer than the twenty-odd years since her actual death. It had always been that way; memories would come to her in the oddest moments, catching her unawares. For most of her life, she'd barely registered her presence, and when she died, it seemed to Diana that she'd already mourned her passing long before. She couldn't remember much about her; her presence in the house had always been overshadowed by Diana's father. She put the cup down with shaking hands. It was odd how she came to mind, not in anything she did or said, but in those little details that were so insignificant Diana had difficulty remembering how she'd come by them in the first place. The bone china cups; the colour of the curtains in the living room; the flowers she favoured – pale, pretty, nothing flamboyant or particularly memorable. Much like herself, in fact. Diana was suddenly unable to swallow her tea. She couldn't even remember the exact details of her mother's death. What was the cause? Dementia, was what she remembered everyone saying, but how old had she been? Sixty? Sixty-five? Did people really die of dementia? Some illness brought on by her drinking was much more likely. What would that have been? Something to do with the liver. She brought her hands up to her face. Her cheeks were wet. How was it that she remembered so little of either of them? She'd principally been afraid of her father; fear was what she'd always associated with him. Fear and the terror of being hit. In more ways than she cared to admit or remember, her ability to live with secrets had come from there. Behind the respectable façade, things had gone on in that house that no one should ever have known about, least of all a child. Her father was a doctor; he knew precisely where and how to hit. Her mother rarely, if ever, showed the scars. She'd taken it all in – the beatings, the rages, the uncontrollable moods, the bullying. All Cathy Pryce ever did was turn the other cheek. From her Diana had learned how *not* to be a woman, not the other way round. Her mother sickened her; she hated the excuses and the way she put up with things, excusing him for everything, even beating her half to death. There were times when she'd hear him hitting her, softly at first, then with increasing anger and rage, and she'd stand at the dining room door, her hands pressed over her ears. It made no difference. His voice and his fists came through the walls as if they were paper. Later, much later, she would hear her mother petting *him*, tending to the bruises on his fists and sometimes the small cuts on his fingers *as if it had been the other way round*. She would do anything to block out the sound of *that*. Her mother's weakness enraged her. In the terrible closeness of such moments, when they were shouting and struggling with each other, it seemed to her like a murder. One day she would kill him, that was what she thought. One day. Soon. It was Rufus who'd first put the words into her mouth. She'd gone next door as she always did when they fought, only this time, there was a faint bruise showing up underneath the lightly freckled skin of her cheek. She'd been in the way of his hand as he reached across the dining table to administer a slap. She sat there, the pain gathering under the surface of her skin, unable to say or do anything until he'd told her to leave the room. She knew what it meant, of course . . . that the beating he was about to administer would be harder and worse, partly to assuage his own guilt at having hit her, even inadvertently. That was the rule – only her mother, never her.

'Did he hit you?' Rufus's voice was low and controlled.

Diana shook her head mutely. 'No. It was an accident. I got in the way.'

'Good. 'Cos if he does, I'll fucking kill him.' It was said with such clarity and assuredness . . . that was the day she'd fallen in love with him. He would protect her in a way that no one else could or would. She'd been wrong, as it turned out. Rufus wasn't capable of protecting anyone, least of all himself. It was Harvey. Kind, gentle Harvey. He'd watched it all silently, never saying anything, no dramatic outbursts like Rufus. Just a quiet, confident watchfulness. When the time came, and she really was in need of protection, it was Harvey who'd stepped forward, not Rufus. But it didn't change a thing. It was Rufus who held sway, not Harvey. No matter that she'd married him.

She picked up the teacup and drank slowly until it was drained. Then she reached into her briefcase and pulled out her phone. She looked at it for a second, then dialled.

'Where are you?'

'The Russian Tea Room. It's on Chalcott Crescent, just—'

'I know where it is. Give me half an hour. And Diana?'

'Yes?'

'Don't run away this time.'

The tea room was almost empty by the time Rufus arrived. Diana was on her third cup; the slice of cake was still untouched. She couldn't bring herself to eat.

'Diana.' She looked up. He was suddenly in front of her. He filled the frame of her vision, as always, larger than life. She felt her eyes suddenly fill with tears. 'Sorry, traffic was heavy,' he said, sliding into the seat opposite her. 'Surprised you're still here, actually. Half-expected you to have gone.'

She blinked away the tears and took a deep breath. 'Nowhere to run to,' she said slowly.

'What's the matter?'

She'd never been able to hide anything from Rufus. Never. She took another deep breath. 'Something's come up,' she said. 'I need to talk to you.' She signalled to the waitress.

His dark brown eyes regarded hers evenly. 'Mind if I smoke?' he asked.

She shook her head. 'No, go ahead.' She waited until the waitress brought a fresh pot and cup over. She took a deep breath. 'Look, I'm not going to beat around the bush. There's no point. I've just come from seeing Geoffrey Laing.'

'Harvey's friend? The oncologist?'

She nodded. 'Yes, the oncologist.'

'Is it Harvey?'

She shook her head again. There was a short silence. She watched him light a cigarette, carefully disposing of the match. 'So, it's you,' he said slowly. 'And it's cancer.'

'Yes. It's me. And yes, it's cancer.'

'Where?' His voice was terse.

'Breast.'

'Operable?'

Diana paused. She pulled her lower lip into her mouth, releasing it slowly. 'There's new treatment available, Geoffrey says. More radical and more invasive . . . but it's too early to tell if it works or not. He wants me to do it, of course—'

'What does Harvey say?' Rufus interrupted her.

'I haven't told him yet.' Diana lifted her shoulders and let them drop again. 'I don't know what's going to happen, Rufus. Obviously Harvey and I will talk it over . . . see what the options are. But I don't want to leave things too late. And I don't want to leave things unsaid. Just in case.'

'What're you talking about? Don't be silly, Diana. You're going to be fine. You'll have the best treatment available . . . Harvey'll see to that, of course he will.'

'This isn't about the treatment I'm going to get, Rufus. This is about what we do if it doesn't work. Or if I opt not to have it.'

'Of course it's going to work. Of course you'll have it. There's no question.'

Diana was quiet. The waitress brought over a fresh pot of tea and poured two new cups. Diana waited until she'd gone before she spoke again. 'It's out of my hands, Rufus. That's what I feel. I'm not religious, you know that. But there's something . . . I don't know how to explain it.' She spread her hands flat out on the table and gave a rather shaky laugh. 'It's as if I've somehow brought this on myself.'

'Don't.' Rufus was shaking his head at her. 'Stop it. That's absurd.'

'Is it? Rufus . . . think about what we did. What *I* did. I can't stop myself thinking about it.'

'And believing that this is some kind of divine retribution is going to make it easier?' Rufus's voice was scathing.

Diana flinched. 'You can mock me all you like,' she said tightly. 'I don't care. All I care about is that we do the right thing.'

'And what's that?'

'We've got to come clean. We have to tell Josh.'

'Why? What good could it possibly do him now?'

'He has to know. He has a *right* to know, Rufus. I can't . . . what if something happens? To me, I mean. What if the treatment doesn't work and it turns out that . . .' She stumbled over the words. 'That I don't have much time left. I can't leave things the way they are. It's not fair.'

'And what if Josh tells Harvey?'

'He won't.'

'How do you know he won't? How can you be so sure?'

'I know Josh. He's my *son*, Rufus.'

'Don't forget, Diana, he was mine first.'

91

MADDY
London, September 2000

Maddy put the phone down and only just managed not to scream out loud. With delight. With joy. She stared at the phone, unable to wipe the grin off her face. The gods were on her side. Smiling down upon her. Her prayers had been answered. She'd missed out on one part but somehow, against the odds, another had appeared. She'd jotted down the address where auditions were being held the following Friday; it was another small role – *very* small, Stef warned – but again, it might lead to bigger things. She wrote down the name of the play – *Phaedra* – hands shaking with excitement and rushed upstairs to the study, where she switched on the computer and tried to find everything she could about the Greek play. She looked at the address again. Goodge Street Studios, just off Tottenham Court Road, a ten-minute walk away. Yes, the gods were truly listening. Auditions would begin at 9 a.m. sharp. She'd be there at 8.30, just to be sure. She would drop Darcy off at playschool first and pick her up at lunchtime, hopefully with a smile on her face.

She printed off a list of books she would buy and devour in the week . . . by Friday, she'd be ready and raring to go. She picked up the phone again. She couldn't wait to tell Julia. She frowned. It suddenly occurred to her that she hadn't spoken to Julia in almost a fortnight. In fact, she'd hardly spoken to her all month. Julia had been very busy in the weeks that followed their return from Mougins; there'd been another conference somewhere, Maddy couldn't remember where. Then she'd had an important case to prepare for; then she'd been unwell for a week – a cold, a stomach upset . . . again, Maddy couldn't remember the details. They'd made loose plans to have dinner and to invite Niela, but there'd been one reason or another why she couldn't make it. Diana had invited everyone to Sunday lunch a fortnight or so ago but then had called to cancel it. Strange. Strange, too, that Maddy hadn't noticed how quickly the time had gone by.

She dialled Julia's number. The phone rang and rang but there was no answer. She left a message and put the receiver down slowly. She hoped nothing was wrong. She suddenly missed their chats. Come to think of it, Julia had been odd since the last few days of their holiday. She'd hardly seen her or Aaron on the last day, or since. They'd all left at different times – Niela and Josh had been the first to go; she, Darcy and Rafe had driven to Cannes the following morning and caught the afternoon flight back . . . Julia and Aaron had driven all the way down from London – they were the last to leave. She looked at the phone again. She hesitated; should she call Niela and share the good news? She'd enjoyed spending time with her in Mougins but there was a natural reserve in Niela that had always kept Maddy at bay. It wouldn't hurt to reach out, though, would it? After all, that was exactly what she'd done with Julia and it had worked . . . She picked up the phone, her fingers hovering over the keypad. But after a few seconds she replaced it gently. Better to wait. Let others come to her every once in a while, not always the other way round. It was the one lesson she'd learned in the nearly four years she'd been in the UK. She *was* an overeager, impulsive and impatient American – but she didn't always have to act that way. She picked up her reading list and began to go through it, her earlier excitement slowly returning as she contemplated what books to buy.

Her part *was* small, just as Stef had warned. Maddy couldn't have cared less. The feeling of being back in a theatre again, surrounded by actors, director, agents and producers, hit her like a thunderclap. The director, a short, intense, energetic man named Jack, looked her up and down, nodded to himself and asked her to read out a few lines of a script that he handed over in his office, just like that. Maddy stared at him nervously, cleared her throat and began. 'No, no . . . it's an English part. Get rid of the American,' he interrupted her almost immediately. She stopped. She felt the cold hand of fear snake its way up her back. She coughed, cleared her throat again and started afresh. She could feel the sweat prickling under her arms. Stef wasn't there; it was just her and Jack in his small, untidy office. She glanced at him, half-expecting him to yell at her to stop again. But he didn't. He nodded to himself several more times and then grinned. 'Yeah, all right. We were right. You'll do.'

Maddy had almost stopped breathing. 'I will?'

'Yep. You'll do. You've got the part. Your accent's near-perfect. I like your hair, too.' And that was it. She stumbled out of his office, clutching her lines to her chest.

Stef was pleased, but not unduly surprised. 'I told you he liked your tape. It's just a small role, Maddy. You've got a handful of lines but you and Carys Douglas complement each other. Good for you. Well done. See you back here on Monday.'

'I play Phaedra's handmaid,' she told Rafe that night, her voice rising with excitement. 'I've only got a few lines but I'm in almost every scene. Carys Douglas is playing Phaedra. You've seen her. She was in that Dickens adaptation that we watched, remember? The dark-haired woman with—' She stopped mid-sentence. Rafe's attention was elsewhere. Anywhere but on her. 'Am I boring you?' she asked stiffly.

'Huh? No, no . . . I was just drifting off for a bit. I'm tired, that's all. We had a hell of a list today. Two similar cases of arteriovenous malformation and a cranioplasty that pretty much took up the whole afternoon. I told Giddens that he could make the primary incision in the afternoon case but he was surprisingly nervous. I suppose I keep forgetting that he's only a year post-qualifiying. It takes quite a while to—' It was Maddy's turn to drift off. No matter how hard she tried to interest Rafe in things beyond the scope of his own world, the conversation always returned to him. She finished the rest of her dinner in silence – not that Rafe appeared to notice. He had some post-operation notes to complete, he said, getting up from the table as soon as they'd finished. And that was pretty much it.

By the time she climbed the stairs to their bedroom, he was already in bed and asleep, one hand still loosely holding a copy of a memo he'd been reading. She glanced at it. It was a departmental circular. *To All Heads of Surgical Wards.* She sighed. There were times when the worlds in which they moved seemed so diametrically opposed, she wondered if they would ever meet. In the beginning she'd found the differences between them fascinating. Rafe's work and the mystery of it had captivated her. Now . . . she hesitated to say it, even to herself. Boring. It was boring. She was no longer interested in the minutiae of his daily life, much less his operations. A cranioplasty was much the same as an endarterectomy.

There'd been a time when she'd dutifully noted all the different terms, struggling to understand the intricacies of each. Now she couldn't even remember a quarter of them. There seemed to be very little point. Rafe probably wouldn't be able to tell her the name of her character or the play's title. He probably didn't even know when the damn opening night was. She climbed into bed beside him, her chest tight with resentment. It occurred to her just as she closed her eyes that Julia still hadn't rung back. She made a mental note to call her again in the morning. It was most unlike her, she thought as she drifted off to sleep. Most unlike her.

92

JULIA
London, September 2000

Julia's first waking thought each and every morning was: *Today's the day. Today I must tell Aaron.* She should tell him. She *ought* to tell him. But what exactly was she going to say? Soon it would be too late and she'd be forced to keep it. Keep *it*? She had to keep reminding herself of the fact that there was no 'it' – there was a child, hers and Josh's, which, if the passing of time had anything to do with it, was slowly beginning to take shape in her body and mind as *her* child, not his. If that meant bringing the child up as hers and Aaron's, well, that was just the way it would have to be. After all, what was the alternative? She and Aaron had been trying for months and it looked increasingly as if nothing would ever happen. It was a lie, but was it really so terrible?

She plugged in the kettle and made herself a cup of tea. Aaron was in the bathroom; she could hear the familiar sounds of the shower being turned on and off, the tap that dripped unless you tightened it all the way and then she'd have to call him to come and loosen it for her again, the sound of the medicine cabinet door being opened and closed; the small rhythms of their daily life that set the day on its course. Now all that was about to change.

She was sipping her tea when Aaron came into the kitchen. He was surprised to see her still in her dressing gown. 'Jules? You're not even dressed. Aren't you going to work?'

397

She gave a start. 'Y-yes, of course. I was just . . . just thinking.'

''Bout what?' He took a slice of bread from the loaf and stuck it in the toaster.

She looked at him, his blond hair still wet from the shower, freshly shaved . . . A wave of mingled guilt and love washed over her, leaving her trembling in its wake. 'N . . . nothing much,' she said, rinsing her cup. 'Is that the time?' She glanced at the clock on the wall. 'I'd better hurry up.'

'D'you want me to wait for you?'

She shook her head. 'No, you go ahead. I'll . . . I'll just have a shower. I'll phone in and tell Liz I'll be late.'

'You're never late. You sure nothing's wrong?' Aaron was looking at her closely. 'You all right?'

To her horror, she felt her eyes fill with tears. 'Y-yes,' she stammered, 'everything's fine.'

Aaron put down the butter knife and pulled her close. 'C'mere,' he said softly, his hand stroking the nape of her neck. 'Something's wrong. You haven't been yourself for weeks.'

She closed her eyes. His touch was more than she could bear. She could feel her lips forming around the words and all of a sudden they were out. 'Aaron . . . there's something . . . I need to tell you something. Oh, Aaron . . . I'm pregnant.' Her words dropped into the silence between them. His hand froze in its gentle caress. She was overcome with relief and trembling, so much so that she didn't even notice he hadn't said a word, or that his hand stayed where it was. She couldn't think about anything other than the fact that the weeks of agonising and waiting were over. She was going to have this child, come what may. She was having a baby, and that was all that mattered in the world.

93

AARON
London, September 2000

'Sperm abnormalities can be caused by a range of factors, including congenital birth defects, disease, chemical exposure, and lifestyle habits.' Aaron put down the report, aware of a faint but persistent pulse beating somewhere around his left temple. He put up a hand to touch it, massaging the spot where the pain was most persistent. He couldn't quite take it all in. The problem lay with him. *Azoospermia*. An abnormally low sperm count. Had they made a mistake? He desperately wanted to believe so. He'd had the report in his desk drawer for almost three weeks now, waiting for the right time to bring it up. Well, now the time had come – but he wasn't sure how to even think about it, never mind open his mouth. There was only one person he could turn to – Rafe. Rafe would know, surely? He scanned the report one last time, blew out his cheeks and picked up the phone.

Ten minutes later, he managed to get hold of Rafe. 'A mistake? How d'you mean?' Rafe was in a hurry.

'I mean is it possible they've made a mistake?'

'Highly unlikely. Unless the results were mixed up with someone else's – that's always possible. Did your client go privately, d'you know?'

'Er, no, I don't,' Aaron said, his heart sinking.

'Well, whatever the case, I'd advise him to have the results done again, maybe privately, or by a different clinic. If it was a simple case of oligospermia, then it's possible that the results change over time. Sperm counts vary for all sorts of reasons, but it's unlikely that someone who's been diagnosed with azoospermia will suddenly start producing healthy sperm. Get him to take the test again. And then if it *is* wrong and they've made a mistake, he's got grounds for legal action. I presume that's why you're calling?'

'Er, yes . . . yes, yes, it is.'

'Anyway, got to run, old chap. Might see you on Sunday . . . no, blast. Maddy's got one of her bloody rehearsals on . . . maybe the week after?'

'Yeah . . . the week after,' Aaron echoed faintly. He put the phone down, aware of a thin trickle of sweat making its way down his back. A second opinion. He picked up the phone again. Half an hour later, it was all done. He had an appointment for the following morning at a Harley Street clinic, where he would go through the same humiliating procedure all over again. He fought back the beginnings of a migraine headache. He hadn't had one in years, not since school. On the rugby field. He couldn't remember how he'd been involved in the scrum, but he'd gone down, almost suffocating with the weight and bulk of the boys around and over him. He'd panicked, of course, and, ashamed of it, not wanting anyone to see, he'd blacked out. The headache had stayed with him for almost two days. Two days of the most excruciating pain he'd ever felt, until now. In a curious way, it was the same prickling sense of humiliation that had brought it on. Julia . . . what had she done? The thought was enough to make him physically sick. He staggered up from his desk and burst into the corridor. He only just made it to the toilets in time. He spewed everything up – his breakfast, the salad he'd had for lunch, two cups of coffee, everything. He staggered back against the wall, exhausted with the effort of trying to keep everything locked down, including his nauseating shame.

94

DIANA
London, September 2000

She stood up and looked at herself in the full-length mirror. The cream linen dress from Stefanel fell to just below the knee. It was only a year old but it already looked different; it was hanging on her. She pulled in the woven leather belt and buckled it. She'd lost weight; the belt-hole wasn't the one she normally used. She flicked her hair away from her face, picked up her lipstick and applied a second coat. She looked tired. Tired and drawn. It had been a fortnight since her appointment with Geoffrey and she'd told no one apart from Rufus. Not even Harvey. She lay awake beside him in bed, night after night, and the words simply wouldn't come. She didn't even know how to begin. *I've been to see Geoffrey? I'm not well? Darling, I'm dying?* Each struck her as more absurd than the last. Dying? She could hear Harvey's voice. *Of course you're not dying. Don't be ridiculous.* Anger and denial would be his weapons of choice. He could take the most horrific illnesses in his capable hands; but not hers. That much she already knew.

She heard the doorbell and gave a little start. She looked at her watch. It was one o'clock. Lunch was nearly ready; she could smell the roast drifting up three flights of stairs. It made her nauseous. There would only be Niela for lunch today. Maddy had a rehearsal and Rafe was looking after Darcy. He'd promised to drop in later on, if he could get away. At the last minute, just after breakfast that morning, Aaron had rung to say that Julia wasn't feeling well. He didn't sound well either. She wondered what was wrong – something they'd both picked up? Come to think of it, she hadn't seen either of them in a while. She quickly squirted a little perfume behind her ears and a dab on each wrist and hurried downstairs.

'Hello, Niela. Lovely to see you. Do come in.' She stood aside to let her pass. 'Would you like a drink?'

Niela shook her head. 'No, I'm fine, thank you.' She stood in the hallway. 'Is there anything I can help with?' she asked politely.

'No, it's all in hand,' Diana said, closing the door behind her. 'It's only the three of us, I'm afraid. Julia's not feeling well and Maddy's at a rehearsal. Aaron rang this morning to cancel. But you can come downstairs, if you like. I've got a couple of last-minute things to do. Come and sit with me.' The invitation slipped out before she could even think about it. It seemed to surprise Niela as much as it had surprised her. She'd rarely spent any time alone with Niela, she realised, leading the way downstairs. There was always someone else present, someone else to talk to, usually Josh. 'Have you heard from Josh?' she asked. 'Did he arrive safely?'

'Yes. He's in Dar-es-Salaam at the moment. They're heading out to the camp tomorrow.'

'And when's he back? Another couple of months, did he say?'

'Yes, I think so. Sometimes they stay a bit longer.'

She glanced at the girl. There was a wistful note in her voice that she hadn't heard before. It was little wonder; Josh was hardly ever around. She shook herself impatiently. It was the first time she'd ever allowed herself to wonder about the sort of relationship they had . . . what had come over her? Thankfully, before she could think about it any further, she heard the front door opening and Harvey's deep voice. She was relieved. She was unused to the sudden empathy that Niela had unwittingly stirred in her. 'We're down here,' she called out, bending down to peer at the roast. She caught a glimpse of Niela's face as she straightened up. She too seemed relieved. Harvey came down into the kitchen, a broad smile already on his face. He was genuinely fond of Niela, she knew. He was fond of all of them – Maddy, Niela and Julia. For the first time ever, Diana was aware of having held herself back. She didn't *want* to be fond of them. Especially not now. She felt the sharp prick of tears and turned away. Something was happening to her that she couldn't control.

All through lunch, Niela found it hard to concentrate. Her mind kept slipping, going back to what she'd seen from the top of the bus. Josh and Julia. Julia and Josh. Julia wasn't well; what did that mean? She listened with half an ear to Diana and Harvey talking, occasionally taking part. It was the first time she'd been alone with them, she realised. There was always someone else present; usually Josh . . . Her mind drifted back again. Why would they have needed to meet – and why in a café, why not here, at Diana's, or at home? She was aware of a great build-up of tension in her throat, an overflow of emotion that she couldn't contain. That was the trouble with living with things that couldn't be said. There was always a well of untapped sadness that, once released, was impossible to contain. The tears in her throat weren't just to do with Josh and Julia, whatever had happened between them. The tears were for everyone – her parents, her brothers, Christian . . . herself. For everything that had happened to her, but most especially for the deep pool of silence that surrounded her life. Anna was right: it was time to bring these things into the open, let everything be said. All of a sudden, the thought of living another day in the shadow of the truth was more than she could bear. She got up clumsily, avoiding Diana's concerned look. She had to be alone, to look her own image in the face. She fled from the room before anything more could be said.

'Can I help with the washing-up?' Niela's soft voice broke into her thoughts.

Diana turned round. 'Oh, no, there's no need. There's a dishwasher,' she said, pointing to the machine. 'But you can help me put the first load away,' she added, touched by the offer. After her abrupt disappearance from the kitchen at lunch, the girl had been practically silent. *What the hell's going on?* Diana asked herself. There was a sadness in Niela's eyes that worried her, but the girl's quiet manner made it almost impossible to ask.

'Where do these go?' Niela picked up two wine glasses by the stem.

'Up there. That's it . . . second shelf. And those ones go over there . . . yes, that one.' They worked together in silence for a few minutes, punctuated by Niela's questioning glance as she held up a bowl or a dish. Harvey had put some music on – it drifted gently down the stairwell and into the kitchen. Something soothing – Stravinsky; it added to the unexpected calm whilst they worked. 'Julia's not well again, did I mention it?' Diana said suddenly. 'I just wondered . . . perhaps you've heard something?' She glanced at Niela. She was holding one of Diana's heavy glass bowls. There was a sudden intake of breath and then the bowl slipped. It hit the ground with a deafening crack, shattering immediately and sending shards of glass flying everywhere.

Niela gave a startled cry and looked at the ground in horror. 'Oh, Diana . . . I'm so sorry, I'm so sorry! I don't know how it happened . . . it just slipped. I'm so sorry!'

'Don't worry about it,' Diana said quickly. 'Don't move. I'll get the dustpan. Stay right where you are.' She hurried to the pantry to fetch the dustpan and brush.

'Everything all right down there?' she heard Harvey call from the top of the stairs.

'Fine,' she shouted back. 'We just dropped something. Nothing to worry about.'

'Diana, I'm so sorry. I'll get you another one,' Niela stammered, bending down to help her pick up the bigger pieces. 'I don't know what happened . . . it . . . it just slipped.'

'Don't be silly, it's nothing, Niela. It's a bowl, that's all. Plenty more where those came from. Be careful . . . here, just let me sweep this bit up.' She quickly swept the floor around them until all the glass had been carefully disposed of. 'Why don't I make us both a cup of tea?' she heard herself saying. 'A nice, strong cup of tea. Don't worry about the silly bowl, Niela. Please.'

Niela nodded slowly, straightening up. Her eyes were glassy with tears, Diana noticed, somewhat alarmed. She herself felt dangerously close; the last thing she wanted was for Niela to see her own. She turned away and busied herself with the kettle.

Ten minutes later, they were seated at the table. Diana took a sip of her tea, her mind racing. She could tell that the dropped bowl had something to do with her question, and what it implied, but she had no idea how to bring it up again. She realised, not for the first time, that she knew next to nothing about the women who'd married her sons. Was Julia pregnant? Ironic that she would hear about it from Niela, if she were, but that didn't explain why Niela was so upset. She took another sip of tea.

'Julia's pregnant.' The words dropped from Niela's lips straight into the silence between them, relieving her of the burden.

Diana's face grew immediately warm. 'Why . . . that's . . . that's good news, isn't it?' Niela's face was partially turned away from hers. It was almost five in the afternoon and the late summer shadows were long on the ground. She could hear the faint chatter of birds in the garden outside. Just visible from the kitchen were the waxy deep cerise and orange dahlias that the gardener had planted earlier in the summer; they were in full, splendid bloom. She looked out over the garden. Suddenly Niela spoke. Her voice was barely audible, so that Diana thought at first she'd misheard. 'What?' she asked, unable to comprehend what Niela had just said. 'What are you talking about?'

'It's Josh's,' Niela repeated, bringing her hands up from her lap and placing them palms down on the table.

'Josh's? Whatever do you mean?'

Niela kept her gaze lowered. She examined her fingers one by one, turning them over slowly. 'He and Julia . . .' Her voice faltered. She lifted her head and brought her face round to Diana's. There was an expression in it that Diana had never before seen – a kind of relief mixed in with the pain. Diana's own eyes widened. Something more was about to be said. 'I think they slept together,' she said simply, lifting her shoulders. 'I think I know when.'

'Oh, Niela . . . no. You're imagining it, surely?' Distress rose in her, sharp and swift.

'I'm not imagining it,' she said quietly. 'I'm not stupid. I know I don't say very much, but that doesn't mean I don't see what's going on.'

'But . . . but have you asked Josh?'

Niela shook her head. 'I tried to, before he left, but he just got angry. I know it sounds absurd. Silly, even. But I *know*. I just know.'

'How? How can you tell?'

Niela brought her hands up to her face. 'I know what living with a secret is like. I've been living with one for the past four years and I know what it does to me. I see it in Josh. I can see what he's going through.'

'What secret are you talking about? What sort of secret?' Diana heard her own voice as if from far away.

Niela took a deep breath. 'I'm married, Diana.' She lifted her head and looked straight at her.

Diana frowned. 'Of course you're married. You and Josh . . .'

Niela shook her head slowly from side to side. 'No, not Josh. I was married before. I still *am* married. Legally. I never got divorced.'

Diana stared at Niela, unable to think of a single thing to say. She'd known all along that there was something different about this girl that Josh had brought so suddenly and unexpectedly into their home. She felt herself gripped by an unspecified panic. She wanted to continue the conversation, and in a way she'd never before experienced, she wanted to unburden herself. 'What do you mean, you're still legally married?'

'An arranged marriage,' Niela said quietly. 'To a relative of my father's. We were married in Vienna, eight years ago. I never got divorced. I just ran away.'

Diana stared at her. 'H . . . how did you marry Josh?' she asked finally, though she knew full well the answer.

Niela shrugged. 'I said nothing. No one asked me for anything, other than my passport. Josh arranged it all.'

Diana nodded. She knew just how easy it was; she'd taken on countless similar cases, years ago, when she was starting out. She, more than anyone, knew just how easy it was to slip between the pages of the law. 'Oh, Niela,' she said slowly. 'But why didn't you just say? We could have done something . . . *I* could have done something.'

Niela looked down at her hands. She shook her head. 'I . . . I don't know. I wanted to . . . in the beginning. But it never seemed to be the right time and then everything happened so fast. I . . . I didn't want Josh to think that I wasn't . . . you know, a *good* person, someone you could trust. And then I met all of you and I just didn't think it was the sort of thing I could ever say. By that time we were married and there didn't seem to be any point in bringing it up. I'd become another person, someone else. Someone who was married to Josh, not . . .' She stopped, swallowing painfully. 'Not to Hamid. Hamid Osman. That was his name. I ran away from him about a month after we were married. I was so afraid they would track me down and take me back. He took me to live with him and his sister in Munich.' She wiped her cheek with the back of her hand. 'I hated her. I hated them both. He caught me talking to someone, a bank clerk . . . I got a beating for it and his sister practically kept me under lock and key. I escaped one afternoon when someone came to read the meter. I just ran away. I came to London because I didn't know anyone here and no one knew me. I'm sorry, Diana. I just couldn't keep it in any longer.'

Something inside Diana shifted at the sound of Niela's words. She put a hand to her mouth. 'You poor girl,' she said, her voice cracking. 'You poor, poor girl.' She slid her hand across the table and touched Niela's forearm. 'There's something I need to tell you, Niela. I know this is going to sound strange – after all, why should I tell you? I've never told anyone else. But I have to. It's time *I* told the truth. *I* can't go on like this any longer, either.'

Diana spoke for almost two hours straight. Niela didn't interrupt her, not once. She didn't dare. At first Diana's voice was hesitant; she seemed to be groping for words. Niela watched her in astonishment. Diana? Lost for words? It didn't seem possible. But as she spoke, slowly unburdening herself of the weight she'd been carrying around for most of her life, her voice grew stronger. Harvey poked his head round the door, saw that they were deep in conversation and left with Rafe and Darcy in tow. Diana seemed not to have noticed. It was nearly seven by the time she stopped. 'H . . . how much of this does Josh know?' she asked quietly.

Niela was still too stunned by what she'd heard to speak. She shook her head slowly. 'Not much, I don't think. Hardly any of it. I . . . he knows about Rufus.'

'Rufus?' Diana's eyes closed with pain. 'How?'

'He saw you once. With him. He was around nine or ten,' Niela said slowly. 'He was hiding in the attic and he saw you. I don't know if he thinks it was just that once . . . he wouldn't say.'

Diana swallowed painfully. She took a large gulp of wine. 'He saw us. Christ. What a mess. What a fucking mess.'

Niela winced. It was so unlike Diana to swear. She looked at her sitting opposite, her feet tucked underneath her, her hands wrapped tightly around her glass as if she were holding on to it for dear life. Diana had lost weight, she realised suddenly. Her face, normally so perfectly made-up and practically wrinkle-free, suddenly looked aged and drawn. 'This . . . this thing with Rufus. Do . . . do you know why it happened? Why you can't break free?' Niela asked after a moment, wondering if it was a question too far.

'Why?' Diana gave a small start. She shook her head and took in a deep breath. 'I couldn't tell you. It was always that way,' she said slowly. 'Always. I can't even tell you when it began. I just know that I've always loved him and in some way that I can't even begin to explain, I always will. Don't misunderstand me . . . I do love Harvey. I married him because I loved him, not because I couldn't have Rufus. I didn't *want* Rufus. He's . . . there's something *damaged* about Rufus and I don't know why. He and Harvey come from exactly the same place. They've had the same upbringing, the same love and care, and let me tell you, there was no one as caring as their mother. If it hadn't been for Dot, I don't know what would have happened to me.' She stopped and took another sip. She looked at Niela and her face softened suddenly. 'Isn't it strange? I've spent my whole life trying to be perfect at everything, and in the end, I've failed with the one thing I'm most proud of . . . my sons. I've failed at being a wife and a mother. Taking care of my family. And you . . . by the sound of it, a family's exactly what you've lost. And yet I'll bet you anything it's the thing you'll do well. Brilliantly, in fact. I know you will.'

Niela shook her head slowly. She could feel the tears beginning to slide down her cheeks. 'It's not up to me. It's Josh's decision too, and he's already made one.'

'Can you forgive him?'

Niela shook her head again. 'I don't know. I don't know anything any more,' she said slowly. 'I don't even know what to think.'

'Give it time,' Diana said, draining the rest of her glass. 'Don't make a decision now. Let him come back, settle in . . . and then the two of you should talk. *I* need to talk to Josh. I need to speak to each of my sons before it's too late.' She stood up abruptly. 'I'll get you some sheets and a duvet,' she said, the briskness that Niela was used to back in her voice and manner. 'You can sleep in Josh's room. It's far too late for you to be traipsing across London. Can you call in late to work tomorrow?'

Niela nodded, relieved. Her head was spinning, and not just because of what she'd heard. There were so many emotions running through her – relief, anger, fear, sadness. Some distant memory of a longing came back to her, and it took her a while to place it. It was Ayanna, and the closeness between her cousin and her aunt. She'd never experienced that kind of closeness between a mother and a daughter before. The gulf between her own mother and the way her life had turned out was too wide and vast to be easily traversed . . . and now it was too late. When she thought of Saira, it was anger she felt, not love or longing. Saira had abandoned her to the sort of fate she'd been brought up to believe she would avoid. Diana was hardly the sort of mother she'd have chosen, either to have, or to aspire to be, but she'd been touched beyond belief by Diana's confession. She followed her out of the room and up the stairs to what had once been Josh's childhood room. Diana quickly and expertly made up the bed. Then she turned to Niela and paused, a small, wistful smile flickering across her face. 'Good night, Niela. Try to sleep. I know this must be hard for you . . . it's hard for all of us. But things will work out, you'll see. You have to have . . . faith. Yes, that's it. Faith. I think we could all do with a little faith.' And before Niela could say another word, she left the room, closing the door behind her. Niela heard her footsteps fall away. She lay in the dark, listening to the faint creaking and settling of the house as it slipped into the small hours of the morning.

Harvey was fast asleep; she crept into the bedroom, taking off her clothes and jewellery with great care. She needn't have bothered. Nothing would wake him. He slept the sleep of the innocent, she thought to herself wistfully; always had. In those first few dreadful months after it had happened, she'd been unable to sleep. She'd lain beside him, night after night, unable to give even the tiniest vent to the double-headed dragon of grief and fear that coursed through her veins in the same way that dread now choked up her throat. It wasn't just the thought of what was happening silently inside her that clogged her mind and made her thoughts heavy with what couldn't be said – it was everything else. The mess she'd made of everything. She who had once had everything so tightly in place now felt things slipping away from her uncontrollably. Even her own body had rebelled against her. She lay stiffly beside him, already feeling lighter, the thoughts and half-fancies coming dangerously close. In her half-dream state, she thought she could hear the beating of mechanical wings, coming to carry her off. She turned over on to her side, pressing her face into the pillow, ashamed of the temporary feeling of sweet relief as she imagined giving herself up to some other agency and slipping away unseen. Don't be ridiculous, she admonished herself, sliding out a foot to touch Harvey. That was all she needed – a touch. The solid reassurance of his flesh against hers. In the dark, her eyes adjusted to the familiar shapes of things around her. The antique dressing table that stood by the open window; the heavy damask drapes and the lighter, floating fabric that billowed gently to and fro. Harvey liked to sleep with the windows open. She did too, although lately she'd felt a kind of fear emanating from the darkness beyond. Silly. Ridiculous. She was being fanciful; the sort of thing her mother, when she had a mind to, warned her against.

Her mind drifted off on its own independent course. She was too tired to stop it. For the first time in years, she gave in, allowed it to roam. Mohammed. Khadija . . . What had happened to them? She could no longer remember the name of the village where Rufus said they were from. Djemmah? Djemba? No, Djemmorah. Yes, that was it. A tiny village high up in the slopes of the Atlas Mountains. She still remembered the tremor of fear that had run through her when Josh told her he'd been assigned to work on a camp in Algeria. She'd stared at him, her heartbeat suddenly accelerating. 'Algeria?' she'd murmured, turning away so that he wouldn't see the heat rising fast in her cheeks. 'Good God, darling . . . what makes you want to go there?' *Please don't say it.* She'd waited, every nerve ending in her body alive to the sound of the name Djemmorah. But of course he didn't and of course he hadn't . . . he'd never been near the place, as far as she could tell. Smara, close to the border on the opposite side of the country, would be as close as he'd ever get. She didn't know how much Rufus had shelled out for everyone's silence – he wouldn't say. Substantial enough, no doubt. She'd never asked where he got the money from. The Keelers were wealthy, but not *that* wealthy. How much did a child cost? She felt the knife-edge of guilt twist a little deeper in her gut. She thought of Josh and of Julia. And of the child about to come. She saw in Josh's dark, glowering face the bewildered child, casting about in his unhappiness, looking for some mischief or naughtiness for which he would make someone pay. He'd been making her pay for thirty years with his choices and his absences and the tug-of-war love between them that refused to rest. Now it was someone else's turn – Julia? Aaron? Niela? Who would pay the ultimate price for what she'd done? She stifled a sob. What a mess. What an unholy, godforsaken, mangled, tangled-up mess.

95

JOSH
Dar-es-Salaam, October 2000

Rain leaned in from the horizon, falling in silent vertical sheets, moving stealthily over the heaving sea. Out there, barely a few hundred yards away from the hotel, waves rose and fell soundlessly. Josh moved about the room gathering his things, stowing them into the khaki duffel bag that he'd come with, picking up the last remnants of his presence. In an hour or so the driver would come for him and take him to the airport. In a few hours, he'd be gone, back to where he'd come from. He'd come to Tanzania to sort out someone else's mistakes – a small project in Buguruni, one of the capital city's many slums – and now he was about to fly back and try to sort out his own. He had no idea what to do. In the three months since he'd been gone, he'd spoken to Niela only a handful of times, short, tense conversations in which nothing of any importance was said. Now it was time to go home and face the music. He was dreading it. He continued to stuff his belongings into his bag with a violence that betrayed him. It was his own emotions he was longing to cut off, to choke before they choked him.

A short, sharp horn-blast announced the driver's arrival. He took one last look around, picked up his bag and slung it over his shoulder. He closed the door behind him and stepped into the heat. Within minutes they were away. He watched the city slip past, a cornucopia of corrugated tin roofs, skyscrapers and mouldy cement, interspersed with flashes of brilliant, riotous bougainvillea, spilling out over crumbling walls and fences along the route. It took them less than thirty minutes to reach the airport. He checked in, watched his bag disappear on the thick black tongue of the luggage belt and then made his way upstairs. He had a whisky in the bar, felt it slide hot and silky down his throat, momentarily calming him, and then made his way on to the plane. It was a ten-hour flight back to London. Somewhere along the journey, he hoped, an answer of sorts would come to him. Or perhaps not.

96

DIANA
London, October 2000

Harvey's car was in the driveway when she pulled up that evening. She parked her little sports car neatly next to his, unsure whether to be relieved or not. It had been a long day in chambers, her mind barely there, listening with a fraction of her usual concentration to the voices of those around her. Whilst everyone else went on talking, she withdrew into herself, her mind focused only on how she was going to tell Harvey – what words she would use, and, perhaps more importantly, where and when she would stop. What did he need to know? What did she need to tell him and what could she leave out? There was only one person who needed to know absolutely everything, and that was Josh. What happened afterwards was up to him, not her. But Harvey? What were the limits of his understanding? Lately she'd been unable to control her thoughts or stop them dead in their dangerous tracks – one wrong move or a tender word and things might start tumbling out that she couldn't afford.

She picked up her bag from the passenger seat and opened the door. She noticed, not for the first time, that little things like getting out of the car or picking up her bag single-handedly were becoming more difficult. All of a sudden, it seemed, she was no longer in proper control of her body – it deserted her at the oddest, weakest moments. She couldn't trust it to obey her commands. She stood for a moment, leaning against the car, breathing heavily. She hadn't expected this – the sudden and frightening decline of her strength. Nor was it constant or continuous. She would have a moment's weakness, a slight shortness of breath, and then things would swing themselves back to normal and all was exactly as before. It made the moments when the weakness took hold of her that much harder to accept. She took another deep breath, steadied herself and then walked up the path to the house. She slid the key into the lock and pushed open the door. It took her a moment to realise that Harvey was standing there in the hallway, a look of agitation on his normally placid, calm face. A tremor of fear ran through her. 'Darling,' she began, putting her bag down and turning to him. 'You're home early.'

'I've been here since one. I cancelled my list. Diana . . . why didn't you tell me?'

She turned to him slowly, feeling the blood slowly draining away from her limbs and face. How did he know? 'I . . . I . . . wanted to . . .' she began, putting out a hand to support herself against the sideboard. Her knees felt weak. 'I . . . I should have, I know, I should have told you. H . . . how did you hear?'

'I bumped into Geoffrey at the Wellington this afternoon. No, he didn't give me the details . . . What is it, Diana? What's wrong? *Tell* me.'

'Harvey . . .' She stopped. She couldn't bring herself to say it. Now that the moment had come, she couldn't speak.

He grasped her wrist, pulling her towards him. 'Come here. I don't know why I didn't notice . . . so stupid of me . . . I could see something wasn't right. Diana . . . what is it? Just tell me. For God's sake, *tell* me.'

*

She had only seen him cry once before, twenty years earlier, in the small hours of the morning. It was the first time a patient had died on the operating table, he told her eventually, his voice hoarse with tears. A young girl; a brain tumour. She'd bled uncontrollably to death in front of them and there wasn't a damn thing any of them could do. She'd held him close to her for the remainder of the night, feeling the tension slowly slip out of his large, supremely capable body. But by morning, he was back to normal. That had been the only time. Until now. He cried silently, his powerful shoulders jerking a little as he struggled to catch his breath. She was the dry-eyed, strong and compassionate one. She patted his hand as she'd done to her children, once. There were no tears lurking inside her, not yet at any rate.

He got up from the kitchen table, wiping the tears from his face with the back of his hand. It wasn't a gesture she'd ever seen him make. She'd always known Harvey loved her, without question or reservation; it had been the touchstone of their life together. For him there'd been no one else; there never would be. She could no more understand it than she dared to bring herself to question it. *This is it, then*, she thought to herself as she finished speaking, her throat suddenly painfully constricted. *This is it. There, I've told him.* A single sentence breaking itself out of the confusion: Harvey knows. There was no turning back, now. Harvey knows. She lifted her gaze to meet his. Curiously, now that it was out, she was no longer afraid.

97

RAFE/MADDY
London October 2000

Rafe stood back to let his registrar close up the wound, keeping a watchful eye on him. The registrar was young and gifted but still unsure of himself, much as Rafe himself had been at the beginning. Through his green mask he could hear the young man's breathing, nice and steady, as he positioned the sucker, draining away the excess fluid and blood. He looked up once – everything OK? Rafe nodded, giving him permission to make the final stitches, then he stepped away and left the team to it, his clogs squeaking on the polished floor. The theatre doors swung shut behind him. He glanced at his watch. It was almost noon. One more case and then he was done for the weekend. He pushed open the doors to the second theatre impatiently. The patient was a young girl with a short history of gradually diminishing sight. The test results were in – a tumour behind the rear ventricle, pressing down on the ocular muscle. It was a delicate operation of the sort he rather enjoyed. He slipped on his mask and gloves and joined the team at the table. Everything was ready and waiting for him. The back of the patient's head had been expertly opened up and he was able to look inside without obstruction. The brain lay exposed before him with all the fragile, lovely beauty of a flower. In that moment, instead of concentrating on his incision and planning his next moves, he thought of Maddy and the soft, sensual entrance into her body. Fortunately, he came to his senses immediately, his whole being flooded with a mixture of desire and embarrassment. He spent the next thirty minutes carefully incising the tumour, taking care not to disturb any of the surrounding tissue. Finally, it was done. He left the assisting surgeon to finish the job and made his way back towards the doors again. He shrugged off his robe and mask and dropped them in the incinerator chute. He made his way to the basement garage, but his mind kept drifting back to Maddy. The image that had come to him disturbed him; it had been so long since he and Maddy had made love. Months, as a matter of fact. Something was going on but he couldn't work out what. She'd changed. She'd lost weight, he realised. That morning, as he left for work and she got ready for her final rehearsal, he'd noticed her crossing the floor to pick up her dressing gown. He'd looked up, about to tell her something – he could no longer recall what – but the sight of her ribs had stopped him. They were showing in a way he'd never noticed before, all the way round her back. He'd looked at her closely but hadn't said anything. Perhaps she was on a diet? He tried to recall what they'd both eaten at dinner . . . pasta with chicken, something like that. But she'd had a second helping, he remembered. And he'd been the one to decline the cheese, not her. A glass of wine or two . . . that was no diet that he'd ever heard of. It had been a while since she'd complained about being fat, too. A cold feeling of unease began to settle all over him. It was as if he knew what was coming, but couldn't see it.

She stared at him as if she couldn't believe what he'd just said. 'Too *thin?*' she echoed. 'Me?'

He lifted his shoulders. 'Yes . . . I don't know, you're much thinner than you used to be. I saw your ribs this morning and . . .' His voice trailed off. An ugly blush had spread itself across her face and neck. He began to wish he hadn't brought it up.

'No, I'm not. I'm exactly the same weight as I've always been. It's the rehearsals, that's all. I don't always have time to eat lunch.' She turned away from him, busying herself with the dishes.

He remained where he was, unsure of himself; should he go on, press the point? There was tension in the way she held herself at the sink, he saw. He'd touched on something raw. But what? He tried again, regretting it as soon as he opened his mouth. 'But, Maddy . . .'

'Drop it, Rafe.' Her voice was a low, tight command.

'But—'

'Rafe.' Maddy turned round. There were two brilliant red spots of anger in her cheeks and her eyes were glassy with tears. She was trembling ever so slightly. She untied the apron and laid it carefully on the counter top. 'Just *drop* it, will you?' she hissed.

'Maddy—'

But she was gone. She walked out of the room, holding herself very tense and still. He heard her climb the stairs and shut the bedroom door. He stood in the middle of the kitchen feeling like a prize idiot, wondering what he'd done wrong and why she'd reacted like that. What was going on? What had he failed to spot? He was a doctor and yet he could do nothing to help her. How could he when he had no idea what was wrong?

Again and again. She retched in almost total silence, removing the last traces of the conversation from her body and mind. She reached up for the handle and tugged downwards, watching the angry swirl with relief. It was gone. All gone. She stood up, feeling slightly dizzy. She put a hand under her jumper and touched her skin . . . she could feel her ribs standing hard and proud underneath her fingertips. Was it true? Had she really lost so much weight? She lifted her jumper up all the way and turned to face the mirror. Her heart was thumping. No, no . . . no change at all. She saw herself as she'd always done. White, alabaster skin, freckled here and there, dimpled at the belly button, the same gross swelling of her abdomen when she turned sideways . . . he was completely wrong. She was *fat*, not *thin*. What the hell was wrong with him? She tugged her jumper back down again. She picked up her toothbrush and began brushing her teeth. Soon the bitter taste of bile was replaced by a pleasingly sweet peppermint. She rinsed her mouth once more, smoothed down her hair and opened the door. The flat was quiet. Fortunately their muted, angry exchange in the kitchen hadn't woken Darcy up. She drew in a deep breath, squared her shoulders and walked downstairs to the living room.

He looked up as she entered. The look of perplexed worry in his face sliced through her like a knife. She walked over to the couch and sat down beside him. She took one of his hands in hers, turning it over slowly. When she first met him, it was his hands that had fascinated her most. She couldn't stop staring at them – less for their physical qualities than for what she imagined their capabilities to be. 'You save people's lives with these,' she'd said to him on more than one occasion, lifting up one of his hands to her cheek. He'd laughed, embarrassed, but it was true. She was in awe of what his hands could do. Now she traced the raised map of tendons, running her fingers in between his own, lacing his hand tightly to hers. She felt in his answering grip his relief. She turned her head and kissed him. 'I'm sorry,' she murmured, pressing herself into him. 'I'm sorry.'

'For what?' He held her tightly.

'Everything. For snapping at you. For not taking better care of Darcy. For not being nicer to Diana . . . for everything.'

'Is . . . is everything all right, Mads?' Rafe used his nickname for her.

'Of course it is. It's just—'

But whatever she was about to say was cut short by the shrill ringing of the phone. Rafe stretched out one hand to pick it up but the other stayed where it was, holding her. She leaned into him gratefully. 'Hello?' He listened to whoever was on the other end for a few minutes. She felt his body stiffen. 'I'll be right there.'

'Who is it?' she asked, looking up into his face. There was a terrible confusion in it, something she'd never seen in him. 'Who is it?' she repeated, suddenly afraid. Darcy was upstairs. She was safe. Who else was there to worry about?

'It's Harvey. Dad. I . . . I've got to go over. Now.' His words came out in short, sharp bursts, as though he were out of breath.

'What's the matter?' Maddy reached out a hand to stop him, but he'd already disengaged himself and was practically running towards the door.

'It's Diana. Something's happened. I'll . . . I'll call you later,' he called over his shoulder, grabbing his jacket. The front door slammed behind him and he was gone. She leaned back against the cushions, perplexed. Something wrong with Diana? What on earth could be wrong with *her*? She passed a hand over her lips, feeling their rough, papery texture against her fingertips. She knew exactly why they were so dry. That was another one of the little side effects of her 'problem' – with the opening night of *Phaedra* only two days away, she'd been feeling even more panicked than usual . . . silly, of course. She had a grand total of eight lines and she'd more or less memorised everyone else's parts. She knew the play inside out, back to front and front to back. She'd read every interpretation going; studied the critics' responses to other, older adaptations . . . she'd fine-tuned her eight lines until they sang. In other words, it was all going to be fine. *She* would be fine. She had tickets for everyone; she'd organised a babysitter for Darcy and there were several bottles of champagne in the fridge for herself and Rafe to celebrate when it was all over. She felt a ripple of excitement rush through her at the thought of the rest of the family seeing her up there on the stage, in some capacity other than the one they knew – Rafe's wife, Darcy's mother, somebody's sister-in-law. For the first time since she'd come to London, she would be herself, who she really was. An actress. Someone with a profession and a talent worth showing. Herself, in other words. *As she really was and as she'd like to be seen.* She buried her face in her hands, suddenly overwhelmed with gratitude and relief. From now on, things would be different. There'd be no need to panic, no need to be afraid or to find herself out of her depth. She would be able to hold her head up amongst them all, yes, even Diana. More than anything, it was Diana's respect she craved. She no longer cared whether Diana liked her or not. That, she realised, was out of her hands and always would be. But respect was another issue altogether. That she could control. Signing up with Stef, getting an audition and actually landing the part were the first, tentative steps towards regaining some control. If she could do that, there was no telling what else she could do. She looked at her hands. They too were dry, the skin paper-thin. It was time to stop that other stuff before it was too late.

98

AARON
London, October 2000

Aaron stared at the young doctor who'd come in to deliver the news. Although he understood what it was he'd said, the lawyer in him fought back. 'So, what you're saying is . . . anything's possible. How is *that* possible?'

The doctor was patronisingly patient. 'Medicine's not an exact science, contrary to popular belief, Mr Keeler. Now, I know this may be hard to grasp, but in your case, we simply don't know. Yes, you've been diagnosed with azoospermia – low sperm count, that is – but, just to complicate matters further, we've also detected spermatozoa that are lethargic but not always consistently so. In other words, yes, you are experiencing difficulty fertilising an egg, but there's an outside chance that you may succeed in doing so one day, and the bottom line is, we've no idea how or why.'

Aaron shook his head slowly. He was aware of his heart lifting in relief. So it *was* possible. The child *was* his – of course it was. Who else's would it be? He picked up the envelope that contained the report and slid it into his briefcase.

Ten minutes later, the bill settled and paid, he was out on Harley Street, walking towards Great Portland Street. His heart slowed to its normal pace; his thoughts, which, for the past few weeks had been so jumbled, so confused, slowly began to right themselves. He wouldn't speak of it again, he knew, now that it was over. He'd sought a second opinion, just as Rafe had suggested, and the result was what he wanted, wasn't it? The child was his. His and Julia's. And yet . . . the tiniest, most fleeting doubt remained. For all his relief and outward assurance, there was a part of him that didn't believe it. He knew himself well enough; he knew he would push the doubt deep down into himself, somewhere so buried he would not be able to get at it. But it would be there, waiting to unsettle him whenever the opportunity arose. He would have to live with it, just as he'd lived with the questions that had tormented him for the past few weeks. He had no other choice, no alternative. He could no more force the truth out of Julia than he could face it, whatever it turned out to be. The medical uncertainty that had emerged over the past few hours had presented him with a stark choice: accept the version of events that was on offer – or not. Accept that she was telling the truth – the child was his. Or not. It wasn't the sort of choice he'd ever dreamed he would have to make.

He walked into his office and sat down at his desk. His phone was beeping furiously; there were a dozen messages, three from Julia, two from Rafe, one from Harvey. He listened to the last, a bolt of fear spreading through him as his father's disembodied voice faded away. He put down the receiver, all thoughts of Julia, the baby, the report, the truth, simply vanishing into thin air. Diana. Diana was ill. He stood up, grabbed the jacket he'd just placed on the back of his chair and fled from the room.

99

JOSH
London, October 2000

Niela wasn't home. He pushed open the front door impatiently; it was just after eight o'clock in the morning. He went into the bedroom – her coat was gone. He must have just missed her. He tossed his duffel bag on to the bed, hurriedly stripped off his clothes and walked into the shower. He felt as though he'd been travelling for weeks. He stood under the blast of hot water, feeling the tiredness and dislocation of stepping on to a plane in the heat of Africa one moment and then off it into the cool damp of England the next sloughing off him. He stayed under for longer than was necessary; by the time he finally emerged out of the steam and fug, the skin on his fingers was wrinkled. He towel-dried his hair and pulled on clean clothes. The living room was quiet; he sat down with a mug of coffee, enjoying the soft light and the scent of coolness. He glanced at the phone; he ought to give Diana a ring. He hadn't spoken to her since he'd left.

A few minutes later he put down the phone, a strange hackle of fear rising somewhere in him. Diana was not in chambers. She hadn't been in all week. She wasn't well, her PA told him. She wasn't sure what was wrong but she'd only been in sporadically in the past couple of weeks. He hung up the phone and brought the receiver to his lips for a few moments before dialling. Diana answered on the third ring. As soon as he heard her voice, he knew something was wrong.

'What's the matter?' he asked.

'Josh.' Diana's voice was weak with relief. 'You're back. When did you get back?'

'This morning. What's the matter? I rang chambers – they said you're ill.'

'It's nothing,' she began, brushing aside his concern, as always.

'It's not nothing,' Josh interrupted her quickly. 'I can hear it in your voice. What is it?'

'Oh, Josh.'

To his horror, he realised Diana was crying. He couldn't recall the last time he'd heard her cry. He stood up, agitated. 'I'm coming over,' he said, already walking towards the door. He picked up his lightweight jacket on the way. 'I'll see you in half an hour.' He put down the phone before she could say another word.

His first reaction was one of relief. Diana didn't *look* terribly ill. She looked more or less the same; a little thinner, perhaps, but he was used to her dropping a few pounds every now and then in response to a dress she wanted to buy or some photograph she'd seen of herself in which she always seemed to claim she was actually much thinner. She was sitting on the chesterfield in the upstairs living room when he arrived, wrapped in a light cashmere blanket although it wasn't cold. Her face was drawn, he noticed, as he bent to kiss her. There was a chemical smell to her that he'd never noticed before – it mingled with the perfume she always wore; his relief began to evaporate.

'Mother,' he said, straightening up. 'What's the matter? What's going on?'

Diana patted the space next to her. She took one of her hands in his, turning it over, examining the dark, tanned skin in silence for a few moments. He felt a tightening in his gut, as if someone had literally turned a screw. 'Josh,' she said slowly, 'I'm so glad you're here.' She looked up at him. She was holding herself in. They sat for a moment like that, Josh all emotion, Diana calmer now. 'I wish I knew how to say this better, darling,' she said, lifting her hands from his and bringing them up to her own face.

'Say what? What is it?'

'I'm not well, Josh. It's . . . well, there's no other way of saying it. It's cancer. It's pretty far advanced, I'm afraid.'

The words slid into him like a knife. He'd been holding his breath, he realised. Cancer. He wanted to put up a hand as if to ward the word off but Diana grabbed it, holding on to it tightly. 'Cancer?' The word spun out of control.

She nodded. 'Breast cancer. I found out about a month ago, just after you left. I couldn't tell you over the phone, especially not when you're so far away.'

'What's the prognosis?' He slipped easily into the medical terminology that had been theirs around the dinner table.

She let go of his hand. 'It's not great,' she said, turning her own hands over, examining her fingernails.

'Just tell me.'

She took a deep breath. 'It's unusually aggressive. It's spreading fast, and despite what everyone says, they're not optimistic.'

'What about Dad? What does he say?'

She spread her hands. 'You know your father. He doesn't give up easily. But he's looking at it like a surgeon would.'

'What d'you mean?'

'Cut it out, clear everything in its path . . . that's the way they're trained to think. Geoffrey – you remember him . . . Dr Laing? – he thinks it's more complicated. Not just a matter of surgery. The statistics are pretty low . . . less than ten per cent, he says.'

'Just numbers,' Josh said automatically. 'Didn't you always tell us that?'

Diana smiled. 'I did. But this time . . . I don't know, Josh. I just don't know.'

'You'll get through this, Mother. Of course you will. You'll have the best treatment available . . . Dad'll see to that. You'll get through it.'

'I wish I had your confidence, darling,' Diana said, looking straight at him. 'But I don't. And it's not that I don't think everyone won't move heaven and earth on my behalf – it's not that at all. There's something else. I . . . I've been speaking to Niela this past month . . . no, let me finish. She's been a great comfort to me, I can't tell you. Took me completely by surprise. And it's because of something she said that I feel I have to talk to you before I talk to anyone else. I haven't told your brothers yet. Only Dad knows. And Uncle Rufus.'

Slowly, as he watched, Diana's face changed. Her eyes, dark like his own, were difficult to meet. The small, taut fold of skin beneath each eye fell away as her face was drawn back over her high cheekbones. It was a feature of hers that he'd known since childhood. Her face tightened, taking on a new urgency. Her mouth opened; words came tumbling out. He felt himself shrinking as the true meaning of what she was telling him began to dawn on him. His whole body felt as though it were turning itself inside out. He struggled to focus on her words. *Khadija. Mohammed. Djemmorah.* None of it made any sense. His mouth opened a moment in unease but Diana took no notice. She was spinning a thread of a story he'd known all along. He didn't belong. *That* wasn't the surprise. What he couldn't have guessed at was the lengths to which she had gone.

100

DIANA
Mougins, June 1969

She lay down just as Rufus had instructed her. Her stomach was churning with fear and the brandy he'd forced her to drink. The sun had come up, advancing its way across the pale gold flagstones of the patio. The blood-red geraniums that stood to attention in the terracotta pots were slowly unfolding their petals towards it; everything coming alive again with the dawn of a new day. Her teeth were still chattering, despite the warmth of the room. Where was Rufus? Her breath caught itself on a sob. Where was Josh? What had he done with him . . . with the tiny body? She closed her eyes in anguish and brought her hands up to her face. From outside came the familiar sounds of the properties around them slowly coming to life: the farting stutter of old Cassoux's motorcycle, the gear-whine of a tractor from the villa down the hill that still had land to till; music from the pool house across the track . . . now and then something came tinkling clear – a woman's voice, the gobbling bark of a dog. She lay on the rug in front of the stone-cold fireplace, her whole body tense with panic, waiting for Rufus to return.

It seemed as though he'd been gone for hours when she finally heard the crunch of tyres on the gravel outside. She sat upright, longing for the whole thing to have been a terrible dream. Her whole body was concentrated in that second when he would walk through the doorway, a laughing, gurgling Josh in his arms. She was wide-eyed with tension when he came in and he carried no child. She felt her own face crumple as though watching someone else. 'Rufus . . . where did you go?'

He didn't answer but strode over to her, bending down so that his face was on a level with hers. He gripped her upper arms, his fingers digging painfully into her flesh. 'Diana . . . I've got an idea. I've just been to see Khadija. We're going to sort this out, all right? Everything's going to be fine.'

'Wh-what are you talking about?' Diana's voice rose uncomfortably in her own ears. 'Josh is dead, Rufus . . . I killed him. I killed him.'

'Stop it. We're going to sort this out. There's no point blaming yourself, Diana. It was an accident. It could have happened to anyone.'

'But it didn't! It happened to me! I made it happen!'

'Shh.' His grip relaxed and he drew her into his arms, stroking her hair. 'Shh. It's all going to be fine, you'll see. I need you to pull yourself together, Diana. Get a hold of yourself. This is what's going to happen.'

She listened to him in growing disbelief. For a sum of money he didn't disclose, Khadija would give up her child. His assurances came flooding out. The child was the same age as Josh. They looked almost identical, hadn't she said so herself? He was even genetically related. Khadija would go back to Algeria and finish her schooling without the burden of this child that she didn't even want. Diana would take the new baby back to London; all would be as it was. Everything would be smoothed over, forgotten about. It would be as if nothing had happened. Mohammed had agreed – he had been as distraught over Khadija's pregnancy as she was. Rufus had taken care of everything – all that remained was for Diana to buy into it . . . and that would be that. It all came down to her. 'It won't work,' she said flatly, her mind racing ahead. 'It won't work. Harvey'll never believe it. It just won't work.'

'Diana, listen to me. Harvey will believe whatever you tell him. You know that. He's always been a fool where you're concerned. You know that about him. If you say there's nothing wrong, he'll believe it. Christ, he wouldn't believe it if he'd seen it with his own eyes. It's up to you, Diana. It's up to you.'

She was silent. In her heart, she knew it was true. Harvey worshipped the ground she walked on. He would no more believe her capable of deceit than he would himself. Rufus was right. It was up to her. If she decided to go along with it, everything would be fine. All she had to do was say yes. She took a deep, shuddering breath. The shivering rose in her like a dog's hair along its back. 'Yes,' she gasped, as if there wasn't enough breath in her to expel the word. 'Yes.'

'Good girl. Finish the rest of that,' he pointed to the half-empty glass lying on the hearth beside her. 'And then come upstairs.'

'No.' She shook her head, still shuddering. 'I can't. I can't go up there again. Don't make me, Rufus, please don't make me.'

'OK, OK. You need to get some rest. Here, lie down on the couch. That's it . . . just close your eyes. I'm here. Everything's going to be fine, d'you understand, Diana? Everything's going to be fine.'

And it was. Three days later the two men arrived late one night and disposed of the tiny body that Rufus had hidden, God alone knew where. She couldn't help herself; she walked out into the night and stood watching them as they prepared the shallow grave. They buried Josh underneath the paving stones of the driveway that she'd told Harvey simply had to be replaced, immediately. Rufus was there; he would help her supervise the workers . . . by the time they all came back in September, it would be done. Harvey agreed immediately. 'You sure it's not too much work for you, darling? After all, you've got Josh to look after.'

'No, n-not at all. It'll be f-fine. Rufus is here. He'll help.'

'All right. Whatever you say.'

And that was that. They buried him; the earth was patted over and stamped upon. The two men left, their silence paid for by Rufus. The following morning, workers arrived with the new paving stones. It took them the better part of the morning; by lunchtime, it was almost done. No one would ever know or believe it.

Towards the end of the afternoon, when the sun was beginning its slow descent towards the horizon and the air was still thick with pulsing insects and bees, Rufus drove up. He got out of the car carrying something wrapped in a bundle of white. He came into the kitchen. For one long, dreadful moment they looked at each other, the knowledge of what they'd done in their eyes, between them; she looked at the beautiful, sleeping infant and then slowly that knowledge disappeared, rolling away in light, empty waves, like the waves at the beach at Antibes where they sometimes went swimming. She couldn't believe how easy it was – she looked at the tight, tiny face swaddled in cloth and fell in love. He was so like Josh – a little darker, perhaps, but nothing that couldn't be explained by the sun. The same dark eyes, dark eyebrows, thick, rich dark hair . . . just like hers. Just like Rufus. Slowly, as she took the infant

423

in her arms, she felt herself dissolving, the terror and guilt of the previous few days suddenly slipping away. He wasn't just like Josh — he was Josh. She hugged him to her tightly, hot, silky tears of relief sliding down her face, unstoppable. Rufus said nothing; just watched her holding him, the only sound in the room the three of them breathing steadily, quietly, as one.

101

JOSH
London, October 2000

He stumbled down the stairs, running from the disclosure that had just been made. He couldn't think straight. Somehow he found himself walking along Northumberland Park Road, turning right on to Ball's Pond Road and walking up towards Highbury, to the station. Interspersed with the creak and sway of the train and the shouts that came from further down the carriage, fragments of Diana's story came back to him, washing over the outside noise. He accepted the facts as she told them; it had happened. This decision followed that. But he couldn't accept their finality. They had pulled his world out from underneath him and now there was nothing left to stand on, nothing to hold. He listened to her with the intuitive understanding of someone who knew the story before it was told, familiarity and distress breaking over him in equal amounts. In the train, sitting opposite him, an elderly gentleman sat reading. Josh blankly followed his eyes as they moved across the newspaper from left to right; he was in his own trance. He got out at Shepherd's Bush and crossed the road without looking. He made it across the road in one piece, God alone knew how.

The flat was empty. He looked at the clock on the mantelpiece. It was almost four. Niela would be home in an hour or so. He felt the need for her wash over him, almost bringing him to his knees. He threw his jacket on the dining room table and walked into the kitchen. He needed something to drink — anything. He found a bottle of whisky in the cupboard beside the cooker. He twisted off the cap and poured himself a glass, looking around him uneasily. It was like being in someone else's home, he realised suddenly. His duffel bag lay on the living room floor, but apart from that and a few toiletries in the bathroom, it was essentially Niela's flat into which from time to time he inserted himself and his strange, peripatetic life. He took a gulp of whisky. Was that part of the problem? he wondered slowly. His inability to attach himself to anything, to anyone . . . wasn't that what Rania had thrown at him, always? 'You don't love me,' she'd screamed at him time and again. 'You *can't* love me. You can't love anyone because you can't love yourself.' He'd dismissed it, of course, lashing back at her in anger and rage . . . he'd put it down to the ridiculous magazines she read or the friends she spoke to – a silly, trite comment of the sort that women always made, a comment that had no place in reality, least of all his. But today, this morning, listening to Diana, a horrible sense of déjà vu had come over him as she spoke. It was Rania he was listening to, and Niela, though Niela's judgements were never as harsh. He had to put out a hand to steady himself. He couldn't wait to see Niela, to explain. She would understand – Niela understood everything. That was why he loved her. Diana was dying; he was not his father's son; his brothers were not his own. He lay down on the couch, his head spinning. Nothing was as it had been; nothing was as it seemed. Niela. Everything would be fine as soon as he saw her. He'd known that about her, always. Right from the start.

She saw him sprawled out on the couch as soon as she opened the door. He was fast asleep, one hand flung away from him as if he was warding off something, even in sleep. She closed the door quietly, hung her bag and jacket on the back of a chair and then crossed the room to where he lay. She looked down at him; his face was troubled . . . there was a flicker of a frown between his brows and the muscle in his cheek clenched and unclenched itself as he slept. Something was wrong. She wondered if he'd been to see Diana. She was just about to turn away and walk into the bedroom, leaving him to sleep, when he woke suddenly. 'Niela.' His voice stopped her. She turned around.

'I didn't want to wake you,' she began hesitantly. 'You were fast asleep.'

'Niela,' he repeated and there was an urgency in his voice she hadn't heard before.

'What is it?' He sat upright and ran a hand through his hair. He was agitated. 'What is it?' she repeated.

'I . . . I . . . there's something . . . I need to talk to you about something. I need to tell you something.' He looked up at her. 'It's Diana.'

'Diana?' Niela repeated, surprised. She'd been expecting something else – someone else. 'What's wrong with Diana?'

He seemed unable to answer immediately. 'It's . . . she's not well,' he said eventually, slowly. 'She's ill.'

'What d'you mean? What sort of illness?'

Again there was a hesitation before he spoke. 'You'd better sit down,' he said, patting the space beside him. Niela stared at him wordlessly for a few moments, then walked back over to the couch and sat down gingerly next to him. He took her hand in his, turning the palm over slowly. 'I've been with her pretty much all day. I got back in this morning and you'd already gone to work so I rang her at the office – they said she wasn't in. I went round to the house, and that's when she told me.'

'Told you what?'

'It's cancer, Niela. Breast cancer.' His voice was strained. He let go of her hand; his own dangled helplessly in front of him. 'We've been talking all day. Niela . . .' He got up suddenly, almost catching her off balance. He strode to the window and picked up his jacket, fishing around agitatedly in the pockets for his cigarettes. He lit up and she could see his hand shaking ever so slightly. She sat back, stunned by the news. Cancer? She couldn't believe it; couldn't take it in. She'd seen Diana only a few days earlier . . . she'd looked tired, yes, and a little withdrawn, but Niela had put it down to the strain of what it was they'd talked about. Cancer? She felt the cold hand of fear travel slowly up the length of her body.

'Is it . . . treatable?'

Josh turned away from the window. 'She says it's not. I don't know . . . I need to speak to Dad . . . to Rafe . . .' He stopped again. He swallowed. 'We talked about a lot of things, Niela. I . . . I don't know what she's told you. She said . . . she said the two of you'd become close.' He shook his head. 'She's changed, somehow . . . she's different.'

'I like her,' Niela said slowly, a note of wonder in her voice. 'I never thought I would . . . or that she'd like *me*. I was always so afraid of her. But she's nothing like that . . . like how I thought. She's . . . she's great.'

'Niela.'

She looked up at him. There was such anguish in his voice. His whole face was contorted with pain. She didn't know what to make of the way he dropped his hands to his sides. He stubbed out his cigarette and came over to her suddenly, pulling her to her feet. He bent his head to bury it in her neck. She could feel his lips moving against her skin; his arms bound her tightly. 'Shhh,' she said quietly, feeling his whole body tense. 'Shhh.'

'Niela.' He was holding on to her so tightly she was unable to breathe. 'There's something else . . . she told me something else. About me.'

'Shhh,' Niela repeated, lifting a hand and running it through his hair. She let her fingers come to rest on the nape of his neck, stroking it lightly. 'Not now. Don't think about that now. Diana's going to get better – that's all. Nothing else matters. Everything else will heal with time.'

He pulled his head away from hers slightly, looking down at her. His eyes were dark pools in which she could see herself reflected. 'Everything else?'

The question hung in the air between them; the slight emphasis on the 'every' was not lost on her. She understood immediately what he was asking. She closed her own eyes for a brief, halting second. When she opened them again, his were still on her. The question was still unanswered. He tightened his grip on her arm.

'Everything,' she said quietly, firmly. 'Everything.'

102

MADDY
London, October 2000

Maddy looked at Rafe in disbelief. She struggled to get her mouth around the word. Cancer? *Diana?* 'No,' she said automatically. 'No. Not Diana. That's crazy.'

Rafe's eyes were half-closed. He looked exhausted, utterly drained. He'd spent the last few hours with Harvey and Geoffrey Laing. In addition to his fears as Diana's eldest son, there was a deeper layer of knowledge that only he and Harvey were privy to that made it difficult to speak. 'Not crazy, Maddy,' he said quietly. 'It's serious. It's happening.'

'Not to Diana!' Maddy blurted the words out. 'No, not to her. Anyone else, but not her.' For all her insecurities where Diana was concerned, Maddy was suddenly aware of Diana's strength. She was the one who held the Keelers together; not Harvey. Diana's hand was everywhere. It was she who organised the Sunday lunches, the dinners . . . she never forgot a birthday, never missed an important event. Why, only the other day Maddy had received a card from her: *Break a leg* – the traditional actor's good-luck greeting. A beautiful hand-drawn card from one of the museum collections; the sort of thing only Diana would chose. She felt a sudden chill pass through her. Diana demanded much of others; you either rose to the challenge or sank beneath it. Maddy had sunk at first – unnerved by the weight of an expectation she sensed in her. But in the past few months, another side to Diana had emerged. It wasn't just her generosity – that was on evidence week after week, at one family gathering or another. That much was easy to see. In Mougins, one evening, they'd sat over a glass of wine, talking about the theatre. Diana was far more knowledgeable than Maddy had ever guessed. Perhaps more important was the way she held herself back, allowing Maddy a chance to show off, and therefore to shine. It was a small gesture – Maddy couldn't even remember who or what they'd been talking about – but it spoke volumes in a way that nothing else could have, or did. She'd come away from the conversation that night with a renewed sense of faith in herself. The resentment she'd harboured towards Rafe and everyone else for forcing her to make the choice between an audition and Harvey's birthday party had suddenly gone out of her. She knew her own best qualities, and after that evening, she trusted Diana to see them. A small triumph, but a significant one nonetheless. And now here was Rafe . . . telling her something she didn't want to believe. Diana was dying. No, it wasn't possible. Not her. Somewhere buried deep down and pushed to the back of her mind was the horribly familiar fear. Another source of strength in her life was about to disappear. She turned to Rafe, gripping his arm fiercely. 'No, it won't happen. Not to her.' Rafe was silent. His eyes were still closed. She could feel the fear of what they couldn't bring themselves to say emanating from him, like sweat. She wasn't the only one whose sense of self had been quietly bolstered all along. She let her hand fall from his arm, lacing her fingers through his instead. They sat there together in the deepening gloom, not speaking or moving, simply holding on. Holding each other. Holding fast.

103

JULIA
London, October 2000

Some things didn't bear thinking about. Not now, at any rate, not whilst the damage had already been done. She sat alone in the kitchen of their flat, her hands going automatically to the hard, rounded dome of her stomach, as if in protection of what lay there. Aaron believed her; *he* had no choice. She did. She alone knew the truth – as did Josh. But if there was one thing she'd learned it was that sometimes the truth wasn't enough. Or, perhaps more accurately, sometimes the truth was too much. What would be gained by telling anyone what had happened? She would destroy two marriages in the process and probably the entire family to boot. Diana was ill; Aaron had gone to her. She didn't know precisely what was wrong but from the garbled messages Aaron had left her, it didn't sound good. No, now was not the time to start making a disclosure of her own. There would probably never be a time.

She got up from the table and walked over to the sink. Outside, the late summer's evening was slowly drawing to a close. It had been an unusually warm September. She looked down into the gardens. A red-breasted robin picked his way delicately across the lawn, dipping his beak every now and then in a sharp, staccato movement to root out a worm or a grub visible only to him. She stood there for a few minutes, her concentration utterly absorbed, lost in a world of buried memories, the sound of her father's voice coming to her as if he were there, standing next to her, watching for what she might do or say. He'd been such a stickler for the truth; that, and nothing but. It was from him she'd learned the true meaning of integrity, grit, determination . . . the stuff she'd always thought herself made of. Her mother's lessons had been gentler: compassion, perhaps, and the importance of feelings. Mike didn't hold with feelings. Feelings got you into trouble – much better to stick to facts, concrete things, concrete concepts like justice and truth. She grimaced. How hard she'd tried to live up to that expectation; her whole life thus far had been to that end – Oxford, law, becoming a barrister . . . even this last unexpected path that her career had taken had, at some subliminal level, been addressed to him. For him. The only time she'd deviated from what she thought he'd expect of her . . . well, look what had happened. She glanced down at her stomach. It was almost ironic. In the end, her child would be her greatest achievement, especially if she and Aaron were unable to have another. This child was *it*; the rest would fall away. She only had to look at Diana to understand what she didn't want to become. Three sons; none of them properly hers. She'd never fully understood what the source of tension in the family was – clearly, it was something to do with Josh – but her own intuition prevented her from enquiring any further. *Dig a four-foot hole and you'll find two bodies; dig a ten-foot hole and you'll find twenty.* The line from a film or a book she'd read suddenly came back to her, startling her. There was a secret at the heart of the Keeler family that was struggling to repeat itself now, with her. But she was damned if she would let it. As painful as it might be to keep the truth to herself, she couldn't allow the same thing to happen to her child as she suspected had happened to Josh. *Feelings.* A half-smile lifted the corner of her lips. That was her mother's voice. She didn't know; she had no proof – but the *feeling* that somehow, in some buried, deeply hidden way, Josh didn't belong in the Keeler family the way Aaron and Rafe did was stronger than any fact she cared to admit. She couldn't allow that to happen again. She wouldn't. The moment of truth was *now*; not back then, not in Mougins, or the café on Gray's Inn Road or the mornings she spent lying in bed with the memory of what she'd done swirling endlessly around in her head. Now mattered; not then. Now, and what would happen next. She turned away from the window feeling strangely lighter than she had done in months. Like Diana, she supposed, her dogged search for the truth in her everyday life had obscured her to a much deeper truth. What was it Dom had said to her once? *People rarely remember what you do or say, Jules, but they do remember how you make them feel.* If there was ever a moment to trust her own intuition about what to do next, it was now. The child belonged to her and Aaron; nothing more would ever be said.

104

DIANA
London, New Year's Eve, 2000

In the corner of the room, a TV screen was dancing with light and static. A reporter was speaking, saying something meaningful, no doubt, about the new year that was nearly upon them. Diana lay back against the cardboard-stiff sheets, her left arm upturned and lying loosely by her side as the nurse skilfully inserted one needle after another in the pale patch of skin of her elbow, producing only the slightest sting as she drew blood. There was a plastic bubble taped to the soft flesh beneath her shoulder and several more plastic discs from which tubes sprouted like a potato she'd once found as a child, playing underneath the kitchen sink. She'd screamed as she touched it and then stood back in horror as it rolled clumsily out of the cupboard and on to the ground, all gnarled bumps and desiccated, wrinkled-looking skin, much like hers would be . . . No, stop it. She made a small sound of impatience within herself.

'Nearly done,' the nurse said cheerfully, deftly transferring the syringe full of bright-red blood – her blood – into one of the purple-tipped vials that stood waiting on the sideboard. 'One more to go and then you're done. Lucky you.'

It was on the tip of Diana's tongue to enquire how this – being prodded and pierced for an hour every other day in preparation for what looked like six months of absolute hell in front of her – could possibly be described as 'luck', but she held herself in. In half an hour, Geoffrey would come through the door with the results of the tests they'd just run, and together, she and he would discuss her options. It sounded like some kind of bedtime drink, she thought to herself drowsily. Or a new kind of perfume. For a whole day the previous week, she'd moved around with a flattish metal canister in a holster that recorded the weather of her body – every drop and rise in temperature, every fluid ounce of sweat, every-thing . . . dreams, thoughts, the taste of metals in her mouth and all. From those records, and from the results they were drawing from her body today, a plan would be made. She turned her head warily to one side. It had all happened so fast. Caught in the middle of some ordinary, mundane act – answering the phone, writing up a brief, perusing her notes, cooking, even – she became aware that her body had deserted her, gone off on its own, haywire course, in much the same manner as her thoughts. She fancied she could feel it engaged in its silent, secret war against itself.

'All done.' The nurse was relentlessly cheerful. 'There, that wasn't so bad, was it?'

Diana shook her head. She lay for a few minutes longer, aware of the blood pumping through her body and the low, steady drumbeat of her own heart. The sound of it filled her ears. The door opened in the corner of the room and someone came in. There was another sound; someone was speaking. It took some effort to listen. It was Geoffrey. She nodded where she thought it appropriate, stretched the muscles of her face in response, although she'd taken in practically nothing. *Treatment . . . promising . . . good preparatory results . . . twice a week . . .* The words drifted round and round. 'Yes,' she murmured drowsily. 'Yes, yes.' Yes to everything they said. Her attention wandered off. The nurses moved about her purposefully; they all had parties to go to, they told her cheerfully. New Year's Eve. She would be able to see the fireworks from her window, they said. She lay back against the pillows, too exhausted to think. She was waiting for Harvey. He would be here any moment now in his theatre robes, ready to take her home.

She woke suddenly. She didn't know what time it was. She sat up cautiously in bed, trying to tell from the quality and sound of the silence outside whether it was day or night. She dimly remembered climbing into bed – Harvey at her side – and then the sound of his voice as he began telling her something . . . and then the rest of it was blankness, blackness. She was so tired; it seemed as if she'd never been more tired. She lay back against the pillows, exhausted. It was night, slipping towards morning. Outside she could just hear the earliest morning birds in the oak tree at the bottom of the garden beginning to stir, their voices rising slowly into the sky. The air around her was dark and still, layers of sleep suspended over the bedroom and the rest of the house. She turned her head – Harvey wasn't there. He must have got up and moved to the spare room. He'd done that several times that week. She knew he often found it too painful to sleep next to her. Poor Harvey. He didn't know the half of it, and already his world had been turned upside down.

There was no moon – the room wouldn't have been so dark other-wise. Suddenly, out of her lassitude, something had changed. She began to think very clearly, as if the emotions of the day had settled in her mind like sediment and all her faculties were suddenly awake and clear. A sudden slow sweep of headlights came into the room; outside, a car was making the turn around the street, heading towards the main road. She heard the engine fall away and then she was cocooned in silence again. She pulled an arm out from beneath the thick, warm duvet and let it fall back on to the cover. She was afraid to look at it, to look at herself. Outside of her body, life went on . . . her family came and went, her sons . . . one of them, Rafe, his filial concern mingling with another, professional kind of angst that made conversation between them, for the first time ever, difficult. They came every day, one or the other. Julia, with her high, swollen belly; Aaron so full of touching, father-to-be pride. Maddy, distracted and distracting as ever, absorbed with some new part she was playing, settled at last. And Niela, of course. She let her mind drift for a moment. How unexpected that had turned out to be. Dear, sweet Niela. On those days when she went into hospital for her twice-weekly dose of chemotherapy, Niela was often waiting for her when she got home. She said very little in those first few hours afterwards, instinctively reacting to Diana's inability to do anything other than just be. She would sit beside the window in the upholstered chair that Harvey had brought in from the study, sometimes reading to Diana in her lightly accented, careful voice, at others just looking out of the window at the garden below, lost in her own thoughts but always attuned. Niela. She'd come to depend on her in a way that she'd never thought she would depend on anyone, ever. There were things she could tell Niela that she dared not utter to anyone, not even Harvey. One morning, a few weeks earlier, she'd come downstairs after a particularly bad night. She'd walked into the kitchen and caught sight of Harvey sitting at the table facing the French doors that looked out over the garden. He was eating breakfast alone, his head bent over a bowl of cereal or some such. He didn't hear her come in. At the sight of him, the childish dread of abandon flowed over her. Did all those years together mean nothing? Forty years – a lifetime. If it happened to her as she knew it would, Harvey would be alone. She turned around and crept back upstairs, unable to bear the thought.

The birds were singing properly now, and in the far corner of the window, the faint light of dawn was beginning to show. She'd been lying awake a long time. She pushed aside the covers and slowly slid her legs out of bed. She stared at them for a moment: thin, pale, white . . . not the legs of a few months previously. Tanned, slim, toned. She'd always been proud of her legs. She slipped out of bed and walked towards the window. She pushed back the remaining heavy bunch of curtain and looked out into the slowly lightening sky. The stars were still out, those hard, blossoming points of light with which she'd suddenly found herself connected. She had the clear-headed sense of being a source of light herself, just like those twinkling above her. The grainy reality of her own life and the certainty of death grew stronger in her as she stood in her nightgown, watching. Her eyes travelled the length of the sky, taking in its richness. She was suddenly overwhelmed. Too many things were happening; too many memories, too much pain and guilt . . . When the stars began to blur in her eyes, it was the welling of a deeper pain that was the overflow of the moment. She raised a hand to brush them away. She'd told Josh the truth. And Niela. No one else needed to know. No one else mattered. Not even Harvey.

She turned from the window and went back to bed. The slow, even beat of her heart played out a steady rhythm . . . alive/afraid; alive/afraid . . . she was tired again. It was time to put down the burden she'd been carrying for so long. She climbed into the soft mass of feather duvet and pillows. She groaned aloud, since there was no one to hear her. She spread her hands out in front of her; her wedding ring and the heavy, solitary diamond Harvey had given her, all those years ago, sat awkwardly on her finger, now that she'd lost weight. The diamond slid to one side, the flesh underneath showing up as a white band against the slightly darker, tanned skin of her hands. She tugged it off and put it down on the bedside table. It settled with a satisfying clunk, the last sound before silence.

Epilogue

Djemmorah, Algeria, October 2001

The car crested the last hill, and suddenly the village and the long, thick line of olive trees opened up in front of them, snaking through the valley, skirting the foothills but hugging the road. The hills around them were dotted with white rocks and the odd, solitary tree. Josh was silent as he shifted gear and plunged downwards. Niela too was quiet as they began to leave the barrenness of the desert and descended into green. The buildings were made of the same pinkish, sandy mud as the hills – square, rugged buildings with the odd curiously elaborate embellishment across the doorway or windows. The air was dry and cool, slowly warming up as they drove down into the valley. The sky was a piercing blue, dazzling in its intensity, broken only by the faintest wisps of white leaning in wide, shimmering streaks towards the horizon. On her bare knees in front of her was the map they'd been consulting ever since leaving Algiers. All they had was the name of the town – to which Josh had once been, unbelievably, en route to somewhere else – and an ages-old letter addressed to Mohammed Ben Ahmed, rue 13 Fevrier, Djemmorah. Rufus had given it to Josh just after the funeral.

'They don't seem to have street names,' Niela commented as they drove slowly into what seemed to be the centre of the village. An open square, surrounded by mud-walled buildings, with a few crooked signs hanging haphazardly above shop awnings and the beautiful walled maze of streets leading away from the square. It was just after three o'clock in the afternoon and the shadows were already long on the ground. A few men looked up curiously as Josh parked the car to one side of the road and opened the door. Niela quickly wound a headscarf around her head and fastened the remaining buttons on her long white skirt.

'Come on.' Josh held out his hand to her. 'Let's start with those men over there.'

She followed him but hung back as they drew near. '*Salaam alaikum.*' The greetings flowed back and forth between them. She stood to one side, acknowledging their curious glances but making no attempt to join in. She half-smiled to herself, listening to Josh's Arabic as he asked the whereabouts of Mohammed Ben Ahmed or his daughter, Khadija.

'Ben Ahmed?' one of the older men asked, squinting up at Josh. 'You sure of that? There's no one in the village by that name.'

'Yes. He worked in France for a while. I think he came back here . . . around thirty years ago?'

They looked at one another, pulling faces and shaking their heads. She could read the disappointment in Josh's stance. 'No, there's no one here by that name. Ben Ahmed, you said?'

'Yes. Mohammed. He had a daughter . . . Khadija . . . they came back together from France.'

'Why d'you ask?' Someone spoke suddenly. Niela watched as Josh turned to him. He was a short, stocky man, in his early forties, perhaps. He wore the same closed, suspicious face that she'd seen in villagers everywhere – a natural defence against strangers and the unknown. Her pulse suddenly quickened. 'Who are you?' he asked, looking from Josh to Niela and back again.

She saw Josh stiffen and his shoulders hunch in the way she knew so well. There was a moment's pause as he gathered himself, and then the words were out. 'I'm his grandson. I'm Khadija's child. The one they left behind.'

The air was thick with the sweet, cloying scent of flowers and herbs. They ducked under one doorway, then another. Josh was holding on to Niela's hand tightly, as if for dear life. Ahead of them, pushing their way impatiently through lines of washing, the two women who'd been summoned by the men outside hurried down the narrow alleyways towards some unknown destination. Niela's heart was thudding painfully inside her chest as she was half-dragged, half-carried along with them. They began the high, excitable ululation that she remembered so well from Mogadishu – a cry of welcome and pain and blessed release. At last they stopped before an intricately carved wooden doorway, but before they could pound on it, it was flung open. A young man stood in the semi-darkened doorway; Niela put a hand to her mouth. It was like looking at a younger Josh, the features oddly familiar, at once different and the same. He looked up at Josh, a slow frown of puzzlement appearing on his face. The women were crying out for Khadija . . . the dialect in these parts was hard for her to follow. There was a great flurry of commotion and noise – Josh and Niela were swept into the darkened rooms and told to wait. The young man, with a stunned backwards glance at them both, was dispatched outside and told to wait. What was about to happen was for his mother's eyes and ears alone.

She was small and dark-skinned. She sat in the middle of the room on an arrangement of colourful rugs, dressed in the soft woven cloth that the women of her village wore. Her eyes were brilliant, outlined with thick black kohl pencil. She listened without saying a word to the excited chatter of her neighbours and friends, and when they'd finally run out of words, she dismissed them all with a quick, imperious wave of her hand. To Niela's great surprise, it was Diana she brought to mind.

'*Viens.*' She said the word out loud, breaking the silence that had descended upon the room as the last of the women had left. Her French still carried with it the sun and the lilt of Provence. '*Pas vous,*' she said, shaking her head at Niela. She looked up at Josh from her seated position. '*Toi.*'

Josh walked uncertainly towards the centre of the room. He knelt suddenly, squatting down beside her, bringing his face almost on a level with hers. Niela's breath caught and held. There was a pause of a few seconds. Khadija reached out a hand from beneath her robes and let it fall beside his. She waited a few seconds, then turned the palm of her hand towards his. A simple gesture. The first touch. The first touch in over thirty years. Niela felt the sharp tug of tears in her throat and turned away. It was a gesture she recognised only too well. One of the last that Diana had made; a mother's touch, both tender and strong. She looked back as she surreptitiously wiped the tears from her cheeks. Josh's hand was held within Khadija's own. The first touch. But not the last.